RED
EARTH
TO
PARADISE

VINCENT GARNER

WHITE MOUNTAIN

White Mountain Books is an affiliate of
The Arcadian Group S.A., Case Postale 431, 1211 Geneva 12, Switzerland
Copyright © White Mountain Books 2017

Database right White Mountain Books (maker)

First published 2017

ISBN 9781941634813

Designed and typeset by Megan Sheer

Printed in Great Britain by CPI UK, 141-143 Shoreditch High Street,
London, E1 6JE
Typeset in Monotype Arcadian Bembo

To my old professors,
and to my family, who influenced my
scientific and spiritual philosophy.

NOTE FROM THE AUTHOR

Since I was a child, I could never quite grasp the idea of the 'soul'. *What is it?* I would ponder. *What is it made of, what is its meaning? And what of its destiny after we die?*

The most troubling thing for me was trying to understand the vague and watery definitions ascribed to the soul of a human. Those offered to us over the years by priests, prophets, and clerics; philosophers, scientists and scholars; they always seemed so nebulous to me. So self-serving. When I was living in Ireland, the force of religion was very strong around me. Whenever I visited the church, I would come away unsatisfied and unconvinced. Far from forging some bond between I and a scriptural god, the only thing it did do was to urge me to muse on what I believed the soul to consist of instead. I had the habit of trying to find explanations for nearly all the phenomena around us. I wondered about those concerning the creation of the earth – the truth of the big bang – and the many-worlds interpretation; the quantum mechanical idea that all alternate histories and futures of our lives are real.

Thinking of the soul as energy was one of the many theories that passed through my mind like shooting stars: *Is the soul a vapour? Is it an ascending cloud? Is it a force that is transient? Has it been somehow resurrected?* These questions – frenzied as they were – would ultimately come to a dead end. I would write them down on pieces of paper and lay them out, trying to find the answer. For years, I tried to come to some sort of conclusion, but, in the end, like a boxer's trainer throwing in the towel, I gave up. The soul was, I resigned myself to think, an unexplainable puzzle; a nut too tough to crack.

However, one day, many years later, I was working as a researcher in physics and chemistry, when the answer came to me in the most unlikely of places: in the back of taxi. We were winding through the leafy suburbs of Geneva, when I got talking to the driver. He seemed eager to make conversation – as was his habit with impressionable foreigners, I suspected. He spoke about the weather, the mountains, the character of the Swiss, and the culinary delicacies of the region. He recommended that for lunch that day I try the canton's favourite dish: *filet de perche*. Assuming that my French was a little sketchy, he quickly explained that this was a tasty white fish pulled out from the shores of Lake Geneva itself.

'From out there!' he confirmed, pointing at the lake which glittered blue outside my window.

'I see, and it's good?' I asked.

'Oh yes. Take it with some crispy fries,' he said, licking his lips; before adding, almost as an afterthought, 'and some salad, if you want,' rolling his eyes.

When I asked why, he told me that it would be an excellent choice to have as my final meal.

'My final meal?' I said, half laughing. 'What are you talking about, old boy? Do you know something I don't?'

It was his answer to this question that inspired the conception of this novel. He said, 'Today, the boffins at CERN are turning on the engines' – I knew this to be the switching on of the Large Hadron Collider on the outskirts of Geneva, a momentous day in science the world over – 'And so,' he continued, with only a slight look of dread flickering over his face, 'we'll be blown up by this time tomorrow. The whole earth will be sucked into a black hole...nothingness...or,' he paused, and raised a finger, like someone about to explain a riddle, 'it's already happened, and we're already *inside* the black hole.'

It was then that I marvelled at such logic. Of the soul transcending space and time, worlds and black holes – transcending everything.

Having paid my fare, I rushed to my research lab, where I decided to take a pen, and attempt to pour my lifetime's musings on the soul into my very first novel. I have written it with the hope that God, and any other supernatural power, will bless it with success, and that you the reader will enjoy it as much as I did writing it.

Finally, I would like to thank my editorial team, the many diligent and passionate people at White Mountain Books, and to extend my special thanks to Elodie Olsson-Coons, whose untiring dedication went a long way in bringing this book to completion.

PROLOGUE

Axel Parker stared at the smoke pouring from the factory windows.

'What… What did you say happened?'

The hand holding his styrofoam cup of coffee began to shake ever so slightly. He had left the Zeta Delta Pi fraternity that morning, just as he had most days this summer, in a good mood: just another day of his internship with the Advanced Electric Company. The sun had been just as bright as the previous day, his coffee just as sweet, and the radio had been playing old rock tunes for him to blare from the radio of his 1984 Mustang. Despite a traffic jam making him a little late, Axel had been in a good mood. When he'd stepped out of his car, however, he'd found the eight hundred factory workers and their bosses massed outside the factory, while black smoke belched from the windows. The air smelled like burning rubber, and small flakes of ash and soot drifted in the air.

The chief engineer, James Slater, sighed. A tall man in a short-sleeved shirt with horn-rimmed glasses and a pencil tucked over his ear, he was not a figure who usually commanded a great deal of authority: to his workers, he came across as a passionate geek, rather than a slave-driver. Right now, however, Axel couldn't help but feel a little scared of his temporary boss. He'd gone looking for him in the crowd, to find out what was going on, but he had regretted that decision almost immediately. Tension radiated from the man, as hot as the heat waves still melting the air above the factory rooftop. Slater ran a hand through his hair.

'It blew up,' he said again, shortly. 'One of the compressors blew up.'

Axel swallowed. The first time, he could have sworn Slater had said '*You* blew it up.' The Advanced Electric Company factory outside Lake Salvation, Texas, was the biggest factory in the world producing compressors for air conditioning units. Eight hundred men worked there full-time, building compressors for enormous air conditioning units that would end up everywhere from skyscrapers in Houston to aeroplane hangars in Seattle. Axel was five weeks into a six-week internship organised by his university engineering course: a summer-long course of practical training to cement the knowledge gained in his sophomore year.

'The firefighters have only just left,' Slater added distractedly, as if talking to himself. 'There were there all night, hosing the kiosks down with water and foam. It's eighty thousand square metres, you know. The factory.' His eyes focused on Axel again.

For some reason, Axel became acutely aware of the coffee cup in his hand. He wished he could set it down somewhere.

'At first I thought it was a strike,' he said nervously. 'All those people standing outside. Then I saw the smoke.'

'It took us hours to work out what happened,' Slater snapped. 'Hours!' Axel jumped a little, surprised at his tone.

'Hours, sir?' he said, feeling stupid.

'In the middle of the night.' Slater closed his eyes, then removed his glasses and pressed his fist into his sockets. 'I don't want you coming back,' he muttered into his sleeve.

'I'm sorry?' Axel felt his stomach tighten again.

Slater coughed a little, put his glasses back on, and sighed. 'Axel,' he said, then stopped. 'The firefighters found the source of the explosion in your kiosk.' After this outburst, he paused again, clearly agitated, then plunged ahead: 'Last night, Axel, you forgot to turn off the pressure on the compressor you were working with. You had it on automatic, and it continued to run on automatic until it couldn't take the pressure and exploded. It blew up the whole eastern section of the factory and started a fire. We're lucky the whole factory didn't burn to the ground.' Catching sight of Axel's expression, Slater remembered himself, and some of his anger seemed to drain away: 'Of course, we have no-one to blame but ourselves: we should never have put an undergraduate in a position of such heavy responsibility. I don't know what we were thinking. People could have died. Eight hundred people are out of work. And I don't even know if our insurance will cover…' With an almost physical effort, he managed to stop. 'I'm sorry, Axel. I don't mean to lay any of this on your shoulders. How old are you, again?'

The first time Axel tried to speak, his voice appeared to be stuck in his throat. 'Twenty,' he finally managed to squeak out, 'sir.' For a minute, he thought he might be sick.

Slater sighed. All at once, he looked very tired and old. 'Axel,' he said, 'I think you should go home.'

The Texas roads zoomed by in a blur of dust and cornfields. Axel pressed down on the accelerator, his heart racing. He'd crawled down the gravel road outside the Advanced Electric factory, heavy with guilt and shame, but as soon as the location of the disastrous incident was out of sight, he wanted nothing more than to drive and drive. The air conditioning, which he usually blasted until the inside of his Mustang felt like a refrigerator, reminded him too much of his compressor accident, so he rolled down the windows and let the hot Texas wind blow through his hair. *Cleansing me of my sins*, he thought to himself, ironically. Axel was not a religious young man, but he had been raised Christian, and some of the reflexes had stuck with him. Atonement, for one. Visions of his kiosk, the high-ceilinged room full of machinery, kept drifting into his mind, but he batted them away and cranked the radio up.

He slowed as he arrived on the outskirts of Lake Salvation, the wheels of his Mustang bumping over the cracks in the pavement. The twenty-mile drive had gone by in a flash. He felt furious that everything in his hometown looked the same; that the weather had stayed glorious on such a terrible day in his life. There was the candy store with its pretty striped awning, there was the library and the coffee shop, there was the Trout Fisher Bar. He drove past the First Lake Salvation Church of Grace and the Lake Salvation Town Hall. As he turned down 27th Street, and the campus swam into view, he felt his heart slow to a guilty thump. His mouth felt dry. *Maybe I should go to my parents' house*, he thought. Or just go back to the fraternity, take a nap, face the professor afterwards... But no: procrastination would only make things worse. He had to own up. He parked his car in front of the Zeta Delta Pi house, stepped out into the blistering heat, and walked slowly down the concrete slab path under the ash and catalpa trees. Now that he'd arrived at his destination, he was in no hurry to get to Professor Bohmann's office. For one thing, he barely knew the professor: but Bohmann was in charge of the internship arrangement with Advanced Electric, and as such, he was the person Axel needed to come clean to. He walked as slowly as he could past the rolling, immaculate lawns, past the manicured boxes of flowerbeds, wondering idly how many times a day they had to water the plants in this heat to keep everything so lush and green. The cafeteria was open, he noticed, despite the fact that the campus was essentially empty this time of year. In just a few weeks, though, the perfect lawns would be trampled across by waves and waves of new and old students...

Without thinking, Axel had walked right up to the door to the Engineering school. He grabbed the handle and tugged it open, deciding to make it down the corridor before his brain could catch up with him. He strode down the linoleum, past the empty reception, past the posters advertising football games and string quartets, past the vending machine. Before he knew it, he was standing in front of the door he so wanted to avoid, staring at a copper plaque engraved with the name MELVIN BOHMANN.

'Come in.' A muffled voice came from inside, and Axel's shoulders slumped. He slowly swung the door open, and walked in.

Axel had never been in Professor Bohmann's office before, having only met him briefly at the start of his internship, and he was surprised by how messy the space was. There were pencils and coffee cups strewn everywhere, and stacks of paper all over the floor. On one wall, a cork board was covered with tacked-up sheets of paper scribbled with mathematical formulas, what looked like a hand-drawn map of the earth, and several iterations of the word ENERGY in capital letters. Bohmann was seated in the centre of this chaos, calm as the Buddha during a storm. His hair was greasy and his shirt was buttoned up wrong, but somehow he radiated an almost spiritual calm that made Axel's stomach loosen a little.

'Hello, sir,' he said. 'Do you have ten minutes?'

Bohmann smiled. 'Axel Parker!' he said. 'What a pleasure to see you again.' He squinted for a moment, then his smile widened. 'You're our intern at the Advanced Electric Company, aren't you. How's all that going?'

'Well actually, sir...' Axel began, but Bohmann waved his hand in the air.

'I'm so sorry, my boy,' he said. 'Come in and sit down. You're not here for an interview. Would you like a coffee?'

His face red, Axel declined awkwardly. 'There's something I need to talk to you about, sir.'

'Please stop calling me sir,' Bohmann said. 'And stop apologising for taking up ten minutes of my time. I'm bored to death with this book I'm working on. It's been the bane of my existence for seven years now.' He gestured at his computer. 'Any time away from this old beast is time I'm grateful for.'

'I have something to confess,' Axel blurted out.

Bohmann laughed lightly. 'I'm not a priest,' he said. 'What kind of sophomore woes would you like to lay at my feet? Did you cheat on a test? Did you break up with your girlfriend?'

'It's about my internship,' Axel continued, doggedly. 'I...'

'Are you bored already? Shouldn't the whole thing be over soon?'

'I blew it up,' Axel said, quite loudly. There was a silence. 'I blew up the factory.'

Bohmann blinked a few times, then erupted in a roar of laughter. He kept laughing for quite a lot longer than Axel was comfortable with. 'I hope you're not joking,' he finally said, wiping a tear from his eye with a stained handkerchief. 'You're not, are you?'

Axel gave a nervous laugh. 'No,' he said. 'I really did. I blew up a compressor. I forgot to switch it off.'

'You mean nobody checked?'

'No, sir. I can't stop replaying the scene in my head. I don't understand how I went away without turning it off. I mean, I turn it off every night. I know you have to do that,' Axel babbled miserably.

Bohmann didn't appear to be listening. 'You mean that Advanced Electric, one of the biggest companies in the USA – no, in the world! – left a dangerously powerful machine in the hands of a sophomore student, with no additional security? It's a wonder it was just one compressor that blew up. Son, you taught those idiots a good lesson.' He laughed again, as if delightedly.

'The fire department was there all night,' Axel added, unwilling to let the matter go so easily. 'All these people, they're going to be out of work for days. And Slater said he didn't know if the insurance…'

'And you think that's your responsibility?'

'No… Well, it certainly feels like it.'

'Well, it's not,' Bohmann said crisply. 'You are no more responsible for Advanced Electric's insurance policies than I am; and between you and me, I'm fairly sure one of the major corporations of the Western world can afford insurance.' He stood up from his chair, and walked over to the coffee machine in the corner, then poured two cups from the warm pot. 'You did say yes to coffee, didn't you?'

Axel nodded, even though he hadn't.

'Lake Salvation University,' Bohmann said, as he put heaping teaspoons of sugar in each cup and stirred them with a pencil, 'truly is a marvellous place to study. So many world-famous doctors and engineers, astronauts and computer technicians started out right in these same halls as you and I. And don't tell me you don't belong here just as much as I do: every Lake Salvation alumnus is as important as the next.'

Axel couldn't handle the change of subject. 'Is this going to go on my record? Am I going to be punished?'

Bohmann laughed, handing him a cup of barely-warm coffee. 'Axel, you really must stop worrying about this silly little drama. What's done is done. All scientific progress comes from trial and error. Because of your mistake, Axel, Advanced Electric will have to tighten their security. You've ensured, in fact, that the company will become safer in the future. Is that something to be worried about?'

'No, sir,' Axel muttered.

'Was anyone injured?'

'No, sir.'

'Listen, son: your future isn't ruined.' Bohmann removed the coffee-soaked pencil from his cup and began chewing it pensively. There was a comforting old-fashioned lilt to Bohmann's voice: later, Axel would learn his mother had been British. 'For Advanced Electric as a company, this is nothing – a Post-It note on the CEO's desk tomorrow morning, crumpled into his garbage can by lunch. Those men will be back at work in a week. And you cannot, I repeat, *cannot*, take responsibility for this yourself. You should think of it as an act of God, like a natural catastrophe. Think of it as… destiny.'

'As destiny, sir?' Axel was beginning to like this eccentric professor. He sipped his lukewarm coffee and began to feel better. 'That's hardly an engineering term.'

Bohmann laughed, a friendly sound. 'You are not the first person to think this, or to tell me so,' he replied, 'but you are wrong. Most of my life's work revolves around an attempt to bring science and the humanities closer together. So much of our educational system is built around false dichotomies!' He giggled, as if this was a very funny joke. Axel couldn't help but smile. 'Facts and opinions. Science and religion. Life and death. None of these dualities are as separate as people think. Even Man and God… I mean, think how powerful you, a sophomore – a babe in arms! – have become. You blew up one of the most important factories in Texas! Isn't that amazing? One boy.'

Startling Axel, Bohmann leapt up from his chair, sloshing his coffee over the edge of his mug, and rushed over to his computer, where he dropped into another chair. For a minute he said nothing, hunched over the glowing screen, clicking away furiously. Axel was just about to ask what was going on, when he looked up with a beatific grin. 'There you are!' he said. 'Just as I suspected: a brilliant student. All of your grades are excellent, Axel Parker. You have two years of fantastic work behind you, and I have just…' He peered at the screen. 'I have just given you an A* for your internship. Congratulations on finishing it in just five weeks!'

Axel couldn't help but laugh. 'But sir, what will Advanced Electric…'

'Pah,' said Bohmann. 'You think Advanced Electric have time to check what I say about their interns? I bet they've already forgotten your name.'

'Not mine,' Axel said sheepishly.

Bohmann laughed loudly. 'Perhaps not. Still, this is the last you'll hear from them, I can guarantee that. It's all water under the bridge, my boy.'

'More like smoke in the sky, sir.' Axel grinned.

Bohmann laughed. 'Exactly! Time to start planning for back to school. No, no, no: I'm forgetting you're just a student. No classes to prepare, unlike the rest of us old fogeys. For you, Axel, it's time to enjoy the end of your summer in peace! Do your parents live nearby?'

Axel nodded. 'My mother lives over by Fairway Creek,' he said.

'Well make sure you go over there for dinner tonight, alright? Bring a pie or something. And don't go over there to wallow in your guilt. Go there to really spend time with your mother. Guilt and brilliance don't mix well, you see. It's unnecessary.' With this blunt pronouncement, Bohmann leapt up from his desk chair. 'I'm so glad you came to see me directly,' he said. 'You do know you're registered for my classes next semester?'

'I do, sir.'

'Well that's bound to be a bit of a shock to the system. You know things become more complex in junior year? It's not quite as overwhelming a transition as it is for seniors, but you'll be grappling with some big ideas. Big ideas.'

Bohmann rubbed his hands together, as if the prospect thrilled him, so Axel felt it was best not to show his apprehension.

'I'm looking forward to it,' he said.

CHAPTER ONE

Bohmann looked nervous, pacing back and forth on the stage as he waited for the undergraduates to settle into their seats. THERMODYNAMICS 101, someone had scribbled on the whiteboard in uneven, blocky letters – Bohmann, no doubt, given the messiness of the handwriting. Axel felt a surge of affection for his tutor, not just because Bohmann had rescued him from the Advanced Electric fiasco, but also because he'd felt a certain kinship with the frazzled old man. There was a real warmth to him, under all that mess. Besides, he was excited to get started on the year's engineering material, which would move further away from basic engineering and closer to the specifics of aeronautical engineering, focusing on thermodynamics, aeromechanics, fluid mechanics, and differential equations.

Term had started up just a week or so previously, startling Axel out of the comfortable rhythms he'd settled into: reading nineteenth-century novels on his own in the common room of his fraternity; walking alone amongst the summer revellers of Lake Salvation to the ice cream parlour, or the library; enjoying quiet dinners of chicken-fried steak, potatoes and collard greens with his mother. Now, the Zeta Delta Pi common room was overrun with Axel's colleagues and friends, talking loudly, sprawled over the sofas drinking cheap wine and smoking. Term-time was nice in its own chaotic way, Axel thought to himself, but the change of rhythm took a little getting used to.

Axel's train of thought was interrupted by a throaty cough from Professor Bohmann, at which point the auditorium fell silent. 'Greetings!' Bohmann boomed, or at least the first syllable rang out impressively: the tail end was a little scratchy. The professor, Axel noted, often sounded like he'd just smoked a whole cigar, even at 8 a.m. on a Wednesday. 'I'm sure you're all very excited to start this lesson,' he continued, sparking a murmur of laughter throughout the room. 'After all, there's nothing like the laws of thermodynamics to clear the cobwebs from your brains!'

'Ain't no cobwebs in my brain,' a young man yelled from the back row, at the top of the bleachers.

'Daddy's moonshine burned 'em all away,' somebody riposted from across the room. A ripple of laughter made its way down the auditorium, and Bohmann gave a little smile.

'Gentlemen, gentlemen,' he said, raising a hand, 'I have nothing against a little humour, but if you could keep it between yourselves… After all, if what you're saying is worth sharing with hundreds of your colleagues, perhaps you should apply for tenure!'

Another quarter of the room, closer to the front – the serious scientists, Axel guessed – laughed heartily at this.

Professor Bohmann walked to the front of the stage and drew himself up to his full height: not a very dramatic movement, but it was enough to make the room quiet again. 'We're here to learn about thermodynamics,' he said, 'but also to explore the wider repercussions of the topic: philosophical, ethical and religious.'

There was some muttering in the front of the class, but Bohmann paid it no heed. 'First, let me give a general introduction to these laws. Today, I will attempt an overview: if you have specific questions, please write them down and save them for next week.' There was tittering in the back of the room, and grumbling in the front.

'Let us begin at the beginning. The first law,' Bohmann began, 'states that the internal energy of an isolated system is constant. This internal energy is modified when either heat is supplied to the system, or work is done by the system on its surroundings. Or, as lyrical geniuses Flanders and Swann put it, "heat is work and work is heat." If I push a bowl across my desk, there are two principal consequences: one, the bowl has moved, and two, I have spent ten calories moving it. In other words, the energy required for this movement of the bowl equals the energy which I have spent: in this case, ten calories. Ten calories have been expended, have been put to use. To use another example, if you burn wood in your fireplace, the energy that you have burnt there is emitted in the form of heat: it is equivalent. That energy has now been consumed: it is no longer present within the once-stable system. It doesn't matter if you count it in British thermal units or calories or joules. Conduction, convection, radiation: there are dozens of ways in which energy can move around in a system, changing, being transformed, but – and this is important – the quantity of energy remains the same until heat and work interfere, and modify the state of the system. The first law of thermodynamics, in short, is an expression of the principle of conservation of energy, and a questioning of it, as well. Importantly, the law states that energy can be transformed, can be changed from one form to another, but cannot be created or destroyed. Energy in equals energy out, if you will. Now if that's not philosophical, I don't know what is!'

Bohmann held up a hand, as dissent rumbled in the front rows. 'This question of destruction, however, is far more complicated than it at first appears. If the first law sounds like a magical, golden rule, the second law quickly comes to undercut it with a little realism. The second law of thermodynamics, thus, is an expression of the universal principle of decay observable in nature. It states that heat cannot spontaneously flow from a colder location to a hotter location.'

'Like Florida?' somebody in the back shouted out.

Bohmann inclined his neck ever so slightly. 'Our friend is not entirely wrong: it is in part because of the second law of thermodynamics that the snowstorms of North America do not cool these sunny streets. I am a physicist, not a meteorologist, but even I can tell you the simple fact that although cold is not attracted to a hot body' – he paused to acknowledge the titters in the auditorium – 'hot bodies can nonetheless cool down. Otherwise we would not survive these Texan summers. Why is that? Because of entropy. The second law, in short, explains that over time, even a perfect system isolated from the outside world will adapt to the external conditions. The temperature, pressure and chemical potential will change: the energy remains the same, but the system is irredeemably transformed.'

The professor was silent for a moment, gazing up at the ceiling of the auditorium. 'Now, the third law of thermodynamics states that, as a system approaches absolute zero, all processes cease and the entropy of the system approaches a minimum value. We will leave this complex law aside for the moment, as the concept of absolute entropy is of little use to us today. However, before we move on, can anybody tell me what this absolute zero signifies?'

Several hands in the front row shot up.

'Minus 273.15 degrees Celsius, or minus 459.67 degrees Fahrenheit,' a student recited.

Bohmann nodded. 'Exactly, young lady. Also known as zero Kelvin. That answers the question of what it is. But what it signifies, what this unknown value represents… is a much trickier issue. Of course, we are basically dealing in science fiction, here, in a quite literal sense: a whole scientific law has been written based on something that is scientifically impossible!' He laughed, a little nervously, as the attendees murmured amongst themselves.

Bohmann wiped his forehead. 'As you can clearly see, we are dealing with vast philosophical concepts here: transformation, destruction and the possibility of eternity. The first law, the golden law, states that a system can be perfectly stable: the second law states that everything in this world is headed for destruction. How can that be? Is this possibility, the internal energy of an isolated system, an impossible fiction?'

The mutters in the front row became louder, and a few hands shot up.

'I thought physics taught us about the real world,' a woman's voice called out from the back.

'Ah,' Bohmann said, 'but that is the catch. The *real* world. You seem to believe the real world is somehow separate from these laws, because their wording is a little complex. But these laws are the real world. They run the real world. Is there an arrogance in this scientific approach, mankind believing we can understand the universe, reduce it to a series of laws? Yes, of course. But is the process valuable, even essential to our ability to live full lives? Yes. There is, of course, a way to temper our human arrogance in science: by acknowledging the hand of God.'

Someone in the front row actually leapt out of their seat. 'God? God?' this individual repeated, his checkered shirt soaked with sweat, his voice growing squeaky. 'We're here to learn about thermodynamics, not for some quack to teach us lessons about religion!'

There was a sort of roar from the back of the room. 'Do not take the Lord's name in vain!' a woman shouted. Axel was unsure whether this was aimed at the crimson-faced student in the front row, or at Bohmann. The professor, he noted, looked a bit worried. The beads of sweat that had been forming on his brow were now dripping down his neck, forming a V-shaped stain down his light blue shirt front.

Bohmann, however, was not finished. 'God is inseparable from the work we do here in the engineering department,' he said quite sternly. 'If the systems that form the world we live in are balanced, and then brought towards entropy, without the whole world collapsing into chaos, it must be that there is some greater stabilising power at work: I call that power God.'

'If God created an ordered world, how would we even have these laws?' a front-row student pleaded. 'Why would we need science?'

'God *did* create an ordered world!' somebody called back from the top row benches. 'You shouldn't be questioning His will!'

'What about war?' the front-row student shot back. 'What about hurricanes?'

'That's just it!' Bohmann said excitedly. 'The world is ordered, and stable overall – despite war, despite natural disasters – but even with all these laws of physics, we cannot explain why. We cannot explain the balance, we cannot explain the conversion, we cannot explain entropy...'

'Bullshit!' a scientist in the front row shouted up at him.

At this, Bohmann appeared to lose his cool, and held up both hands as authoritatively as he could, as if to end the session. However, the comments kept fusing.

'God has better things to do than get involved in mathematical formulas!'

'Those mathematical formulas work out when hurricanes are going to hit! Those hurricanes that your *benevolent God* created! Science saves lives.'

'God isn't a scientist! God created the world just as it is, four thousand years ago!'

'God has nothing to do with thermodynamics!'

'God has no place being mentioned in a scientific class!'

'God's world is perfect!'

'God doesn't exist!'

'CLASS!' Bohmann finally bellowed. 'Enough! If you have questions, write them down and leave them in my pigeonhole. I will read through them ahead of next week's class, and respond... to anything I deem interesting enough to merit engaging with.' A roar of disapproval rose up throughout the classroom, but the professor kept speaking over it as loudly as he could: 'I expect all of you to have studied the first ten pages of your thermodynamics textbook. There will be a quiz in two weeks.'

But some of the front-row students had already left the auditorium, quickly followed by the rest of the students. Axel stayed in his seat, a little stunned, staring down at his sparse notes. 'First law: constant energy. Second law: entropy. Third law: absolute zero.' And then, underneath, in wavering, uncertain script, '*Hand of God?*'

'I thought that went rather well,' Professor Bohmann said, interrupting his thoughts. Axel looked up to find that he was the last student left in the auditorium, with Bohmann beaming down sweatily over his row of desks.

'It was a very interesting class,' Axel said uncertainly.

Bohmann grinned. 'Thank you, my boy.'

'To be honest...' Axel's voice trailed off. 'Never mind, sir.'

'No, no, by all means!' his tutor encouraged him. 'If you think I can't handle criticism, you must have been somewhere else for the last hour.'

Axel laughed gently. 'Well, sir, it's just that I don't think I agree with your theory.'

Bohmann laughed even more loudly. 'You're hardly in the minority there,' he said. 'I'm beginning to think you weren't here at all. Didn't you hear them all shouting at me?'

'I did, sir,' Axel replied, 'and I didn't like the way they treated you. It seemed very disrespectful.'

A smile creased Bohmann's sweaty cheeks. 'That's a kind thing to say, Axel,' he replied. 'I appreciate it. I know it's difficult for a hardcore scientist like you to hear what I have to say, but I need you to keep an open mind. You're such an intelligent young man, Axel Parker. Don't be like the others. So many of these students live limited lives, and leave this university with an incredibly limited vision of the world around them: either limited by science, or limited by religion. I mean, they are studying thermodynamics, energy, entropy: these incredible ways of looking at the unbelievable *power* of this world! And they keep holding themselves back, out of fear. Perhaps I should stop courting controversy by using the G-word all the time, at least in this city of kooks and holy rollers... And the scientists, my colleagues, they're just as bad! Just as critical, just as limited, just as fearful. None of these people want to listen to what I have to say. But it's what I believe, as a religious man and as a scientist. If nothing else, at my age, you'd think I've earned the right to be true to myself.'

'Is this what your book is about, sir?' Axel asked curiously.

Bohmann beamed. 'It is, Axel. Perhaps you'd like to read it one day! I mean, right now it's a mass of files full of notes on my computer... But up here,' – he tapped the side of his head, 'it's a finished book. A book that could change people's lives, if they'd only listen to me.' He sighed and shook his head. 'But you've already had to listen to an hour of this madness. Go on, get out of here. You're dismissed.'

'I'll write my questions down for you, then,' Axel joked.

Possible questions flooded through his mind. *What do you think energy is, then, Professor Bohmann? Why do you believe we need God to understand thermodynamics? Are you a religious man first, or a scientist? Why have you stayed in Texas all your life? How did you end up teaching this class?*

'I have a lot of questions,' he added seriously.

'So do I, my boy,' Bohmann replied. 'So do I.'

CHAPTER TWO

Sun blazed down on the Lake Salvation University campus, on the elm and catalpa trees, on the immaculate lawns, and on Axel Parker's gown, mortarboard and tassel. Axel grinned as he walked towards the sandstone walls of Williams Hall, the oldest building on campus, joining the throngs of students heading towards the graduation ceremony. The atmosphere was light and joyful, his fellow students whooping and clapping each other on the back, running around with their gowns billowing behind them like superhero capes. As they entered the hall and were herded into alphabetical order, the atmosphere grew more serious, and was almost solemn by the time everyone had been ushered to their seats. As he walked to his place in the auditorium, Axel caught a glimpse of his mother, looking lovely in lilac and dabbing at her eyes with a handkerchief, and his girlfriend, Patti-Ann, fixing her shining blonde curls in her pocket mirror. His heart swelled with joy as Elgar's 'Pomp and Circumstance' began to play from the speakers.

Four years! He was barely able to focus on the solemn speeches, so busy was he going over all of his memories of his time as an engineer. There was the Chancellor, Langdon, his familiar hawkish profile surveying the rows, smiling like every person sitting in that auditorium was his favourite child. What a wonderful university! How he'd loved his time here, Axel thought warmly. Every bit of it. How nervous he'd been in his first lectures as a freshman. How happy he'd been to discover he loved the course. The canteen camaraderie, the fraternity practical jokes. The long nights studying, and the early coffee-fuelled practicals. He looked around him at the faces of his classmates, some serious, some still grinning, and the mass of people blurred a little as a tear came to his eye. All at once it was time: Chancellor Langdon began calling students to the front. The As went first, Posy Adams and Jim Appleby, and before he knew it, Axel was standing too, and walking to the front of the line, and looking up into the Chancellor's eyes as his diploma was handed to him. Axel felt his heart pounding as he walked off the stage. A handshake and a piece of paper in a tube: so little, and yet in that moment, they meant the whole world to him.

It seemed just a minute later that he was standing blinking in the sun, as someone handed him a glass of wine and a platter of canapés. Dazed, he selected a deep-fried shrimp. Satin hangings emblazoned with the lone star were blowing in the light summer breeze above a large buffet table, while family members milled around, chatting and congratulating each other's offspring on their academic success.

'Summa cum laude!' Axel's mother Felicia kept repeating to everyone that greeted them, in this case, several of Axel's classmates. In her pale violet silk dress, her ample bosom seemed to puff out like a proud mother hen. 'I just can't believe it! Always knew he was a clever boy. But an aeronautical engineer, graduating with full honours from Lake Salvation University, one of the best in the country? Well I never.'

'Mom,' Axel murmured, blushing.

The two classmates, Wally and Bob, jostled each other with their elbows and grinned. 'You're right, Mrs Parker,' Wally said.

Bob tipped his mortarboard in a mock salutation. 'He's a very special boy.'

'Guys!' Axel turned a deeper shade of crimson, and Felicia rounded on her son. 'Stop trying to hide behind me! Was there ever a better day to embarrass you?' she asked, before planting a big sticky kiss on his cheek. 'You're just going to have to put up with it, my darling.' She pulled him into a tight hug, then held him by the shoulders and looked into his eyes. 'I'm just so proud of you! And your father would be so proud too! I just wish he could be with us today.'

As his heart squeezed from the compliment, Axel felt a cool, slender hand slide into his, and turned to find his girlfriend Patti-Ann had returned from her trip to the bathroom to freshen up.

'Sorry, am I interrupting?' she asked Felicia, who smiled.

'Not at all,' she replied. 'Come join the party! We're embarrassing Axel, for a change,' she added with a wink.

'Gosh, you just look so beautiful today,' Axel said. The expressions on his classmates' faces mirrored his. In just a short absence, Patti-Ann had managed to pin her loose curls up into a graceful bun and to reapply eyeshadow, mascara and lipgloss. She looked luminous; positively glistening.

'Can't be looking sweaty and tired on your special day, can I, sweet pea?'

Axel laughed. 'Late night last night?' He grabbed a miniature hotdog from a passing platter.

Patti-Ann shook her head ruefully. 'You know what Pamela's like. You agree to come out for a Coke and five hours later you're riding off to a ranch in somebody's pick-up truck full of...' She clasped her hand to her mouth, but Axel reached up and lowered it slowly.

'I'm glad you had a good time,' he said reassuringly.

Patti-Ann still looked a little nervous. 'I didn't mean... You're not mad at me, honey?'

He smiled. 'You know I like you to have fun. And I trust you! I don't have to know all the details of your nights out. I'm just sorry you're stuck with an old man like me.'

'You *are* an old man!' Bob chimed in. 'Do you know, I've seen him sitting in an armchair cool as a cucumber, reading a newspaper and not even looking up when all those freshmen ladies from Kappa Gamma Phi were dancing around in their—'

'Bob!' Wally cut in. 'That's not a story for... a day like this.'

Patti-Ann laughed. 'Oh, don't worry about me, I've heard all the stories. I know about your little trip to Dallas and everything!' Bob choked on a mini hamburger, making Axel laugh. 'I know I can trust my fiancé,' Patti-Ann continued, unperturbed. 'I'm a lucky girl.' She winked outrageously: this time, it was Wally's turn to go bright red.

'And we're lucky to have you in our family,' Felicia added, interrupting the discussion to put an arm around Patti-Ann's waist. 'Or almost!'

Patti-Ann gave a dazzling smile, and squeezed Felicia's hand. 'I'm looking forward to being a Parker girl,' she said warmly. 'But first we have to wait for this one to get himself a job!'

Axel sighed, only half in jest. 'Do we have to talk about this at my graduation?' he asked.

Patti-Ann pouted. 'But honey, aren't you excited to be done with your degree? And you did so well, too! You could walk into any company you wanted.'

'We've talked about this, sweetie. I'm still thinking about going on to do a PhD.'

A cascade of high-pitched laughter announced that a new arrival had joined the conversation. 'Oh hi, Pamela!' Patti-Ann said, as her friend teetered over, her silvery dress shimmering in the sun, her stiletto heels sinking into the lawn.

'Hi, Patti-Ann. Hi Axel. And who are these charming gentlemen?' Pamela batted her false eyelashes at Wally and Bob, who fell over each other in their enthusiasm to introduce themselves.

'I've leave you two Ps to it, then,' Felicia said, seeming a little disgruntled as she left the group.

'Wait, Mom...' Axel said, but she waved him away with a smile.

'PhD, huh,' Pamela said, squinting at him. 'I thought you nipped that old chestnut in the bud, Patti-Ann.'

Axel shivered a little: a few rare clouds had drifted across the blazing sun. He wished he'd gone after his mother.

Patti-Ann shrugged. 'I'm not his mother,' she said, smiling a little. She turned to Axel. 'And if you don't want to talk about this today, that's fine.'

Pamela made a grunting sort of noise. 'Well I don't mean to piss on your parade, but I was really looking forward to coming to all your swanky dinner parties when you guys finally got a house. I mean, where are you going to live? What are you going to do for money?'

'I'll be staying with my mother for the rest of the summer,' Axel said firmly, *though it's none of your business*, he added in his head.

'So what would your PhD topic be, Ax?' Wally asked, clearly trying to be helpful.

'I… I'm not sure. I have a few ideas.' Axel looked around desperately, seeking some form of escape: his mother, perhaps. All he found, however, was a platter of tiny cups of macaroni and cheese, one of which he grabbed gratefully. 'Look, can we just enjoy today without worrying about the future? I feel like today is about celebrating the last four years.'

'I feel like today is about free food,' Pamela retorted, grabbing some mini macaroni. 'Is all of it so small?'

'Hear hear,' said Bob, though Axel was unsure whether he was replying to Pamela or himself.

'What are we agreeing to?' Felicia inquired, reappearing with none other than Professor Bohmann on her arm.

'Professor!' Axel said happily, partly grateful for the change of topic. The professor's idea of dressing up for a fancy occasion appeared to be inherited from the nineteenth century, involving a tattered tweed waistcoat and a ludicrous gold tie pin.

'What an utterly charming mother you have,' he said, giving an old-fashioned bow. Felicia blushed.

'You old rogue! If you weren't my son's favourite tutor…'

But Axel's mother didn't finish her sentence, as a tall, glittering figure practically threw herself at the professor, quite nearly knocking him to the ground.

'Hi, I'm Pamela,' she said quite loudly.

Axel inhaled deeply, counted to five, then breathed out slowly. 'Professor Bohmann,' he said, deciding to ignore Patti-Ann's friend. 'It's so nice to see you!'

Bohmann extricated himself from Pamela's grip, looking even more dishevelled than usual, and awkwardly shook Axel's hand. 'Wonderful day, wonderful day,' he said. 'I can never believe how fast those four years fly by. It's seems just yesterday you were showing up at my office, looking terribly shame-faced—'

Pamela, seemingly unfazed by Bohmann dismissal, had somehow moved around and was now draping her arm across Axel's shoulders. 'Blown anything up lately?' she asked. 'I haven't blown anything...'

Felicia rolled her eyes.

'Pamela,' Wally said, catching the expression on Axel's face, 'why don't I introduce you to some of the boys from the football team?'

Pamela gave a noise best described as a squeal, and let Wally lead her away without any resistance. Bob followed, grinning and waving back at Axel. 'Free food *and* boys,' Pamela could be heard exclaiming, as they disappeared into the crowd.

Axel sighed, relieved.

'Goodness,' Bohmann said, brushing his suit off as if to rid it of dust. 'Are all young women like that nowadays?'

'Absolutely not,' Felicia replied firmly. 'Our Patti-Ann is a sweetheart.'

Patti-Ann gave a wavering smile. 'I'm so sorry about my friend,' she said. 'I thought it was nice that she wanted to come along today, I didn't think...'

'It's OK,' Axel said. 'It's not your fault.' He kissed the top of his girlfriend's head.

'She's certainly entertaining,' Felicia added dryly. 'Where did you meet this charming young lady?'

'She lives just down the road from me,' Patti-Ann said anxiously. 'I'm sorry, Mrs Parker. And I didn't mean to pressure you about getting a job, Axel,' she burst out, obviously overcome by a surge of guilt. 'I know it's your decision to make.'

'Oh, sweetie!' Axel said, putting his arm around his girlfriend. 'I've been trying to decide if I should go on to do a PhD,' he explained to Professor Bohmann, who was looking decidedly uncomfortable.

'Oh, right!' he said. 'Well, you know how I feel about that, my boy. I'd love nothing more in the world than to keep you in my department another few years.'

'Of course, I have to take a lot of factors into consideration,' Axel continued, smiling down at Patti-Ann. 'Sometimes, I feel like it's time for me to head out into the real world, get a job, maybe think about having kids.' He added the last bit almost without thinking, knowing it would make Patti-Ann smile, but he hadn't factored his mother's presence into the equation.

'Oh!' Felicia said, waving her hands in the air as if there was a great deal more she wanted to say, but obviously trying to retain decorum. A glance exchanged between his mother and his girlfriend told Axel all he needed to know: if reproduction became a part of his plan for the near future, it would certainly be well received.

'Don't have kids unless you're truly ready,' Professor Bohmann said, unexpectedly. Seeing the surprised and disappointed glances of his audience, he seemingly remembered himself. 'I just mean... a lot of people get carried away by young love, and make decisions too quickly. I just want you to be happy,' he concluded awkwardly.

'You know I'll support you no matter what you choose,' Felicia said warmly. 'You can live with me as long as you like, or go back to Zeta Delta Pi. Some of those boys are just so nice, and I know you like a little freedom! And you know that the minute you find a house you like, I'll help you out with the deposit.'

Patti-Ann beamed, and Axel felt a wave of love for all these people wash over him. Which made it a perfect moment for Pamela to return, Wally and Bob trailing behind her like downtrodden lackeys. 'Where are those little macaroni pots?' she demanded.

Felicia gave a very warm smile. 'I think the snacks and wine are finished, sweetie.'

'Hey, do you guys want to go to Big Boy for a half a pounder? Or wait, maybe we could go to Kraft's, they have all you can eat for three dollars. Why don't we head over there, maybe grab a cocktail after? What do you say?'

'We already have plans,' Patti-Ann said firmly.

'Oh, come on,' Pamela sighed. 'Don't be boring.'

'We have a reservation at the steakhouse,' Axel said. 'For three,' he added pointedly.

'Yeah, I'm having dinner with my dad,' Bob added, sounding embarrassed.

'I'll come!' said Wally to Pamela.

'What about you?' Pamela said seductively to Professor Bohmann, ignoring Wally. 'Does a big boy like you like Big Boy?'

'No,' Bohmann blurted out, before seemingly gathering his spirits. 'I too have plans.' There was an awkward silence, in which Bohmann clearly tried to make up a pretend plan in case he needed to defend his decision to decline a date with a twenty-year-old stranger.

'Fine,' Pamela replied, shrugging. 'Come on Wally. Why don't you buy me a burger.'

'Let me walk with you, Pammy,' Patti-Ann suggested. 'Give me chance to say goodbye.'

'Give me a chance to catch up on your gossip, you mean, in double time,' Pamela retorted, 'before I dedicate myself entirely to this sexy young man.'

'Axel!' Bohmann said suddenly, as the three wandered away, Wally looking distinctly dazed. 'Will you be coming to my lecture on Saturday?'

'A lecture, Melvin?' Felicia asked politely. 'What's it about?'

'Don't get him started,' Axel said hastily.

Bohmann laughed. 'God and science, God and science, I'm like a broken record, aren't I.'

'How fascinating!' said Felicia.

'Actually, I'm not sure I can come,' Axel added. 'Patti-Ann and I were thinking of heading into Austin for the weekend. There's this new Mexican grill she really wanted to try.'

'Oh, right,' Bohmann said, looking crestfallen. 'Well, no matter, no matter, I'm sure I'll see you soon enough.'

There was an awkward pause.

'I mean, I don't know yet,' Axel said slowly. 'I might be able to—'

But Bohmann waved his hand in the air. 'Forgive me. You're a graduate now, Axel, and I'm just a selfish old man. You don't have to come to any lectures you don't want to! Anyway, I didn't come here to blow my own trumpet: I wanted to congratulate you.'

He stuck out his hand for a handshake, and Axel pulled him into a hug, which the professor returned with more warmth than he'd expected. 'I'll see you soon, Professor,' he said, his voice muffled by Bohmann's musty shoulder.

Bohmann pulled away a little abruptly, coughed, said 'Well,' patted Axel on the shoulder, and walked away.

'Axel!' Felicia chided him, as the professor disappeared from view. 'This lecture sounds like a big deal. Why did you have to hurt his feelings like that? The professor's obviously very fond of you, and I thought you liked him too!'

Axel sighed. 'I know, I know, that was really rude of me. I probably should go. It's just… Well, his theories are getting crazier and crazier. None of the scientists in the department will listen to him anymore, and I'm worried about this public lecture – I don't think it'll go down well with the Defenders of Grace.'

Felicia made a tsking sound. 'You know those holy rollers are crazy,' she said.

'I know. To be honest, I love the man to pieces,' Axel continued, 'but it's hard to watch him go on like this. This lecture, it'll be like throwing him into the gladiator's arena with a bunch of lions.'

'Well you should be there, then, to show him some support! I mean, you care about this man. You've been close. Are you even going to see each other anymore, now that you've graduated? For shame.'

Axel blushed. 'You're right, Mom. I'm being selfish. I should go to the lecture.'

Felicia patted him on the shoulder. 'That's my boy,' she said. 'And here's your girl!'

'Is it time for dinner yet?' Patti-Ann asked, reappearing with pink cheeks. 'Those snacks were pretty tiny.'

'I think it might just be. Looks like the crowds are dying down. Why don't we walk?' Axel suggested. 'Downtown's only twenty minutes away…'

'That sounds real nice,' Patti-Ann said.

'Let me just get my coat out of the car,' Felicia said. 'It might get chilly later.'

'We'll wait by the main entrance,' Axel told her.

The young couple walked in silence for a few minutes. 'Listen, sweetheart,' Axel began reluctantly, 'I don't want you to get upset, but I feel like I have to tell you I don't understand why you brought Pamela along today. It's a bit like bringing a pet tiger to Sunday school.'

'She's basically family!' Patti-Ann said defensively. 'You know we've been friends since we were kids. She lives just down the road from me.'

'OK, I understand that, but why did you have to bring her to my graduation? That's the part I don't understand. I mean, you were out with her last night.'

'I don't know,' Patti-Ann said quietly. 'I guess I was just nervous.'

'Nervous?' Axel stopped and turned to look at his girlfriend. 'Why would you be nervous?'

'You know I don't like your big fancy college things! I'm just a… technical college bimbo to them, like that professor of yours. He probably doesn't think you should have kids with me cause I'm too stupid for you.'

'Patti-Ann!' Axel said, mortified. 'My darling! How could you think such a thing? Professor Bohmann, he's weird with everybody. All my friends love you.'

'They like Pamela better,' Patti-Ann said remorsefully.

'That's because she's a—' Axel stopped and sighed. 'Look, what's done is done. I guess I've just never understood your friendship, that's all. I mean, she's such a party girl!'

'I'm a party girl too,' Patti-Ann said, sounding hurt. 'And if you were going to call her… I don't know, an airhead, or worse, well the same goes for me. We're two peas in a pod. Two Ps!'

'But Patti-Ann,' Axel said, getting exasperated, 'she spent the first few months of our acquaintance flirting outrageously with me. Why would you think she'd be able to behave at a graduation?'

'You know that's just how she is! She can't resist a man she can't have. Even a gross old professor, I guess.'

Axel laughed. 'I guess it's a lost cause, trying to understand a female friendship. Anyway, I guess you realise you made a mistake. Let's not talk about it anymore. Look, there's my mom with her coat.' He took Patti-Ann by the shoulders and kissed her gently.

'Hey, lovebirds. Who's ready for a nice tenderloin steak?' Felicia called out.

'I'm hoping for a club sandwich,' Patti-Ann replied, smiling. 'Or maybe a salad.'

'And a nice glass of wine,' Axel added. 'Come on, ladies: the night's still young.'

He slung an arm over each of their shoulders and walked off the university campus lawns. Unbidden, the thought drifted through his mind: *Would this be the last time?*

CHAPTER THREE

The day of Professor Bohmann's lecture dawned bright and warm, with just a hint of autumn in the breeze. Now that the September term was starting up, it was strange to walk past the LSU campus. If he sent in the paperwork now, Axel found himself thinking, he would be able to register for a PhD in the spring semester…

As he entered the town hall, Axel didn't see any of his fellow students, but he did see a few professors from the science department, clustered in the back rows. They looked uneasy, as if they weren't sure they were in the right place. Axel raised a hand to wave as he walked by, but none of them acknowledged him. He shook his head and kept walking down the central aisle. It would be nice if Bohmann could see him, he thought, given how disappointed the professor had sounded when Axel had told him he might bail on the lecture. The hall was packed, though, which would surely make his old tutor happy. Looking around at the crowd as he settled into his seat, Axel was a little surprised to find a sea of unfamiliar faces – and a few undesirable ones.

With a sinking heart, Axel recognised Ichabod Potts, the leader of the Texas Defenders of Grace, surrounded by twenty, maybe thirty, of his disciples. Potts was a minor local TV celebrity, preaching fire and brimstone to housewives and gas station attendants from Waco to Abilene. His followers were well-known for their intense devotion and mob-like behaviour. He hoped Bohmann wouldn't provide any fuel for their fire. Where was Bohmann, though? Axel finally spotted him hunched behind the podium, pawing through his notes as if revising for an exam. When the bell of the nearby First Lake Salvation Church of Grace began to toll, he sat up, startled, looking remarkably like a mad scientist. Then he banged his pile of notes on the podium to straighten it, and stood up.

'Good afternoon, everyone,' he said. 'I'm Melvin Bohmann, from the Physics department at Lake Salvation University. Some of you will know me from class, others from the first of these lectures I gave, some ten years ago.' He looked a little nervous, and there were whispers throughout the room, but he ploughed on with his script. 'I guess it can't have been so bad if they asked me back!' The whispers grew louder, and not all of the laughter was sympathetic. Axel felt a worried feeling creeping back into the pit of his stomach. 'Don't worry,' Bohmann continued, visibly sweating, Axel noted, less than a minute into his speech, 'I'll try to steer clear of controversial topics. Today, I'd like to talk to you about the sun.'

There were murmurs throughout the room, some of them approving. Axel relaxed a little.

'Look outside, through these big windows,' Bohmann began. 'What do you see?' He paused, waiting for answers.

'Grass!' a young man finally called out.

'Trees!' an elderly woman added.

'Light,' said Bohmann. He left a long pause for emphasis. 'The light shining through these windows, those long golden rays making the dust motes shine, are a blazing, visible form of converted energy.' In moments such as these, Axel understood why the man had a reputation as a prophet. A sweaty, nervous prophet, admittedly, but a prophet nonetheless. There was an intensity to his gaze, a solemnity to his voice, that sent shivers down his spine.

'Where does that energy come from?' Bohmann continued. 'The sun.' He began pacing up and down the stage, as if he was in one of his university lectures. 'The sun – the poets' golden orb – is our central processing unit, our solar system's source of energy, the patriarch of all the planets. What would our lives be like, here in Texas, without the light of the sun? The sun, in fact, is our lone star.'

He paused, obviously awaiting some kind of reaction, and a few confused cheers rang out. 'The sun's a star?' an older woman whispered loudly to her neighbour.

Bohmann ignored the reactions and continued. 'The state of Texas has between 200 and 300 days of sunlight a year. That's 100, 150 days of full, bright sunshine, and another 100 of partial sun. Can you even conceive of that quantity of energy? Our planet revolves around the sun, bathing in that light. It's our wealth, like the oil we have below the earth, our gold.'

Here, a scattering of cheers rang out across the room. Even if they weren't following all of Bohmann's line of argument, some of the audience were clearly moved by his oratorical skills.

'Now, if you forgive me for talking about hard science for a minute, I want to explain a little about the power of that sun. I know some of my students are in the room: they can ignore the next section, which will be familiar to them. After all, I'm not here to teach a class on thermodynamics.'

A few giggles and mutters were heard, and Bohmann's eyes cast around the room, as if he was looking for his students but having trouble locating them. Axel sat up a little straighter, wondering if he was the only one of his class who had showed up, and after a moment the professor's eyes met his. Bohmann nodded and smiled.

'I'd like to talk about energy. What is energy? You're no doubt imagining a fire, or a combustion engine, but there is all of fluid mechanics to take into account as well, and electromagnetic energy... There's the kinetic energy of an object in movement, the thermal energy of changing temperatures, the elastic energy of stretching solid objects, the nuclear energy of splitting atoms. But your first instinct, I'm guessing, is to think of the most powerful manifestation of energy, the most visible to the human eye: burning. The chemical energy released by burning fuel, and the radiant energy embodied in a ray of light.'

He gestured at the sunlight streaming in through the town hall's windows, as if awestruck. Bohmann's relationship to science, it was clear, bore an almost religious intensity.

'We think of the sun as fertile, as benevolent. It makes our crops grow. It tans our farmers' necks. It makes us smile in the morning, like a glass of fresh orange juice. It fills us with vitamin D. But these rays of light coming straight from the sun, 150 million kilometres away, are produced by a flaming ball of gas. At its core, the sun has a temperature of 27 million degrees Fahrenheit.'

Bohmann paused for a moment to let this sink in.

'Now, as any of my students will tell you, the laws of physics say that energy can neither be created nor destroyed: it can only be transformed. But – and this is a question that has preoccupied me for nigh on thirty years – what happens to the energy in the core of the sun? What happens to those twenty-seven million degrees? Where does all that heat go? What happened to all that energy, that, as we know from Newtonian physics, cannot disappear or stop, only be transformed? What happens to the energy of fires that go out, or the burning rays of the sun that strike the earth? Do they just come to a dead stop? And how is humanity allowed to survive the power of the universe? I mean, we burn our hands badly when we get splashed with boiling water. That's 212 degrees Fahrenheit. So why aren't we all being fried up like pigs on a barbecue? Why haven't we all turned to cinders? I'll tell you why: because of God. God has intervened, to save us from the heat of the sun. God is protecting us.'

There was an uproar in several parts of the room: a cluster of science professors from the university began raising their hands, and somebody shouted out something about the atmosphere. In another part of the room, shouts of 'Praise the Lord!' and 'God is great!' were echoing out. Axel felt his stomach sinking.

Professor Bohmann held up both his hands, and silence slowly fell across the auditorium. 'Now, I know my theories have been seen as controversial, but I'd like you all to hear me out. I'm working on a book, in which my thoughts will be laid out at great length, but today is just an introduction.' The pleading note in his tone worried Axel. 'One thing I'd like to clarify first and foremost is what I mean by 'God.' I am a Christian, like most people in this fair town, but my religion is not what inspires my scientific theory. It is the other way round: through the study of science, I believe I have proved the existence of God.'

There was a louder roar from the Defenders of Grace and, this time, some of the scientists simply got up and filed out of the auditorium, but Bohmann kept talking. 'As the writer C.S. Lewis said, "I believe in Christianity as I believe that the sun has risen: not only because I see it, but because by it I see everything else." God is an obvious truth; a postulate, if you will, in scientific terms. God shows us the way in our scientific research, and is simultaneously an integral part of it. God cannot be separated from life on earth. God is light, God is energy, God is a protective force. Some of my colleagues would like to call that the atmosphere: that's fine!' He raised his voice, here, as if to appeal to the scientists, but not one of them turned back. The door slammed loudly.

'Some others call this force Jehovah, or Allah, or they call it the big man in the sky. I'm not interested in debating the appearance of this superpower, this ultimate energy. I'm not interested in the face of God: I'm interested in the hand of God.'

A voice rose from the back of the room, louder than Bohmann's. 'Shut your blasphemous mouth! You heathen. How dare you speak about Our Lord in this way?'

Shouts of 'Amen!' rang out, like a chorus in call and response.

Axel turned around: it was Ichabod Potts, towering over the rows of chairs as if they were the pews of his church, the faces of his devotees turned to him like flowers to the sun. His face was pale, his hair was floppy and dark red, and his eyes burned, in Axel's opinion, with a quite unholy fire.

'What do you know of our Lord's mysterious ways?' he cried out, as if performing in a play. 'How can you stand in front of the people of this good town and spew out your ugly, atheist lies? I've never heard such a twisted rendition of faith in my life. Go hence and be baptised, before you flood the ears of the believers with your heathen filth!'

Bohmann appeared to have gathered his strength and steadied himself enough to speak. 'I'm not baptised, Ichabod,' he said slowly. 'I've never pretended anything to the contrary. My faith does not have a name. It is a private matter.'

'Then why are you here preaching it?' Potts bellowed triumphantly.

'Because I want to share what I've learned,' Bohmann said simply. 'Because I want to discuss, and debate it. It's why I became a university professor. Go on, then, share your challenges. I welcome them.'

'My challenges?' Potts repeated with a sneer. 'I have no need to challenge you, only to correct you. You've lost, Melvin Bohmann. Your science followers have deserted you. The faithful have no interest in your mad, made-up version of religion.'

The chorus of 'Amen' that followed was sprinkled with laughter.

'You're right about one thing, Bohmann,' Potts said sarcastically. 'God does protect us. God keeps us safe. He keeps us safe from crazy old professors like you, preaching that the universe is millions of years old, and that all life evolved on its own, magically, without a helping hand. He keeps us safe from all the liberal loonies who think we're the grandchildren of monkeys. How can you raise your voice to challenge God, when God has already answered all our questions?'

'I don't...' Bohmann tried to interrupt, but it was no use. His talk had been hijacked. Potts' voice was smooth and oily, a resonant tenor that could be heard clearly from every seat in the room. Axel had no doubt that the preacher had calculated his seating based on this assumption.

'If true believers want to think about God's relationship with men on earth, if they want to contemplate the generous beauty of his creation, then they can come to church. They don't have to sit here and listen to your improvised pseudo-religious, pseudo-scientific bullshit. The Bible isn't just a text you can ignore, or give your own interpretation of! The Bible is the word of the Lord, laid down in stone and passed down through the centuries to help us through our life on earth.'

'Amen! Amen!' the followers cried out. The shouts were perfectly coordinated: so much so that they sounded rehearsed. Axel closed his eyes: of course they were rehearsed. This whole intervention had been seamlessly planned by old Ichabod Potts to fire up his old faithfuls and turn some wavering hearts. A recruitment drive, Axel realised.

Potts still wasn't finished. At this point, everyone in the town hall had swivelled to face him. 'The truth of our life on this earth is not something we can just make up as we go along. How can you be so arrogant, so foolhardy, as to stand in front of all these people and ramble on about your fallible, changing views? How can you try to reconcile the irreconcilable? The true believer doesn't change his mind: he accepts the world just as it is, as it was made by our Lord God in heaven. He doesn't ask questions, and he doesn't give talks about his crazy personal theories.'

A young man sprang up from his seat at Potts' right hand, his face contorted with fury. 'Shut up! Just shut up! You're not in your safe little university now,' he shouted, 'spreading your liberal lies.'

Something about the viciousness of the youth's tone made Axel turn around and look at Bohmann, just in time to witness the last shred of composure vanishing from his face. Axel's beloved professor looked like he'd been punched in the stomach. He opened his mouth as if to say something, and one quiet syllable emerged – a name, perhaps? – but no more. Axel turned back to look at the boy, a lanky youth with long, dark hair and a sallow face, and saw that Ichabod Potts' had put his hand on his shoulder, as if to curb any further outbursts.

'See,' Potts' said. 'Out of the mouths of babes.'

There was a long pause. Then, heartbroken and astonished, Axel watched as Bohmann began to collect his papers into a stack. After a few minutes' silence, a few people began leaving the room in awkward gaggles, though the Defenders of Grace stayed where they were. 'Thank you all for coming,' Bohmann muttered in the microphone, barely raising his eyes. 'That'll be all for today.'

CHAPTER FOUR

'Maybe I should postpone the meeting,' Axel said, slowly stirring his coffee, his eyes glued to the TV.

Grainy shots of the façade of Lake Salvation University, slashed in graffiti, were underlaid with running ticker tape: *Science scandal hits Lake Salvation. Professor Bohmann embroiled in religious controversy. Science department targeted by Defenders of Grace group.* The shots of the campus made Axel so sad, the paint probably still wet on some of the slogans the Defenders of Grace had managed to drum up over the weekend. DIE YOU COMMUNIST and ATHEIST MAGGOT sat alongside BOHMANN MUST GO.

Bohmann has to walk past this every single morning just to go to work, Axel thought drearily.

'Honey, it'll probably do Professor Bohmann good to talk about something other than this craziness.' Felicia was concentrating on the waffle iron, which she was wiping down with a paper towel. Hot, buttery steam rose from the metal, making Axel's stomach growl.

'I'm just so worried about him!' he said. 'Mom, you just can't imagine how badly that talk went. I wanted... You know how sometimes you want to sink into the ground? Well, for the first time in my life, I wanted that for another person.'

'I know, honey. You've told me already.' Felicia poured the batter into the waffle iron, then closed it with a satisfying hiss. 'Look, you two set up this meeting two days after the talk, so he was already stressed. Besides, you've made your decision, you're ready to start your PhD. Why miss this deadline and have to wait a whole semester? Bohmann will probably welcome a break from this media madness.'

She gestured at the television, where Ichabod Potts' unwelcome face had appeared, glowing a truly worrying shade of orange and giving a slimy smile.

'Thank you for having me, Mr Klauser,' he was saying ingratiatingly. 'It's always a pleasure to reach a wider audience than my own faithful congregation.' He laughed softly, an unpleasant sound.

'Do you think that horrible man wears a toupee?' Felicia asked. She patted her own strawberry blonde locks. 'It makes me feel ashamed of my Irish blood.'

Keith Klauser, a smart Scandinavian-looking newscaster, had been an anchor at the local television station for as long as Axel could remember. He was glad Klauser had been chosen to take on the preacher, rather than one of the younger women – no accident, surely. Potts could be brutal, at times.

Axel smiled against his will. 'I hope he does,' he said, forcing himself to look away from the TV. 'I hope it comes flying off in the middle of one of his crazy sermons. I don't understand why they let him on TV.'

'Why have you picketed Professor Bohmann's lectures?' the newsreader asked, as the screen cut away to pictures of various figures from the Defenders of Grace group carrying placards. THE SCIENCE DELUSION, one of them read, and DON'T LET THIS MAN TEACH OUR KIDS.

'We think it's irresponsible to let a man so obviously confused and corrupt anywhere near the young minds of this city,' Potts said smoothly. 'Bohmann has a history of—'

'I'm not interested in hearing your views on Professor Bohmann, Mr Potts,' the newscaster cut in. 'This is a short interview, not a debate.'

'Certainly, Keith—'

'That's Mr Klauser to you,' the newscaster said shortly.

'I've always rather liked that Klauser,' Felicia said. 'Smart-sounding young man.' She popped a waffle out of the iron, and began pouring another ladle of batter in.

Axel tuned back into the preacher's stream-of-consciousness-style account of Bohmann's speech. 'There were young children in that town hall,' the preacher was saying melodramatically, his red hair flopping around. 'Innocent souls. Good Christians. And there he is, this madman with his big pile of notes for his book, telling them God is the sun, or God doesn't exist, or God is some mathematical theorem.'

'No there weren't! There weren't any kids,' Axel cried out in frustration, but of course Potts' pixelated face didn't react.

'As if children can't make up their own minds about God,' Felicia huffed, 'or tell who's crazy and who's not.'

'You can't just go around spouting made-up theories about God to innocent ears. The man's not even a Christian, and he's standing up in the town hall telling us God is some big ball of gas! It's a disgrace that he was given a public platform, right in our town hall. We're already being punished: there's a tornado headed right towards the innocent and righteous homes of Lake Salvation, and Melvin Bohmann is to blame. All he wants is to sell copies of his book!' Ichabod Potts ranted on. 'He's a liar and a narcissist, an atheist fool.'

'Mr Potts, your followers are blocking the streets and the university campus. The city has ground to a halt. People are missing important appointments, buses are running late, and student exams are being cancelled. Can you tell us when you expect this to end?'

'As soon as Professor Bohmann is fired,' Potts said with a smile.

Axel let out something like a growl.

'What would you like with your waffles, sweetie?' asked Felicia. 'Syrup or blueberries?'

'I just can't believe it!' Axel groaned, ignoring his mother's attempt to cajole him out of his bad mood. 'Poor Professor Bohmann. All he wanted was to share his ideas with the world, or at least the city. Now it must feel as if everyone's turned against him.'

'Honey, the professor's no spring chicken. I'm sure he's keeping his head above water. Now, one more time: syrup or blueberries?'

★ ★ ★ ★

Bohmann looked up at Axel from behind his desk, a panicked look in his eyes. Crumpled papers spread around him in all directions. There were four or five dirty mugs visible, propped precariously under open books, and a pizza box under the desk.

'Did you forget...' Axel asked, before he could stop himself.

'Oh God,' said Bohmann, bleary-eyed, 'did we schedule a meeting for today? I'm such an idiot.'

'Professor, please don't worry!' Axel pleaded. 'Remember, it was just to look through the paperwork for a PhD. Nothing pressing.'

'But you're already late. When is the deadline again, next week?'

Axel nodded hesitantly. 'But I realise you've got other things on your mind, Professor.'

Bohmann looked like he hadn't slept in days, or changed his clothes to do so. His shirt was buttoned up wrong, and there was a large stain on the front. Axel also noticed a blueish smudge on his forehead, which looked rather like a line of type – perhaps, he surmised, the result of dropping a sweaty face onto a newspaper in despair.

'It's just...' Bohmann ran a hand through his messy hair, 'I've been having trouble with my computer.' He stared at the screen blankly for a minute.

'Your computer?' Axel repeated.

'I can't seem to access any of my book files. It was fine yesterday, I was working on a new chapter, something to show those heathens...' His breath caught in his throat, and for a terrible moment Axel thought he might be about to cry.

'Don't worry, Professor! Why don't we ask somebody in the computer lab?'

Bohmann looked up as if Axel had just solved some mathematical theorem. 'The computer lab!' he exclaimed. 'I hadn't thought of that. Yes, surely Tippetts will be able to help me. Come, come, my boy.'

As he dragged himself laboriously from his chair, Axel caught a whiff of his ripe aroma. 'Professor,' he asked hesitantly, 'have you been living in the department?'

Bohmann barked out a laugh. 'Have you seen those crowds? Savages. The last time I set foot outside the department, I got hit with a rotten tomato.'

'So you're hiding in here,' Axel concluded.

Bohmann shrugged. 'Maybe someone as young and as full of energy as you couldn't understand, but I just don't have it in me to face them. The fight's gone out of me. I could lose my job.'

'Surely Chancellor Langdon wouldn't let that happen!'

'Chancellor Langdon's a coward and a demagogue,' Bohmann said, walking slowly down the hallway. 'He wants to keep Lake Salvation University's reputation spotless. If these lunatics keep blocking traffic and picketing lectures, and if this ends up on national news, he'll give in.'

'That's awful!' Axel exclaimed. 'That's so unfair!'

Bohmann cracked a sad smile. 'I appreciate the sentiment, Axel, but you should know that I'm not innocent. I made the choice to give a controversial lecture on an inflammatory subject in the town hall of a city ruled over by holy rollers.'

'The Defenders of Grace don't rule me!' Axel retorted. 'And they shouldn't rule anyone. Just because that old fool Potts can get himself on television...'

'Enough, Axel,' Bohmann said gently. He stopped in front of the door to the computer lab. 'Believe me, I've been over all of it too many times already. What's done is done.'

'I'm sorry, Professor,' Axel said guiltily. 'I didn't mean to speak out of turn.'

Bohmann smiled as he opened the door. 'That's quite alright, Axel,' he said.

Several professors from the science department were sitting together in the computer lab. They looked up, startled, when Bohmann and Axel came in. Axel wondered if they'd been gossiping about their colleague. Tippetts was sitting in the corner, tinkering with one of the older computers, while McMahon and Schumacher were sitting conspiratorially side by side.

'Hi, Melvin,' McMahon said cheerily.

'Hi,' Bohmann said hesitantly.

'How are you holding up?' Schumacher said, his tone not unfriendly.

'OK, I guess,' Bohmann replied. 'It's been a tough few days.'

'God I hate those Defenders of Grace guys,' McMahon contributed. 'Those women in their long skirts – they look like they should be churning butter. And don't get me started on those virginity rings or whatever they're called. Loons, the lot of 'em!'

'They may be crazy, but they're powerful,' Schumacher replied. 'And, well, they have a point.'

'A point?' Axel repeated, flabbergasted. He had expected the professor's colleagues to be supportive at least, if not kind.

Schumacher shrugged. 'Don't take it personally, Melvin, but if you're going to go public with that crazy science-and-religion stuff, you've got to expect some controversy.'

'It's like oil and water,' McMahon added. 'Science and religion will never mix.'

Schumacher and McMahon turned to each other and laughed chummily.

'Don't you realise how serious this is?' Axel burst out. Bohmann laid a hand on his shoulder, but he couldn't stop. 'You're just as bad as the Defenders of Grace!' he said.

'Who is this kid, anyway?' McMahon asked, amused.

'I'm soon to be a PhD student in this department,' Axel replied, standing up straight, 'and if I was one of Professor Bohmann's colleagues, I would be standing up for him, not laughing at his adversaries.'

'If this is about your petition, Melv,' Schumacher said, while McMahon rolled his eyes, 'I'm real sorry, but I just can't put my own work at risk.'

'What petition?' Axel asked, confused.

Bohmann sighed. 'Some of my… A select few of my colleagues have put together a petition asking Chancellor Langdon not to fire me. It's unlikely to work. But I must say I'm disappointed at the ridiculously small number of signatures.'

Schumacher looked a little guilty, but his tone was defensive: 'You're all over the TV, Melv,' he said. 'We can't associate ourselves with this scandal! You're going down in history as a madman, a radical…'

'A radical?' Bohmann raised his voice. 'A radical? Aren't radical theories exactly what we scientists are meant to be pursuing? Pushing back the frontiers of human knowledge, questioning everything we hold true? How is my work any more controversial than your discoveries in chemistry, McMahon, or yours, Schumacher: how crazy did people say you were when you started writing about goose intestines?' He turned to Axel. 'Professor Schumacher's research claims that some of the protein found in goose guts could help strengthen human immune systems, and ultimately cure several forms of cancer, or even act as a sort of fountain of eternal youth.'

'That's hopelessly simplifying my thesis—' Schumacher tried to intervene, but Bohmann wasn't finished.

'As if every one of you wasn't hopelessly simplifying mine! None of you even came to my lecture. I bet you didn't even read the abstract. You're basing your opinion of my work on some graffiti, on the hatred of a television preacher.'

'And where else are we meant to get information?' McMahon cut in. 'You've been working on that damn book of yours for years, and not a page published.'

'Not all of us have twenty books self-published on Amazon,' Schumacher interrupted, and the two professors started laughing again, as if all of this was just a game.

Axel's blood was boiling. 'I can't believe you're standing here mocking Professor Bohmann, a man with more integrity than the rest of the department put together, and you won't even consider signing the petition,' he burst out. 'You think the Defenders of Grace are the intolerant ones, you call yourself rational men—'

'Enough, Axel,' Bohmann said, squeezing his shoulder. 'We're wasting our breath here. I appreciate your support, but my colleagues' minds are clearly made up. Tippetts, could you come to my office, please?'

Tippetts, who had been staring intently at his computer, as if hoping no-one would notice him, jumped a little in his seat, then sat up straight. 'Of course,' he said in his soft, scratchy voice. 'Anything to help a colleague.' He flushed bright red, and scurried towards them.

Without another word, the trio left the computer lab.

'I'm sorry, Professor,' Axel said. 'I just couldn't help it. How can they be so selfish? They're your colleagues!'

'Don't apologise, Axel,' Bohmann said. 'I really appreciate how passionately you feel about all this. But those two… They're snakes in the grass. If I'm fired, you see, they have a better shot at tenure. They wouldn't defend my case to the Chancellor if you put a gun to their heads.'

'They're afraid.' Tippetts suddenly spoke up, quite unexpectedly. 'Cowards. Afraid of the Chancellor, afraid of the Defenders of Grace, afraid for their paltry little careers… Do you know Schumacher takes a taxi to work every morning, just so he doesn't have to walk past the pickets?'

Bohmann shook his head. 'We live in a strange time,' he said. 'Where self-professed men of God and men of science are bullies and cowards and fools. Worst of all, where they refuse to listen to each other! Intolerance rules this city, and intolerance is, more than anything, what I want to fight with my book. I want the two sides to stop fighting. Not for them to stand back to back, either, with their fingers plugged in their ears, but to listen to each other. For fertile dialogue.' He sighed as they arrived in front of the door to his office.

'Spent a lot of time in here lately, huh,' Tippetts said with a mousy grin.

'It feels like an eternity,' Bohmann replied.

'No family waiting for you at home? Lucky man,' Tippetts joked, but Bohmann looked sad.

'No,' he said shortly. 'Not for a long time.'

There was an awkward silence as the three men entered the room and gazed over the chaos of paper.

'Ah, there's the beast!' Tippetts joked, upon finally locating the computer. He gingerly made his way through the boxes and mugs, and lowered himself into the desk chair. 'So you said you were working on a book?'

'Yes,' Bohmann replied, 'so I can share my theories with a wider audience than this bigoted crew. But I just can't seem to log on correctly. When I type in my passwords, all of my personal files show up empty.'

'Can you come over here and give me your access codes?' Tippetts asked, and Bohmann waded through the paper to stand next to him.

Tippetts was quiet for a while, clicking around and typing in lines of code, his expression worryingly serious. With his cloud of wiry white hair, he looked like a mad scientist from a cartoon.

'Melvin,' he finally said, 'I don't mean to alarm you, but if these are really your access codes, and this is your database, then you've been hacked.'

'But everything is empty!' Bohmann said, uncomprehending. 'Nothing is…' He seemed to be struggling.

'Do you have backups?' Tippetts said gently.

'Of course, everything is in the Cloud!' he said.

'That's the problem,' Tippetts replied, sounding embarrassed. 'Whoever did this got access to everything. They wiped your hard drive, and they wiped your Cloud.'

Professor Bohmann blanched.

'Now, let's not get ahead of ourselves. *Everything* can't be gone. I'm sure there are records of a lot of the work: emails sent, printouts, anything you can think of.'

'I have some of the first draft on a USB key,' Bohmann said in a very small voice, 'but ever since I set up the Cloud account, I've stopped making hard copies.'

'Bohmann,' Tippetts said seriously, 'I don't want to leap to any conclusions, but did anyone in the department have your passwords? Or is there someplace else you access this database from, a VPN on your home computer, perhaps? If it happened here in the department, this is grounds to launch a serious investigation.'

'There's no need for an investigation,' Bohmann said hollowly. 'I know who did this.'

There was a silence, in which neither Tippetts nor Axel dared ask the obvious question. It was Bohmann who finally broke the silence. 'Is there any way to recover any of the data?' he asked.

Tippetts nodded. 'I'll do everything I can, Melvin. But it'll take time. I'll need to run checks on all the faculty servers, to see if parts of your private database might have been backed up somewhere. It's something I usually see as a fault in our system, this access the university has to our private work, but in this case, it might save your ass. Meanwhile, go find and save everything you can. Your computer still works perfectly fine, so you can start loading up all the data you have.'

Axel nodded. 'If there's anything I can do, Professor, just ask me.'

Tippetts smiled. 'Ask your colleagues, your friends, anybody you might have sent chapters to...'

Bohmann nodded several times, looking dazed. 'Thank you, Michael,' he said. 'I think I need some time to process this.'

'Of course,' Tippetts said, scrambling out of his seat. 'Just let me know if you need anything, alright?'

Axel smiled at the professor as he left the office, but his face fell when he turned back to look at his tutor. Bohmann looked physically crushed, as if a terrible blow had been struck to his body, not just his work.

'It'll be alright,' he told his professor. 'I know it will. I know you'll be able to put your book back together.'

Bohmann shook his head, as if in shock. 'It's Kyle,' he said. 'Kyle did this to me.'

'Kyle?' Axel asked.

'Kyle...' Bohmann sighed deeply, as if wondering where to begin. 'Kyle is a young recruit amongst the Defenders of Grace. He's become Ichabod Potts's right hand man.'

'And he wanted to prove himself,' Axel thought aloud. A memory of the brooding, dark-haired young man at the talk sprang into his mind.

'He wanted...' Bohmann began, but this time real tears sprang to his eyes, and Axel felt compelled to shush him very gently.

'We don't have to talk about this now,' he said softly. 'You can tell me about this Kyle another time, and explain why he would do such a terrible thing. But first, why don't we focus on fixing this? Tell me about the most recent chapter you were working on. Maybe we can try and piece it together.'

'It's no use. It's the product of days and days' research at CERN, in Geneva, with one of my esteemed colleagues... Well, soon to be ex-colleagues.'

'Don't be morbid,' Axel chided him. 'If Langdon fires you, he's an idiot. Why don't you just call up this guy in Geneva, then?'

Bohmann sighed deeply. 'I can't just call him. We worked together at CERN for a week collating the data. If it's all lost, I'd have to go back to Switzerland,' he said.

Axel couldn't help but laugh. 'And that's impossible because?'

Bohmann laughed too, some of his old twinkle returning to his tired eyes. 'You're right, Axel. Gosh, I really need to remember to keep you youngsters around.' He sighed, some of the tension seeming to go out of his shoulders. 'Maybe you're right. Maybe if you help me, I can put that last chapter together. But first things first: I also lost the PowerPoint I'd made for Chancellor Langdon. I have a meeting with him tomorrow, and I have to be prepared to defend my position here.'

'Well let's begin with that,' Axel said firmly. 'Let me make you some coffee, and you tell me what was in your presentation. Let's fix this thing, one small step at a time.'

CHAPTER FIVE

'So it's done? You've handed in the paperwork?'

Axel and Patti-Ann were sitting in a booth by the window at the Cherry Pie Diner, sipping their drinks as they perused the menus printed on their paper placemats.

Axel nodded. 'Yep,' he said. 'I'm now officially a PhD applicant.'

Patti-Ann clapped her hands in delight, her sparkly bracelets jangling together. 'I'm so proud of you,' she said. 'Dr Axel Parker! It sounds so glamorous. Like a Bond villain.'

Axel laughed. 'I won't be Dr Parker for a few years. If I even get in!'

'You'll get in,' Patti-Ann said sweetly. 'I just know it.'

'I sure hope so,' Axel replied, a grin spreading across his face. 'With Professor Bohmann's help, I think I was able to put together a pretty solid application.'

He reached across the table and clasped Patti-Ann's hand in his. 'And you're not too disappointed I'm not going to be your working man just yet?'

Patti-Ann shook her head, her blonde curls bouncing emphatically. They seemed particularly shiny, Axel noted, as if she'd sprayed each one with varnish. 'I'm glad you made your mind up and chose what you wanted to do.' A worried expression flitted across her face. 'This doesn't mean you're going to be a professor like Bohmann, does it?'

Axel smiled. 'I don't think that's for me, sweetie,' he said. 'You don't have to worry about that.'

'Oh, good!' Patti-Ann replied, smoothing down her pink flowered blouse. 'It's just... Imagine all the awful dinner parties we'd have had to go to!'

Shaking his head, Axel returned to his menu. 'I think I'll have the meatloaf special,' he said.

'Oh, I just can't make my mind up!' Patti-Ann sighed. 'You know I love a club sandwich, but maybe it'd be nice to have soup, but then soup's not really that filling…'

'Why don't you have half a sandwich and a small soup? That way you get the best of both worlds?'

Patti-Ann smiled. 'See, I knew it would come in useful, having a real smart boyfriend.'

'Oh, so you planned this all out when we met in high school?'

'Of course,' Patti-Ann replied, with mock seriousness. 'I just knew the guy I wanted to be with would be a boring old professor, reading his newspaper while I go drink cocktails with my girlfriends…'

'Hey,' Axel replied, pretending to be offended. 'Don't professors get to drink cocktails too?'

The waitress appeared, briefly interrupting their banter, and held up a pitcher of lemonade.

'Can I get you a refill, hun?'

Patti-Ann smiled. 'Sure!'

'Thanks,' said Axel, sipping the fresh, tart drink. 'And I think we're ready to order.'

When their food arrived fifteen minutes later, Axel realised he was starving.

'Until I met you,' Patti-Ann commented, watching him pile his fork high with meatloaf, mashed potato and gravy, 'I never met a guy who could forget to eat. But I swear if I didn't keep you on your toes, you'd live off cereal.'

'I pretty much did, during finals,' Axel replied through a mouthful of potato.

Patti-Ann took a dainty bite of her sandwich, then wiped her pearly pink nails on her napkin. 'I'm always hungry,' she said. 'I swear when I'm stressed out, or nervous, or upset, I eat twice as much. I mean, this weekend, watching the news… It's just so terrible! And there I am with a big bowl of potato salad, and almost half a pack of Oreos gone.'

Axel laughed. 'I've never seen you eat half a pack of cookies in your life.'

Patti-Ann pouted. 'Well, alright, maybe three or four, but they're so sugary! Anyway, all I'm saying is that we have different approaches to stressful times.'

Alex wiped his mouth with his napkin. 'Can I confess something weird?' he said.

'Go on,' said Patti-Ann.

'In a way, I'm almost grateful for this tornado.'

Patti-Ann raised her eyebrows. 'You'd better keep your voice down,' she said, not sounding amused. 'People here lost their crops, their cars. A couple of kids ended up in hospital.'

'I know, I know. It's just... You know how that crazy Ichabod Potts said on TV that the tornado was a punishment for Bohmann's talk? Well, in the end, the tornado broke up the picket, and also took over the news. We didn't hear anything about the Defenders of Grace all weekend!'

Patti-Ann shook her head. 'You're the only person who could think a tornado is good news.'

'No, no, of course I don't really think that. It's just that I'm glad all this madness with the Defenders of Grace is done.'

'I wouldn't be so sure they're done,' Patti-Ann said, inspecting her nails. 'Bohmann hasn't been fired yet.'

'And I hope he won't be!' Axel replied, a little aggrieved by her tone. 'I helped him patch up his presentation, so hopefully he has a chance of convincing Chancellor Langdon to let him stay.'

'Do you know,' Patti-Ann said thoughtfully, 'the tornado missed my parents' house by about ten yards. All our garbage cans flew away into the sky. Those big clunky aluminium things, tossed like paper! We were really lucky.'

'I'm sorry,' Axel said after a pause. 'I didn't mean to sound dismissive.'

'I know, honey,' his girlfriend replied. 'I just think you've blown this whole Bohmann thing way out of proportion. It must be because you two spent so much time together last week. I know you're close to him, but he's just a teacher. What do you care if he's fired?'

Axel opened his mouth to disagree fervently, then realised he didn't want to have a fight with his girlfriend. 'I didn't mean to start an argument,' he offered instead.

Patti-Ann shrugged. 'Me neither,' she replied. 'Now eat your meatloaf before it gets cold.'

★ ★ ★ ★

After lunch, Axel dropped Patti-Ann off back at her parents' house, and began driving back to his mother's. The clouds in the sky still looked grey and menacing, although the tornado was long gone. He briefly felt bad for joking about the violent storm, then rebuked himself for such superstition. After all, it was just a meteorological phenomenon: no-one was being punished for anything. And if you couldn't comment on current events, where was the world going? It wasn't like anyone had died. His phone rang, startling him out of his reverie. It was an unfamiliar number.

He picked up. 'Hello?'

'Axel?' There were indecipherable muffled sounds in the background, and it took Axel a moment to recognise the voice.

'Professor Bohmann?' he asked, confused.

'Axel, my boy!' The professor's voice sounded weak and strange. Axel pulled over on the side of the road.

'What's wrong, professor?'

A sound rather like a laugh came down the line, followed by a choking sob. 'I was wondering,' the professor finally said, 'if you could come to my house. It's 229 Lakeshore Drive, over by the library.'

'Of course!' Axel said at once. 'That's not very far from where I am right now. I'll be there as soon as I can.' He paused. 'Do you need me to bring you anything?' A vision of the state of Bohmann's office sprang unbidden into his mind.

'No, no, I'm fine,' he said. 'I'd just like to speak to you about something. In person.'

'I'll be there as soon as I can.'

Axel hung up and switched the motor on. As he drove, he wished he'd asked more questions: every scenario that popped into his overexcited brain was worse than the last. Bohmann had been fired. Bohmann had to leave the country. Bohmann had been stabbed in a parking lot by the Defenders of Grace, or whoever Kyle was. He shook his head, trying to clear his mind. There was no point wasting his time in speculation: he'd be there soon enough. Lakeshore Drive was as far north as you could go and still be in Lake Salvation: a quiet cluster of houses right by the lake that felt more like a village than the outskirts of a city. The water glistened quietly by the side of the road, reflecting the clouds, oblivious to the cars and weather alike.

There it was: 229. Axel locked the car and walked slowly towards the front door. Professor Bohmann's house was old and dilapidated. There were a few roof tiles missing, and the gate squeaked as he pulled it open. Everything could do with a fresh coat of paint, Axel thought, and the garden was overflowing with weeds and wildflowers: but the roses were blooming bright red.

Bohmann's face appeared, blurry behind the front door glass, and with a jangle of keys, the door swung open.

'Professor!' Axel exclaimed, almost against his will. It had been less than a week since he'd last seen Bohmann, but in that time, something terrible had clearly happened. The professor looked gaunt and worn, his skin sallow and sagging. There were stained bandages in the crook of his arm, and he smelled of disinfectant. 'Are you… ill?' Axel ventured.

'Come in, come in,' Bohmann said, his voice muted. 'Can I get you some coffee?'

Axel followed as he walked heavily down the corridor, their footsteps echoing on the bare wooden floor. 'No thanks,' he said.

He didn't want to push the professor, but he had to know. He put a hand on Bohmann's shoulder as they arrived in the living room. 'Professor, what happened?'

'I had a… well, a sort of minor heart attack,' Bohmann explained, sinking into a leather armchair. 'Tachycardia, they called it. My heart just went crazy. They were worried I was going to go into cardiac arrest, so they kept me at the hospital all the way till Wednesday evening.'

He sighed deeply, and ran a hand over his face. He looked very old.

Axel's mind was racing. 'And Langdon?' he asked, fearing the worst.

'He fired me on Monday morning,' Bohmann said gloomily. 'All weekend, I'd thought things were changing for the better – that tornado kicked the damn Defenders off the TV, and, well, you and I managed to piece my presentation back together… I really thought I had it nailed.'

'That coward!' said Axel. 'And the Defenders?'

'Langdon said he'd give me a week before making a public announcement. I guess he felt kind of sorry for me, or maybe he just wanted to avoid another scene on campus. He told me I had to get my stuff out of the university by Friday evening.'

'That's tomorrow,' Axel said, quite angrily.

'It's alright,' Bohmann said heavily, 'I really only needed my books and my computer. The rest can go to hell. I got almost everything into the car after the meeting on Monday. Come to think of it, maybe it was the strain of carrying all those heavy boxes… But I just collapsed in the parking lot. Tippetts had to call an ambulance.'

'Oh, Professor, how awful,' Axel said.

Bohmann shrugged, then suddenly seemed embarrassed. He pushed himself back out of his chair. 'Please, let me make you some coffee.'

'Why don't I do it?' Axel said, his heart going out to his old professor.

Bohmann shook his head. 'It's an old machine,' he said with a shadow of a smile. 'Let me: it'll do me good.'

Axel opened his mouth to protest, but the professor had already made his way to the door and back towards the kitchen. He looked around the lounge, taking in the view of the lake, the framed certificates on the wall – Princeton University, University of Chicago, Lake Salvation University. There was a simple wooden table with four chairs around it, much in the same unvarnished style as the scuffed floors.

The bookshelves, of course, were heavy with old books stacked in all directions: historical and religious texts piled on top of chemistry and physics manuals. There were three full shelves of *National Geographic* magazines, no doubt going back forty years. Something else caught Axel's eye, though, as his eyes wandered along the shelves: a framed photograph of a young boy with dark hair, smiling brightly. There was something familiar about the child's face, although he couldn't put his finger on it.

Professor Bohmann came back into the room carrying a tray with two steaming mugs of coffee, and immediately saw what had caught Axel's attention.

'Professor, who is that?' Axel asked curiously.

There was a silence. 'That's my son,' Bohmann said at last. 'Or at least, that was my son. The photo's from a few years ago.'

Seeing Axel's expression of shock, he laughed sadly. 'No, he's not dead. Well, I suppose you may as well know,' he said. Setting down the coffee on a wooden side table, he crossed the room and took down another picture, hidden away on the top shelf of a bookcase.

'This is what he looks like now. This is Kyle.' Bohmann handed Axel the framed photograph of a sullen, dark-haired youth, and everything clicked into place. The Defenders of Grace at the town hall. The computer hacking.

'Oh my God!' Axel exclaimed. 'Your son!'

'He hasn't lived with me for years, of course,' Bohmann explained. 'We're... estranged. I don't really talk about him because it breaks my heart.'

'How did...' Axel was struggling to process this information. 'But the Defenders...'

The professor sighed deeply. 'When his mother died, Kyle was just a teenager. He didn't cope very well. I suppose he blamed me – for what, I'm not sure, for still being alive, for not saving her... Well, he was a vulnerable soul, brimming over with emotions, and the Defenders of Grace, those vultures swooped right in and dug their claws into him.

He started going to meetings several times a week, not coming home at night... And one day he just packed a bag and said he was leaving. I fought him, of course, I tried to get him to stay, but he said Potts was looking after him now, that I wasn't his father anymore...' All of this story had come out in a rush, and when the flood of words stilled, Bohmann buried his face in his hands. 'He never came back,' he said through his tears. 'My own son despises me, and now he's played a major role in wrecking my career, forever.'

Axel knelt down in front of the professor, overcome with emotion. 'Professor, your career isn't wrecked,' he said gently. 'It doesn't matter that you've been kicked out of the university. It doesn't matter that you've lost your files. Everything that matters is right here, in your head. All you need to do is put your book back together. You could find work at another university, maybe somewhere on the East Coast!'

Bohmann put a damp hand on his shoulder to stop him. 'I appreciate your enthusiasm,' he said, smiling through his tears, 'but I don't have the energy for it. My mind... It's not what it used to be.'

'You've just come out of hospital, Professor,' Axel protested. 'Of course you feel diminished. Take your time recovering. But I refuse to let you give up like this. Look, with all due respect, you son sounds kind of like a dumbass. He's not your responsibility anymore. I mean, did he even come see you in hospital?' Axel tried to control the anger that was flooding through him. 'I'm sorry, I know Kyle's none of my business.'

'It's alright,' Bohmann said. 'He *is* kind of a dumbass. But I love him, and I miss him every day.'

'Of course you do,' Axel replied, chastised. He was silent for a moment. The two stayed frozen in place, Bohmann hunched over in his chair, Axel kneeling at his feet. A ray of sunlight streaming in through the windows gave Axel an idea. 'Why don't you show me your garden, Professor?'

Bohmann raised his head and smiled weakly. 'I have a better idea,' he said. 'Let's go sit on the patio.'

Having warmed their coffees in Bohmann's ancient microwave, the pair crossed his big, messy kitchen and opened the sliding door out onto the patio. A cool breeze was blowing, a welcome change from the stuffy air inside.

'Another benefit of the tornado,' Axel joked: 'free air conditioning!'

'It's a tremendous force, you know, a tornado,' Bohmann replied. 'Have you ever seen one?'

Axel shook his head. 'The only one I lived through was in the early '90s, when I was just a kid. We were in the basement the whole time. I saw the footage on TV, though: whole buildings just gone, and cars flying through the air like toys.'

Bohmann shook his head ruefully. 'And my colleagues want to tell me there's no higher power.'

They sat down in the rickety deck chairs, looking out over the dandelions and daisies that sprinkled the lawn. In the distance, a sliver of the lake was visible.

'Kyle used to love this garden,' Bohmann said softly. 'The birds and squirrels that come visiting. There are even badgers and possums sometimes.'

'It's beautiful out here,' Axel replied.

'I like to sit out here and meditate early in the morning, before work,' Bohmann said. 'Of course, now I'll be able to meditate all day if I want to.'

'I know it must be hard, losing your job,' said Axel, 'but it doesn't mean your career is over.'

There was a silence. The men sipped their coffees.

'When I was in the hospital,' Bohmann said, 'the doctors told me I was at a high risk of brain haemorrhage. I can't stop thinking about it. I mean, I'm a professor. My brain is my livelihood. If anything goes wrong... Of course, our brains are all our livelihoods.' He gave a short laugh. 'But I'm worried. I can't take this kind of pressure anymore. I can't handle the politics of teaching, I can't handle the religious pressure, the media... This research, it's everything to me. I want nothing more than to finish my book and publish it, so people can understand what

I've been on about all these years. But I'd not even finished the research, and everything I've done is lost.'

'Did you do what Tippetts suggested?' Axel ask. 'Did you look through the files you have saved?'

Bohmann nodded. 'I found drafts of the first five chapters, and some notes from the interviews. I lost everything from CERN, though, and the whole last third of the book. I have to be honest with you, Axel, I don't know if I can put it back together again. Not on my own.'

There was a silence. 'Are you asking me for my help?' Axel finally asked. 'Because I'd happily give it. I'll do anything for you, Professor. I can't stand to watch you give up.'

'You're starting a PhD, Axel,' Bohmann said quietly. 'I don't know how much I can ask you for.'

'I haven't even been accepted yet,' Axel pointed out, 'and even if I do get in, surely I can defer for a year?'

Bohmann nodded hesitantly. 'That's true,' he said. 'We've had several requests for deferment over the years, and I've never heard of one being turned down.'

'Let me be your research assistant,' Axel said passionately. 'I'll help you piece together your book, so you can finish it. Let me work for you for a year.'

The turn of phrase made them both pause. 'What about money?' Bohmann asked. 'Under better circumstances, I'd see what the university could do for you...'

'I'll ask my mother,' Axel said firmly. 'She'll understand. Besides, my father left us enough for us to get by. I haven't touched a penny of my inheritance: I should be able to use a little for this special project. All I'll ask in return is that you help me with some grant applications for next year.'

Bohmann smiled. 'I'll pay for your flights and accommodation in Europe,' he said, 'if you think you'll be able to afford your own expenses.'

'Europe?' Axel repeated, impressed.

'There's a conference,' Bohmann replied, 'in London next month, on the heritage of Islamic spirituality. It's something I really wanted to work into the chapters I was working on: since medieval times, you see, Middle Eastern culture has integrated science and religion.'

A sudden wave of panic went over Axel. 'Professor,' he blurted out, 'you know I don't believe in any of this stuff?'

Bohmann laughed, a real, warm laugh. 'You're a scientist,' he said. 'I'm not asking you to believe. I'm just asking you to help me with my research. Why, don't you think you can listen to a couple of talks about Allah without converting to Islam?'

Axel laughed too, relieved. 'OK,' he said. 'I just thought it seemed important to point out that I'm not… a convert to your theories. I respect your research, but I don't understand it. I actually disagree with a lot of it.'

'That makes your commitment to me all the more moving,' Bohmann answered honestly. 'I also believe it will make you a much shrewder research assistant. I'm no Ichabod Potts: I'm not looking for a disciple. I'm looking for a colleague. Of course, I can't help but hope that in the course of your work, you'll come to understand what I've been blathering on about all these years. But I also respect your right to disagree with me until my dying day.'

Axel sipped his coffee thoughtfully. 'London,' he said out loud. 'I've never even been to Europe.'

'We'll need to get your visa sorted, and have your name put on my plane ticket. I've already booked a hotel.' Bohmann stopped suddenly. 'You're sure about this?' he asked. 'Would you like a few days to think things over, talk to your mother? I don't mean to rush you into anything.'

'My mind's made up, Professor,' Axel replied. 'I'm ready to get started.'

CHAPTER SIX

Axel opened the curtain of his small hotel room window to find rain pouring down outside. He shook his head, impressed. In late October, weather like this would be unimaginable in Texas. He picked his phone up and took a picture, which he sent to his mother. *Don't wish you were here! The weather is terrible*, he wrote, adding in a grinning smiley face. *P.S. I miss you.* He wasn't just being a loving son: his first trip overseas had had a strange effect on him, and he had found himself pining for his mother, Patti-Ann and even Professor Bohmann all through the transatlantic flight. Even now, he wished the professor could be with him, explaining what he needed to do in the coming days.

He'd had a whole weekend to acclimate to the jet lag and explore London before the day of the conference dawned grey and miserable, and still he didn't feel ready. A little overwhelmed by the scale of the city, Axel had stuck to tourist landmarks and major museums, but he'd still been struck by how cosmopolitan the city felt compared to a little American place like Lake Salvation. There were restaurants serving Vietnamese street food and Korean-American fusion and Jamaican barbecue, next to bookstores selling books in Spanish and Japanese and Arabic as well as English. It was thrilling and overwhelming all at once.

He turned from the window and glanced down at the handwritten notes Bohmann had left him to prepare for the conference. 'Please pay particular attention to any conferences discussing the power of God, Nature or the superpower. I would also appreciate it if you'd go see as many people as you can speak about Sufism, the mystical and philosophical side of the Islamic faith. The Sufi vision of God as a powerful force totally compatible with ancient and modern science interests me a great deal, as you can imagine.'

The conference, Bohmann had explained, would be accompanied by an exhibit of calligraphy manuscripts, which he'd suggested Axel have a look at for a bit of extra culture.

'After all,' the professor had said, smiling to himself, 'this is a bit like your Grand Tour.' Seeing Axel's confusion, he'd explained: 'When young, upper-class British men finished university, they were traditionally shipped off to explore continental Europe in order to… expand their minds. It was a rite of passage, a time to come of age, to have one's viewpoints challenged, to learn about different cultures and come home both humbled and illuminated. Of course, it was terribly elitist, and many of those men just went and spent all their money on gambling and whores. But I don't think there's too much of a risk of that happening with you.'

Axel laughed at the memory. So far, overwhelmed by the unfamiliar array of choices, he'd spent his money on two cheap burgers, a Turkish kebab and a single pint of English ale – which he'd struggled to finish, finding it flat and warm. He didn't feel particularly at risk of elitism.

Checking his watch, he realised it was time to make his way to the conference. Making sure the Google map was loaded on his phone, he tucked Bohmann's notes into his small leather briefcase and set off. 'Sir, sir!' the doorman called out, as he headed towards the front door. Axel turned around, feeling worried, to find the doorman briskly walking to the front desk. He followed sheepishly, wondering what he'd done wrong, only for the doorman to turn around, grinning, clutching a black umbrella. 'It's pissing it down out there,' he said in his rough North London accent. 'Take this, or you'll drown!' Seeing Axel was hesitating, he added: 'Oh, it's from the Lost and Found. We have about a hundred of these. People forget them all the time. It won't be missed, sir. Go on!' Axel nodded, then, and accepted the umbrella.

* * * *

Axel arrived at the conference venue with a good half an hour to spare, having padded his schedule generously out of nerves. Mentally thanking the kind doorman for the tenth time since he'd left the hotel, he shook out the drenched rag and contemplated his surroundings. The Brunei Gallery, Bohmann had explained, was part of SOAS, the School of Oriental and African Studies of the University of London. A blocky brick building, it reminded Axel a little of the library on the Lake Salvation campus, which he found comforting. Seeing his nervous, wet face reflected in the many panes of glass that made up the front entrance, he decided it was time to go in. Passing between the two classical columns and swinging open the door, he found himself in a luminous space, with tasteful framed photographs hung on the walls and several posters announcing the conference title: SUFI SPIRITUALITY & THE SOUL.

'Good morning, sir,' the receptionist greeted him. Startled by her politeness, Axel gave a sort of bow, then immediately stood up straight again, realising how silly that looked. 'Good morning,' he said. 'I'm here for the conference.' He cursed himself inwardly. *Why else would I be here?* he thought.

Unfazed, the receptionist nodded. 'If you could just head up to the first floor, sir,' she said, handing him a leaflet. 'The first talk will begin in twenty minutes. Refreshments will be served at half eleven. You can leave your umbrella here, though,' she added with a smile, gesturing at a vase by the door.

'I thought that was a piece of art!' Axel joked, dropping his sopping, borrowed umbrella in.

As he ascended the stairs, he found himself wishing desperately for Professor Bohmann's company. He felt like an imposter: an American in Britain, a scientist at a spirituality conference, a twenty-four-year-old taking an older and wiser man's place. *Bohmann wanted to be here*, he had to remind himself. *It's a privilege that you get to be here. And they allowed him to transfer his invitation to you. You're allowed to be here – "sir,"* he added in his head, smiling. Straightening his shoulders and his blazer, Axel arrived on the first floor.

There was almost no-one there, just an older woman in a headscarf and three middle-aged men in crumpled suits, so Axel sat down and began to read through the programme. A tap on the shoulder interrupted him after a minute or two.

Axel looked up to find a pair of bright white sneakers in front of him. Looking up, he found chunky jeans, an oversized blazer, and a smiling older man. 'You must be Axel!' the man said, in a broad East Coast accent. 'I'm Chester. Chester Mackenzie.'

A surge of relief went through Axel, and he stood up to greet the new arrival. 'It's so nice to hear an American accent!' he said. 'How do you know who I am? Are you a friend of Professor Bohmann's?'

'Melvin and I were at Princeton together,' Mackenzie explained. 'I sent him an email a few days ago, and he told me he'd had to send a replacement. Such sad news! I can't believe anyone would fire old Bohmann. But then, it was his idea to move to cowboy country...' Mackenzie paused. 'No disrespect, of course.'

'None taken,' Axel replied. 'I can't believe what happened either.'

'But you volunteered to help him put his research back together. That's pretty cool,' Mackenzie added.

'I'm just an engineering student,' Axel said. 'I can't pretend to understand all of his spiritual ideas.'

Mackenzie laughed. 'You're not the first to feel that way, and you won't be the last. But it'd be nice for poor old Melvin to finally get his ideas out there, publish his book, get people talking about him outside Texas. Besides, you don't need to understand his research to help him with it. I certainly take that approach to my own students' work!'

Axel smiled. 'I do think it's interesting,' he felt obliged to add, 'I just don't... get it.'

Mackenzie shrugged. 'Well, I'm sure you'll come to understand Bohmann's work, even if you don't agree with it.' He checked his watch. 'Now, shall we head in and get ourselves some good seats?'

Axel agreed readily, and the pair made their way into the busy auditorium. Settling into the plush seat, Axel found himself beginning to relax. All he had to do was listen.

'Man, Bohmann would have loved this conference,' said Mackenzie, leafing through his booklet. 'It's right up his street.'

'I'm still worried I'm a bit out of my depths here,' Axel confessed. 'I mean, look at these titles – "The Beauty of the Sufi Soul" is not something any scientist in all of Texas would be caught dead at.' He peered closely at the programme. 'I sure hope this Doctor Midana guy isn't some kind of insane religious nutjob, like those we have at home.'

A soft, sweet voice came from the aisle, very close to his ear. 'Doctor Midana certainly hopes not,' a woman said. Blushing, Axel turned to look at his new interlocutor, but the woman was already walking towards the front of the room. Axel caught a whiff of perfume as she left – jasmine and something earthy, like sandalwood.

'Who was...' His question trailed off as, mortified, he watched the woman – Doctor Midana, he realised – climb up to the podium.

Mackenzie smothered a giggle.

'I'm Doctor Safiya Midana,' she said, 'Professor of Theology at the University of Istanbul and Visiting Fellow at SOAS. I'd like to thank Sylvester Robadin for being so kind as to organise this conference, and to invite me to speak to you all about a subject I hold very close to my heart.'

Dr Midana's voice was smooth and low, confident yet gentle. She looked severe yet stunning in a conservatively cut cream linen suit and silver jewellery.

'Today, I'd like to talk to you about the core of my research interests, as well as the heart of my own private faith. The ancient philosophy known as Sufism happens to hold that place for me.'

She spoke without notes, Axel noticed, with a warmth that gave credence to her claims of personal involvement with the topic.

'I am a theologian, yes, but before that, I was my grandmother's child, I was a young girl finding God, I was a woman coming to a personal understanding of the soul. I find it impossible to separate my research interests from my life experience.'

This stung Axel for a moment. However, he reminded himself that he was there as Bohmann's eyes and ears, and to try to listen to the talk as if he were the professor himself.

'For this reason, this is not an academic talk, although I am an academic: this is something a little poetic, largely personal – an introduction, if you will, to the Sufi conception of the soul.

Were all lectures like this in Europe? he found himself wondering. Or was this just what it was like in the humanities?

'Now, I don't know if all of you have already been to see the calligraphy exhibition which Mr Robadin has so brilliantly put on in parallel with this series of talks, but you absolutely must. There is no more powerful artwork: the Sufi poets used calligraphy as a way of elevating their thoughts, elevating their souls to communicate with the superpower. It is a deeply moving art form. Calligraphy is the meeting place of the intellectual and the aesthetic, the poetic and the religious. In the early days of the art, a thought had to be pure to become poetry, and it had to be beautiful enough to deserve to be written in these flowing, golden scripts. It had to be eternal.

'And what text is more eternal than a holy one? The Quran, in a way, is the ultimate collection of poetry in Arabic. It is also the source text for much of my research into the Sufi conception of the soul. You see, Sufism is a philosophy running in parallel to religion, not a religion itself: it focuses on the mystical aspects of faith. Sufism is, in a sense, the poetics of Islam: its most beautiful and pure expression.'

She paused for a moment and gazed out across the room, then gave a small smile.

'Now, if the ratio is consistent with other talks I've given, maybe ninety per cent of you are Christians, and just a few of you are familiar with the Quran: you are all welcome at my talk, of course, don't worry!' There was a scattering of laughter across the room. 'London, after all, is such a cosmopolitan city. Here, it matters little which of the superpower's names you choose: Jehovah, Allah, or simply God. I myself tend to use the general expression "the superpower" – a Sufi preference that expresses how unknown the eternal is to us all.'

Here, once more, Axel thought he detected a Bohmannesque undercurrent.

'If you have not come across the texts of the Holy Quran before,' Safiya continued, 'you may be surprised at how closely related they are to your Bible. Even the atheists here will recognise that. The stories, however, are not all quite the same. Let me read a passage, for those of you who speak Arabic.'

There must have been a hundred, two hundred people in the room at the Brunei Gallery, but Axel felt as if every word was spoken to him personally. The Arabic words rushed over him in a wave, like a lullaby heard just before drifting off to sleep. He was almost startled by the return to English.

'In this passage from the Quran, 5:110, Jesus sculpts a bird out of wet clay and then breathes life into it. He heals a leper and a blind man, and – this is important – he brings men back from the dead. Think about that bird, and about those dead bodies, for a moment: the prophet took the lifeless and gave it life. In one case, there had never been life – the bird of clay – in the others, life had been taken away. The Bible gives those dead men names, or at least stories: Lazarus, the son of a widow, and Jairus' daughter.'

There were murmurs of agreement throughout the room.

'In the text, Allah or God himself is imagined to be speaking, telling Jesus he has accomplished these miracles "with My permission." The power, it is clear, is not Jesus's: it is far larger than the prophet, extends far beyond his human comprehension. Jesus does not create life. He… works with life, channels life, accepts the superpower's permission to give life. That life does not come from nowhere. Nothing comes from nothing.'

Axel's scientist ears perked up at these words. He could see why Bohmann was interested in this talk. This sounded similar to the professor's slightly radical take on the laws of thermodynamics.

'What is life? Life is the soul. The soul, then, exists outside the body. It can be taken from thin air and given to a bird of clay, or it can be found and returned to a human body it had left. This means that the soul is all around us, in the air, in life. The soul is everything, and everywhere.'

Dr Midana smiled beatifically, but she had lost Axel again. Some parts of this talk reminded him of nothing else than the church sermons he'd had to sit through as a child.

'There are 115 references to the soul in the Quran,' Dr Midana continued. 'This omnipresent energy takes several forms in the text: the holy spirit, and the life all around us, and the human soul. Now, who was the first human to be given a soul? In both the Quran and the Bible, it is Adam. And afterwards, every human being born was born with a soul. Or perhaps we should say "with some soul," or "with a part of the universal soul," for this conception of the soul as an individual thing is quite a Western one.

'To me, one of the most interesting aspects of the Eastern conception of the soul is its permanence. Throughout Islam, the soul is presented as if there was a circle, a route for the soul, just like the rain cycle. When a body dies, there is a specific route for the soul to take to exit the body, moving up from the feet towards the throat: in 75:26, there is a mention of the soul reaching the collar-bone, and in 56:83, it is said "when the soul at death reaches the throat." At birth, the soul leaves the superpower and enters a body; in death, the soul leaves the body and comes back to the superpower. The mechanism of this ascent and descent is pictured as a stairway, with angels climbing up and down it.'

Dr Midana smiled. 'Beautiful, isn't it? I suspect these angels to be more metaphorical than magical, but I love the image nonetheless. In the verse or surah known as al-Ma'arij, "the ascending stairway," 70:4, it is said: "The angels and the Spirit will ascend to Him during a Day the extent of which is fifty thousand years." The angels carry the spirit: they are the process, the instrument for carrying energy away from earth by Godly decree. Thanks to this stairway, the soul moves from one source to the next. For the scientists and sceptics in the audience, it is worth noting that this passage bears a close relation to your Einstein's theory of relativity. The soul travels back to its sources – to God in heaven, across the sky – in a day that is equivalent to fifty thousand years. Isn't that exactly what would happen to astronauts, if they managed to travel across space-time?'

She smiled again, and Axel realised that his jaw had dropped open. He closed it, and shook his head. Either this Dr Midana was crazy, or she and Bohmann both were, or was he the one who was out of the loop? Of all the things he had expected from his engineering studies, discussing time travel in the Quran had not been one.

'The second most fascinating facet of the soul, to me,' Dr Midana continued, 'is how profoundly unknown it is to us. In the Quran, 17:85, to paraphrase, Muhammad (peace be upon him) says of the soul that it is the Lord's business, and that mankind has really only been given a little knowledge. In short, the soul is not ours to know: it lives inside each of us, but is ultimately inaccessible and mysterious. I have always found this idea incredibly compelling.

'Accepting our ignorance is one of the fundamental pillars of the Muslim faith. Allah alone is all-knowing: he alone decides when we live and when we die. There is a beautiful passage, 31:34, which reads "Allah alone has knowledge of the Hour and sends down the rain and knows what is in the wombs. And no soul perceives what it will earn tomorrow, and no soul perceives in what land it will die." God knows, and we cannot, do not, will not. Only by accepting our ignorance of what is to come can we live good lives on this earth. Another word for this acceptance of God's power is destiny: if we believe that our course is charted, is it not much easier to surrender to it?'

Dr Midana looked around the room. 'I know I am covering a lot of ground, here, but this is what happens when you let someone who has studied Islamic ideas of the soul her whole life give an introductory talk at SOAS!' She smiled. a wide, warm smile, and friendly laughter spread across the room. 'Now, before I hand the stage back over to our charming Mr Robadin, let's recap what I've covered so far. In the Islamic conception, the soul is a life force, one that a prophet can breathe into a clay bird, or that is given to a newborn. The soul, however, does not belong to the body it inhabits: it is a part of an immense and eternal whole, a rain cycle of life and death. It is a gift from God, and at the moment of our death, it returns to God, carried up and down the staircase by angels. The soul, in short, does not belong to us, but it lives within us, powerful and unknown. It drives us, it inspires us, it connects us to God and makes us a part of all life across the surface of this world. Is that not true beauty?'

She bowed her head as a ripple of applause spread across the room. 'Refreshments will be served in the atrium,' she said, 'where I will be happy to answer any questions you might have.'

Dr Midana descended from the podium and crossed the room. Hoping to catch her eye, Axel turned towards the central aisle, but she did not turn to look at him, striding confidently towards the exit.

'Well, isn't she something!' Mackenzie exclaimed. 'What a talk!'

'I didn't understand the half of it,' Axel replied hesitantly. 'That's a lot of thoughts about the soul to process for somebody who doesn't believe in the soul.'

Mackenzie laughed. 'Maybe you should go ask Dr Midana your questions.'

'And apologise,' Axel added ruefully. 'I mean, she's not a religious nutjob. Maybe a little crazy, but not in a harmful kind of way.'

'Go on then,' said Mackenzie, 'what are you waiting for?'

CHAPTER SEVEN

Just talk to her. Taking his courage in both hands, Axel walked towards Dr Midana's linen-clad shoulders. She was standing at one of the drinks tables with a champagne flute in her hand, apparently in animated discussion with two elderly gentlemen.

Arriving behind her, Axel coughed, but received no reaction. 'Dr Midana?' he finally said, slightly more loudly than he'd planned.

The professor turned slowly, without much interest.

'Yes?' she said. Her dark eyes travelled slowly to his face, like a cat studying her prey.

'I'm so sorry about earlier,' Axel said in a rush. 'I didn't know who you were.'

The professor gave a tolerant smile. 'That's quite alright,' she said.

'I just didn't think you'd be...' Axel blustered.

'A woman?' Dr Midana finished his sentence, her tone sharp. 'Of course not. There are no female professors in American universities, are there?'

'Of course there are,' Axel said, embarrassed.

'Ah, so it's the Middle Eastern name? Or the fact that I'm a theologian?' Dr Midana was giving Axel her full attention now, and her conversation partners had drifted off towards another table laden with drinks. Axel found himself wishing he could sink into the beautiful wooden parquet. Why hadn't he stopped talking after the initial apology?

'No, no,' he said quickly. 'I didn't mean that.'

Dr Midana stared at him for a moment, as if expecting more, then she sighed. 'Well. Did you enjoy the talk, at least?'

'Yes!' Axel said. 'It was interesting.' Nothing else came to mind, so an awkward silence followed.

'Interesting.' Dr Midana repeated, narrowing her eyes curiously. 'I see. And why did you come to my talk, exactly? Were you expecting something else?'

'I, er,' said Axel, 'am helping my professor with his research. He's a scientist, you see, but he's also really into these ideas about God and the soul,' he concluded lamely. 'I'm helping him write a book about it.'

Dr Midana laughed, not in an entirely friendly fashion. 'And you are not... *into* these ideas?'

'I don't really believe in all this spiritual stuff,' Axel replied awkwardly. 'I thought your talk was really interesting and... personal. This is just very different to the sort of academic conferences I'm used to,' he tried to explain.

'Personal?' Dr Midana repeated, raising an eyebrow. With a sinking feeling, Axel realised he'd made yet another gaffe. 'I, for one, do not believe you can separate the personal from the academic. After all, how could I write a PhD about the soul, study the soul, read about the soul, think about the soul every day of my life without being in touch with my own?'

Axel felt a rush of anger rise up in him, against his will. 'I don't believe that anyone would have to "know" their own soul to study the topic in a historical or scientific context,' he replied. 'After all, I didn't need an... emotional relationship to aeronautical engineering to commit to a PhD on the subject.'

'And how is that PhD going?' Dr Midana asked, a little slyly.

'I'm starting next year,' Axel sputtered, caught off guard.

His interlocutor seemed unimpressed. 'And where will you be studying?'

'Lake Salvation University, in Texas. But I've committed this year to this research project...'

'That you don't believe in,' Dr Midana cut in.

Just as Axel was about to burst out in a defensive tirade, she surprised him by taking his hand. 'I'm sorry,' she said, 'now I'm the one baiting you. I don't even know you: I didn't mean to start a fight.'

Axel swallowed. 'That's OK,' he said.

'Look,' Dr Midana said after a pause, 'I feel like we got off on the wrong foot, here. You came here from Texas? To hear my talk?'

Axel nodded. 'That's why I'm in London,' he said.

'Why don't I show you some of the calligraphy?' Dr Midana offered, seemingly mollified. 'You've come a long way. Maybe I can help you understand why I'm so interested in this conception of the soul, even if you don't subscribe to it yourself.'

A little intimidated, Axel agreed, and found himself following Dr Midana's linen-blazered shoulders up the stairs to the top floor of the Brunei Gallery.

★ ★ ★ ★

Entering the room, which was lit by a wide skylight, Axel found himself surrounded by manuscript pages in glass cases.

'Impressive, isn't it?' Dr Midana said, turning back to him with a smile.

He nodded.

'See these, on your left? That's a set of ornamental *sajdahs* from a collection of Ottoman Qurans. Prayers, if you will.'

'The writing is so beautiful!'

Dr Midana smiled, all animosity seemingly forgotten, a woman at ease in her world. 'It's incredible, isn't it? And look, it's not just paper and parchment: see those silks on the back wall? They have calligraphy woven into their very fabric.'

Entranced, Axel moved closer to the hangings, studying the narrow bands of gold and the swirling embroidered script. 'I've never seen anything like that,' he confessed.

'Then just wait till you see this!'

As she took Axel's hand and pulled him to the opposite corner of the room, he realised that the professor was younger than he'd first imagined – maybe only a few years older than he was. There was a youthful energy to her here, totally different to the stern impression she gave off from the rostrum.

'Here,' she said breathlessly, 'this is one of the most famous calligraphic manuscripts in the world: the Blue Quran.'

Fascinated, Axel peered through the glass at the deep blue parchment.

'It is an incredibly luxurious piece,' she explained. 'The ink is gold, and the calfskin is dyed with indigo.'

'Wow,' said Axel, mesmerised. 'Who made it?'

'Somebody in the tenth century,' Dr Midana replied, 'it was discovered in North Africa, in Qairawan, and was listed in the thirteenth-century inventory of the Great Mosque. But its exact authorship and provenance is disputed. Some say it could well have been made in Andalusia, based upon the Byzantine gold-on-blue mosaics of the Great Mosque of Cordoba.'

'That's amazing!'

Clearly pleased by his enthusiasm, Dr Midana gave a trilling, bird-like laugh, a sweet sound that made Axel grin. Their earlier animosity seemed to have been entirely forgotten.

'Oh, and this one is by Yaqut al-Musta'simi – arguably the most famous calligrapher, who was known for developing a particularly beautiful form of *naskh* script.' She stared at the beautiful piece of illuminated text for a moment in silence. 'They say he copied out the text of the Quran more than a thousand times. Such a graceful devotional act!'

'A thousand times!' Axel repeated. 'I don't even think the monks in Europe did that in the Middle Ages.'

Dr Midana smiled, pleased. 'No, they didn't,' she said. 'In Western Europe, the monasteries would be incredibly proud of their, say, twelve or fourteen books, whilst the Ottoman and Persian libraries often contained hundreds, even thousands of manuscripts!'

Axel stared at the yellowed vellum, the crimson swirls of ink, the beautiful gold lines. 'It's incredible,' he said. 'And every one of the manuscripts in this room is so intricate! Is all of this writing from the Quran?' he asked curiously.

Dr Midana nodded. 'Almost all of it. Calligraphy is often used as a religious art form in Islamic culture, and it is very closely associated with the Quran. There is also another issue: the fact that figurative religious art has long been seen as potentially idolatrous. It has been done, of course, but usually in secular contexts, like the interior of palace walls, or in a poetry manuscript. Most explicitly religious Islamic art takes the form of abstract decoration, including calligraphy, as well as tiles, carpets and woodwork. Oh, come see this!' Safiya beckoned Axel to a cabinet in the corner, where several wood panels were softly lit. 'These are from the ninth century,' she said, admiration shining in her voice.

'It must have taken hours and hours to make those,' Axel said, staring. 'Days!'

'Probably months,' Dr Midana replied.

'All those swirls and curls...' Axel added, lost in a reverie.

'Arabesques,' Dr Midana offered the proper term. She stopped for a moment, as if embarrassed to have slipped into a professorial role. 'Am I boring you?'

'Oh, no!' Axel exclaimed, then he blushed too. 'No, this is incredibly fascinating. I feel like such a boring scientist; I hardly know anything about art!'

Dr Midana laughed. 'I guess they don't have much Islamic calligraphy in Texas.'

Axel laughed with her, and met her eyes. 'No, they don't teach us about this kind of stuff. Certainly not on an engineering course.

There was a pause, as a far warmer current passed between the two. 'Would you like to come up on the roof for a drink?' Dr Midana asked. 'I feel like I've given you enough of a mini-conference here. After all, you've already had to listen to my talk.'

Axel felt his ears grow red, but Dr Midana was laughing as she led the way from the room. At the top of a luminous staircase, they found themselves emerging into a quiet, green rectangle.

'This is the Japanese garden,' Dr Midana said. As a man in a suit came up to them, she nodded graciously. 'He's with me,' she said, and they were allowed to proceed.

She smiled at Axel. 'There's much nicer wine up here,' she said, 'but only for professors. And yes, I do drink,' she added, her tone implying a challenge, which Axel was smart enough not to rise to.

'So do I,' he said instead, conciliatory. What a mystery this woman was!

They walked over to a low table set with a white tablecloth, where the professor selected a bottle of white wine and slipped it into a bucket of ice. As she picked up two delicate glasses and began walking towards the back wall, Axel could wait no longer.

'Dr Midana,' he began, but his companion held up the hand full of wineglasses to silence him, turning around to smile.

'Safiya, please.'

'I'm Axel,' he said, surprised and pleased. 'Axel Parker.'

'Very pleased to meet you, Axel Parker,' Safiya said, with a little mock bow. They walked on to a little wooden bench, and the professor set down the silver bucket and glasses on a low stone table. 'Now, what was it you were going to say to me?' she asked in a teasing tone.

'I'm sorry I was rude to you earlier,' he burst out.

'Which time?' Safiya interjected, but seeing his expression, she waved her hand in the air. 'I'm joking. Please, go on.'

'You were right – I don't belong here.' After a moment's silence, he added: 'Truth be told, I guess your accusations stung a little because I think they might be true; about not having an emotional relationship with my topic. I don't know if I'm qualified to undertake this research: I'm not a spiritual or religious person at all. But it doesn't mean I won't be a good research assistant to Professor Bohmann.'

'I'm sure it doesn't,' Safiya replied. 'I've not had the privilege of meeting your professor, but he sounds like someone with some groundbreaking ideas. You should be excited to be involved, even if you don't agree with them.'

She sat down, and Axel followed suit, feeling the knot in his stomach finally unwind.

'There were several elements of your philosophy that reminded me a lot of Professor Bohmann's actually,' Axel said. 'For instance, when you were explaining about the Sufi notion of, what was the word you used, the superpower?'

Safiya nodded. 'In Sufi philosophy, the superpower is unknown. We guess its name, its face, its form; call it Allah or God, but ultimately it is so far beyond our human grasp… I believe the Sufi approach to be the most respectful.'

Axel nodded. 'Professor Bohmann described God as energy – he's a scientist, after all. His idea seemed to be more or less the same as this.'

'There is an old and lovely saying I've always been quite partial to,' Safiya said thoughtfully: 'many pools, one moon.'

She gestured across the garden, and Axel found himself looking at the waterlilies scattered across the ornamental pond, looking for traces of godliness in the reflections.

'Where I grew up,' Safiya continued sadly, 'treating religion as a rulebook, as something limited, led to nothing but violence and exclusion. It is an indescribable tragedy that people kill each other over beliefs that are so similar! I mean, so much of the Quran and the Bible share the same stories, the same ideology.' She shook her head.

'One moon,' Axel repeated thoughtfully. 'But what if I don't think there's any moon at all?'

Safiya gave her little birdlike laugh. 'Just because you don't think there is a moon doesn't mean there isn't one. After all, can you see the wind?'

'No, but I can feel it.'

'Yes, but what if you lived somewhere where the wind never blew? Or what if you'd never opened your windows at night, and had never seen the moon? You have not *felt* the superpower's presence. That does not mean it is not real.' She paused for a moment. 'It is not a gift that is given to all: many of us have to move through life, trusting we are not alone. It is, in many ways, more difficult to live happily as a man or woman without faith.'

'I disagree,' Axel said, before hastily adding, 'respectfully.'

Safiya shook her head. 'Let me pour you a glass of Chablis,' she said, 'before we start fighting again.'

★ ★ ★ ★

The cold white wine relaxed Axel and Safiya, and for a while they chatted companionably in the shade of the wisteria.

'So your Professor Bohmann believes he can prove the existence of God?' Safiya asked, her eyes lost in the distance.

Axel nodded, leaning back into the wooden bench. 'He believes that the laws of thermodynamics are the key to this. His vision of God, as I understand it, is as a force, an energy.'

'A superpower,' Safiya added, smiling.

'Yes. Bohmann believes that the way energy... exists, and is transformed, on earth, could demonstrate the existence of a force beyond our perception. The rays of the sun, for instance, are somehow stopped from burning us.' He stopped and frowned, but Safiya seemed unfazed.

'How interesting,' she said. 'Your Professor Bohmann's theories sound absolutely fascinating. And this is your first trip to Europe?'

Axel nodded. 'I've been here four days and I'm still jet-lagged,' he joked.

'How long are you staying?' Safiya leaned forward and refilled their glasses from the bottle, now dripping with condensation.

'Three weeks,' he replied. 'I'm here in London for another few days, photocopying some manuscripts at the British Museum and setting up meetings with some of Professor Bohmann's Swiss contacts.'

'Swiss?' Safiya asked curiously, looking up as she set the bottle down.

'Bohmann had a lot of Swiss colleagues,' Axel explained. 'He did a major chunk of his research at CERN, so that's where I'll be headed next.'

Safiya's eyes sparkled. 'Geneva? How incredibly exciting.' She took a sip of her wine.

'I'm really looking forward to it,' Axel replied. 'Some of the most brilliant scientists in the country work on the Large Hadron Collider underground at CERN, and I get to meet with them!'

'To talk about the soul?' Safiya said a little mockingly, but Axel only shrugged.

'To talk about Bohmann's research,' he corrected her. 'The professor is particularly interested in domains of physics studying the unknown and the unseen. He believes that particles like the Higgs Boson are signs from God; that they prove his idea of an organised universe.'

'And you think you can participate in these meetings without sharing his vision of God, or God's hand?' Safiya said dubiously.

Axel instinctively sat up straight, prepared to defend himself, but then he let his shoulders slump. 'I don't know,' he said honestly. The wine had made his brain a little fuzzy, and he found it difficult to summon up the confidence he usually felt when discussing scientific topics. 'I mean, he's drawing a parallel between his idea of God's hand modifying energy and the Higgs Boson.'

Safiya frowned, intrigued. 'How?' she asked.

Axel paused and thought for a moment. 'Do you know much about the Higgs Boson?' he asked, wary of patronising the professor.

His caution elicited a smile from his companion. 'Only that it's known as the God Particle,' she said, 'and that they discovered it last year in Switzerland.'

'Exactly,' said Axel. 'The particle has always been present, all around us, but for the first time, in 2012, the Higgs Boson was definitely identified in the tunnels beneath CERN. Scientists were able to prove, in a carefully monitored environment, what they'd known for a century without having anything to show for it: that this particle was a real and powerful force of physics, one that affected the very fabric of our universe. You can see why this appeals to Bohmann,' he added.

'I can,' Safiya replied. 'So tell me, then, mister science man, what *is* the God Particle?'

Axel paused. 'For decades,' he finally said, 'we've suspected the Higgs Boson existed because of the way it affects the objects around it, not because we could see it. For a long time, we were only aware of the particle's gravitational field, not the particle itself.' He took a long swig from his glass of white wine. 'So, think of a beam of light, and how it travels through the air, unchanged, all of its wavelengths moving together. When that beam of light touches water, or glass, it splits, and different wavelengths appear to have different velocities: it splits into a rainbow.' He swirled the last sip of wine in his glass for emphasis. 'Now imagine if we couldn't perceive that water or glass, but only the change it wrought. Well, the Higgs Boson is visible to us in a similar way, by breaking the fields of other particles, changing their masses, and generally affecting them.'

Safiya nodded, her gaze no longer abstracted, but intensely fixed on Axel. 'Like the hand of God,' she said, as if in amazement.

'Yes,' Axel replied. 'But how exactly this would operate, or why...' His voice trailed off, a little intimidated by the force of her reaction.

'Do you remember what I was saying earlier about the moon?' she said, clearly excited. 'It is a deep human instinct to be wary of what we cannot see or touch.'

Axel smiled. 'Yeah,' he replied, 'it's a little like that.'

'But don't you see? This is such an incredible opportunity!' Safiya said animatedly. 'To bring this radical spiritual theory about the existence and the power of God to the greatest scientific minds in the country, even in Europe... After all, you don't have to understand Bohmann's research perfectly in order to harvest the answers he needs. You said yourself he'd already spent time at CERN.'

'Yes, and part of what I'll be doing there is simply going back through the research he did with one of the Swiss scientists. The physics I can handle.' He took another swig of his wine, then set his glass down on the wooden bench.

There was a long silence as the pair stared out over the London skyline, which was slowly sinking into shadow. 'I could handle the spiritual part,' she said, sounding scared and excited. She hesitated for a moment, letting what she'd just suggested sink in before continuing: 'I mean, I know this is crazy, we've only just met... But I feel like you're holding something incredible in your hands, Axel, something you've only barely begun to understand. A powerful, revolutionary theory that could change the world. All you need is the theological background to bring it all together.'

Safiya had been looking at the ground at their feet during this whole tirade, then she shifted and turned towards Axel, taking his hands. Her dark, luminous eyes met his. 'Axel, this is an incredible opportunity. You have the physics; I have the spiritual knowledge. Together, we're like two halves of your Professor Bohmann. I mean, I've studied God and the soul all my life; I could help you. Let me come with you to Switzerland?'

Axel let out a nervous laugh. 'Are you sure?' he asked, looking over out of the corner of his eye at the bottle of white wine they had finished between them.

'Please!' she replied earnestly. Following his gaze, she gave her little bird laugh. 'It's not the wine,' she said. 'I mean it. I want to come with you. I won't get in the way.'

He looked into her eyes in silence for a moment before making his decision. 'Come with me,' he said. 'My flight leaves for Geneva on Saturday morning.'

Safiya clapped her hands together joyfully. 'I've always wanted to travel to Switzerland,' she said happily. 'To see the mountains and the lakes…'

'To have boring scientific debates,' Axel added, a wave of confusion and joy rising up in his chest.

'Yes!' said Safiya. 'And spiritual ones, too.'

As if overwhelmed by the craziness of their decision, the pair began laughing uncontrollably, sitting in the half-darkness of the Japanese garden, as evening fell around them.

CHAPTER EIGHT

The plane swooped down low over the snow-capped mountains, then followed the curve of the vast silver lake towards the green plains. There it was, at the very tip of Lac Léman, a semicircle of a city, with the tiny white plume of the famous Jet d'Eau fountaining up from the waters: Geneva. Axel tried to take a snapshot of the view to send to his mother, but only managed to capture the plane wing and a rectangle of sky. One of the professors at CERN had assured him that the flight route went right over the research facility, but Axel didn't recognise the dome of the museum. Before he could really take stock of his surroundings, there he was, hitting the tarmac.

'Welcome to Switzerland,' the flight attendant said with a smile as he disembarked, but Axel was barely paying attention as he made his way through security and out through the gates. He was meant to be meeting Safiya in town for a quick breakfast before heading over to CERN, but his flight had been delayed, and he was worried the professor would be impatient. Would she be sitting in the hotel lobby, drumming her fingers on her armrest, regretting her decision to come at all? As soon as he was on the bus from the airport, Axel gathered his courage and called the number she'd given him.

'Dr Midana,' she replied, her voice stern and more adult than he remembered. 'To whom am I speaking?'

Axel swallowed. 'It's Axel,' he said.

'Oh, Axel! Hello! Have you landed? I saw your flight was delayed.' Safiya's tone changed instantly to something warm and kind.

'Yes, I'm so sorry,' he said. 'I should have sent a message before we took off. I'm just on my way into town. Do you still want to meet for coffee?'

Safiya's laugh remained just as distinctive, even through the crackling of the phone line. 'Of course I do,' she said. 'Would you like me to call our contact at CERN to say we're going to be late? I have his office number here on my laptop in front of me.'

Axel felt relief flooding through him. 'That would be so helpful, thank you,' he replied.

'Look, why don't you get off the bus at the train station?' Safiya continued. 'My hotel isn't far from there: text me when you get in and I can come meet you. We'll go for a quick coffee and croissant, and then get the tram to CERN. How does that sound?'

'That sounds perfect. I'll be there as soon as I can.'

Hanging up, Axel couldn't have been happier that Safiya would be on this leg of the trip with him. Up until that moment, he'd had to manage everything himself, obsessively checking Professor Bohmann's notes and panicking about every schedule change. With two people working together, he realised, the full weight of responsibility for this project didn't fall on his shoulders. He and Safiya were a team now.

He leaned his head against the bus window and let the rumbling sound of the wheels on the road soothe him as he rode into the centre of Geneva.

★ ★ ★ ★

As he stepped off the bus at the train station, he felt the cold autumn air hit him full force: a sharp, bright wind that blew in off the lake, deeply unfamiliar to Axel's Texan blood. He pulled his coat around him and shivered, looking for Safiya. A minute later, he saw her waving from the side of the road, wearing a dark green tweed coat and a cream scarf. He walked over to join her.

'There's a little *boulangerie* just over here,' Safiya said briskly, freeing Axel from the question of whether to hug, or kiss her cheeks, or shake her hand. 'Let's get out of this cold!'

'It's freezing!' Axel agreed, walking quickly to keep up. 'I've never felt anything like it.'

Safiya smiled as she pushed open the glass door of a little bakery. 'You and I are warm-blooded people,' she said. Her cheeks were flushed, and as she unwound her scarf, her hair fell onto her shoulders in a mass of curls.

'I suppose we're both from the South!' Axel replied, trying not to stare. Dr Midana was even more beautiful than he'd remembered. 'A very different kind of south, but still.'

A short man with a potbelly came over to their table, wiping his hands on his apron. '*La bise!*' he said, shaking his head. '*Quel temps pourri!*'

Embarrassed, Axel was about to reply that he only spoke English, when Safiya smiled and said several sentences back in French. The waiter nodded and walked back to the counter. From Safiya's amused expression, Axel figured he must have been staring again, and he blushed.

'I didn't know you spoke French,' he said.

Safiya shrugged. 'Not particularly well,' she replied modestly, 'and I probably have a heavy Turkish accent, but we all learned it in school.'

'What was he saying?'

'He's talking about the local wind, *la bise*, a very cold wind that blows in from the mountains. I guess even the locals aren't used to it.'

'Well, I guess that's good news!' Axel said with a smile. 'I mean, it'd be a shame if it was this cold and grey the whole time we were in Geneva. I've never seen a lake this size: I'd love to take a boat out across it!'

Safiya smiled, a genuine expression that made her look even younger. 'Oh, I'd love that!' she said. 'When I was younger, I used to go sailing on the Bosphorus with my friends...'

'I've never been sailing,' Axel confessed. 'My uncle used to say he'd teach me – I mean, lots of people go sailing on Lake Salvation, but I've never tried. Did your family teach you how to sail?'

'Oh, no!' Safiya exclaimed. 'My family disapproved horribly. It's not something a respectable young woman should take on as a hobby, you see.' She grinned. 'But I loved it: one summer, my friends and I went every weekend.'

The waiter returned with two small black coffees and buttery almond croissants.

'You like almonds, right?' Safiya asked.

'I've never had a croissant that wasn't from a gas station,' Axel replied, 'but I do like almonds.'

The pair laughed, and breakfasted in companionable silence.

'Well, I guess it's time,' Safiya said when they had finished, checking her watch.

Axel brushed the crumbs from his clothes. 'Let's do this,' he replied, more confidently than he felt.

* * * *

A tall, olive-skinned man was waiting for them at the reception, lounging against the front desk and stirring a styrofoam cup of coffee. 'Emilio Tericiano,' he introduced himself, holding out his hand. 'You must be Axel Parker and Safiya Midana. My colleague Albert Straussfeld, whom you're here to meet, is currently giving a conference to some visiting university students,' he explained.

'We can wait,' Axel replied politely.

'I have a better idea,' Tericiano said in turn, a cloud of cologne wafting from his arms as he gestured vaguely towards the inside of the building. 'Why don't we stop in and listen? It's in the main lecture hall. I'll grab him afterwards and introduce you: the conference room is booked and ready. Let me just get you your visitors' badges...'

After thanking Tericiano profusely, and pinning their badges to the front of their coats, Axel and Safiya found themselves following him down several sets of stairs, and down a series of long underground corridors, trailing perfume in their wake. At last, they arrived at a small open door, which they quietly swung open to find themselves in the back of a large auditorium. A large colour photo of a galaxy was projected on the back wall, with swirling white stars and mounds of indigo cloud. In front of this image, a man with white blonde hair was gesturing with a laser pointer.

'That's Straussfeld,' Tericiano whispered. 'The head of our department.'

'For centuries,' the man on the podium was saying gravely, 'no-one believed that gravity had any effect on light: this was why the first ideas of "dark stars" or black holes were widely ignored. Einstein, having discovered that gravity does influence light's motion, came up with the theory of general relativity just one hundred years ago.'

Dr Straussfeld was tall and thin, cutting a professorial figure on the stage. His accent had a slight German edge that made him sound tremendously serious. He waved his hand at the wall, and the slide changed to a photograph of the Milky Way.

'General relativity describes gravity as a geometric property of space and time, or space-time. The way space-time operates, Einstein worked out, is directly related to the energy and momentum of the matter and radiation present. You've studied differential equations, right?' There was scattered agreement throughout the hall. 'Well, Einstein used those to prove that relationship. Before Einstein, as you know, Newton's model showed that gravity was the result of an attractive force between massive objects. But there were a lot of questions left to answer, many of which Einstein tackled, and some of which he successfully resolved. Like any man, of course, he reached his limits.'

Dr Straussfeld began pacing the stage. 'However that may be, it's difficult to emphasise strongly enough how groundbreaking the theory of relativity was in its day. We've all seen a hundred science fiction films in which space-time is warped, and spacemen return to Earth having barely aged while time on the planet sped by. But we're talking about rewriting the laws of classical physics: changing the way scientists thought about the passage of time, the geometry of space, the motion of bodies in free fall, and the propagation of light. Einstein was a radical thinker: he changed modern science forever. If you find yourselves disagreeing, you must have slept through most of my talk.'

Laughter and applause mingled as Dr Straussfeld concluded his introduction, handing out a printed summary and taking questions on a one-to-one basis from a few of the students. As the room emptied, he switched off the projector and microphone, put away his notes, and walked towards the exit.

'Albert!' Ticiano called out. 'Bohmann's protégé is here!'

Before Axel could protest, Dr Straussfeld was shaking his hand warmly, his eyes crinkled in a friendly smile. 'It's wonderful to meet you.'

'Likewise,' Axel managed to say quietly.

'And this is your theologian friend?' He turned to Safiya, who took his hand warmly and professionally, once more saving Axel from embarrassment.

'I hope you don't mind me tagging along,' she said sweetly.

Dr Straussfeld, quite unexpectedly, blushed. 'Not at all, not at all,' he blustered. 'I can't say I'm quite as knowledgeable as my American colleague about philosophy or religion, but I'll do my best to answer any questions you might have.'

Ticiano made a slight coughing noise, and Straussfeld turned to him with eyebrows raised. 'What is it, Emiliano?'

'Could we stop by the coffee machine before we go to the conference room?'

Dr Straussfeld rolled his eyes affectionately. 'My colleague here does not have access to all of the same areas as I do,' he explained. 'Apparently, our coffee machine is far superior.' He shrugged, teasing Ticiano. 'What do I know? I do not come from a long line of pure Italian blood...'

Ticiano made a disgruntled noise. 'Don't mock me! Just because my parents lived in Lugano does not mean I have not done my research. My ancestors were nobles of Pisa,' he added. 'I have visited the castles. I know my roots.'

Axel was curious. 'So you are Swiss-Italian?' he asked.

'Italian-Swiss,' Ticiano retorted.

'We are all Swiss,' Dr Straussfeld intervened, 'and I'm fairly sure our Nespresso machine was made in China. Come: let us get to the conference room before we lose our booking.'

* * * *

'I really enjoyed your talk,' Axel ventured as they made their way back along the corridors.

'Thank you. Einstein truly is a fascinating figure,' Dr Straussfeld said thoughtfully. 'I've never quite got over my teenage admiration for him. I seem to recall our friend Melvin Bohmann being particularly interested in some of his views. What is that famous quotation of Einstein's? Oh yes: "I want to know how God created this world. I'm not interested in this or that phenomenon, in the spectrum of this or that element. I want to know His thoughts, the rest are details." I believe that is how you might render it in English.'

Axel and Safiya exchanged a glance.

Dr Straussfeld paused and turned to them. 'In other words, what he is saying is: I want to know *why*, not just how.' He began walking and talking again. 'When Einstein talks about God, what he's really talking about are the laws of physics. His vision of God is not an interventionist one: not a shepherd looking out for his sheep, listening to their prayers or picking sides in their wars. He is the Creator.'

'The superpower,' Safiya replied.

Dr Straussfeld looked at her and smiled. 'Exactly,' he said. 'A great and eternal power, far beyond the comprehension of humans, who set the world in motion and then let it go.'

They walked in silence after that, each lost in their own thoughts. After a time, Dr Straussfeld stopped and took a cluster of keys from his pocket, then opened a wooden door to their left. The conference room was a small one, which reassured Axel: he'd been quite daunted by the auditorium they'd just left, which reminded him more of being a freshman in lectures than a graduate attending seminars.

'Oh, not this room!' Tericiano sighed. 'It's so small!'

'There are only four of us,' Dr Straussfeld pointed out, settling into a chair by the side of the lacquered wooden table.

'Five, if Fabien decides to show up,' Tericiano argued.

Axel and Safiya settled into their seats and exchanged amused glances.

'Fine. I'll go get the coffee,' Tericiano finally pouted, reaching out his hand for Straussfeld's keys, which he promptly received. He disappeared in a cloud of cologne.

Dr Straussfeld sighed and shook his head. 'I do not know why I am burdened with this buffoon,' he said affectionately. 'I mean, he's an incredible technician, very focused. As he'll no doubt tell you himself, he studied in Sankt Gallen and Lausanne.'

'How long have you worked together?' Axel asked politely.

'Oh, three, four years?' Dr Straussfeld replied. 'He came here as a trainee in, let's see, 2010 I believe.'

The door opened, and Axel turned, expecting Tericiano to have returned, but instead, a short man in a smart navy suit entered the room.

'Oh my God,' he said in a heavy French accent, 'are we talking about Emi again?'

Dr Straussfeld laughed. 'Hello Fabien,' he said. 'Axel, Safiya, this is Fabien de Grand-Maizelle, my research assistant.'

De Grand-Maizelle spread his arms out, as if expecting applause from a bullfighting arena, then gave a high-pitched laugh. He had salt-and-pepper hair, which was immaculately styled and combed over. 'Emiliano is the brawn, and I am the brains,' he said. 'I come up with the theories in the library, and the Italian tries them out for me. Dr Straussfeld is our master, of course. He is the one in charge.' He bowed like a judo master, causing his superior to shake his head.

'I'm afraid my assistants do not seem very preoccupied with giving a serious image of the work we do here at CERN,' he said sternly, though the corner of his mouth was trembling, as if he was trying not to smile.

'Oh my God,' de Grand-Maizelle said, looking genuinely horrified. 'I am so sorry. I have spent too long in the stacks.'

Dr Straussfeld gave a forgiving smile. 'That is quite all right. But shall we get started?'

De Grand-Maizelle nodded emphatically and slid into his chair just as Tericiano re-entered the room with a tray of steaming cups.

'Hi Fab,' he said, setting the coffee down. 'Are you telling people that I'm the brawn again? Because I am definitely the brains.' He slid into his seat. 'Just because you smell like an old book does not mean you are the smart one.'

'Oh,' de Grand-Maizelle rolled his eyes, 'so how many minutes will it be before you begin telling us about your *diplôme de polytechnique* from Lausanne and your PhD from Rome? Go on, I'm counting.' He dramatically uncovered his watch.

'Gentlemen!' Dr Straussfeld intervened, quite loudly, and the Italian and Frenchman started.

'Sorry,' said Tericiano.

'Sorry,' said de Grand-Maizelle.

There was a sheepish silence. At last, the team was assembled: Axel looked around the room and found only friendly faces. He felt tremendously reassured.

'Let me begin by telling you about the work Professor Melvin Bohmann and I carried out here last year,' Dr Straussfeld began. 'We were working at the intersection of physics and philosophy, something we are quite comfortable with here at CERN. Professor Bohmann came to CERN at a very exciting time in our research, just before the Large Hadron Collider was first launched. It was a time of great scientific excitement, a time of chance, and worry too. You'll no doubt remember how the newspapers reacted to the news of our experiments.'

Tericiano laughed. 'People were so worried that the world was going to end when our little atom smasher here was first fired up. They thought we'd be able to spawn a little black hole, one that could suck the Earth into itself. Boom!' The scientists exchanged amused glances. 'Of course, this was highly unlikely. The laws of gravity alone keep us safe.'

'And if we had, by some miracle, created a mini black hole,' Dr Straussfeld added with a tolerant smile, 'it would have been so unstable that it would have collapsed in on itself and disintegrated before it had had time to consume the Earth.'

'Dan Brown loves that stuff,' de Grand-Maizelle added, rolling his eyes. 'As if he was the first person to come up with crazy theories about the universe! I mean, try the Venerable Bede, or Ptolemy, or Bishop Oresme!'

'The Large Hadron Collider,' Dr Straussfeld continued, 'is the world's largest and most powerful particle collider.'

'The largest machine in the world!' Tericiano added.

Straussfeld turned to Safiya. 'The collider was built in a tunnel twenty-seven kilometres in circumference, running underneath the border of France and Switzerland. You will have crossed over it when you took the tram here earlier.'

Safiya smiled.

'The physicists who had it built, and the many countries who engineered and designed and financed it,' Dr Straussfeld continued, 'hoped that the Large Hadron Collider would help answer some of the fundamental unanswered questions in physics, to do with the laws that govern the interactions and forces governing elementary objects, as well as the profound underlying structures of space and time.'

'And quantum physics,' de Grand-Maizelle chimed in, 'and general relativity.'

Dr Straussfeld nodded. 'As you may have guessed from the talk you walked in on, we deal in enormous unanswered questions here. General relativity and quantum physics, as our French friend here pointed out, are full of philosophical questions. Questions about the existence of the universe and its ability, say, to remain balanced rather than collapsing in on itself. How did our universe come into existence, and us with it? What are the conditions in terms of gravity, for instance, that allow life? Are we humans only able to live in these planes, in these dimensions, or will we eventually learn to bend space-time and travel further?'

De Grand-Maizelle and Tericiano, Axel noticed, were absolutely captivated by Dr Straussfeld's talk, despite having no doubt heard it a thousand times before. He and Safiya, he knew, were hardly the first people to come in here with only basic knowledge of what went on in those tunnels. Still, he was tremendously grateful for the explanation.

'The Higgs Boson particle,' Straussfeld continued, 'lies at the heart of many of these questions, or at least is able to shed some light on them. The Higgs Boson is not an answer, but it is evidence that some answers are right. It is, if you will, a ripple in the force fields of space that emerged at the birth of the universe – at the Big Bang – spanning the cosmos to this day. If we could identify this particle, we would prove that our theories about the origin of the universe and its very composition, its fundamental balance, were right.' He paused for a moment. 'You are familiar with the Higgs Boson?' he asked. 'The God Particle? I don't want to bore you.'

Axel said yes hesitantly, while Safiya replied that she knew only the basics. The three men nodded, as if pleased that the explanation could continue.

'The Higgs Boson is incredibly elusive,' Dr Straussfeld said. 'It is not easy to study, being essentially invisible. In fact, it can only be witnessed in the way it affects the particles around it: in short, some begin to act as if they have mass, while others are unaffected. It is similar, in that sense, to an electrical field, where charged objects are affected and moved by the energy while neutral objects fly through unaffected.'

'Like light in a water glass,' Safiya said quietly, smiling at Axel.

'And nobody here calls it the God Particle,' Tericiano added.

'Yes, scientists hate that name,' de Grand-Maizelle chimed in.

Dr Straussfeld agreed: 'I know,' he said, 'but in the case of Professor Bohmann's research, it is actually of some relevance. You see, the Higgs Boson has affected the fundamental symmetries of this universe from the moment of the Big Bang to the present day. That apparent chaos of structures and forces and particles that somehow resolved into the cosmos we now call home… Well, we have some notions of *how*, but very little of *why*.' He smiled. 'Your Professor Bohmann, in this sense, is a kind of Einstein. He is only interested in the phenomena and the experiments inasmuch as they might lead to more profound answers about life on this earth, and how and why it exists. Leon Lederman, the man who coined the term 'God Particle' in his book—'

'*If the Universe is the Answer, What is the Question?*' Tericiano quoted the subtitle with a roll of his eyes.

'It's a good question,' de Grand-Maizelle said defensively. 'One philosophers have been asking since the dawn of time. If you ever set foot in the library, you little grease monkey—'

Dr Straussfeld held up his hands, and the two men grumbled into silence. 'Lederman himself, as I was saying, asks the following question in his controversial work: whether the Higgs Boson was a kind of joke, a trick or a puzzle that exists only to confuse those of us trying to understand the universe, or whether it is the key to understanding – these are his words – how beautiful is the universe God has made.'

'A puzzle set up by God?' Safiya asked, her first question since they'd entered the room. Glancing over, worried that she had been offended, Axel saw that her eyes were shining with excitement.

Dr Straussfeld smiled. 'That is one theory,' he said. 'It is not entirely crazy, if we posit that the universe is in any profound way rational or organised. After all, the Higgs Boson's aspect as a puzzle or key is only an anthropocentric perspective – a metaphor, even – but it doesn't mean that it couldn't give us the answers we need to understand our place in the universe.'

'The control, if any, we have over space-time,' de Grand-Maizelle added, getting caught up in the excitement.

'Our place in the universe,' Safiya repeated breathlessly.

'As Einstein put it,' Dr Straussfeld said, 'to know the mind of God.' He paused. 'As you can imagine, it is quite a useful framework.'

There was a silence, one positively humming with energy, as all the minds in the room raced together. It was an incredible atmosphere, Axel realised, one he felt tremendously privileged to be soaking in. But in the midst of all this, nagging doubts began to surface.

'So Professor Bohmann was studying this philosophical aspect of the discovery of the God Particle?' he asked.

'Yes,' said Dr Straussfeld, 'and much of his research is still saved on our computers here. The information cannot leave the laboratory, of course – we have very strict policies on our data – but you are welcome to collect and transcribe as much as you want, as long as I can cast an eye over your research before you leave.'

'And please, no viruses,' Tericiano joked.

Dr Straussfeld shook his head. 'Fabien will take you to the library,' he said, 'where you can stay as long as you like today. He will also arrange for you to have a pass, so you can come back over the next few days if you need. Emiliano has set up a small desk for you in the computer laboratory, with an internet connection, so you can Skype Professor Bohmann if you need to ask him any questions. The library and computer labs stay open till ten p.m., so you should be able to communicate with the US just fine. If you have any questions, just call me on my office line during the day, or my mobile in case of emergencies.' He drew a small white card from his jacket pocket, which Axel took gratefully.

Safiya cleared her throat. 'Excuse me,' she said, 'but do you have any… older works of philosophy relating to this area of study in your library?'

De Grand-Maizelle looked up at her with wide eyes. 'The CERN library only goes back to 1950 or so,' he said regretfully, 'but there are several libraries in Geneva I could show you. Of course, right here we have online access to any journals you might need,' he said, quite adoringly. 'Whom would you be interested in studying?'

'I've mostly worked on Albumasar and Alfraganus, at least since my days at university,' she replied.

'Oh my!' de Grand-Maizelle exclaimed, his eyes widening. 'You mean Albumasar's studies of the great conjunctions of Jupiter and Saturn? How unusual! How wonderful! I know very little about the Islamic scientists of the Middle Ages. Who was the second one you mentioned?'

'Alfraganus, a student of Ptolemy's,' she said, 'who happened to be an engineer as well as an astronomer. Of course, my own research interests lie in the Middle East, but perhaps I could serve this project better by focusing on the European texts relating to the history of these questions. For instance, whom would Einstein have studied?'

De Grand-Maizelle looked like Christmas had come early. 'Galileo is my personal favourite,' he burst out, 'though of course Kepler is equally fascinating. I actually have some manuscripts checked out from a private collection, there's this one incredible map of the heavens you simply must see...'

'Oh dear,' Tericiano intervened, 'you've encouraged him.'

Ignoring the Italian, Safiya smiled thoughtfully. 'That would be wonderful,' she said. 'Perhaps we could meet tomorrow? Do you think it would be possible to arrange access to some of these libraries for me at the last minute?'

'Of course!' de Grand-Maizelle sputtered, 'for a reputed theologian from the University of Istanbul, anything is possible. I will make some calls.' He puffed out his chest. 'Besides, I have my badge. We can go anywhere you like.'

'As long as it's in the Old Town of Geneva,' Tericiano whispered to Axel, who giggled.

'Well!' Dr Straussfeld exclaimed. 'I feel like this has been a fruitful introductory session. Questions have been asked, groundwork has been laid, and contacts have been made. Now who would like some lunch?'

CHAPTER NINE

Axel and Safiya stood on the Pont des Bergues, watching the waters of Lake Léman swirl as they were channelled into the Rhône river.

'What time are you meeting de Grand-Maizelle?' Axel asked.

Safiya checked her watch. 'In two hours,' she said, 'in the Old Town. Apparently there's a private library there with some manuscripts I absolutely must see…'

Axel smiled. 'I guess that leaves us time for a little lunch, right?'

'Absolutely! I was too busy doing preparatory research to take advantage of the hotel buffet,' Safiya said. 'Perhaps we could do a little exploring first, then have a bite of something before I have to head off?'

'This city is incredible,' Axel said, still staring into the river. 'The water is so clear and blue, and just look at these flowers!' He gestured the length of the bridge, where dark green vines were bursting with white blossom.

'It's unusual for November in Europe,' Safiya commented. 'They seem to have quite clement weather here. At least when the *bise* isn't blowing!'

Axel shivered. 'Yes, I'm glad the weather has cleared up today,' he replied. 'I hope it doesn't rain: I left my coat at the hotel.'

Safiya smiled. 'Even without any rain, this river is so powerful,' she said, as they looked down into the Rhône together. 'The force of a whole lake moving… It's incredible.'

'So is that why you've wanted to come here for so long?' Axel wanted to know. 'The river, the lake?'

Safiya shrugged. 'There are a lot of aspects of Switzerland I've been attracted to for a long time: I've always loved high mountains, but I've never seen the Alps. I love hiking, you see.'

'I didn't have you down as an outdoors woman,' Axel commented, before blushing, worried he'd offended again, but Safiya only grinned.

'Oh, the Sufis have always been big walkers,' she said. 'We're not just bookworms. Walking in the great outdoors is the best time to meditate, to be alone with one's thoughts and one's spirituality, to feel connected to the universe around us.' She laughed gently. 'Maybe that sounds silly to you.'

Axel shook his head emphatically. 'I love being outside,' he said. 'I don't know if it's a spiritual thing, exactly – I mean, it's not – but I've always loved the lake in Lake Salvation. There's something so reassuring about watching water ripple.'

Safiya nodded. 'It's a universal awe,' she said. They stood in silence for another minute, watching the powerful flow.

'Come on, then,' she said at last, 'shall we walk up to the cathedral?'

Axel nodded. 'So what else?' he asked, as they began walking. 'Why Geneva?'

'Well, during my studies one of my professors of Islamic History in Istanbul was Swiss,' Safiya replied. 'He taught me about the fascinating intersection of early Swiss Protestantism and traditional Islam. You see, Martin Luther, for one, was very interested in the Quran: he had the text translated so he could study it. He did this, of course, to argue with Islam and criticise it, but the results were more interesting than he'd perhaps foreseen, and a certain amount of struggle is visible in his writing on the subject. At first, Luther argued against resisting the Ottoman invasion, explaining that they were a scourge sent by God to punish the sinful, and that it was God's will that they take over Europe.'

Axel whistled, and Safiya smiled. 'He changed his mind, of course. The more he studied Islam, the more conflicted Luther became. In fact, he was quite taken with many Eastern ideas, and often refers in his writing to the idea that "the Ottoman" or "the Turk" is both more peaceful and more intelligent than many Christians. In his tract *On War Against the Turk*, he memorably says "A smart Turk makes a better ruler than a dumb Christian".'

Axel laughed. 'That can't have been a popular point of view.'

'It certainly wasn't. You have to remember that this was a period of serious territorial expansion on the part of the Ottomans. In the end, the tract argues for resistance to invasion, but it certainly makes for an interesting read – an overture to the East disguised as a pamphlet against its evils. I'll stop with the history lesson now,' she added, smiling, 'but I always thought it was interesting to note that the East–West interest was reciprocal: Suleiman the Magnificent actually sent letters to Luther's followers across Holland and Germany, suggesting that they shared a mission, since they believed in one God, did not worship idols, and intended to fight against the power of Pope and Emperor. In other words, they were opposed to secular power and they hated Catholics and Jews, so they were natural allies.'

'Of course,' said Axel, smiling as they began climbing up a small cobbled street. 'So do you believe this yourself? That Swiss Protestantism and Islam have a... relationship?'

Safiya pursed her lips. 'It's perhaps historically not quite as strong as that,' she said, 'but I do think there is much to be gained by their study in parallel. For instance, both place the idea of simplicity at the centre of their faith. The way the Protestants of the Renaissance dressed, for instance, is very similar to traditional medieval Muslim dress, despite the separation of centuries and oceans.' She paused thoughtfully. 'More broadly, I also feel that the world would benefit from Christians and Muslims admitting how closely their religions are linked, historically speaking. After all, it could be said that Islam is the first Protestant religion, since it accepts the existence of the Bible, both Old and New Testaments, and retells many of its stories with some corrections and additions. For instance, the recognition of Jesus is of great importance in Islam, as indicated by the many chapters in the Quran dedicated to his stories. One of the longest chapters is about the virgin birth.'

'Yes, you mentioned this in your talk,' Axel said, eager to show he was following her argument. 'Jesus bringing a clay bird to life and all that.' He paused. 'To be honest, I was amazed. I'd never heard about that before.'

'I guess they don't teach that in Texas,' Safiya said wryly. 'It's true, though. All the old books – the Quran, the Torah and the Bible – share the same Old Testament, and much of the New Testament also filters into the Quran in a changed form.'

The pair had arrived at the top of their narrow street, winding between little boutiques and bakeries.

'I can't see the cathedral anymore,' Axel commented. 'How weird!'

'We must be close,' Safiya replied.

'Maybe we can't see the wood for the trees,' Axel joked. 'Hey, look at these canons!' Like an excited child, he ran up ahead to a covered portico where several immense black canons stood, impressive in their black paint.

Safiya laid her hand on the cold metal. 'I wonder how many men these killed in their day.'

Axel stayed silent, a little embarrassed by his enthusiasm. 'I guess I've never seen a canon,' he tried to explain, but Safiya smiled warmly.

'I understand,' she said. 'These are three or four centuries old. Any deaths they caused are in the distant past. They are displayed here to be admired as relics, of course, but I don't think that should stop us from remembering their power.'

Axel was quiet as they retraced their steps and turned down a shadowy side street, their footsteps echoing on the cobbles. All at once, there it was, towering over them: the impressive facade of the cathedral.

'This was Jean Calvin's cathedral,' Safiya said quite reverently. 'We're standing in the heartland of European Protestantism.'

'It looks almost Greek,' Axel observed, 'with all those tall columns.'

'So it does!' said Safiya, sounding pleased. 'Like most European cathedrals, you see, the Cathédrale Saint-Pierre is a mishmash of different eras, destroyed and rebuilt a hundred times over the centuries. You're right, of course: the entrance portico is neoclassical, but that copper spire is Gothic. And in the basement, I've read, there are ruins dating back to Roman times, even prehistory: stones that have lain here since the first settlers built huts on the bank of the lake...'

Axel let his eyes travel up the immensity of the cathedral, all the way up to the green needle of the spire. 'It's beautiful,' he said. 'Shall we go inside?'

'I heard an amazing story about this cathedral once,' Safiya commented as they swung open the heavy wooden door. 'You know how during the Reformation, there was a lot of violence? Many Protestants were protestors in quite a modern sense of the term, smashing up statues because they deemed them idolatrous, and incidentally destroying centuries of precious religious artwork. But the Swiss were different. They lived up to their reputation for tidiness and order, even in the midst of this chaotic period: instead of destroying the Catholic art, Calvin had it removed in an orderly fashion. So all the sculptures, the gilding, the stained glass, was gently packed away in the basement, and now it's exhibited there, in the museum.'

Axel laughed. 'You mean they kept it just in case?' he said.

'Of course, there are many Catholics in Geneva now. That particular religious conflict, at least, has ended. But the cathedral is still a Protestant edifice. See how there's no gold, no unnecessary decoration?'

Looking around, Axel found this to be true. The cathedral was impressive, an echoing stone interior glowing with sunlight. For a moment, he found himself wishing Bohmann was here to see the gentle rays streaming down through the white glass panes.

'I find it difficult to understand how anyone could not be moved by a religious space such as this, no matter their background,' Safiya said almost dreamily, her eyes on the high ceiling.

Axel kept his mouth shut, but he could see her point: there was something quite overwhelming in the light, the silence... *Just beautiful architecture*, he told himself, *nothing more*. He checked his phone: twelve thirty, and two texts from Patti-Ann. He'd read them later, he told himself.

'We should probably go find some lunch soon,' he said quietly to Safiya, who nodded slowly, as if waking from a deep sleep, and walked with him out into the cold November sun.

★ ★ ★ ★

Tucking into crisp salads with a savoury vinaigrette and hunks of crusty bread, Axel and Safiya relaxed on the terrace of the Restaurant Les Armures.

'I don't understand why nobody is eating outdoors,' Axel commented, looking around.

Safiya shrugged. 'I guess the Swiss think this is an odd time of year to sit outside. You have to remember that it's probably usually raining, or snowing.'

Axel's eyes widened. 'Wouldn't it be amazing if it snowed?'

Safiya smiled warmly. 'You mean you've never seen snow?'

He shook his head. 'I've never left Texas,' he confessed.

'You should see the snow in Istanbul,' said Safiya. 'It's very delicate, but so beautiful, as if lace has fallen from the sky, coating the cupolas and rooftops. The snow in the mountains, here, must be something else entirely: thick drifts, solid enough to ski down...' She sighed dreamily and finished her salad.

As Axel sipped from his glass of sparkling water, thinking about winter, the waiter reappeared and cleaned away their salad plates. Five minutes later, he returned with a steaming tray.

'Wow!' Axel exclaimed as his perch filets were set down in front of him, the smell of grilled almonds and butter rising to his nostrils. 'It's so beautiful!' Indeed, the little breaded fish were decorated with almond slivers and lemon peel, while the side of roasted courgettes and red peppers had been assembled into a bright red and green tower, which sat neatly next to a little cup of rice.

Safiya seemed to take her meal in her stride, barely glancing at the delicate slices of pink beef, the thinly shaved parmesan, the dark green salad, before assembling her first forkful. 'White truffle oil,' she said approvingly, as Axel gaped. It occurred to him as he watched his sophisticated companion tuck into her meal that he'd spent very little time with older women. Sure, he knew his mother's friends, the dowdy, cake-baking crew, but a cosmopolitan being such as this had never crossed his path.

'Would you like to try a bite?' Safiya asked, a twinkle in her eye.

'Is it... raw? The meat?' Axel asked hesitantly.

'Just try it.' She held out a perfectly composed forkful, droplets of oil glistening on the rocket leaves.

Axel closed his eyes and gave in. It was incredible, of course: tender, delicately-seasoned beef; salty parmesan; peppery leaves. And a note of something sweet, almost musky – the truffle oil, perhaps. He opened his eyes wide. 'Wow,' he said at last.

Safiya laughed joyfully, the birdlike sound trilling in the air. 'Eat up,' she said, 'Fabien will be here soon.'

Indeed, de Grand-Maizelle appeared before they had finished their desserts: a creamy chocolate torte with hazelnuts for Axel, a lemon sorbet for Safiya. 'Bonjour!' he greeted them, placing a hand on his double-breasted blazer. 'How wonderful, you tourists are so unafraid of the cold.'

'The sun is so beautiful,' Safiya replied with a smile. 'Even we warm-blooded Southerners couldn't resist.'

De Grand-Maizelle sat down and ordered an espresso. 'So, Dr Midana, are you ready for your tour?'

'Of course,' Safiya said, wiping her lips with her white napkin.

'And Mr Parker, will you be joining us today?'

'Oh no,' Axel said, staring at his dessert.

'You should come!' Safiya said unexpectedly.

'Yes, come!' de Grand-Maizelle said generously. 'The proprietor has given me the keys: we can look at anything we want. It's the opportunity of a lifetime.'

Axel looked up at Safiya, and found her smiling with genuine warmth. 'As long as you don't think you'll be bored,' she said.

And so, de Grand-Maizelle having downed his espresso in a single gesture and paid for both their lunches, the three found themselves walking down a street hung with enormous flags.

'You'll know the big cross,' de Grand-Maizelle explained, 'but are you familiar with the flag of Geneva? It stands for the whole canton, of course, nowadays, not just the city, but it's very dear to our hearts. In the Middle Ages, however, it belonged quite firmly to the city.'

Axel looked up at the red, black and gold flag.

'That's a two-headed eagle,' de Grand-Maizelle continued, 'an imperial symbol, and Saint Peter's key…'

'Saint Pierre, like the cathedral!' Safiya exclaimed, and de Grand-Maizelle nodded.

'I can only see one head,' Axel said, puzzled.

De Grand-Maizelle laughed. 'Ah, the scientist, limited by his powers of observation. You're a real doubting Thomas, aren't you?' Seeing Axel's embarrassment, he put a hand on his shoulder. 'I'm only joking, of course. See how the shield is split in half? It's *half* a two-headed eagle: so you're entirely right, it really only has one head.'

Cheerily, the three descended the street, past the fountain, and past the Musée d'Art et d'Histoire. 'Nothing particularly mind-blowing in their collections,' de Grand-Maizelle commented dismissively, 'although they occasionally showcase some excellent expositions.'

At last, they arrived in a quiet street, where each house seemed to have an immense front garden – at least, when Axel could see anything over the high walls. De Grand-Maizelle stopped in front of one of the gates, drew a key from his pocket and opened it. 'Welcome to the home of Jean-Pierre Picot de Larmon,' he said, beckoning them into a quiet lawn surrounded by some kind of thick coniferous hedge. An immense sculpture stood in the centre, casting complex shadows across the grass. 'And this is his sundial, based on the Prague astronomical clock,' he said, rolling his eyes. 'Quite unnecessarily extravagant, in my opinion, but then I suppose Picot de Larmon wishes his guests to know what kind of a man he is.'

'And what kind of a man is he?' Safiya asked. 'Rich?'

De Grand-Maizelle let out of a bellow of a laugh. 'That he certainly is,' he said, crossing to the front door and entering a complex series of numbers on a keypad, no doubt disabling an alarm. 'He's one of the chief financial officers at CERN. The irony is, he's incredibly stingy in his line of work: makes everyone fly EastJet or take overnight buses… But in his private life? My God, the parties.' He shook his head as the door swung open. 'I once was invited to an event at which he was entertaining the head curator of one of the big London museums, and the entire library was full of crates of Moët. Anyway! Before he started working in the finance department – the sell-out! – he was a researcher like me.'

He entered the hallway, and Axel and Safiya followed, gaping at the lavish decoration. The floor was marble, and the high ceilings were painted with skies and clouds. The stairway that wound up to one side seemed to be gilded: on closer inspection, it was in fact covered with a fine pattern of little golden stars.

'I didn't know CERN gave out such generous salaries,' Safiya commented, looking around in astonishment.

De Grand-Maizelle barked out his laugh again. 'Trust me, they don't: in fact, old Larmon's job is to make sure they don't. No, Jean-Pierre Picot de Larmon was born with a silver spoon in his mouth, maybe even a gold one: he's from a very, very old French family, one who emigrated to Geneva after the Edict of Fontainebleau, dragging their piles of gold with them.'

'The what of Fontaine-what?' Axel asked, immediately wishing he'd stop asking foolish questions.

But de Grand-Maizelle seemed pleased. Axel supposed he shared Safiya's professorial instincts. 'Of course,' the Swiss man said, 'I forget that you are from abroad. 'I presume you have not heard of the Edict of Nantes either?'

Axel shook his head.

'The two are something of a pair. The Edict of Nantes,' de Grand-Maizelle explained, 'is a treaty king Henry IV of France wrote in 1598, granting the Protestants of France amnesty. We actually have the original text here in Geneva!'

'The treaty,' Safiya continued, 'has widely gone down in history as marking the end of the French religious wars, but in fact it really only offered Protestants very basic rights—'

'And, much worse, it was revoked ten years later,' de Grand-Maizelle concluded, smiling. 'Furthermore, Louis XIV, the grandson of Henry IV, who wrote it, declared Protestantism illegal in 1685 with the Edict of Fontainebleau. At this point, Protestants were persecuted all across the country, and many fled across the borders, to England, Holland or Switzerland. Many came to Geneva.'

Axel nodded. 'So Larmon's family were Protestants.'

'Exactly!' de Grand-Maizelle crowed. 'He also claims that they were Renaissance astronomers, but it's hard to tell if there's any truth in that. Can you believe he's put that in his bio on the CERN website?' He rolled his eyes. 'In any case, no matter what the provenance might be, he's certainly amassed a very impressive collection of early astronomical texts and objects. If you follow me, I'll show you the library.'

Their ascended the oak staircase, Axel tiptoeing, for fear of scratching the immaculately polished wood. There were planets and solar systems painted on the wood, he saw now, along with the tiny stars.

'Just one more flight of stairs,' de Grand-Maizelle said, rounding a corner. This staircase was much narrower, and made of ancient wood. They ascended the creaking stairs gingerly, and found themselves under a ceiling stripped with very old beams.

'This is the oldest part of the house, as you no doubt can tell. The western wing burned down in the 1700s, but all three stories on this side emerged unscathed. Picot de Larmon had his private study set up here where nobody could bother him.' He retrieved a rusty-looking key from his pocket and swung open a small door. 'This is also where he keeps his most valuable antiques.'

Axel couldn't help but gasp as they entered the room. Dusty light streamed in through the thick, warped glass of the windowpanes, soaking everything in gold. The room was immense, a loft stretching the whole length of the house, each of its walls a tall pine bookcase. Glass cases in the centre held particularly ancient-looking manuscripts.

'This, for instance,' de Grand-Maizelle said proudly, following Axel's gaze, 'is an illuminated manuscript by Johannes von Gmunden, a fifteenth-century Austrian astronomer.'

In the centre of the page, the sun had been painted as a gilded orb with a human face and a rather wry expression. It was surrounded by simple golden stars on a blue background, and several concentric wheels. Axel leaned closer.

'Those are the astrological signs,' Safiya explained, her face very close to his shoulder, 'and the corresponding days and months of the year.'

'Picot de Larmon takes a very romantic view of these manuscripts,' de Grand-Maizelle said with something like affection. 'He simply cannot get over the fact that these learned men of ancient times were looking up at the same stars as we are now. The planets will have moved over the centuries, but not the sun, not the stars.' He shook his head thoughtfully.

'The sheer, beautiful order of it all,' Safiya muttered, as if forgetting the men were there with her. 'Each star placed in the firmament by the hand of the superpower, each planet's orbit drawn into perfect balance...'

De Grand-Maizelle and Axel exchanged a glance.

'Power indeed,' de Grand-Maizelle replied, smiling almost flirtatiously at Safiya. 'Do you know that the power of even the smallest black hole is enough to swallow entire passing solar systems?'

'A dead star consuming other stars, drawing them into itself,' Safiya replied, as if she were quoting some beautiful Sufi poetry. Maybe she was, Axel found himself thinking.

'The energy of a star ten times the size of our sun, collapsed into a space the size of a city...' De Grand-Maizelle shook his head, obviously not immune to the poetry of space either.

'Did scientists in the Middle Ages know about black holes?' Axel asked, wishing to break the spell. He felt increasingly ill at ease with this wishy-washy mystical atmosphere. After all, he told himself, black holes were just gravity. Where was the magic in that?

'There is some debate on the subject,' de Grand-Maizelle said mysteriously, 'but there is one manuscript in Sankt Gallen, in the Stiftsbibliothek...' He paused. 'Wait a minute, I believe I know where I can find a picture of it.' He strode over to the enormous desk that took up the wall on the left side of the attic, turned to the bookshelf immediately next to it, and began running his hands over the volumes. After a moment, he pulled down a large hardback. 'Here it is,' he said, beckoning them over, 'the astronomical clock of Pacificus of Verona.'

The page was covered in a scribble of script, with several columns of text that obviously served as a kind of rudimentary calendar. But in the centre, there was a perfect black disk, and in the corner of the page, a man is pictured looking at it through a telescope. 'It's no doubt apocryphal, a joke amongst scholars, but I've always wondered if it might be true,' de Grand-Maizelle told them. 'I mean, the force of black holes is such that they affect everything around them. It's entirely possible a scientist ahead of his time might have suspected their existence.' He sighed. 'Of course, we had to wait for Einstein to have any sort of proof; and still almost nobody believed in black holes until the 1960s!'

Safiya laughed. 'We are all doubting Thomases,' she said, with a smile.

'Like with God's Particle,' Axel chipped in, not wanting to be left out.

De Grand-Maizelle nodded. 'Exactly,' he said. 'Much of our work at CERN has to do with convincing people to believe things we know to be true. It can be very frustrating.'

Safiya's bird-laugh came quite loudly. 'Try theology,' she said wryly.

As they looked from ancient manuscript to gorgeously bound book, Axel found himself letting go of his scientific reticence, and simply letting the beauty of the illustrations wash over his imagination like the Milky Way. How incredible it was that all those centuries ago, people were looking up at the same sky, pondering these vast questions! And still humanity was looking for so many answers. Black holes were still unseen and essentially unknown. So much of the universe remained untouched, mysterious, untravelled. Perhaps – Axel found himself thinking as he stared at a map of the solar system, the orbits of the planets mapped out in perfect concentric circles of indigo and turquoise – scientists hundreds of years into the future would look at the hard disks of CERN as charmingly primitive, and exhibit print-outs of emails in their fanciest museums! The thought made him laugh quietly.

'What is it?' Safiya asked.

'Nothing,' Axel replied. Indeed, he thought to himself, perhaps that was the truth: we, as humans, after millions of years on this earth and under this sky, still knew almost nothing.

CHAPTER TEN

'Those Galileo sketches were just incredible,' Safiya said dreamily, gazing up at the night sky.

Axel nodded. 'It's so strange to think that he was looking at exactly the same moon as we are, sketching it on that ancient parchment...'

They were sitting a little ways apart from the crowd at the Bain des Pâquis restaurant, a small local fondue place right on the water. It had been three days since they had first arrived in Geneva. Axel had had several long sessions of work in the computer lab at CERN, while Safiya had toured several libraries and museums with Fabien de Grand-Maizelle. That afternoon, the Frenchman had invited Axel along to view another private collection of manuscripts, this one involving Galileo's drawings of the moon.

'Galileo,' Safiya commented, 'another man struggling to get anyone to believe him. It's the danger of finding out the truth before your peers.'

'So he was the first person to get a good look at the moon through a telescope?'

'Yes. He was the first person to stand up and say that it wasn't smooth, as people thought all heavenly bodies were; that a planet could be imperfect and rough. It challenged people's assumptions about God and the heavens.'

'Because it wasn't perfect?'

'Exactly,' said Safiya. 'In those days, it was widely thought that God's perfect balance had no room for chaos or ugliness. Somehow, Earth's imperfection was seen as an exception: therefore, Earth could not be a heavenly body. Galileo suggested it might be otherwise, that we might be just one amongst many planets, orbiting the sun. That was pretty radical, in his day. He went to prison for it.'

'Heliocentrism,' Axel said, remembering something from a lesson.

'Right,' said Safiya. 'Galileo and Copernicus were right, of course: the sun is the central force, and we are just one of the planets orbiting around it.'

The little pebble beach was deserted this time of year, but the inside was packed, the air rich with the scent of garlic, white wine and melted cheese. From their table in the very back of the restaurant, they could look out over the water through the windows, watching the moon reflected in the lapping waves. Axel found himself thinking back to their first conversation in the Japanese garden – many pools, one moon. The moon, after all, was just an imperfect rock reflecting the light of the sun. *What if I don't think there's any moon at all?* he remembered asking, and his impetuous cynicism embarrassed him in retrospect. Of course there was a moon: it was right there, pearl-white, glowing for anyone to see, its light divided into fragments by the current pulling the lake into the river.

Suddenly overcome by a mixture of emotions, Axel blurted out: 'Will you come with me to Bern?'

Startled, Safiya laughed. 'Bern?'

Mortified, Axel cast around for the right words to backtrack, or explain that he'd just meant to compliment her or thank her for her help in Geneva, or try to tell her about the obviousness of the moon, but before he could say anything more, she smiled.

'I'd love to,' she said, decisively. 'We've been a good team. It would be a shame to give up on working together before we've made any breakthroughs. Besides, I could use a little time to write up the last few days' worth of manuscript reading before I head back home to Istanbul. My flight is very flexible,' she added demurely.

Axel glanced up from the tabletop, his cheeks still burning, and found her staring studiously at her fingernails. Then she looked up, and their eyes met.

'Breakthroughs?' he asked, smiling.

Safiya gave a mischievous smile. 'Well, didn't our first meetings go well at CERN? Don't you feel that we are learning from each other?'

'They did,' Axel agreed. 'We are. We *are* a good team.' Everything seemed to be softened around him, from the heat or the evaporating wine, he wasn't sure. The pair fell silent for a moment, contemplating their new plan, as the waiter arrived with an enormous pan full of melted cheese.

Axel gawped. 'The volume of it!' he exclaimed, making Safiya laugh.

'As I said, ever the scientist.' She began tearing the slices of bread into small pieces, then speared one on her fork and dipped it into the cheese.

'That's all there is to it?' Axel asked, impressed. 'It's just bread and cheese?'

'Now you're failing me, Mr Scientist,' Safiya teased. 'The laws of physics should tell you this can't just be cheese, or it would be much denser. No, the cheese is melted and whipped with lots of garlic and white wine. Some places add stronger alcohol, but I saw on the menu that this place uses crémant, sparkling wine.'

'That sounds like a waste,' Axel commented, struggling to get the strands of melted cheese to wrap around his piece of bread.

'Wait till you taste it,' Safiya replied.

It was delicious, of course. 'Patti-Ann would love this,' Axel said without thinking, then he blushed without quite knowing why.

'How is your girlfriend? Have you spoken to her lately?' Safiya asked without much curiosity.

'I'm calling her on Skype tonight,' Axel replied, more defensively than he'd intended. The truth was, he hadn't answered any of Patti-Ann's text messages that day, including a photograph of her in a short dress and cowboy boots, no doubt getting ready for a night out. He'd be in trouble for that when they spoke. For reasons which remained obscure to him, he'd also failed to mention meeting Safiya, or inviting her to come with him to Geneva, and Bern, or sharing fancy meals by moonlight.

Axel poured them both a little more wine, pushing the thoughts aside. 'This is nice stuff,' he commented. 'I'd never heard of Swiss wine.'

'Surely you only drink Californian?' Safiya teased, and Axel blushed.

'I don't know a lot about wine,' he said defensively, 'but I know what I like. And I like this… Chasselas,' he read out from the label.

'So do I,' Safiya said in a conciliatory tone. 'It's well-deserved after another day of research.'

'I don't know if it's been much a day of research for me,' Axel replied, still feeling a little bit peeved by the thoughts of Patti-Ann. 'It was more like another day of trawling through files, and another bit of tourism, with another private museum visit thrown in.'

Safiya shook her head. 'Always such a scientist! As if you're only working when you're hunched over your computer. Just wait till you tell your professor what you were looking at today, and see if he isn't pleased with your work.'

Axel shrugged. 'Maybe,' he said. 'I guess I feel a little frustrated with the Geneva leg of the trip so far. All I'm doing is copying down notes and sending files by email. It's hardly ground-breaking research.'

'Maybe things will be different in Bern,' Safiya said politely. Something about her expression implied she was disappointed with his reaction.

Axel frowned. 'I still feel like I'm missing something, when you talk about our research,' he said slowly. 'I mean, I'm just here as Professor Bohmann's research assistant, and you've somehow ended up studying all these old manuscripts… Which don't really, as far as I can tell, have much to do with the soul.'

Safiya's eyes twinkled. 'Only a scientist would think one's research interests should be narrowed down to the field of one's PhD. I'm much more interested in cross-disciplinary research. I'm learning a lot.' She paused and finished her glass of wine. 'After all, I am very familiar with studying old manuscripts. These ones just happen to be about the sky, the sun and the stars.'

'And the moon,' Axel added, feeling a glow return to his chest. 'So you are… helping me – helping Professor Bohmann?' he corrected himself.

Safiya cocked her head to the side. 'Perhaps,' she said. 'We shall see.'

★ ★ ★ ★

Axel walked back to his hotel in a daze. The lake water was dark now, the moon having disappeared behind the clouds, or perhaps sunk behind the distant mountains. He had to tell Patti-Ann about Safiya, he realised: after all, what was there to hide? He'd made a professional contact, found a very productive research assistant of his own, an experienced one who opened doors for them. Couldn't a man make friends with a woman in all innocence? He arrived at the hotel both energised and disgruntled. When he stopped at the front desk for his key, the polite man checked his ledger. 'Monsieur Parker?' he asked. Axel, confused, nodded, only for the man to reach down under the desk and pull out a cardboard box. 'A delivery for you!' he said, smiling. 'Just sign here.'

Axel recognised Patti-Ann's handwriting at once, and his heart tightened. Thirty-five dollars shipping! He really should have answered more of her messages, sent more pictures... Arriving in his bedroom, he sat down on the side of the bed and pulled open the package. The box was full of crumpled pink tissue paper and smelled of his fiancée's perfume so strongly that it made his heart feel strange. Inside, there was a smaller glossy box wrapped with a red satin ribbon. He opened it and found it filled with square chocolates; or at least, chocolates that had once been square. Transatlantic shipping had not been kind to them. Axel chose one of the least crushed pieces and bit in, then made a face. They were made of dark chocolate, his favourite kind, and filled with pecans, his favourite too, but were somehow dry and quite bitter. Axel found himself laughing as he struggled to swallow the creation. Patti-Ann had never been one for the kitchen. He wondered how long this whole enterprise had taken her, and felt his heart go out to her. He crossed the room to the hotel room's small desk and opened his laptop to boot up Skype. While the hotel WiFi was connecting, he read back through his messages from the day. There were seven, he realised with another pang of guilt. Patti-Ann's graduation photograph appeared in a square on his screen, a little orange light blinking in the corner. Maybe she wasn't in. He called her, and the familiar Skype tune rang out through the Swiss hotel room.

'Hello? Hello?' The screen was black, but that was Patti-Ann's voice, her sweet Southern twang.

'Patti-Ann! Sweetie! It's me, Axel!'

There was a pause, then something like a squeal. 'Axel!' she said, then in a more muffled tone, 'Everybody, it's Axel!'

Axel was confused. 'Where are you?' he asked.

'Oh, I'm in town! I have Skype on my phone now, Pamela showed me how to download it.'

There was a scuffle, and another voice was heard: 'Hi, Axel! Having fun in Europe?'

Axel sighed. 'I'm sorry I didn't answer your messages today,' he said. 'I was really busy with my research.'

'That's OK,' Patti-Ann said sweetly.

'And thank you for your package!' he added. 'The chocolates are really delicious.'

'You sent *chocolates* to Switzerland?' Pamela again, and he heard the sound of women laughing.

Axel felt himself growing angry, but forced himself to keep his voice soft. 'Patti-Ann, why don't you step outside for a minute? I can't hear you very well.'

He heard her assuring the assembled company that she would be 'just five minutes' then there was silence. 'Can I see your face?' he asked. 'I really miss you.'

After a minute's pause, Patti-Ann switched the video on and her lovely face appeared, her heavy makeup apparent even on the grainy screen. 'Do you like my hair?' she asked, turning her head and shaking her glossy curls.

'You look beautiful,' he said. After a pause, he added: 'What time is it over there?'

Patti-Ann giggled. 'Why, what time is it in Geneva?'

He checked the corner of the screen. 'Almost midnight,' he realised in surprise.

'It's five in the afternoon here,' she replied.

'And you're out already?'

'Pamela had a brunch party, and it turned into an afternoon party, and we'll probably go out this evening.' She giggled.

Axel decided to drop the subject and cut to the chase. 'Listen, I'm sorry I've not been in touch more, I met a professor and we're travelling together now.'

'What's his name?' Patti-Ann asked.

'She's... a theologian from Istanbul.'

'Oh, cool!' said Patti-Ann. 'So have you almost finished your project? Have you booked your flight home?'

Axel sighed. 'Not yet,' he said. 'I'm heading over to Bern the day after tomorrow, and it kind of depends how things go there. I should be home next week, though. Maybe the week after. I promise I'll let you know as soon as I book.'

'OK,' Patti-Ann said, a little sadly. 'Well, everybody's just getting in Pamela's truck, we're heading over to a house party, so I gotta go.'

'Do you really...?' Axel asked, before realising he was in no position to be guilt-tripping Patti-Ann. She'd been in touch with him constantly: he was the one who hadn't made time for her. 'OK, sweetheart,' he said, 'you have fun. Can I call you again soon?'

'Yeah,' his fiancée replied, 'I'd like that. OK, P., I'm coming! I love you so much, sweetie.'

'I love you too,' Axel replied, and with a beep, the line went dead. He stared at the screen for a while, at Patti-Ann's grainy photograph – much sweeter and more innocent than she'd looked just then. What had she been doing this last week? All her messages just told him what she was wearing, what she was eating, and that she loved him so, so much. Had she been spending all her time with Pamela? Was she lonely?

His worries were interrupted as the Skype sound rang out again, and a black-and-white photograph of Professor Bohmann appeared. He picked up immediately.

'Professor!' he said.

'Axel, my boy!' The connection was bad, and the professor's face seemed to move from one frozen snapshot to the next.

'I was just going to call you!' Axel said, smiling.

'Well I hope so! It's all very nice, receiving these emails from CERN, but I thought it would be good for us to speak in person.'

'Of course,' Axel replied, feeling chastened. 'I've been busier than I thought I would.'

'That sounds promising,' Bohmann replied. 'Tell me everything!'

'Well, sir, I think I've managed to retrieve everything I could from CERN. I'll be spending another day in the lab there tomorrow, but I think that should be sufficient.'

'Then you'll be off to Bern?'

'Exactly.'

'Fantastic, just fantastic. I was there years and years ago, you must realise, so it's entirely likely they'll have forgotten who I am, but their department – it's at the cutting edge in energy research. Oh, remind me to send you the name of the professor I knew there... Some German guy, absolutely brilliant. Maybe I still have his card somewhere.'

'Dr Straussfeld from CERN set up the meeting, so I think it should all go pretty smoothly.'

'Fantastic! I can't wait to hear all about it.'

'And are you feeling alright?' Axel asked.

Bohmann's face – or at least, the grainy video footage of Bohmann's face – split into a crinkled grin. 'Better,' he said, 'now that you're my eyes and ears. I've actually been quite enjoying this retirement business!'

'You're not retired,' Axel retorted, feeling worried. 'You're working on a book!'

'And tending my garden, and spending more time cooking... Retirement isn't a curse, my boy. In fact, it feels rather like a blessing.'

'Well, OK,' Axel said hesitantly. 'Just as long as you don't drop everything and move to California or anything.'

'I was really thinking more in terms of a small Greek island...' They both laughed, then Bohmann's face fell. 'To tell you the truth, it's not all been blissful. Things have got worse in town since you left.'

'In town? You mean the Defenders of Grace?'

'Those guys never take a vacation,' Bohmann said. 'I mean, it's been nice, hanging out at home, but whenever I end up in town...'

'They're still hassling you?' Axel asked, his stomach tightening.

'Oh, you know, the usual hate mail.' Bohmann's voice sounded light, but Axel could see the sadness in his face. 'That idiot Ichabod Potts is still talking about me too, for some reason. I guess they haven't found another straw man to go after.'

'You're famous!' Axel said weakly.

'He's crazy, that man,' Bohmann said quite vehemently. 'Do you know he's claiming he has healing powers now? Going on live TV and performing "miracles".' He held up his hands, drawing sneer quotes in the air. 'It's all total hooey, of course, but the TV stations let him come on air because their ratings go through the roof. I think it's downright criminal, little old ladies watching this at home and thinking he's a real magician.'

'Try not to worry about it,' Axel said, trying to make his voice soothing. 'I'm sure they'll forget about you before long.'

But Bohmann wasn't finished. 'Kyle was on one of the shows, you know.' He said this lightly, but as he continued, his voice began shaking. 'I couldn't watch. Goddamn Potts thought it'd do his new fundraising campaign good to have a young face involved. He's on a poster, too, plastered all over the centre of town. His face is up in the library! And do you know what it says on those posters? "Save Our Town: Give What You Can". As if Potts hasn't conned every sanctimonious fool in Lake Salvation into giving up their savings already!'

'I'm so sorry to hear that,' Axel said, at a loss. He still found it astounding that Bohmann had a son, let alone such a wayward one.

Professor Bohmann rubbed his eyes, then sighed. 'You're right, there's nothing gained by worrying about it. Let's talk about your trip instead. How are you finding Europe?'

'Beautiful,' Axel said happily. 'Geneva is just amazing.'

'And it's not too cold for you?'

'It was pretty rainy in London,' Axel confessed. 'I bought a coat. But it's been sunny here!' He paused for a moment. 'There's something else: I've been travelling with one of the professors from the conference. Dr Midana. Safiya.' Why was it so hard to confess this perfectly innocent fact?

'Safiya!' Professor Bohmann raised an eyebrow.

'She's a theologian,' Axel hastened to explain. 'After hearing her give a talk about the Sufi spiritual conception of the soul, I told her about your theories, and, well, she asked to come along to Geneva.' How unlikely it seemed, he thought to himself, and yet... 'We've been working together,' he concluded seriously.

'Well! That sounds just wonderful,' Bohmann said, a twinkle in his eye. 'You're moving up in the world, getting your own research assistant...'

'Oh no,' Axel said hastily. 'She's not my assistant. We're a team.'

Bohmann raised his eyebrows so high they disappeared into his messy hair.

'We're going to Bern together,' Axel confessed, feeling embarrassed.

'How incredibly exciting,' Bohmann said, his tone apparently genuine. 'I can't wait to hear how your research progresses.'

'I'll keep you updated.'

After a few pleasantries, Bohmann hung up, but despite the late hour, Axel wasn't remotely ready for bed. Lying fully clothed on the hotel mattress, he stared up at the plaster ceiling, visions of Patti-Ann in cowboy boots mingling with paperwork from CERN and sketches of the moon.

CHAPTER ELEVEN

The train rolled through the green countryside, but neither of the travellers were looking out the window. Safiya was leaning towards Axel, both of them engrossed by his telephone screen.

'It's so awful,' Safiya was muttering, her eyes wide, while Axel was simply shaking his head.

'These poor stupid people,' he said. 'I wonder how much they paid just to go hear this maniac talk.'

On the screen, a video was playing in rather low quality, showing a scene in what appeared to be an American football stadium. A figure was standing on the stage, his arms raised high, like the statue of Christ the Redeemer, though his face was greasy and his hair was lanky and red, and he consequently cut a far less impressive figure than the Rio de Janeiro statue. Ichabod's face, usually so sallow, was an ugly shade of orange in the video, whether from the quality of the recording or the work of an overzealous makeup person, it was hard to tell. It was difficult to ignore, though, as every word he spoke was projected onto an enormous screen behind him, on which his face had been enlarged a hundred feet high. The words currently read MIRACLE-MAKER. The effect was quite terrifying.

Axel had stopped listening to his toxic and incredibly repetitive speech, though he'd gathered the gist of it: America was going to the dogs, the end of the world was near, and the solution to this crisis was to pledge money to the Defenders of Grace. The camera panned around the stadium, showing a crowd of hundreds, maybe even thousands, in throes of rapturous applause.

'Who are all these people?' Safiya asked, half-sadly, half in genuine confusion.

'I don't know,' Axel replied. 'Bored people. Devout people. Lost souls.'

'Oh no,' said Safiya, 'now he's singing.'

Indeed, Ichabod Potts had begun the first line, his warbling luckily quickly drowned out by the crowds:

Jesus paid it all,

All to Him I owe;

Sin had left a crimson stain,

He washed it white as snow.

Axel shook his head. 'He seems to think that the song is about actual money.'

'If Jesus paid it all,' Safiya said wryly, 'who are they to keep their money to themselves, rather than pledging it to a just cause, like Ichabod Potts' pockets?'

'That's probably a direct quote from his speech,' Axel said sadly. Safiya laughed.

'So have you found one with Professor Bohmann's son in it yet? I really want to see what he looks like…'

'Not yet,' Axel replied, 'and I'm getting kind of tired of watching these. Do you think I'm going to get brainwashed? Like, if you see me getting out my credit card, stop me.'

Safiya laughed and took his phone out of his hands. 'OK, you can stop,' she said. 'Why don't we look at the beautiful scenery for a while?'

They both turned and looked out the train window, where the low green pastures and sparkling lakeside of Geneva had slowly evolved into darker hills and forests.

'We must be getting close now,' Axel said, checking his watch.

'Our meeting's at two o'clock: I guess we'll go straight to the university?'

'Sounds good,' said Axel. 'That just about gives me time to go through Professor Bohmann's notes…'

'Again,' Safiya teased.

'Again,' Axel agreed with a smile.

★ ★ ★ ★

Bern, despite being a major city and the de facto capital of Switzerland, felt quaint and lovely. It was crowded, though: incredibly so for a Monday in November.

'Isn't it a bit early in the year for a Christmas market?'

Yet a market it seemed to be, with stalls selling mulled wine and delicious-smelling snacks.

'Why are there so many braided onions at this Christmas market?' Safiya asked curiously.

'I have no idea...' Axel replied.

The university, it turned out, was directly across from the train station, so Axel and Safiya left their suitcases in a locker and spent their spare half hour walking around the bustling old city centre, carried by the joyful crowds. It was beautiful, even when busy: the ancient sandstone buildings encircled by a lovely river and hung with flags emblazoned with black bears.

'I bet de Grand-Maizelle would have something to say about those,' Axel said, gesturing up at the yellow, red and black flags.

'I mean, it's a bear,' Safiya grinned.

'Ah, but not any bear,' Axel joked, imitating the CERN scientist's professorial tones. 'It's actually a quarter of a four-headed bear.'

'Alright, shall we head over?' Safiya asked. 'I'm starting to get nervous, and I swear these crowds are getting more rambunctious.'

Inside the university, it was far quieter. The main building was an impressive structure, a turn-of-the-century palace presiding over the immaculate lawns. There were a few students wandering around, but most must have been in lessons, for the place felt quite deserted.

Entering the building, they were directed to the Institute of Physics, where the Laboratory for High Energy Physics was housed. This building, sober in white-grey steel, looked more like the laboratory Axel had been expecting, and he found this reassuring. When he shared this thought with Safiya, she laughed. 'You're not used to old buildings, are you?'

Axel thought about this. 'I suppose Texan universities are very modern, yes. The cities, too.'

They swung open the door and found themselves in a quiet reception area. A woman looked up from the front desk and smiled. She had big, dark eyes, Axel couldn't help but notice, with a softness to them, and a long ponytail of black hair. 'My name is Sunling. How can I help you?' she asked in perfect English.

'We're here to meet Dr Althauser,' Axel replied. Was he just paranoid from nerves, or had he detected an expression of worry, flitting across the beautiful receptionist's face?

'I'll let him know you're here,' she said smoothly. 'Why don't you sit over there and wait?'

Safiya and Axel exchanged glances, and made their way to the chairs and table in the corner of the reception. Before they could even sit down, however, a tall man charged into the room, a lit cigarette in his mouth.

'Dr Althauser,' the receptionist said sweetly, 'your visitors are here.'

The doctor removed the cigarette from his mouth and exhaled smoke, then walked over to one of the open windows and tossed the butt out.

'So!' Dr Althauser barked, sizing Axel up. 'The American!' Axel held out his hand, trying to keep it from shaking, and Althauser shook it very firmly. 'Welcome,' he said. He then looked over at Safiya for the first time. 'And this is your wife?'

Before a wave of embarrassment for her could spur Axel into any kind of reaction, Safiya had held out her hand. 'Dr Safiya Midana,' she said very professionally.

'Doctor!' The Swiss–German man looked her up and down. 'Well!' Without saying anything more, he turned around and walked away from the reception. Axel looked back nervously at the receptionist, who discreetly motioned that they should follow him. She looked, he noticed, quite apologetic.

He glanced over at Safiya as they followed the doctor down the corridor, but her gaze was fixed straight ahead. 'You can smoke in Swiss universities?' she finally said, her tone curt.

Dr Althauser spun around. 'In my private office, yes,' he replied.

There was silence until they arrived in front of the door, and entered a room that smelled of stale smoke and cleaning products. Althauser went straight to his desk, vaguely motioning that they should sit. This put Axel and Safiya in the rather unfortunate situation of sitting down at one of the lab tables, as if they were students.

'It is very rare that I accept this type of interview,' Dr Althauser began, 'but I have the utmost respect for my colleague Dr Straussfeld, so I accepted his recommendation.'

'You've never met Professor Bohmann?' Axel asked with some trepidation. 'I thought he said he knew you...' His voice trailed off.

'Absolutely not,' Dr Althauser replied. There was a silence. 'So, why don't you tell me why you are here, in one of the highest-powered research departments in the whole of Switzerland, and indeed the world?'

Axel swallowed. 'I am Dr Melvin Bohmann's research assistant, and a PhD student at Lake Salvation University in Texas.'

'And what is Dr Melvin Bohmann's research about?' Dr Althauser asked, with false patience.

'Thermodynamics, sir,' Axel said, the honorific slipping out quite accidentally. He noticed, however, that it seemed to have a placating effect on Althauser, who almost smiled. 'Professor Bohmann is working on using the laws of thermodynamics to prove the existence of God.'

If Dr Althauser had briefly looked amenable to hearing them out, that was over the moment those words left Axel's lips. But the storm did not break immediately.

'God?' Althauser simply repeated.

'Yes, sir. I mean, he doesn't necessarily mean God in the Christian sense, but in terms of a supreme power. In terms of energy,' he finished rather lamely.

'A force that keeps the universe in balance,' Safiya offered.

'The laws of physics keep the universe in balance,' Dr Althauser shot back. 'Or do you disrespect science so much that you don't *believe* that?'

Axel bristled. 'As a scientist,' he said, leaning on the word, 'Bohmann has spent his life studying the mechanisms of the universe, how everything works. Now he is interested in studying *why*. Surely even you must admit this is not a question that even the most cutting-edge science has answered.'

'How everything works?' Althauser sounded almost amused, though the glint in his eyes belied that interpretation. 'How *everything* works?'

'In a philosophical sense,' Axel replied hesitantly, trying to placate him.

Althauser positively glared at him. 'The Laboratory for High-Energy Physics is not a playground for wannabe philosophers,' he said. 'Not a place for some amateur to march in, pretending he's found the solution to all of the toughest, more complex, most fascinating questions in science... And that answer is God? Rubbish.' He pulled a cigarette from his pocket and lit it, then took a deep drag. 'What is it you think we do here, Alex?' he exhaled in a cloud of smoke.

Not daring to correct him, Axel found himself unsure what to reply. 'Physics,' he finally said. 'Cutting-edge physics.'

Althauser made a sound that, in some ways, resembled a laugh. 'Maybe you should have done a little research before turning up here. Have you heard of our Jason Project, for instance, in which we are studying dark matter? Does your professor just think it is sufficient to say that black holes are the work of God? Does he think that will lead to scientific advancement or understanding?' Axel tried to intervene, but it was no use: the doctor was on a roll. 'And what about the Minus Experiment, in which scientists from across the world are conducting research on the fundamental nature of matter? Have you heard of that groundbreaking work we are doing here?'

'Doctor Althauser,' Safiya intervened, 'these two approaches are not exclusive. On the contrary, the domains of science and philosophy – even theology – can enrich each other almost infinitely.'

Althauser, obviously offended at having his rant interrupted, took several deep drags on his cigarette before responding. 'I take it you're a devout Muslim,' he said.

'I'm a theologian,' Safiya replied, obviously stung, 'and a Sufi.'

Althauser laughed. 'That's ridiculous,' he said. 'What, those whirling dervishes? Do they want to come do a dance in my lab, and say they've answered all the questions in modern particle physics?'

'Modern particle physics is not a club,' Safiya replied. 'It is not a closed room that only old white men can participate in. Scientists in the Levant have been studying the same questions as you and your peers here in Bern and in Geneva. In fact, for centuries we were far ahead of you.'

Ignoring her words entirely, Althauser asked: 'And what is it you study, my dear? Physics and theology?'

'I'm currently working on a postdoctoral thesis studying representations of the soul in literature,' she replied, a little deflated.

Althauser shook his head. 'And you think this is science? Do you even know what any of the equipment in this room does?' Safiya didn't reply, but the doctor continued anyway. 'Science is an experimental discipline, based on empirical data. You cannot just sit at home, gazing up at the clouds, or reading about the soul, and come up with the answers to the most difficult questions in the world. You cannot just make things up. You have to have proof.'

'Oh, and do you have proof that black holes exist?' Safiya retorted. 'Did you have proof of the Higgs Boson, until just a year or so ago? No: science is predicated on a great deal of guesswork, some of it just as fanatical and wrong as religious interpretations of the world.'

'Bullshit!' Althauser roared. 'Knowing something without having yet been able to prove it is entirely different to religious *belief*.'

'Knowing something you cannot prove is the core of religious belief,' Safiya said quite calmly. 'Science, in a sense, is simply the ultimate modern religion.'

'Get the hell out of my office,' Althauser said suddenly. 'I don't know why on earth I agreed to see you. I assumed you were carrying out serious research at CERN, or that you wanted to learn in more detail about the extremely cutting-edge experimental science we do here in Bern. I was obviously mistaken. You're a bunch of lunatics. Get out!'

Startled, Axel stumbled up from his chair. He looked over at Safiya, checking how upset she was, and found to his astonishment that she looked perfectly calm and poised, a slight smile on her lips. The door slammed behind them the second they left the room, and they walked slowly back towards the reception, processing what had just happened.

'Are you OK?' Axel asked. 'You look really calm. That was so horrible! I'm so sorry I asked you to come with me!'

Safiya looked over at him in surprise. 'But we won!' she said. 'We won that argument.'

'What do you mean?' Axel asked, astounded.

'He gave up. He got angry and kicked us out because he didn't have an answer. Oh Axel, it doesn't matter that we didn't get more useful information out of him. We planted the seed. Even if he hates it, he'll go home tonight and think about that, and question everything he believes.'

Axel shook his head. 'Well, that's great, but we didn't get anything for Professor Bohmann. I don't know what I'm going to tell him. I'm supposed to be here in Bern for another three whole days.'

As they turned to the front door of the building, a soft voice surprised them. 'Excuse me,' the receptionist said.

They turned around and faced her.

'I'm so sorry about Dr Althauser,' Sunling said. 'He's always like that. I should have warned you. I didn't realise you were a theologian.'

Axel frowned. 'How did you know that?'

The receptionist blushed. 'I could hear him shouting,' she confessed. 'He's... quite intolerant of religion in general.'

'Intolerant indeed,' Safiya commented. 'And we believers get the bad rap.'

'Listen,' Sunling continued, 'I don't know why you were scheduled to meet Althauser. You really should have been talking to Professor Schmidt Hennessey. He works in the Institute for Theoretical Physics.' She permitted herself a small smile. 'He's actually Dr Althauser's boss.' Safiya and Axel exchanged glances. 'He's currently away, finishing his research project in Saint Moritz, but perhaps I could call him?'

'Oh, don't worry about it,' Axel replied, 'there's really no use.'

'Just let me call him,' Sunling said, a pleading note in her voice. 'I really think you should see him.'

'Well, alright then.'

'Look, I have an idea,' the receptionist continued, 'why don't you leave me your card, and I'll get him to call you? I'm fairly sure he'll get back to you today.'

Axel sighed. What harm could there be in accepting a phone call? He handed over his card. 'Thank you, Sunling,' he said.

'I'd expect the call this evening,' she replied with a smile. 'Now go out and enjoy the Zibelemärit, and forget Dr Althauser.'

'The Zibel-what?' asked Axel.

Sunling looked puzzled. 'The Onion Market!' Seeing their confused faces, she burst out laughing. 'You didn't know? It's a traditional folk festival that takes place every year in November. Didn't you see the onions everywhere?'

'There *were* a lot of onions for a Christmas market,' Axel admitted, as Safiya and Sunling laughed.

'Go out and enjoy yourselves,' Sunling said, waving a slender hand towards the door. 'Make sure you try the onion tart.'

Smiling, Axel and Safiya bid Sunling goodbye and walked out into the sun.

'I guess that explains why there are so few students around,' Safiya commented. 'They're all out drinking cheap beer.'

'Doesn't sound like the sort of thing Althauser would be into, does it,' Axel said drily, as they reached the end of the university quadrant.

'It certainly doesn't,' Safiya agreed as they stepped out into the busy street, only to be showered with confetti by a passing child.

Now that he knew it was an onion market, Axel noticed the braided strings of onions hanging everywhere, and the sweet, caramelised scent in the air made sense. There were stands selling bright ceramics, farmers selling produce from carts, and children playing everywhere.

The contrast with the quiet university, and the unpleasantly smoky professor's office, was impressive.

'People really are a mixed bag, aren't they,' Axel commented, dodging a middle-aged man carrying a tray of ten beers. 'The ones you expect to be helpful are horrible, and then somebody like that turns up out of the blue and wants things to work out for you, like Sunling.'

'The universe is more ordered than you believe, Axel Parker,' Safiya replied, a mysterious smile still on her lips. 'If you spent less time questioning how things happened, you might be more grateful for why. Now, shall we try one of those onion tarts?'

CHAPTER TWELVE

After nightfall, the revels at the Onion Market were becoming messier and louder, and Axel and Safiya had sought refuge in the vaulted cellar of a local bistro. The noise from the street was muted here, beneath the dome of the old brick ceiling, and there was a light, musty smell in the air that reminded Axel of some of the libraries they had visited.

'I can't believe I'm still hungry after all that onion tart,' Safiya grinned. They had ordered hearty Germanic food, and Axel had to admit he was starving as well.

'That was a pretty exhausting day,' he said. 'I think we deserve a break.' The onion festival had been a welcome distraction, even fun, but Axel hadn't been able to stop replaying Althauser's comments in his head. Mentioning the disastrous meeting brought the day's misery flooding back.

Seeing Axel's face fall, Safiya reached across the table to take his hand. 'Don't take it so personally! The man was obviously a bigot. Besides, it didn't go that badly. Let's forget about him and go meet his colleague – no, his boss!'

'I don't know,' Axel said hesitantly. 'I mean, he's right, in a way. What am I doing here? I'm only twenty-six. I've not even started my PhD. I don't even understand Bohmann's theories properly. How can I do him justice?'

'You are doing him justice by being here,' Safiya said firmly. 'Who cares if Bern was a failure? Didn't you do well at CERN? Didn't you get the information you needed – the information Professor Bohmann needs?'

Axel nodded slowly.

'And who knows, maybe this Schmidt Hennessey will be able to help us. You can't give up after just one failure!'

The food arrived, interrupting the conversation for a moment: crispy, golden potato cakes Axel remembered as *rösti* from the menu, along with veal cutlets glistening with mushroom cream sauce, sprinkled with parsley. He took a bite, enjoying the warm, savoury flavours.

'My flight home leaves from Geneva at the end of the week,' he said, not raising his eyes from his plate. 'I don't know if I have time to spare to go on another wild goose chase. Not one that might end in humiliation. I mean, I know she was nice, but are we really supposed to trust this Sunling? Straussfeld set us up with Althauser, and Althauser thought we were idiots.'

'Well, we're not,' Safiya said lightly, setting down her fork. 'Idiots, I mean. Don't waste our time beating yourself up.'

Axel bristled. 'Our time?'

'I'm sorry,' Safiya replied, her tone softer. 'I just meant… You're not alone in this.' She was silent for a moment. 'Look, I feel privileged to be your partner on this expedition. Please, let's go together to Saint Moritz. Let's talk to this Schmidt Hennessey. Delay your flight just a few days.'

'I'll miss my birthday,' Axel said, but he couldn't help smiling.

Safiya laughed, a warm sound. 'I'll buy you cake, OK? Listen, Axel, I know you don't believe in this way of thinking, but I have a good feeling about this trip. A gut feeling. Besides, I've always wanted to see the Alps.'

Axel took another bite of the rich, comforting food, and felt the knot in his stomach finally begin to unwind. 'I guess if Bohmann can handle the Defenders of Grace, I should be able to handle one mean scientist.'

'That's the spirit!' Safiya replied. 'There are plenty of scientists with an incredibly limited world view. The academic community has always traditionally been opposed to radical new ways of thinking. I'm sure it's the same thing in Texas, in Istanbul, and here in Bern. You can't let that stand in your way.'

'I also get the feeling the Swiss aren't sure how they feel about foreigners. I mean, did you see how those guys at CERN were always ribbing each other for coming from different regions? And they were all Swiss!'

'*Ah, the American,*' Safiya said sternly, mimicking Althauser's greeting.

'*And the devout Muslim!*' Axel laughed back, then paused. 'I'm sorry,' he said, 'I hope that wasn't offensive.'

Safiya shook her head. 'Not coming from you, it wasn't. Anyway, Althauser was pretty mild compared to some of the criticism I've faced,' she said. 'For being a Muslim, for being Middle Eastern, for being a woman... Of course, it's just as bad at home: they think I'm a free thinker, that I've been Europeanised, corrupted.'

Axel was surprised. 'I guess it can't be easy being a woman teaching theology in such a traditional country,' he said slowly.

'I'm not looking for sympathy,' Safiya said brightly. 'I've had a very successful career. I'm sure the abuse I've received is no worse than what you might get for being a religious person in a very scientific community... or the reverse.'

'Bohmann gets both,' Axel observed. 'It's like everybody expects professors to just sit in their little office, writing some boring book repeating the theories of their predecessors...'

'As if planets were discovered, or diseases were cured, by thinking inside the box,' Safiya scoffed. 'No, you can go ahead and call me a radical if you like, but I will continue to support freedom of thought – for everyone.'

Seeing her animated expression across the candlelit table, Axel tried to imagine Safiya as a radical: this immaculately-dressed, beautiful, polite woman who was, no matter what else she might be, a devout Sufi. He certainly couldn't imagine her spray-painting any university buildings, no matter how angry she got. He could, however, easily picture her destroying an opponent with her intelligence and wit.

'What are you thinking about?' Safiya asked curiously. 'You have a very mysterious smile.'

'Oh, just enjoying the food,' Axel said evasively. 'I don't understand how Swiss people aren't all fat. I mean, I see more obese people on a walk to the Lake Salvation drugstore than I have in this entire European trip.'

'It must be in their genes,' Safiya replied, smiling wryly. 'Or maybe it's the mountain air. In which case I think I might just have a chocolate mousse for dessert...'

* * * *

By the time Axel and Safiya left the restaurant to walk back to the train station to pick up their bags, the revels in the street had quietened.

'I hope it'll be alright, us checking in this late,' Axel worried aloud. 'I kind of lost track of time.'

'Don't worry,' Safiya reassured him, 'with this festival and anything I doubt anybody in Bern will have had an early night.'

They were walking slowly back to the riverside, following its curve to the hotel they had booked, when Axel felt his phone vibrating in his pocket. Startled, he pulled it out to see an unknown number; one prefaced with the Swiss code.

He picked up.

A warm, bright Germanic voice greeted him. 'Hallo, is this Axel Parker? I am Professor Helmut Schmidt Hennessey.'

'Professor Schmidt Hennessey!' Axel exclaimed. 'Yes, hello!'

In all the stress of the afternoon, and the chaos of the Onion Market, Axel had almost forgotten Sunling saying Schmidt Hennessey would call that evening. And yet here he was, the sound of his voice crystal clear, and the distinct sound of birdsong in the background.

'I'm sorry to be calling you so late, but I only just received the message from my assistant.'

'That's fine!' Axel replied.

'Are you still in Bern, then? Enjoying the Onion Market?'

Axel smiled. 'Yes we are,' he said, casting a look over at Safiya, who was grinning.

'Well I won't keep you young folk from the revels, then, but I would like to invite you and Dr Midana to come stay with me at my chalet.'

'At your chalet?' Axel repeated, astounded. He and Safiya exchanged wide-eyed glances.

'Oh, there's plenty of room,' Schmidt Hennessey assured them. 'There's the library, and the lab, and three spare bedrooms. Or one of you could take the basement *carnotzet*, if you fancy a bit more privacy.'

'We'd love to come,' Axel said, as Safiya nodded enthusiastically.

'Excellent!' Schmidt Hennessey exclaimed. 'In that case, why don't you take one of the morning trains over? That way you can explore Saint Moritz before the sun goes down. Just send me a message when you're about to leave. I'll pick you up at the train station, and we'll get to know each other over drinks and dinner. My treat, of course.'

'Thank you so much,' Axel replied, quite overwhelmed.

'*Gute Nacht*, then, and I look forward to meeting you both tomorrow!'

After he'd hung up, Axel and Safiya looked at each other and burst out laughing. 'Can you imagine more of a contrast with Althauser?'

'How do they even work together? I mean, I know we've not met him, but it sounds like day and night...'

'I bet they look like Greek masks for comedy and tragedy when they're sitting together.'

'I bet they avoid each other all day. I bet Althauser sends Schmidt Hennessey rude emails instead of walking over to his office.'

This imaginative game continued for the rest of the walk to the hotel, where the reception door was still luckily open. As the evening had grown rather chilly, the pair stepped onto the plush red velvet carpet of the lobby gratefully.

'*Gruetzi!*' the receptionist welcomed them. 'Can I take your names, please?'

Safiya gave her details, and waited for the receptionist to find them on her computer.

'One room. Is this correct? With a kingsize bed.'

Safiya blushed. 'Oh, no,' she said. 'Two rooms, please.'

'Yes, separate rooms,' Axel added quickly.

The receptionist looked from one to the other surreptitiously, but only apologised politely, and retrieved two keys from the wall behind her.

'472 and 473, then,' she said very sweetly. 'Across the hall from each other.'

Bidding the receptionist goodnight and picking up his bag, Axel walked towards the elevator feeling inexplicably flustered. Safiya, he noticed, after issuing a weak laugh, didn't make any of her usual jokes, and they stood side by side in silence as the numbers flashed white on the panel.

'Well, goodnight!' Axel said, quite heartily.

'Yes, goodnight,' Safiya said, not meeting his eyes. Were her cheeks a little pink?

They turned and walked into their separate bedrooms without another word.

★ ★ ★ ★

Setting all his muddled thoughts aside – Althauser and Schmidt Hennessey, science and religion, Safiya and elevators – Axel collapsed gratefully on the bed. An old frame, it sagged under him and creaked a little, but the mattress was very comfortable. There was a wool blanket folded up at the foot, which he also appreciated. The nights were far colder than anything he'd experienced in Texas, even in the pleasantly middle-class hotel rooms which Bohmann was still paying for. Checking his phone, he realised with a pang that Patti-Ann hadn't sent him a single message that day. And now he would have to tell her that he was delaying his flight home. He switched on Skype with some trepidation, and called Patti-Ann. She picked up after what felt like an eternity.

'Hi, Axel,' she said, quietly. She kept her eyes cast down – a signature move of hers when she was upset – but he could tell by her pink cheeks that she was pleased to hear from him.

'Hi, sweetie! I'm sorry I haven't called. I've been running around doing research and meeting scientists.' *And drinking wine and going to museums and looking at the moon,* he added guiltily in his head.

'Where are you now?' Patti-Ann sounded a little forlorn. With her face scrubbed clean of makeup, she looked years younger than she had the other night. 'What time is it? Are you coming home soon?'

'I'm in Bern,' he replied. 'It's just past midnight.'

'You're out late these days.' It didn't sound like an accusation, but Axel felt his stomach clench all the same.

'There was this festival,' he tried to explain. 'We had kind of a rough day. We met this scientist and he thought Bohmann's ideas were awful. It was kind of hard to get through to him.'

'I mean, doesn't almost everybody think Bohmann's ideas are terrible? Just look at what happened to him here.'

'Well sure, but that's just the Defenders of Grace.' If Patti-Ann was trying to be comforting, she wasn't doing a very good job.

'...all bad,' Patti-Ann murmured incomprehensibly.

'Sorry?' A wave of fatigue suddenly went over him, and he wished he could just curl up in bed.

'They aren't all bad,' Patti-Ann repeated, a little louder. 'I met some of them at Pamela's birthday.'

'Pamela's?' Axel repeated in disbelief, sitting up straight, all sense of fatigue electrified away. 'She's fallen in with that crowd?'

'Ha! Not in a million years. But her sister Carol, well she's really nice. We got talking the other night, you know, at the house party, and she invited me along to a meeting, and I had fun. There's not all crazy, you know.'

'And was Potts there? Ichabod Potts?!' Axel couldn't believe his ears.

'Of course not! It was just a little local meeting!'

'When was this?'

'This morning. And don't you go all high and mighty on me, Axel Parker. What am I supposed to do with my time when you're away like this?' Axel was too stunned to respond. 'Now can you please stop avoiding the topic of this conversation?'

'What topic?' he asked, still angry and confused.

'When you're coming home. I've organised a birthday party for you,' Patti-Ann said, mustering a weak smile.

Axel felt his heart melt. 'Oh sweetie,' he said, 'that's so nice! But listen, I don't think I'm going to make it home in time. There's this other scientist, you see, he...' He stopped himself from saying *invited us to his chalet*. 'He can't see us for a few days. He's up in Saint Moritz.'

'Saint Moritz?' Patti-Ann repeated. 'Is that a church?'

'Oh no,' said Axel, 'it's a glitzy ski resort. You should look it up! It's meant to be very beautiful, and lots of celebrities come to hang out there.' He paused, contemplating how odd this sounded. 'There's a professor I have to visit there for my research,' he explained.

'You and your professors,' Patti-Ann pouted. 'Well, I'll Google this Saint Moritz of yours and see if it really looks worthwhile.'

'Listen, sweetie, this is a once in a lifetime trip. I can't let this opportunity pass. Not after what happened today. It's just one more stop, then I'll be coming home. I promise, I'll let you know as soon as I've rebooked the tickets.'

Patti-Ann was quiet for a minute, then she nodded. 'I guess I can change the date for the party.'

Axel smiled. 'See? We'll be back together in no time. I'll bring you home something nice. Some chocolate, maybe.'

Patti-Ann's face fell, and Axel remembered her gift too late. He felt even worse when he realised he'd left it in the garbage at the last hotel, deciding there was no use in carrying around a large box of inedible chocolates. 'You didn't like mine?' she asked.

'They're perfect,' Axel lied. 'Delicious. You're right, they're better than anything I could get you here.' The thought flashed through his mind that maybe that was overdoing it, but Patti-Ann's smile looked genuine. 'Give me a few more days to find you a really nice gift, OK?'

'Just wait till you see what I got you for your birthday,' Patti-Ann replied happily.

'I can't wait,' said Axel, smiling as brightly as he could.

CHAPTER THIRTEEN

The view from the train window was stunning: even from a distance, the sharp peaks of the Alps were impressive, their crags and snowy summits towering high above the valleys and cities. According to the map on Axel's phone, they had just passed the border of Liechtenstein. Leaving behind the lakes of Zurich and Walen, they were entering a region of high peaks and deep green forests. He was a long way from home, he reflected to himself, snapping blurry photographs through the window to send to his mother. What would Felicia make of the pictures, opening them in the Lake Salvation mall or the drugstore, or sitting in her air-conditioned car as heatwaves rose from the asphalt? Would it look like another world to her, or just like a postcard?

Safiya made a small sound in her sleep, and her head settled onto Axel's shoulder. It had been a long, early train ride out of Bern, the day after a stressful meeting and a late night, and Axel almost envied her the rest. That was not, however, the emotion that rose foremost in him as he listened to her breathing and smelled the faint sandalwood perfume of her hair. Turning back to the mountains, he took another picture and sent it to Patti-Ann.

Soon afterwards, the train pulled into Chur station and Safiya started awake. Gathering their bags, Axel and Safiya crossed the platform and stepped onto a little red train emblazoned with the words 'Rhaetian Railway' and 'Glacier Express' in several languages. Groggily, Safiya rubbed her eyes. 'How many hours were we on that first train for?'

'About three,' Axel replied. 'Another two to go. But don't worry, you're awake for the mountains.'

For a while, the two of them simply stared out the windows, watching the rock faces loom higher and higher above the train, and the distant snow-capped peaks inch closer and closer up the valley.

'I guess they have mountains like this in America?' Safiya asked, unable to keep the awe from her voice.

'Maybe in Colorado, or Alaska... but I don't think they're as tall or as sharp as these.'

'They're so beautiful,' Safiya said in wonder, then yawned and stretched like a cat.

'So what kept you up so late? Were you reading about Galileo?' Axel teased. Safiya had been carrying around an immense hardcover biography of the scientist, courtesy of de Grand-Maizelle.

Safiya smiled ruefully. 'I wish,' she said. 'No, I was on the phone to my parents in Istanbul.' She paused. 'They do not... understand this trip.'

'Are your parents not supportive of your career?' Axel asked cautiously.

Safiya was silent for a while. 'They allowed me to pursue my studies, and supported me financially when I needed it. For this, I will always be grateful.'

She hadn't answered his question, but Axel decided to leave what was clearly a sensitive subject aside. He pulled his own paperback from his bag.

'What is that you've been reading?' Safiya asked curiously.

'It's called *Mountains of the Mind*,' Axel replied, 'by Robert MacFarlane. It's a history of mountaineering, exploring the question of why humanity has always been drawn to the highest peaks.'

'That sounds fascinating,' Safiya replied, drawing out her incredibly heavy book.

Axel grinned. 'I'll lend it to you when you're done with old Galileo,' he offered.

Safiya laughed. '*If* I'm ever done with Galileo.'

They read in companionable silence for the next hour or so, as the train's course tilted further and further uphill, and the mountains drew close enough to finally envelop them. With a squeal, the train finally halted at the neck of the valley, and Axel and Safiya gathered their bags and climbed down onto the platform.

It was cold: far colder than it had been in Geneva or Bern, and there were snowflakes in the air. Axel immediately started shivering, but was distracted from these wintery feelings by a tall figure striding down the platform towards them.

'Axel Parker? Dr Midana?' a friendly Germanic voice called out. 'Welcome to Saint Moritz!'

Axel smiled in relief. 'Professor Schmidt Hennessey?'

The professor was wearing what appeared to be a bearskin coat and a kind of cowboy hat, and was grinning from ear to ear.

Everyone shook hands, and the professor looked them both up and down. 'I see you come from warmer climes,' he observed. 'Did nobody tell you it was cold in the mountains?' He threw his head back and gave a roar of a laugh. 'Come, come to my car! I will take you to the chalet, and you can sit by my fireside. Don't worry, you'll still be able to see the mountains!'

'I can't believe how immense and beautiful they are,' Safiya confessed, as they clambered into his tiny old car. 'The Alps, I mean. I've dreamed of seeing them my whole life...'

Schmidt Hennessey gave a warm smile. 'The Alps are really very young mountains, in geological terms,' he mused aloud. 'They're still alive, still changing, unlike your Jura or your Appalachians.'

'Have you lived here your whole life?' Axel asked. The car, he noticed, had several pairs of hiking boots lying around on the floor, and the mud and leaves from those hikes did not seem to have been cleaned out for months.

'Oh yes, I'm a mountain man through and through. This is my grandparents' chalet, which was my parents' chalet, and, well, now is mine... We lived in Zürich when I was a child, but we used to come here as often as we could: for weeks in the summer and winter, and weekends in between. I've never stopped coming back, no matter where I've been based.'

'How long have you been in Bern?' There was something about the professor that made you want to chat to him. Safiya, it seemed, felt the same.

Schmidt Hennessey squinted thoughtfully. 'Twenty years, give or take a few?' He smiled. 'Quite a commitment. The good news is my retirement will be coming up soon, and then I'll never need to leave the chalet again.'

They drove around the side of the deep blue lake for a little while, then took a sharp turn and began climbing up the mountain. Fifteen minutes later, they turned into a driveway, and arrived in front of an immense wooden chalet. Stepping out into the sharp scent of the pines, Axel and Safiya stared at the house. The wood was old, stained dark with polish, giving the place a quaint energy, but to the side, there was an immense glass conservatory, which looked much more modern.

'Come inside!' Schmidt Hennessey motioned for them to come to the door, where he had brought their bags and was fiddling with the keys.

They stepped inside, and found warm, golden pine, wide windows, and beautiful rugs everywhere. The place was dusty and cluttered with books, papers and trinkets, but exuded a homey charm that made Axel feel comfortable at once.

'Is this a Bergama carpet?' Safiya asked, impressed.

Schmidt Hennessey smiled, clearly pleased. 'It is indeed! I travelled in the Izmir province three years ago, and I just couldn't get over how beautiful the weaving was. All handwoven, and dyed with natural plants. Oh, and you must see this Persian rug, it's actually an antique, over here...' He knelt down by a red and white rug with an interlocking pattern of flowers.

'How gorgeous!' Safiya exclaimed.

Schmidt Hennessey leapt up. 'But I am being a terrible host, showing off my purchases when I should be making you coffee. You do both drink coffee, yes?'

They nodded, and Schmidt Hennessey scrambled off towards another luminous room, calling back 'Come with me!'

The kitchen had a high ceiling and enormous windows, overlooking a breathtaking view of a nearby gorge.

'We're right on the snow-line here, as you can see,' he commented. 'You don't have to walk very far to reach the permafrost, though, or the deep snow. It's all a question of choosing the right paths. You must walk around today, while the weather is good! There's a warm front blowing in overnight, which will change the quality of the snow. Not very safe for walkers, you see. But today? That biting cold is excellent news.' He paused, a twinkle in his eye. 'I will lend you some coats.'

'Oh, you don't have to,' Axel said, but Schmidt Hennessey waved his objections into silence.

'Nonsense!' he said. 'You cannot stay with me here, overlooking this gorgeous valley and these even more gorgeous mountains, and not have a walk around. I mean, you just sat on a train for almost five hours. Have a coffee, tell me a little about yourselves, and then go explore!'

He fiddled around a little with an enormous, glistening coffee machine. Seeing Safiya's interest, he smiled. 'Have you ever seen one of these before? It's a very special machine for very special coffee. It's a bit of an indulgence – I really am getting old. The coffee, you see, doesn't touch anything except crystal.

Axel laughed out loud in surprised delight, and Schmidt Hennessey seemed pleased at his reaction.

'Yes, I am a bit of a mad scientist,' he said. 'The coffee never percolates, which is key to its delicate flavour : it is simply filtered very gently.'

'It smells great,' Axel commented, as the machine whirred and dripped.

Schmidt Hennessey smiled. 'Just wait till you taste it!'

When the machine had finished its process, he took the three cups and set them on a silver tray along with a plate of little cookies, and carried everything into the lounge. 'I found this at a market in Morocco!' he said, gesturing to the tray, 'When I was hiking in the Atlas Mountains. What a gorgeous trip that was.' A fire was burning in the centre of the room, Axel noticed gratefully as he sank into the comfortable sofa.

'So you've travelled a great deal?' Safiya asked admiringly. Something about her expression sent a little spark of jealousy through Axel, though he couldn't have said why.

'Oh, I don't know,' the professor replied dismissively. 'I was quite the globe-trotter in my youth, that's for sure, but these days I barely manage anything outside Europe. I do miss it, though. It's why I keep all these little souvenirs lying around, gathering dust. Like this little thing,' he said, leaning back and picking up a small golden object. 'Axel, you might like this: it's a model of one of the earliest astrolabes. Do you know what that is?'

'I saw a picture of one once,' Axel replied, picking up the elaborate metal disc, intrigued out of his momentary grumpiness. 'Early astronomers used them to navigate by, right?'

'Exactly! It's the original twelfth-century GPS! It's a type of inclinometer, if we're being technical – and I do love to be.' He grinned happily. 'Astronomers, navigators and explorers of all sorts used them to work out the positions of the sun and stars. Some of the most accurate one can operate within a scale of yards. Yards!'

'In the Islamic world,' Safiya added, 'it was traditionally used to work out the prayer times from the position of the sun, as well as the relative position of Mecca.'

'How fascinating! Well, this is only a replica from a museum shop,' Schmidt Hennessey admitted. 'I picked it up in Greece, where the locals told me it was an invention of Hypatia's.'

'A famous early mathematician,' Safiya explained to Axel.

'And a woman,' Axel replied. 'I know.' He handed the astrolabe back to Schmidt Hennessey and sat back into the couch, which let out a comical creak.

'This couch is nearly eighty years old,' Schmidt Hennessey said affectionately, patting the plush so a little cloud of dust puffed out. 'Have an almond crescent!' He held out the plate, and Axel took one. It was delicious. He took another one.

'Orange blossom water,' the professor said. 'That's the secret. Now try a sip of the coffee. They're so delicious together!'

'This chalet is beautiful,' Safiya said softly.

Schmidt Hennessey beamed. 'Isn't it? I love being here, waking up to the bright light and opening the windows to the cold mountain air.

I love taking long walks, I love chopping wood…' He gave his roaring laugh. 'I don't know why I became a scientist instead of a lumberjack.'

'Do you ever get stuck in the snow up here?' Axel asked curiously.

'Oh yes,' Schmidt Hennessey replied. 'All the time. There's only so much you can shovel away. But I have plenty of supplies hidden in the *carnotzet*. Batteries, milk, tinned fish… I could survive an apocalypse out here!'

'What's a *carnotzet*?' Safiya asked, before Axel could.

'Ah!' Schmidt Hennessey leapt up in excitement, then sat right back down. 'I will show you, but first you must finish your coffees. Sit, sit. A *carnotzet* is a traditional Swiss wine cellar, used for storage and degustation. There is also a bed in mine, for guests who have too much of the grape nectar. I presume you'll be wanting separate quarters?'

'Please,' Axel said, prompting an eyebrow raise from the scientist. He didn't look at Safiya, but he sensed her nodding.

'Dr Midana, I will set you up in the upstairs bedroom, which has the best views of the surrounding peaks: the Piz Ot and the Piz Julier. Ladies first, of course.'

'Please, call me Safiya,' she replied warmly. 'And thank you.'

'Axel, you can choose between the smaller guest bedroom – the children's room, I like to call it – and the *carnotzet*.' He winked at Axel, who did not find any of this particularly funny. 'The basement offers more privacy but it can get a little chilly.'

'I'll take the… wine cellar,' Axel said, a little pettily, resenting the offer of the children's room, although of course he would have given Safiya the better room himself. He just wished he'd been given the opportunity to.

They sipped their coffees in silence. After a moment, Safiya asked: 'So, Professor Schmidt Hennessey, could you tell us a little bit about your research here?'

The professor looked thrilled. 'I'm so glad you asked. Let's get right to the heart of the matter!' He rubbed his hands together. 'I work, in a nutshell, in energy. To be more precise, I study the transformation of energy: how it changes, what is gained and lost in those transformations. I am particularly interested in what is lost.'

Axel and Safiya exchanged excited glances. 'That's fantastic,' Axel said. 'That's exactly the sort of thing Professor Bohmann is interested in.'

'Bohmann?' Schmidt Hennessey asked curiously. 'Melvin Bohmann? An American, about my age, who visited us in Bern a few years back?'

Axel's jaw dropped. 'Yes!' he said. 'I'm his research assistant. I'm... We're here to help him write his book.'

'How fantastic!' Schmidt Hennessey exclaimed. 'Yes, we had some really interesting discussions. Shame we lost touch. You'll have to give him my best wishes. How is he, these days?'

Axel hesitated. 'He had a heart attack a few months ago,' he finally said, 'but he's in recovery.' There was a silence as he tried to figure out where to start: the speeches, his university colleagues, the Defenders of Grace, his son, the computer hacking, the firing by Chancellor Langdon... 'It's a long story,' he finally said.

'Maybe you can tell me over dinner tonight, then. Let's stick to the professional subject matter for now, shall we? Long stories require lubrication, of the alcoholic variety.' He took another sip of his coffee with a wink. 'Caffeine, on the other hand, is perfect for scientific stories. To begin with the theoretical aspect of my research, I am particularly interested in the inexplicable; in what lies outside the generally accepted laws of physics. As you imagine, this does not sit me in good stead with many of my colleagues.' He smiled like a naughty schoolboy. 'However, I have made tremendous breakthroughs over the course of my career – some of them begrudgingly accepted by the community, some challenged, rejected or ignored. But perhaps I am approaching this from the wrong angle: let me tell you, for a start, that I am particularly interested in solar and wind energy. The natural forces of this world. Much of my early work revolved around comparing the effectiveness of various energy sources. I seem to recall talking about the sun quite a lot with your friend the professor, would that be right?'

Axel nodded enthusiastically.

'Yes, yes,' Schmidt Hennessey said thoughtfully, 'he was a really interesting fellow. Our research was complementary, for, you see, I am more of a wind guy.' He laughed. 'Let me explain: the last few years, I have been working on developing a new kind of battery for wind turbines, in hopes of finding a better means of storing the energy generated by the spinning blades. As you may know, wind energy suffers from the highest percentage of loss in the energy industry, despite being one of the cleanest sources. There have been a few interesting projects over the years, including one that recycled electric car batteries, but not enough have tackled the theoretical aspects of this research. Not *how* the energy is being lost, in short, but *why*.'

He set his coffee cup down. 'The very basic laws of thermodynamics state that energy cannot be created or destroyed. Yet the loss and destruction of energy is a constant in our daily lives. Physicists have traditionally edged around this by speaking in terms of closed systems and whatnot, but I am not interested in these theoretical frameworks, interesting or useful as they may be: I am interested in practical applications. And surprising as it may seem, the best way to answer these practical questions is to go back to much more philosophical, even theological ones.' Here he nodded at Safiya. 'I seem to recall this was something your Professor Bohmann and I discussed over schnapps,' he added with a laugh.

'I'm quite sure it was,' Axel said, incredibly pleased with the turn this conversation had taken. Here was a real ally, someone who would be able to answer many of his questions. *Their* questions, he corrected himself, glancing over at Safiya.

'What an incredible coincidence,' he said aloud.

'There are no coincidences,' she replied, a mysterious smile playing over her lips, as if she were waiting for Axel to catch up.

The revelation struck Axel suddenly. 'Bohmann must have meant us to come to you,' he said excitedly. 'He just said that we needed to visit the department in Bern, but he couldn't remember any names... When Straussfeld from CERN put us in touch with Althauser—'

'You assumed he was the person you were meant to see.' Schmidt Hennessey shook his head. Safiya was smiling. 'Well, what's done is done: I hope your run-in with my unpleasant colleague didn't go too badly?'

'It wasn't great,' Axel said, just as Safiya said: 'It was alright.' They exchanged looks and laughed.

'You made it out alive, in any case,' Schmidt Hennessey joked, 'and right to my doorstep. That's the important thing.'

'It was meant to be,' Safiya said very quietly.

Professor Schmidt Hennessey smiled, a gentle smile. 'Yes, I believe it was meant to be.'

★ ★ ★ ★

They sat for a long time in front of the fire: after a while, Schmidt Hennessey went into the kitchen and came back with thick sandwiches made on rye bread and stuffed with smoked meat, cheese and grain mustard. Suddenly realising he was starving, Axel wolfed his down as Safiya and Schmidt Hennessey ate more demurely, discussing her work. The conversation had been going on for some time now, and Axel was getting a little bored.

'So you're a Quranic scholar? How fascinating,' Schmidt Hennessey was saying, leaning forward towards Safiya.

Safiya was smiling, leaning back nonchalantly into the soft couch. 'My research interests are much wider than that now, but yes, that was certainly how I began my career. Like you, though, I was always drawn to ideas that lay slightly outside the beaten track.'

As the two smiled at each other, Axel found himself wishing he had something philosophical to contribute to the discussion. Outside, it had started to snow.

'Broadly speaking,' Safiya continued, 'my work centres on different notions of the soul. Cultural ones, historical ones, religious ones. A caveat: I know it may sound odd to say this as a professor of theology, but I'm far more interested in thinking about the universe – the cosmos – than God.'

Schmidt Hennessey nodded, obviously fascinated. 'But you were raised in a religious household?'

'Oh, very much so. My father is very devout. My mother... became more so when she married him. At least that is what my grandmother tells me. She was a Sufi, you see.'

'And you were close to her.' Schmidt Hennessey's voice was gentle, and Axel was surprised to hear a tightness in Safiya's voice when she replied.

'Very close,' she said, and Axel saw a profound sadness in her eyes. 'She taught me everything I know, or at least the emotional, instinctive part. She told me to read everything, and question everything. She was a brilliant, wonderful woman.'

'I know what it's like to lose a woman like that,' Schmidt Hennessey said quietly. 'My wife died four years ago.'

'I'm sorry,' Safiya said, looking up at him, her eyes brimming with shared pain – something intimate and tender.

Axel coughed, and Schmidt Hennessey and Safiya looked up at him in surprise. 'Sorry,' he said weakly. 'Crumbs.'

'In any case,' Safiya said, turning back to the professor, 'the loss of my grandmother was a major inspiration for my life's work. I thought about her all the time: what had made her the woman she was, given her that magical energy? Was it God, was it nature, was it life? And so I started studying the soul, to try to understand how poets and prophets had thought about it.'

'The life force,' Schmidt Hennessey said, nodding, deep in thought. 'It seems our interests are intertwined.'

'And Bohmann's,' Axel interjected, a little more loudly than he'd intended.

This time, Safiya smiled at him. 'That's why I've come on this trip, of course,' she said. 'I saw a spark in Axel – or in his approach to Bohmann's ideas – that I wanted to encourage. To feed off.'

'To be inspired by,' Schmidt Hennessey said, smiling at the pair of them.

Axel's emotions performed something akin to a backflip off a diving board. Schmidt Hennessey's smile suddenly appeared avuncular, supportive, without a trace of rivalry. Axel felt his cheeks burning with embarrassment.

'I'm so glad you've come to me,' the professor said. 'I can't help but feel that you are on the brink of a major philosophical breakthrough – both of you.'

'I feel the same,' Safiya said. 'I just know we'll get there together.'

Schmidt Hennessey, grinning, stood up from the couch. 'I think that's quite enough intellectual stimulation for one day,' he said. 'Why don't you two go out into the snow, and let all these new ideas filter down? Don't try to rush your conclusions, just enjoy the scenery in good company. Come, let me show you to your rooms, and then you can walk before the light begins to fade.'

★ ★ ★ ★

Axel's heart was still beating a little faster than usual by the time they made it out into the snow, bundled up in Schmidt Hennessey's enormous old winter coats.

'I don't think I've ever been anywhere this cold in my life,' Axel said, wishing to keep the conversation to more mundane topics than teamwork, inspiration or breakthroughs, at least for the moment.

'I have,' said Safiya, 'but not for a long time.'

Axel squinted at a signpost to their left. 'Is this the turn Schmidt Hennessey meant?' he asked.

'I think so,' Safiya replied. 'I mean, it certainly looks like it's going in the right direction. Surely it will loop around behind that mountain over there?'

'That sounds right. I mean, Schmidt Hennessey told us the walk would take two hours up, one and a half down, right? An energy transformation in itself!' Axel laughed, trying to imitate Schmidt Hennessey's gruff, friendly tones.

'Like caffeine and sugar,' Safiya retorted, her imitation even weaker than his.

He checked his watch. 'It's only two pm. I guess we got here pretty early from Bern. You always wake up early.'

'I like to see the sun rise while I do my morning meditation,' Safiya replied. 'Even if I've been up late.'

Axel gave her a sympathetic smile, but Safiya's gaze was lost in the distance. Their boots crunched through the snow.

They walked for a time in silence, up into the thick, dark pines. It was still in the forest, fewer snowflakes swirling there, the sounds of Saint Moritz below muffled almost into silence. A small, red squirrel darted in front of them, skittering across the whiteness. As they climbed, the forest began to thin, the trees became more scattered and the light brighter. The snow changed too, Axel noticed, from something thick and crunchy like sugar, to a deep, soft powder.

'This is excellent snow for skiing,' Safiya commented, breaking the silence. Her cheeks were pink, and the walk seemed to have cleared her mind, for she was smiling again.

'Can you ski in the wilderness?' Axel asked curiously. 'I mean, could you ski down one of these slopes?'

'You could if you were experienced,' Safiya replied, 'and if you knew enough about the area to be safe.'

They continued in silence, lost in their thoughts.

'I think we're on the right path,' Axel said after a while. 'I mean, we must be on the far side of that mountain by now. We should be able to look out across the other valley soon.'

'You're right,' said Safiya, 'look over there.' She pointed and, following her outstretched finger, Axel saw another ridge of summits just peeking over the ones they had been steadily walking towards. 'If we keep walking up, we should be able to see even more mountains.'

'We'll have to ask Schmidt Hennessey the names of these peaks,' Axel said breathlessly, his every step sinking deep into the snow.

'I like Schmidt Hennessey,' Safiya said suddenly. 'He seems like a really brilliant man.'

Trying to ignore the flare of jealousy in his stomach, Axel nodded. 'His research sounds like it's right up our alley. I think Bohmann will be really excited about this meeting. I'll have to look back through his notes, see if there are any specific questions he can help us with.'

'Maybe you can Skype him this evening, or tomorrow,' Safiya replied.

'Maybe we could even get them to Skype together!' Axel said, and the two grinned at each other excitedly.

'So what do you think the central philosophy of Bohmann's work really is?' Safiya asked curiously. 'Is it really about God, or is the scientific aspect the most important one?'

'I think he's more of a philosopher, really,' Axel replied, 'like you.' Safiya rewarded him with a warm smile. 'I mean, it's what we were discussing at CERN: he just wants to know *why*. That's part of the reason I think Schmidt Hennessey will be such a good source. Plus, this whole natural energy thing is a new angle for the project. We don't have much of that going on in Texas.'

Safiya laughed. 'Which is funny,' she said, 'considering that one of Bohmann's central theses is about the power of the sun, right?'

Axel grinned. 'I guess it is.'

'This is the whole point of the trip, isn't it,' Safiya said thoughtfully: 'holding Bohmann's ideas up to different kinds of light, turning them around and looking at them from different angles. It's why research, even for a scientist, involves reading so many books.'

'It seems to me...' Axel said hesitantly, 'I mean, this is something I'm still just working out, but on this trip, I've been thinking that the scientific community is just way too isolated. I keep thinking about Althauser's reaction — not just to torture myself anymore, but to try to figure out what we can learn from it — and my main takeaway is that most intellectuals are allowed to hole themselves up in labs and libraries instead of actually having to debate with their colleagues, and especially people in other departments. I mean, this is why Bohmann has suffered so much, and why I think he's so brave: he's been fighting against the current, trying to broaden the conversation, but being shut down at every turn.'

'That's why it's so wonderful that you've come to Europe on his behalf,' Safiya said quietly.

The path was steeper now, drawing them along the curve of the hill. They were indeed overlooking a separate valley, now: no more lights of Saint Moritz down below, only virgin snow and dappled grey rock. 'There isn't even a road here,' Axel breathed. 'Not a single house.'

Safiya looked delighted. 'I guess it's still early enough in the season that not many people have been here. Think how different it would look if snowshoers and cross-country skiers had trampled all over the ground! We're very lucky, Axel.'

They stopped and stood side by side, looking out over the sweeping white and the granite bowl of the valley.

'I feel like we could just walk on forever,' Axel said a little dreamily. 'Like we could easily walk right up to that peak.' It seemed so close, as if he could reach across and touch it.

Safiya smiled. 'Maybe we could,' she said, 'but not before nightfall.'

'It's getting dark, isn't it,' Axel said suddenly. He checked his watch. 'But it's only four p.m.'

Safiya looked up at the sky, a little worried. 'You're right,' she said. 'I hadn't been paying attention; I just figured it was late in the day. I think the weather's changing. We should probably hurry up.'

'Do you think we've gone far enough that we should keep going and finish the loop? Or are we better off turning back?' There was a sudden, ominous grumble in the distance.

'We've been walking more than two hours,' Safiya said hurriedly, gazing up into the distant mass of clouds, 'so we must be more than halfway. The path seems fairly easy to follow: I think we should carry on.'

It's only a little storm, Axel told himself as he picked up his pace. Adrenaline was rushing through him, and something else: worry for Safiya. It was ridiculous, he knew, given that she had more experience with snowy wilderness than he did, but he couldn't help it. The feeling surged through his belly like stomach ache.

With the first real roll of thunder, a flock of crows rushed from the tree-line with a clapping sound, startling Axel and Safiya. 'Animals are very wary of danger,' Safiya said in something like a whisper. They walked on quickly. Another thought sprung into Axel's head: he'd left his phone at the chalet, in the pocket of his lightweight coat. Trying to keep from panicking about this, he reassured himself: the path was still visible, it would be light for another few hours. Besides, this was Switzerland. They were surely very good at rescuing people, if they did somehow get lost or stranded. Schmidt Hennessey knew exactly where they were: he could probably find them himself.

There was another crack of thunder, much closer this time. Safiya stopped dead in her tracks, and said something under her breath in Turkish. 'Look!' she said, grabbing Axel's hand and pulling him into her line of sight. On the other side of the valley, small black dots were bounding across the stone, and then the snow, sending little rivulets of snow rushing down.

'Mountain goats,' Axel breathed aloud, realising what he was looking at. They must have been startled by the thunder. But Safiya squeezed his hand tighter.

'The snow, the snow!' she said. 'Look at the snow!'

With a growing sense of dread, Axel understood what she was saying. It wasn't just little rivulets. The mountain goats, in their panic, had run right into the deep snow, which was rushing in waterfalls, and then a cloud, and then something he didn't understand. There was a terrific cracking sound, a rumble a thousand times louder than any thunder Axel had ever heard, and he felt his heart drop into his stomach. In slow motion, he finally understood what was happening: *avalanche*. A wave of powder exploded down the bowl of the valley with a roar, snapping trees in its path like matchsticks, obliterating the black dots.

My God, my God, Axel found himself thinking, *that wave is going to wash right across the valley and kill us. We'll be buried alive.* In its immensity, it looked so close – even in the depths of his terror, Axel felt a tremendous sense of awe. *Nature is incredible,* he thought vaguely, squeezing Safiya's hand so tightly he thought he might break her. The thought flickered through his mind, even more wildly, that he was going to die hand in hand with Safiya, and a little moment of warmth seeped through the fear. He watched the snow rush and billow, growing and growing as if it would swallow not just the valley and their two figures but the lights of Saint Moritz and the land beyond, devouring all of Switzerland until it rolled into the sea.

Then, just as quickly as it had started, the avalanche ended. It simply… stopped. The cloud of snow drifted down for a moment, settling on the tremendous wash of snow that had shifted down the valley, leaving the upper stone naked and grey, and the valley filled like an ice cream bowl with rock and dirt and snapped trees. Total silence fell.

Overwhelmed, Axel burst into tears, and Safiya very gently wrapped him in her arms. 'It's all over now,' she said very softly, like a mother hushing her child. 'It's all over.'

CHAPTER FOURTEEN

Schmidt Hennessey rushed out of the chalet the second he saw them approaching.

'*Mein Gott!*' he cried out. 'Oh my God, I thought you were lost! I heard the avalanche report on the radio and I feared the worst. Oh, Axel, I called your phone at once but then I heard it ringing in the lounge and I realised you'd left all your things…'

Safiya let go of Axel's hand and took the professor by the shoulders. Offering comfort seemed to be very much in her nature: there was something so matter-of-fact, so adult about her, that no-one could help but be calmed by her presence. 'It's alright, professor,' she said very gently, looking into his eyes. 'It was over in a few minutes, and on the other side of the valley. No-one was hurt.'

'Except some mountain goats,' Axel said shakily, and Professor Schmidt Hennessey gave an emotional, throaty version of his wild bear laugh.

'Come into the house,' he said after a moment. 'I think we could all use something to drink.'

Axel didn't think he'd ever been so happy to see a roaring fire in his entire life. They had walked home so quickly it had been more like a run, and been drenched by the storm along the way: he was freezing and exhausted. Shivering from shock and fatigue, he stripped off Schmidt Hennessey's coat and sunk into the soft couch. It seemed like a lifetime ago that they had sat there eating sandwiches and drinking crystal coffee. Schmidt Hennessey sank into the couch next to him, leaving Safiya standing above them like a worried mother, girlfriend, wife. It would have been comical if Axel hadn't been in shock.

'It was just incredible,' Axel confessed, staring at the rug in front of him. 'The power of it. I've never seen anything like it in my life. And to be triggered by those tiny dots, those little animals...' He shook his head, bewildered.

Safiya laughed softly. 'Do you mean mountain goats?'

Axel nodded.

'Any kind of vibration can set off an avalanche,' Schmidt Hennessey explained, professorial even in the depths of guilt and worry. 'I'd never have let you out there if I knew the storm would be coming so early. The cloud front wasn't supposed to arrive till late tonight! Thunder alone can cause an avalanche, you see, even without scaring mountain goats into a panic.'

'I feel sad for those mountain goats too,' Safiya said, leaning on the back of the couch. 'Shouldn't mountain creatures know about avalanches, just instinctively?'

Schmidt Hennessey shrugged. 'Fear is very deeply engrained in mammals in particular. Whole flocks of sheep have been known to run off a cliff in a panic.'

'It happens in Hardy's novel *Far From the Madding Crowd*,' Safiya said thoughtfully. 'I guess you're right.'

'In fact,' Schmidt Hennessey continued, 'there is a very famous site in France — Solutré, I believe it's called — where they found the bones of tens of thousands of horses from prehistoric times. Historians suspect our ancestors might have chased them off the mountain as a hunting technique.'

'They used to hunt buffalo like that across the American plains,' Axel piped up. 'By driving them off cliffs.' He stared into the fire. 'It's horrible, really.'

There was a silence.

'There's always a lot of new snow, this early in the season,' Schmidt Hennessey said at last. 'I should have thought of that; known there was a risk. I should have checked the radio, the météo, the websites... I was just so excited for you to see the scenery!'

Safiya laid her hands on his shoulders. 'Please stop trying to blame yourself,' she said. 'Let me make us some coffee.'

'I'll come with you,' Schmidt Hennessey said, staggering upright. 'That machine is pretty complicated to the uninitiated.'

Axel was left sitting quietly with the roaring fire. His bag and coat were still lying in the corner, and he went to pick them up. *Mountains of the Mind* was in his inside jacket pocket, along with his phone. There were three missed calls on his phone, two from Schmidt Hennessey, one from his mother. He would not be telling her about the avalanche, he decided at once. She would only panic. Instead, he typed out a quick text message. *Sorry I missed your call. I'm staying in Saint Moritz and very busy with work,* he wrote. *The mountains are very beautiful here, and it's snowing! I'll be home next week. Love you.* He hit send. Texas seemed very, very far away.

Safiya and Schmidt Hennessey reentered, holding aloft a tray of coffee cups identical to the one they had enjoyed that afternoon, except that a slender glass bottle now sat alongside the cups on the silver platter.

'I thought we could all use a little fortification: this is cherry schnapps, which I have made every summer from the sour cherries in the small orchard outside. They're just bare trees this time of year, of course, but in summer, they're heavy with bright red fruit. Unless the blackbirds get there first.'

'I don't know,' said Axel, 'I've never tried it. Maybe just a little sip?'

'I'll just put a little splash in all our coffees. Chalk it up to trying a local tradition,' he added with a smile.

Safiya tasted the hot drink and grimaced. 'It's strong,' she said.

Axel coughed when he sipped his. 'Oh wow,' he said. 'You mountain men aren't kidding around.' He had to admit, however, that the rush of warmth that went through him was pleasant. He steeled himself and took another sip.

'What's that you're reading?' Schmidt Hennessey asked, picking up the MacFarlane from the coffee table. 'A book about mountains?'

'A history of mountaineering. It's fascinating, a very personal book about the appeal of mountains.' He paused. 'I have to say, it seemed a lot more romantic when I was reading it safely on the train. It's almost ironic, thinking about it now: I mean, the author talks a lot about how in modern days, the danger of mountain exploring has a large part to play in their appeal.'

'Mountains are not a hospitable environment,' Schmidt Hennessey replied. 'I mean, one could question whether the desire to live out here can be anything but masochistic.'

Safiya smiled. 'A more tolerant soul might say romantic.'

'They're so violent, all these stories of exploration,' Axel exclaimed. 'The Arctic explorers, you know, Shackleton and all those nineteenth-century guys, they're constantly losing limbs, starving, freezing to death, and the Alpine ascents are even worse!'

'And yet people keep climbing,' Schmidt Hennessey replied, 'no matter how many are lost in ravines, no matter how many cords are cut. There is certainly an almost irresistible force drawing people to the mountains.'

Safiya was quiet for a moment, then spoke. 'The French writer Théophile Gautier said something on the subject: "A peak can exercise the same irresistible power of attraction as an abyss." I remember thinking about that when I was in Nepal as a young woman.'

'Nepal?' Schmidt Hennessey asked. 'How wonderful. I was there myself in the '70s.'

'It was still wonderful in the '90s,' said Safiya, smiling.

She was so well-read, and so well-travelled, Axel found himself thinking in awe. *I mean, I'd never even left the US until now.*

'I lived in a monastery,' she continued, 'amongst the Buddhist monks, near the border of Tibet. It was a meditation retreat, of sorts. I've never found such peace in all my life, such closeness to the superpower. The Annapurna mountains changed my entire life.'

'Mountains have that power,' Schmidt Hennessey replied. 'There is a kind of purity to be found here. A closeness to nature I could easily imagine is similar to a closeness to God.' He paused thoughtfully. 'I am not a religious man myself, but I certainly consider myself spiritual. There have been a number of times in the course of my life when I have felt… touched by something outside myself. Looking up through my telescope, for one, and remembering our relative insignificance within this universe.'

'What can you see with your telescope?' Axel asked curiously. He drained his coffee cup.

'Oh, whatever is visible. The moon is always quite spectacular, even on a cloudy night. On a clear night, you might see Jupiter, or Mars, which is really just like looking at a piece of orange confetti. But the moon, the moon always amazes me, how you can see the craters and little pockmarks in its surface. So clearly you could map it. Just out of reach.'

'It must be a similar instinct,' Safiya mused aloud, 'to want to see and know that which we cannot. I don't think humans were really meant to climb to the top of mountains, but the instinct for conquest is irresistible. And so we set foot on the moon, too, and soon I'm sure we'll fly to distant, unknown planets…'

'Maybe we *are* meant to,' Schmidt Hennessey replied. 'Maybe it is part of our purpose in our time on this earth.'

Safiya nodded thoughtfully. 'God's plan,' she said. Schmidt Hennessey stood up and walked to the window. 'The storm has cleared,' he said, 'and it's dark outside. Would you like to give the telescope a try?'

'Oh, yes please!' Axel exclaimed.

'Follow me, then,' the professor said, leading them across the room.

Opening the door, they found themselves in an immense luminous room. A conservatory, Axel thought first, noting the glass walls, but then he saw the tables set up with half-finished experiments, and the desk covered in papers, and the bookcases heavy with books. A laboratory and a library, he decided.

'This is my office,' Schmidt Hennessey said. 'Do forgive the chaos. I've been up to my neck in work for weeks now. In fact, I must admit I was quite grateful to have unexpected guests.'

Axel peered at the paraphernalia lying around: electrical circuits, lightbulbs and several types of batteries. There were various mobiles hanging in the air, made of thin strips of wood, and sheets of paper taped to the windows. 'For the study of sunlight,' Schmidt Hennessey said vaguely, noting his interest.

Progressing towards the bookshelves, Axel saw a photograph hung on the wall: a wedding photograph, an informal portrait, with a young couple gazing into each other's eyes.

'It was the most beautiful day of my life,' Schmidt Hennessey said wistfully, following him. 'We were married in an orchard, deep in the valleys of the Grisons... There was local wine and cheese, and dancing, and the guests went skinny dipping in the evening!' He sighed. 'I'm sorry, you must think me such a romantic old fool.'

Safiya put a hand on his shoulder, and this time Axel saw that the gesture was kind and sweet rather than seductive. Why had he been so worried about Schmidt Hennessey flirting with Safiya? Was it because he felt protective of her? Was it because he was old?

'Have you found the telescope?' she asked gently, interrupting Axel's muddled train of thought.

'Oh yes, yes, the telescope. It's terrible; I come into this room and I can only think about my research.' He opened a cupboard in the corner and drew out a thick black instrument. 'Here you go: an old model, but it's as good as new.'

There was a door in the conservatory glass, Axel now realised, and soon they were standing outside, shivering.

'Goodness, it's cold. I should have grabbed us some coats,' Schmidt Hennessey realised.

'I'll go get them,' Safiya said, closing the door behind her as she went back into the lab.

There was a silence as Schmidt Hennessey fiddled with the dials. 'You're very lucky,' he said after a while, not looking at Axel. 'I'm not sure I believe in fate, but I can't help but feel that there is something special between you and Safiya. Intellectually speaking. This research of yours sounds fascinating.' He turned to look at Axel and winked. 'I hope you find what you're looking for,' he added.

Safiya having returned with the coats, Axel was unable to respond. He didn't know what he would have said, in any case. Yes, he felt lucky. But what did that mean? And what were they looking for?

* * * *

An hour or so later, dazed by the incredible spectacle of the moon's shadowy surface, shivering from the winter air, they stumbled back inside. After bidding them good-night, Schmidt Hennessey vanished upstairs to his bedroom, and Axel got ready to head down to his basement quarters. But as he picked up his bag, he felt Safiya's presence by his side.

'Can I sit with you a while?' she asked softly. 'I won't be able to sleep. I'm too... exhilarated.'

'By the moon?' Axel asked.

'By the avalanche,' Safiya replied.

'Yeah,' said Axel. He had to admit he understood. 'Why don't you come hang out in the carno... carnu... wine cellar. I had a look earlier, and there's a couch down there. And a TV.'

He walked down the stairs slowly, and entered the dark room. Switching on the lights, he found himself in a golden room, glowing with polished pine and smelling faintly of dust. Like the upstairs, the room was decorated with trinkets from around the world and exotic carpets, but the walls, instead of being covered in bookshelves, were filled with rows and rows of wine bottles. He kicked off his shoes and settled into the comfortable couch, and Safiya joined him shortly after, tiptoeing down the stairs. It was very quiet in the *carnotzet*.

'There's no noise here,' Axel said aloud. 'Not a sound.'

Safiya smiled, taking off her shoes, sitting down and tucking her feet under her on the couch. 'You're right,' she replied. 'We're far from everything and everyone, out here.'

Axel shivered. 'It felt that way this afternoon,' he said. 'Like we'd fallen off the surface of the earth. Like we were alone. Like we were lost. I… I was scared.' *For you*, he stopped himself adding, aware how ridiculous it was when he'd been the frightened one.

'Nature can be ferocious in its power,' Safiya mused. 'Tsunamis, earthquakes, avalanches. But it's only frightening if you're afraid of dying.'

'You're not afraid of dying?' Axel asked, raising his eyebrows.

'As I see it,' Safiya explained, 'everything that happens is part of God's plan. If you and I were meant to die together out there in the snow, hand in hand, I would have accepted it gladly.'

In the rush of warmth that coursed through him at those words, Axel found it hard to argue. 'What about the mountain goats, though?' he asked. Then he thought a little longer, and felt the warmth dissipating. 'Those innocent animals, were they going to accept that fate so gladly? And what about avalanches that destroy whole towns, or hurricanes back home, or tsunamis that wreck Japanese cities, or earthquakes that turn schools to rubble in California?'

'Fate is blind. I mean the superpower. I mean… Nature, if you will. I mean the forces of geology and meteorology and time and space.'

'The laws of physics,' Axel added, finding himself smiling against his will.

'There is a balance,' Safiya continued. 'A natural equilibrium throughout the cosmos. Tsunamis retreat back to the ocean, trees grow back after avalanches. The ash from volcanic eruptions is so fertile that new species grow there. Even in the aftermath of Chernobyl, the trees and ferns grew back stronger, and animals live there quite safely now.'

'You think Chernobyl was part of God's plan?' Axel asked, half-awed, half-horrified.

'You misunderstand my idea of a plan. I mean a *balance*. I mean that anything is possible, and that we as people can choose any path: mass murder, nuclear disaster, walking on the moon. It's entirely possible that in a century we'll have wiped ourselves off the surface of the earth. But the Earth, Nature, the cosmos, will survive, will find its balance again.'

'I think that's quite a dark theory,' Axel replied. 'It sounds like you're embracing chaos.'

'On the contrary!' Safiya exclaimed. 'You're not listening. True chaos is impossible in this universe, because the cosmos is essentially, profoundly balanced. That is how such power and beauty is allowed to exist, as well as horror and loss.'

There was a silence, then Safiya put her hand on his knee and met his eyes. Softly, she asked: 'Tell me you weren't moved by the power of that avalanche. Tell me it was nothing to you, just snow.'

'Of course I was moved. It was… incredible.'

They were silent for a while, lost in their own visions of the snow washing down the hillside, majestic and terrible, destroying everything in its path.

'The stillness that followed,' he finally said. 'Wasn't that strange? I had a sort of… vision during the avalanche, that the snow would just sweep across the country forever, never stopping. Instead, it was over so quickly. Such tremendous force and then just… gone.'

Safiya nodded. 'It was strange,' she said. 'I'm sure our professor friends will be able to illuminate us as to the laws of physics that are in operation here.'

'But that's exactly what's strange. Energy shouldn't be lost like that, not just fading into nothing. The laws of thermodynamics don't account for it.' With a start, Axel realised who he sounded like. 'Oh my God,' he said, 'I'm talking like Bohmann.'

Safiya laughed. 'Good,' she said. 'That means you're truly beginning to understand his research.'

Axel shook his head. 'It doesn't mean there isn't a scientific explanation,' he said stubbornly. 'I mean, look at how the scientists at CERN thought. It's taken us centuries to get this far, and still we know almost nothing. There's room for many unanswered questions in this world.'

'Of course,' said Safiya. 'But there's room for God's hand, too. I happen to believe they're compatible, rather than exclusive. Two sides of the same coin.'

'Many pools, one moon,' Axel said wryly, and he was rewarded with Safiya's very gentle smile.

'Do you know, I've never seen the moon like that,' she said, putting her legs up on the low table and shifting her weight so that she was snuggled into Axel's side. 'The detail, the... geography! It's just incredible.'

'Just like Galileo.' Axel felt so comfortable, so happy, so full of warmth.

'Better than Galileo. I bet Galileo would have given his right eye to see what we can see now. He probably knew it would be possible, in some kind of magical future...'

'Imagine what he'd think of Google maps,' Axel giggled, 'or virtual reality. Or apps where you can order pizza.'

Safiya laughed. 'I think it would be very difficult to explain the world we live in, even to our great-grandparents. To be perfectly honest, I don't understand it all myself. Everything feels so chaotic, so violent... Sometimes I long for my youthful faith, when I believed everything was ordered. These days, I only find true peace in meditation.'

'Maybe you should go back to Nepal,' Axel said sleepily.

Safiya smiled. 'Oh, I wish you could see it there, Axel. It's so incredibly beautiful. Like these mountains, but even more remote. It was just so wonderful, the prayer scarves fluttering in the wind, the towering peaks. We meditated every day at dawn, we walked in the surrounding mountains, we ate lentils and rice...' She paused, lost in her memories. 'I was just a teenager, you know, unsure what I was doing with my life, trying to figure out if I was a Muslim, if I even believed in God... It was the first time I'd been away from my parents' home. My grandmother paid for the trip for my eighteenth birthday.'

'She sounds so wonderful, your grandma.' Axel was having to make an effort to keep his eyes open.

'She really was. She helped me find my own path.' After a silence, she added: 'I remember it being by a lake, Phoksundo Lake I think it was called, and the waters were so turquoise and beautiful. We swam there sometimes, in the cold, and when you came out of the water, it was like being reborn.'

'I grew up by a lake,' Axel said, dreamily. 'It's so beautiful. I wish you could see it. So blue.'

'Let's go walk by the lake in Saint Moritz tomorrow,' Safiya suggested brightly. 'Unless you've been put off walking…'

'I'd love that,' said Axel.

'I bet Schmidt Hennessey would take us to see some of the highlights,' Safiya added.

'The moon,' said Axel. 'Coffee.'

Aware he was half-asleep already, and talking nonsense, Axel felt his eyes drifting closed, and he let his limbs go slack. He was aware of nothing but Safiya's warmth against him, and the luminous pine, and the wonder of everything they had seen together that day. With visions of waves of snow dancing through his mind, he slowly fell asleep.

CHAPTER FIFTEEN

Axel started awake at the sound of his phone ringing. Where was he? A crack of bright light was flooding in the narrow window, and he remembered that he was in the *carnotzet* in Schmidt Hennessey's chalet. In a flash, he remembered falling asleep next to Safiya... How long had they stayed that way, before she had switched off the light and returned to her bedroom? Minutes, an hour, all night? Bleary-eyed, he scrambled from the couch and picked up the phone. *Patti-Ann*, it said on the screen, sending a flood of complex emotions through him. He picked up.

'Hi, sweetie!' he said groggily.

'Good morning honey!' she said, quite loudly.

'Good morning! What... What time is it in Texas?' he asked, confused as to why she was calling so early in the day. 10.20, his phone had said. Wasn't it the middle of the night over there?

'Surprise!' Patti-Ann crowed. 'I'm in town!'

'In town?' Axel asked, a worried feeling creeping into the pit of his stomach, but still not understanding. 'In Lake Salvation?'

'In Saint Moritz, silly!'

Axel leapt out of bed with a shock of adrenaline.

'Now, which hotel are you staying at? Let me come pick you up!'

'I'm... I'm a little ways out of town,' he said, trying to think straight. 'I just woke up. What are you doing here?' he couldn't stop himself asking.

There was the tiniest of pauses. 'It's a surprise,' Patti-Ann said brightly.

'Right,' Axel said, his mind struggling to catch up. 'Great!'

'The taxi driver says we'll get there in about ten minutes,' she added.

'That's fantastic! Let me… go shower and pack up my stuff,' he concluded lamely.

'You're not up yet?'

'It was… kind of a late night,' Axel tried to explain. *I was in an avalanche. We were looking at the moon. Safiya and I…*

'I'm staying at the Royal Palace,' Patti-Ann finally said. 'Why don't you come meet me there at noon?'

'That sounds perfect,' Axel said, trying to keep his voice normal. 'I can't wait to see you.'

Hanging up, he stood for a moment in shock, then he hurried up the stairs.

Safiya and Hennessey looked up, smiling, as he entered the kitchen.

'Good morning!' the professor said, holding up a pot of coffee. 'Did you sleep well?'

'You're still wearing yesterday's clothes,' Safiya teased, her eyes warm. Her expression shifted slightly as she met his gaze. 'What is it?' she asked.

'Were you dreaming about the avalanche?' Hennessey chimed in.

'Patti-Ann is coming,' Axel said vaguely, the words sounding weird in that chalet kitchen.

Safiya raised her eyebrows. 'Your girlfriend?' she asked, her voice neutral.

Axel swallowed. 'Yeah,' he said. 'It's… a surprise, I guess.'

Hennessey gave his booming laugh and clapped him on the back. 'How wonderful!' he said. 'Your Patti-Smith can stay here with us, of course, she is very welcome!'

'Patti-Ann,' Axel corrected him, smiling, before adding against his will: 'She's already booked us a room in town. At the Royal Palace.'

Now it was Hennessey's turn to raise his eyebrows. 'Dear God!' he exclaimed. 'Is your lady some kind of heiress?'

'No,' Axel said with trepidation. 'Why?'

'You've not heard of the Royal Palace? Well, the name is a clue.'

Axel's stomach sank. 'Patti-Ann likes nice things,' he said lamely.

'Well,' Hennessey said after a short pause, 'she will be well served in the way of nice things. It is not really my kind of place, but it's worth a visit once in a lifetime. You two go enjoy yourselves, then.'

'Will you still be working with us?' Safiya asked cautiously.

'Of course!' said Axel. 'I mean, I guess I should go spend today with her. She did come all the way from Texas. But tomorrow.'

'Of course you should!' Hennessey said magnanimously. 'Safiya and I will prepare everything, and then we can all Skype Melvin together tomorrow. How does that sound?'

'I'll help you prepare,' Axel replied. His brain still seemed to be working sluggishly. 'I don't have to go for another hour or so. Is there a bus or something?'

Hennessey waved his hand in the air. 'I won't hear of it. Let Schmidt Hennessey be your taxi. First things first, however: some coffee?'

★ ★ ★ ★

An hour later, Axel found himself sitting in the back of Hennessey's muddy car as they pulled into the centre of Saint Moritz, and then into a small street near the lake. They stopped.

'*This* is the hotel?' he asked in awe, looking up at the vaulted white porticoes, the doormen hovering in their gold-trimmed hats and gloves, the polished wooden doors with their brass knockers.

Hennessey met his eyes in the rearview mirror sympathetically. 'You have fun,' he said.

'I'll be back tomorrow,' Axel said, feeling an odd pang of regret as he stepped out of the car. He retrieved his suitcase and waved Hennessey off, feeling rather lost. His arrival in Saint Moritz felt like centuries ago.

'Hello, sir,' he said at last to the nearest doorman, feeling oddly formal. 'I am meeting someone here.' He was glad he had showered and changed out of the avalanche clothes.

'But of course, Monsieur,' the doorman said, whisking his suitcase off him. 'Let me take you to the front desk.'

There she was: he recognised her at once, even from the back, even in a long caramel coat he'd never seen before. Patti-Ann turned around slowly and smiled. 'Oh my God!' she cried out, running into his arms. 'Axel!'

Holding her tight, Axel was quite overwhelmed by her sudden closeness: her warmth, the fake fur on her coat, the scent of her fancy shampoo. 'You look great,' he said.

She did a little twirl for him, showing off her new winter clothes. 'I did some shopping,' she said with a smile. 'Thank you, Marius,' she said, turning to the doorman and nodding. He bowed and set down Axel's bag, then hesitated for a moment.

'Will there be anything else?' he asked, catching Axel's eye.

'Er, no thank you,' he said as politely as he could, turning towards the elevator. After punching the button, Patti-Ann turned and gave Marius a merry little wave. Marius waved back without enthusiasm.

As they stood in the golden mirrored lift, Axel suddenly understood. 'I think we should have tipped that guy,' he said guiltily.

'What, the doorman?' Patti-Ann said, her expression haughty. 'No way. It's only a tiny suitcase. Besides, I sure paid enough for this room to have service included.'

'How much… did you pay?' Axel asked.

Patti-Ann waved a hand in the air. 'Don't worry about it!' she said. 'It's my treat.'

'Your treat? But you…' *hardly make any money*, he stopped himself from saying. The sentiment, however, was clearly understood.

'My Dad's treat,' she corrected, clearly a little disappointed at her magnanimous gesture being deflated.

'Oh! Well, that sure is nice of him,' Axel said, smiling. The elevator dinged and the doors slid open. They walked down the carpeted hallway, their footsteps soundless on the buttercream plush. Patti-Ann turned the key in the door to room 514.

'I haven't been inside,' she said, her girlish excitement having returned. 'I wanted to wait for you to get here.'

'You weren't waiting long?' Axel asked anxiously.

'Oh no! Don't you worry.'

She pushed the door open, and they stepped into an immense room. Axel's first reaction was to wonder how such a beautiful room could be so stifling. Everything was shades of cream and dusky pink, from the rose-embroidered curtains to the tasselled satin cushions. Patti-Ann clutched his hand tightly. 'It's so beautiful,' she whispered, and turning, Axel saw that she had tears in her wide eyes.

His heart melted. 'I'm so glad you like it, sweetie,' he said, kissing her cheek. It was exactly the sort of décor she would have chosen, he realised: the kind of bedroom every little girl dreamed the fairy tale princesses of Europe must sleep in.

But Patti-Ann's mind was not on tender moments. She let out a squeal and ran across the room to an impressive oak doorway Axel hadn't noticed. They were staying in a suite, he realised, slowly following her across the carpet to the open door. Patti-Ann's father had certainly been in a generous mood.

The bedroom was wood-panelled, a more somber room that instantly reminded Axel of Hennessey's chalet. Far more deluxe than the *carnotzet*, and less dusty, he smiled to himself. Patti-Ann was lying sprawled face-down across the champagne satin of the bed, as if overwhelmed by the grandeur. The curtains were a delicate shade of blue, and the room's windows looked out over the silver surface of the lake – but Axel didn't see this for quite a while, for Patti-Ann was pulling him down onto the jacquard satin sheets and kissing him.

★ ★ ★ ★

Dazed, Axel awoke from a deep slumber a few hours later. Shadows from the branches outside moved across the pillows. With Patti-Ann nestled into his shoulder, it took him a while to understand that he wasn't back in the Zeta Delta Pi fraternity bedroom in Lake Salvation. He groped for his phone and checked the time: two p.m. What a disorientating few days it had been, between the exhausting afternoon hike, the late night moon-gazing and the confusing morning at the chalet. Twice now today he'd woken without knowing where he was or who with. The comparison made him blush guiltily, and he leaned down and kissed Patti-Ann's hair until she woke.

'Hi, honey,' she said sweetly, sitting up and stretching. 'I didn't mean to fall asleep! It must be the jetlag.'

'Don't worry,' he said, with a wink. 'You tired me out too.'

Patti-Ann rolled out of bed. 'Let me just shower and fix my hair,' she said, 'and we can go exploring! You can show me all the best spots in town.'

'I've not actually seen much of Saint Moritz,' Axel confessed. 'I've been… working.' He decided not to tell her about the avalanche.

Forty-five minutes later, the couple were leaving their plush hotel room, taking the mirrored golden elevator down, traversing the echoing marble lobby and letting the doormen guide them out through the oak doors into the street. The fresh November air was a pleasant change, clearing Axel's mind, but Patti-Ann shivered dramatically.

'This weather is crazy!' she said. 'Is it always like this in Europe?'

Axel laughed. 'It's winter, sweetie,' he replied.

'I know it's *winter*, Axel, but I'm cold even with this cashmere sweater and my new wool coat. Don't you think that's weird?'

'You're a Southern girl.' He put his arm around her shoulders and kissed her. 'Have you even seen snow before?'

'When my Daddy took me skiing,' she pouted, 'in Aspen. But that was different.'

'Why don't we walk down to the lake? I'll bet you'll warm up in no time.'

They walked together in silence past the bars and restaurants, past the outdoor skating rink and the fairy lights in the trees. Axel bought Patti-Ann a hot chocolate and a cinnamon donut from a quaint wooden stall, and before long they were down on an old bench by the lake, looking out across the rippling waters.

'So tell me about all this work you've been doing,' Patti-Ann said, daintily licking sugar from her fingertips.

Axel glanced at his fiancée, checking for sarcasm, but she was smiling happily. 'Well, I got a lot of work done at CERN,' he said.

'Is that the library?'

'It's a research centre,' he explained. 'You remember, in Geneva?'

'Oh, right,' she said without much interest. 'The science place.'

'Then we went to Bern and, oh my God, you wouldn't believe how badly that meeting went. Nobody even wanted to talk about Bohmann's research, let alone give us access to any useful resources.'

'Why?' Patti-Ann asked curiously.

'Well, you know some of Bohmann's theories are seen as pretty controversial.'

'I sure do.'

Axel glanced up at the strength of her reply. Remembering their last conversation, he hesitated. 'Do they still talk about Bohmann a lot, the Defenders of Grace?'

Patti-Ann looked aggrieved. 'It's not like they're my best friends,' she said. 'But yeah, they were talking about him at the meeting. I mean, he attacked them pretty violently. They have every right to be upset.'

'Attacked them?' Axel was flabbergasted. 'What do you mean?'

'With his speech,' Patti-Ann said stubbornly. 'The one he got fired for.'

Axel was silent for a moment, processing this interpretation of events. 'I mean,' she continued, 'I told them you were working on something completely different with him. That's true, right?'

'More or less,' Axel lied, trying to quell the wave of anger rising in his chest. 'But I have to say I really don't like you going behind my back, talking about my work. Bohmann hasn't even written the book yet. I'd appreciate if you could keep what I tell you between us.'

'Well what was I supposed to tell them?' Patti-Ann retorted. 'You're working for him for a year on some mysterious project, and I'm supposed to, what, lie about it?'

'I'm not asking you to lie, Patti-Ann. I'm just asking you to respect what I'm doing.'

They gazed out at the lake for a while, watching the cold waves ripple across the surface.

'Anyway, Safiya and I have been making excellent progress,' Axel finally said, feeling like he was playing with fire.

Patti-Ann frowned. 'Who?'

'Safiya. Dr Midana. You remember, the professor I met in London.'

'And you're still travelling together?' she asked, confused.

'It turned out her research was along the same lines as ours,' he said, not entirely untruthfully.

'So she's a scientist?'

Axel paused. 'She's a theologian,' he said. 'From Istanbul.'

'A theologian! Cool!' said Patti-Ann. Before Axel could intervene, she'd ploughed on cheerfully. 'So is she still in town? We should all go out for dinner! Maybe she'll be better at explaining the work you're doing, without getting all high and mighty about it.'

'Sure,' Axel said hesitantly. 'I'll send her a message.' He didn't reach for his phone.

'Go on, then!' Patti-Ann said. 'If you want her to have time to get ready, you can't just tell her ten minutes before.'

'Did you have somewhere particular in mind for this evening?' Axel asked as graciously as he could.

'Oh, I booked us a table at the hotel,' Patti-Ann said airily. 'I was hanging out with Marius and the others for a while before you showed up – they made me a free coffee and showed me the dinner menu and it all sounded so delicious, I booked us a table for six thirty! I'm sure they'd allow us a guest, though.'

'Six thirty?' Axel asked. 'That's pretty early for Europe.'

'Oh, who cares? That's when I like to eat dinner, and I'm not going to change just because I'm on vacation.'

'Sure. Let me just text Safiya.' He pulled out his phone and stared at the screen for a moment before beginning to type. *Dinner at the Royal*

Palace? he typed. After a moment, he added: *with us* and *6.30 tonight,* then hit send. 'Shall we head back to the hotel, then?' he asked. To his embarrassment, he realised his heart was beating fast.

'There was just one thing I wanted to talk to you about,' Patti-Ann said, taking his hand in hers. Axel had the sudden paranoid thought that she might be able to feel his accelerated heartbeat.

'What is it, honey?' he asked, meeting her eyes, but after a moment, she turned and looked out over the lake, and dropped his hand. There was a silence.

'Um, when are we gonna get married?' Patti-Ann finally asked. She sounded bashful.

Axel frowned, startled. 'We agreed we'd wait till I finished my PhD, remember?'

Patti-Ann's eyes didn't leave the surface of the lake. 'I know,' she said faintly, 'but it's been almost two years since you proposed now. And now you've postponed your PhD until next year.'

Axel leaned over and kissed her. 'I know, my darling. It's just hard to organise anything when I'm so busy with work.'

'I could do the organising,' Patti-Ann said, looking over hopefully. 'It's just... I don't want to be an old bride.'

Axel tried very hard not to laugh. 'Old?' he said. 'You're twenty-three.'

'Yeah, but I'll be twenty-seven at least, probably twenty-eight, by the time we get around to actually having a ceremony. I'll probably have loads of wrinkles. My engagement ring won't fit anymore.'

'Yes, you'll be an old woman by then, a big, fat old lady.' Axel grabbed her by the shoulders playfully, but she wrestled away.

'I'm not playing, Axel. If you've changed your mind, you should tell me. You can't just keep me waiting around forever.'

Axel realised that her eyes had filled with tears, and he felt his heart wrench. 'Oh, Patti-Ann, I didn't realise you felt that way,' he said. 'Of course we can get married sooner. Whenever you want.'

Patti-Ann let out a squeal and threw her arms around his shoulders. 'Oh, Axel, I can't wait!' she said. 'There's this venue I found online the other day, this vineyard...'

With a sinking heart, Axel realised that Patti-Ann had made this decision long before coming. She'd probably already printed out lists of caterers and cupcake recipes.

'We'll talk about dates when we get back,' he said. 'Come on, shall we head back to the hotel?'

'I definitely think it should be a spring wedding,' Patti-Ann said firmly, getting up and brushing some invisible dirt from her coat, and proceeded to monologue about decorations and table settings and theme colours most of the way back to the hotel.

★ ★ ★ ★

At 6.30 on the dot, Axel and Patti-Ann were standing by the doorway to the dining room, waiting to be ushered to their seats.

'We should wait for your doctor friend,' Patti-Ann insisted, fixing her hairpins.

'You're right, that would be polite,' Axel agreed, unable to take his eyes off his girlfriend's outfit. Patti-Ann was wearing a bright purple silk dress that tied at the waist and had a long slit up the thigh. Her high heels appeared to be made of crocodile skin, and she was wearing sparkling jewellery.

'Patti-Ann, are these diamonds?' Axel asked, touching the encrusted strands around her neck in wonder.

Patti-Ann giggled. 'Don't be silly, they're rhinestones.'

'Oh,' said Axel, feeling stupid. 'It's just, with the room and everything, I wondered if your father had struck oil!' Patti-Ann blushed, and he regretted the crassness of his comment immediately. 'I'm sorry,' he said straight away. 'It's just... I'm kind of overwhelmed by all this. You turning up out of the blue, your dress, the suite...' He put his arm around her shoulder. 'I couldn't be happier,' he added, unconvincingly.

She smiled and kissed his neck. 'Neither could I,' she beamed.

Hesitant footsteps approached them from behind, then paused. 'Hello, Axel,' Safiya said hesitantly. 'And you must be Patti-Ann.'

Turning around, Axel was floored by Safiya's beauty: she was dressed in a sharp navy suit, with pearl earrings. Her dark hair lay in simple waves, falling down across one shoulder. 'Safiya!' Axel exclaimed, unable to keep the warmth from his voice. 'This is my girlfriend, I mean fiancée, Patti-Ann.'

Giving no acknowledgement of his awkwardness, Safiya shook Patti-Ann's hand firmly.

'Wow,' said Patti-Ann, obviously a little intimidated. 'You really are a professor!'

Safiya smiled tolerantly. 'It's so nice to meet you at last,' she said. 'Shall we sit?'

Axel trailed behind as the women followed the waiter towards their table. The ceilings were sky-high, with polished oak beams running the length of the dining room – easily the size of a ballroom, Axel thought. He was glad Patti-Ann had talked him into putting on a jacket and tie. Though no other guests had arrived in the dining room, he had a suspicion he would still be underdressed. Flowers and cattails planted in tall Grecian urns towered over the white-clothed tables, a candle glowing on each one. With every step across the thick indigo carpet, Patti-Ann's rhinestone bracelets made a little jangling sound, like glass breaking. How on earth had he ended up in this situation?

The waiter seated them in a corner of the room, for which Axel was grateful: it made the immensity of the dining hall seem a little less daunting. He took his leather-bound menu with a nod and a smile, which he had to work quite hard not to lose when he opened it. 300 dollars, it said on the first page: *Menu Dégustation, neuf plats*. Nine courses?

Flipping through the pages, Axel was only slightly relieved to find lobster for eighty dollars, *foie gras* for seventy, and beef carpaccio with roasted something-or-other for sixty-five. The cheapest thing on the menu was a *millefeuille de champignons* for forty-five, and he didn't know what either of those words meant.

'Oh my God,' Patti-Ann said, and Axel felt a surge of relief: so she'd seen the mistake she'd made, coming here, and she would suggest they go out for pizza. He'd seen a little bistro just down the street that seemed quite cosy... 'Everything looks just amazing!' Axel blinked. Patti-Ann, he realised, was thrilled.

'Is your menu in English?' he asked, holding back from asking what she thought of the prices.

Safiya leaned her copy towards him: 'The English is at the back, see?'

Glancing over at Safiya's menu, a realisation hit Axel: his was the only copy with prices. They'd given the ladies of the table menus without prices. He was the only one who knew what this was going to cost. At least, he told himself, he would also know what the food was now. His high school French hadn't prepared him for this kind of occasion. There was a choice of lobster salad, he now saw, with lemon thyme mayonnaise, or a *foie gras* terrine with blackcurrant and fig *coulis*, and beef carpaccio with roasted hazelnuts and truffle dressing. A *millefeuille de champignons*, he gathered, was an elaborate mushroom pastry. It still cost forty-five dollars, though.

'The main courses are on the next page,' Safiya added.

'Oh,' said Axel, feeling foolish once more, then immediately panicking in anticipation of the cost. *Thank God*, was his first thought on turning the page, *there's a soup!* For just twenty-nine dollars, a barley soup from the Grisons region, with cream and smoked meat. That sounded nice. The risottos and pastas weren't too expensive either, he realised. Maybe one of the women would settle on a salad.

'Let's have the degustation menu!' Patti-Ann exclaimed.

Axel felt his heart sinking, but to his delight, Safiya intervened. 'I'm afraid that'll be a bit heavy for me,' she said. 'I don't eat very much meat.'

Patti-Ann smiled benevolently. 'Oh, you don't have to eat it!' she said. 'You can get whatever you like.'

'I think the whole table needs to get that menu,' Axel intervened. 'Otherwise you have some people eating one or two courses, and one person eating nine. You need a minimum of two people for that menu.' He grinned, as if this was a very funny joke, but in truth he was quite worried. He, for one, did not have 300 spare dollars floating around, let alone 900. That was more than he'd spent on the whole trip thus far. And it didn't even include wine! He was going to need wine to get through this experience, that was for sure.

'You can still pick two or three courses of your choice,' Safiya suggested to Patti-Ann, 'and that way you know what you're getting.'

'Ooh!' said Patti-Ann, 'that's true! I hadn't thought of that. Suppose they serve something I don't like, like chicken-fried steak?'

Though this seemed unlikely, at the Royal Palace Hotel, but Axel held his peace. 'I think I'll have the barley soup,' he said lightly.

Patti-Ann stared at him. 'Just the soup?'

He sighed inwardly and scanned the menu. 'And a beetroot risotto.'

'That sounds great,' said Safiya, who had clearly worked out what Axel was so anxious about. 'I think I'll have the sole with asparagus, and the salmon salad as a starter.'

'What is up with you guys?' Patti-Ann pouted. 'When did everybody become vegetarian?'

Checking the prices of Safiya's dishes, Axel found with relief that, like him, she'd steered towards the bottom range. 'You can have whatever you like, sweetheart,' he said warmly. One extravagant dinner, his budget could handle. Just not three.

'I want the *flambéed* Simmental beef, with cream pepper sauce and balsamic roasted carrots and—' she squinted at the menu – 'puree. What's pour-ee?'

'*Purée*,' Safiya said in her immaculate French, 'is just a fancy way of saying mashed potatoes.'

'Oh!' Patti-Ann said, charmed.

The *maitre d'* appeared by the side of the table. 'Good evening,' he said in smooth Oxford English. 'Is there anything I can help you with? Any questions?'

'Well I know what *purée* is now,' Patti-Ann beamed, with a sparkling smile, 'so I think we're all set!'

The *maitre d'* gave a little bow of acknowledgement. 'As you know, we cater to guests from all over the world, and can recommend specialities from Switzerland, France, Italy, even Spain! The lady of the house is Spanish, you see.'

'I really like Italian food,' Patti-Ann said, clearly charmed by the attention. 'Do you have any *gnocchi*?' She pronounced it in two syllables, with a hard 'g', but the waiter was unfazed.

'Of course, Madame! We have homemade *gnocchi di patate* with a very special cream and mustard sauce, and a watercress salad on the side.' His Italian, in contrast, rolled flawlessly off his tongue.

'Ooh! That sounds great. OK, well I'll have that. And the beef.'

Axel kept smiling as best he could. They placed the rest of their orders, along with a bottle of the second-cheapest wine on the menu.

'So, Safiya,' Patti-Ann said curiously, 'where is it you're from, again? Iraq?'

'Turkey,' Safiya corrected her gently. 'I've lived in Istanbul most of my life, apart from the time I've spent studying in London.'

'London!' Patti-Ann was impressed. 'Wasn't it really cold for you there? I mean, coming from the desert and all?'

Safiya gave a sweet smile. Axel realised this wasn't the first time she'd had to put up with these sorts of questions, and his heart went out to her. 'Oh, it was a change of pace, that's for sure,' she said. 'But I grew to love the rain. It's easier to work long hours when you have the soothing sound of the drops falling on the windows. Otherwise, the sun can be tempting, shining in through the library windows...'

'So you're really serious about your work.' This set alarm bells ringing for Axel: he knew how insecure his fiancée was about her career. But he needn't have worried: Safiya was a diplomat born and bred.

'I love my work,' she said, 'but it hasn't always been easy. It took me a long time to be sure of what I wanted to do with my life. My parents were quite resistant to the idea of me being a professor, you see.'

Patti-Ann smiled sympathetically. 'Oh, do women not normally have jobs over there?'

Luckily, at this point the *maitre d'* reappeared with a bottle of wine and their starters, and for a moment the three were absorbed in their beautiful dishes. Axel's soup was so rich and smooth that he forgot about his troubles for a whole minute, and let out a low 'mmm' sound. Patti-Ann laughed. 'I guess you like your soup?'

'You have to taste it! Safiya, would you like to try?'

'No thank you,' she replied.

After another few minutes of silence, filled only with the scraping of knives and forks, Patti-Ann piped up again. 'So I did a bunch of research before heading over here. You know, when you mentioned Saint Moritz on the phone, I just thought, what a cool name! So I did some Googling, and then I headed to the public library. What?' She pouted, seeing Axel's expression of surprise. 'I have a lot of time on my hands. I did some research, just like you. Turns out FDR and Eleanor Roosevelt used to come here all the time! This very hotel, I mean. She brought trunks of her gowns from Paris, and by the time they arrived here, their clothes were all rumpled. So the *maitre d'* refused them entry to the main dining room! They had to eat outside. This was before she was the First Lady, of course. But it's still funny. That's why I figured I'd better dress up real fancy! It's way too cold to eat outside.'

Safiya and Axel laughed. 'I didn't find too many other funny stories,' Patti-Ann continued, 'but it sounds like all the celebrities come skiing here. Hitchcock and Chaplin in the old days, and Robert de Niro and Liz Hurley and John Travolta and Paris Hilton… It just sound so glamorous!'

'The Shah of Iran had his own villa here,' Safiya replied, getting into the spirit of the conversation. 'I've heard it's worth about thirty million.'

Patti-Ann's eyes popped. 'Wow!' she said. 'Is that a friend of yours?'

'I'm pretty sure I saw George Clooney on my way down the mountain yesterday,' Axel intervened hastily. Once more, he was saved by the bell as the *maitre d'* reappeared and whisked away their clean plates.

There was a brief silence. Everybody drank some wine.

Safiya set down her glass. 'So how did you two meet?' she asked politely.

'Oh, we've known each other a very long time,' Axel began, but that was as far as he got.

'We're childhood sweethearts!' Patti-Ann burst out happily. 'And we're getting married next year!'

Axel swallowed. 'I don't know about that, sweetie,' he said as quietly as he could. 'It's not like we've settled on a date.'

Patti-Ann appeared unperturbed. 'Well, we're getting married as soon as possible, then.' She planted a noisy kiss on Axel's cheek, then made a great show of wiping the lipstick off with her napkin.

'Congratulations,' said Safiya, her eyes on the table.

Axel willed the *maitre d'* to reappear, but had no such luck.

'So do you have a special someone?' Patti-Ann asked Safiya.

Safiya gave a thin smile. 'I don't really have time for that sort of thing these days,' she said.

'Oh, so you're too busy being a professor? Or wait, are you even allowed to have a boyfriend over there?'

'Of course,' Safiya replied, and Axel saw that her patience was wearing thin. 'There have been... opportunities. But not the right ones.' There was a bitterness in her voice that he hadn't heard before. 'You two are very lucky,' she added. Axel felt his heart twist in his chest.

The *maitre d'* finally made his appearance, with an immense loaded silver tray of plates.

'Oh my God!' said Patti-Ann, as her immaculate medallion of seared beef was set down in front of her, drizzled in golden sauce. 'It's tiny!'

The *maitre d'* blinked. 'Madame?' he inquired. 'Is everything alright?'

'Oh yes!' Patti-Ann blushed. 'It's just that... I'm from Texas, you know. We have really big steaks at home.' She lowered her voice and leaned towards him in a conspiratorial fashion. 'Do you think you could get me some fries?'

'But of course,' said the *maitre d'*, smiling. He set down Axel's risotto and Safiya's sole, then disappeared.

Patti-Ann picked up her steak knife and began sawing into the meat with gusto. She took a bite, swallowed and grinned. 'Wow!' she said. 'These Swiss guys really know what they're doing. Even if it's really small.' She took the little silver pitcher of sauce and poured it all over her plate.

'How big are steaks in Texas, then?' Safiya asked curiously. 'That looks like plenty of meat to me.'

'Oh, they're usually about the size of a plate, and weigh about half a kilogram,' Patti-Ann said, holding out her hands for scale. 'We even have a restaurant in my home town where they give you a three-pound steak for free if you can eat it all in one sitting. But then of course you've got all the different kinds: T-bone and tenderloin and porterhouse...'

'Goodness. So you don't ever eat fish?' Safiya asked lightly, dipping her fork into her side salad.

'My father raised me on steak,' Patti-Ann said proudly. 'He's a rancher, you see.'

'I guess your part of Texas is quite far from the sea.' Safiya took a delicate bite of sole.

'Oh no!' said Patti-Ann. 'We're really close to the Gulf of Mexico. We have the best beaches. I mean, we hardly ever go there.'

'Even though they're polluted with our oil slicks...' Axel commented under his breath.

'I don't think I could be a vegetarian,' said Safiya. 'I like fish too much. Meat, however, I could live without.'

'Well I sure couldn't,' said Patti-Ann, sawing another bite of steak and dipping it in sauce.

They ate for a while in silence, Axel trying to pay attention only to his delicious beetroot risotto, which was flavoured with sharp goat's cheese and a touch of honey.

'So Safiya, tell me about the work you do,' Patti-Ann said. 'Axel isn't very good at explaining things to me.'

Safiya smiled quite sympathetically. 'Well, on this trip, we've been studying energy,' she said. 'Energy from the sun, from the wind, from the snow.'

'The conversion of energy,' Axel added. 'How energy changes, and what happens to it when it does.'

'With Professor Schmidt Hennessey, we began thinking specifically about how energy comes to a stop.'

'This sounds a whole lot like Bohmann controversial stuff,' Patti-Ann said hesitantly. 'I thought you said you were working on something else.'

'Have you met Professor Bohmann?' Safiya asked. 'He sounds like such a sweet man.'

'Yeah, I've met him,' Patti-Ann said defensively. 'He's pretty weird.'

'Patti-Ann!' Axel intervened, then he softened his tone, not wishing to start an argument. 'I mean, yeah, he is pretty weird. But he's kind of a genius.'

'So you're now working together on his theories,' Patti-Ann said, looking from Axel to Safiya. 'And what did you say your own work was on?' she asked Safiya.

Safiya hesitated. 'I study the soul,' she said finally.

Patti-Ann paused, and Axel worried that she would ask the question he dreaded – but instead, she smiled. 'Oh, so you're a Christian? I'd assumed you were…'

'Muslim?' Safiya didn't look so patient now. 'I am, yes.' After a pause, she added, something crackling like sparks in the undertone: 'A very devout Muslim.'

Patti-Ann looked worried. 'But you're not, like, a terrorist, right? I mean, you don't have anything against Christians?' Her expression showed clearly that she would feel much the same if she had ended up at dinner with a vampire, and cut her finger on her steak knife.

'Of course not,' Safiya said shortly, then she sighed, clearly sharing Axel's instinct for peacekeeping. 'Most Muslims are very tolerant, you know. I grew up around many Christians, many atheists too; there was never any trouble.'

'Oh, OK!' said Patti-Ann, brightly. She ate her final fries and sat back, her worries clearly soothed. 'Well, that was delicious. So does anybody want some dessert?'

'I should be getting back to the chalet,' Safiya replied. She pushed her chair back and stood up. 'Patti-Ann, very nice to meet you.' She shook her hand – was Axel imagining it, or did Patti-Ann wince a little at the strength of it?

'Let me walk you to the door,' Axel said, standing up.

'I'll wait here and get the dessert menus,' said Patti-Ann.

They walked across the carpeted room, where still only a scattering of couples sat dining. The distance felt interminable. At last, they were crossing the lobby and standing on the other side of the oak doors. The snowy wind was a welcome change from the stuffy atmosphere, and Axel closed his eyes for a moment.

'Thank you for inviting me, I guess,' Safiya said frostily.

'I'm sorry about—' Axel began, but Safiya cut in:

'Patti-Ann is very sweet. I'm sure you two will enjoy the rest of the night together.' There was a silence. 'What time should we expect you at Schmidt Hennessey's chalet?'

She was obviously not in the mood for apologies, nor did she give any sign of the alliance Axel had felt with her all night – as if the two of them were a team. For some reason, he'd expected them to immediately burst into laughter upon arriving outside, making fun of the whole awkward evening and Patti-Ann's many faux pas together. Thinking back, it seemed insane that such a thought had crossed his mind at all. He took a step back.

'I'll come as soon as I can.' He blushed, suddenly. 'Late morning, I guess.'

Safiya didn't comment. Now that they were finally out of that situation in the dining room, Axel wished he had some reason to keep her there with him, but he could think of nothing more to say.

'How are you getting home… I mean, back to the chalet?' he finally asked.

'Helmut is picking me up,' she said shortly. 'I sent him a message ten minutes ago: he should be here soon. Good night, Axel.'

And with those words, Safiya turned on her heel and disappeared into the snow, leaving Axel alone on the steps of the Royal Palace Hotel.

CHAPTER SIXTEEN

Breakfast at the Royal Palace Hotel was no sedate affair. As Axel stumbled into the dining room, bleary-eyed, his hair still wet from his shower, his first impression was displeasure at being back on the scene of the previous night's unpleasant dinner, but he couldn't help stopping in his tracks and gawping at the sight of the buffet table. Grapes and flowers spilled from an enormous basket of apples, oranges, pears and pomegranates. Silver platters of cheese and smoked meats were arranged in beautiful overlapping patterns, with not a single piece appearing to be missing or out of place. Pastries, too, studded with raisins and chocolate and glazed with sugar syrup, were piled in baskets lined with pretty napkins. There were dried apricots, figs and dates, fresh yoghurt in an immense cut-glass bowl and fresh bread glistening with butter and little bowls of honey…

'Wow,' was all he could say.

Patti-Ann smiled demurely as she took in the *tableau*. 'I knew it was a good idea, staying here,' she said. 'Though those Swiss people sure eat some weird stuff for breakfast. Who wants smoked fish first thing in the morning?' She wrinkled her nose.

'They'd probably find it weird to eat waffles with syrup every Sunday…'

'I like waffles,' Patti-Ann said defensively. 'Hey, I wonder if they do waffles here?'

Axel stopped himself from commenting that if they did offer waffles, they probably cost sixty dollars and came with truffle oil and gold leaf.

The *maitre d'* appeared and took their order for coffee – 'a nice big one with lots of creamer' for Patti-Ann and an espresso for Axel.

'Look who's gone all continental,' Patti-Ann teased.

Axel shrugged. 'They just do really good coffee here,' he said. He set his napkin back on the table and stood up. 'I guess we should help ourselves to some of this food!'

When they returned from the buffet table, Patti-Ann's plate laden with almond pastries, cheese and fruit, while Axel chose a bowl of muesli with yoghurt and some toast, he couldn't help blurting out what had been on his mind since the previous night.

'I don't think you were very polite to Safiya yesterday.'

Patti-Ann looked up from her breakfast, surprised. 'What?'

'She was supposed to be our dinner guest. You saw how she left in a huff.'

'I thought that was just the way... people like her did things. Or that she was tired. I don't know!'

'She left like that because you offended her,' Axel couldn't stop himself from saying, holding back his private belief that she had left simply because she had spent a miserable evening. It was easier, after all, to lay the blame on his fiancée.

'Because of the Muslim thing? I mean come on, Axel, you could have warned me. How was I supposed to know?'

'You're saying I have to inform you about the religious beliefs of our dinner guests?'

'I'm saying you put me in an awkward situation. I mean, I couldn't have guessed she was mixed up in that crazy stuff! She seems so nice and serious.'

'Crazy stuff? Sufism is the gentlest, most mystical form of devotion I've ever come across. You're the one hanging around with those holy rollers!'

'What in the Lord's name is Sufism?'

'Never mind.' Axel angrily bit into his toast.

'I went to *one* meeting with the Defenders of Grace, Axel. And they were really nice to me. Which is more than can be said for my own fiancé.'

Axel sighed. 'I'm sorry,' he said. 'I didn't mean to start a fight. I just felt bad about last night.'

'That's OK,' Patti-Ann replied, her voice muffled by the pastry into which she had bitten.

'So what would you like to do today?' he asked, making his tone cheery. 'Is there anything in particular you'd like to see before I have to head over to Schmidt Hennessey's to work?'

Patti-Ann made a face. 'Do you really have to go over there today?'

He reached across the table and squeezed her hand. 'I'm sorry, sweetie, but we have a Skype planned with Professor Bohmann. We have to update him on all our progress, and I'm really excited to hear him chatting with Schmidt Hennessey.'

'Fine,' said Patti-Ann, 'but first there's this jewellery auction I really want to go to.'

This caught Axel off guard. 'What?' he asked.

'A jewellery auction,' Patti-Ann repeated cheerily, 'right here in the hotel! Doesn't that sound fun?'

Axel bit his tongue. 'Honey, are you sure that's the sort of thing people like us can go to? I mean, we won't be able to afford anything.'

'Don't be silly,' said Patti-Ann. 'We're guests at the hotel. We can go to any event we want. Besides, I've been to jewellery auctions in the States before, they're really fun and rowdy, and you get to look at lots of beautiful jewels. Who knows, you might even find something you'd like to pick out for me.' She winked.

His heart sinking, Axel agreed. After all, he was abandoning his fiancée to go work with Safiya. Didn't he owe Patti-Ann a nice treat, after she'd come all this way? Maybe they'd have something he could afford, a little bracelet or something.

★ ★ ★ ★

The second they stepped into the hall in which the jewellery auction was being hosted, Axel deeply regretted agreeing to the venture. The atmosphere was deadly serious, hushed voices echoing from the high vaulted ceiling and off the mirrored tiles. Almost everyone was dressed in sober navy, black or grey suits. He tried not to glance over at Patti-Ann, who had gone for a glamorous but youthful look with a sequin vest top over jeans and her crocodile skin heels. She looked, he knew, like new money. *She isn't even new money*, he panicked internally; *she works in a clothing shop!* Catching her eye at last, however, he realised Patti-Ann shared none of his embarrassment: she looked thrilled and excited. 'Look at the jewels!' she whispered in his ear, clutching his hand and leading him to the display cases that lined the side of the room.

A tall man in a Sikh turban leaned towards them. 'These are the prize pieces,' he said smoothly, smiling at the newcomers and spreading his copper-coloured hands. 'As you know, we don't usually have our best pieces out for show except on the table during the auction, but today, given the setting and the international turnout, we are using the Royal Palace Hotel as our showroom.' The Sikh man gestured at a dull blue rock the size of an orange. 'This sapphire here is uncut. It is the largest precious stone currently at auction.'

'What's the starting price?' Patti-Ann asked, sounding quite confident, as if she were the sort of woman who regularly bid on million-dollar gems.

'Three million,' he informed her, without condescension. After all, Axel told himself, the daughters of Texan oil magnates no doubt often came to such events, keen to flash their family cash.

'And who would I be up against?' Patti-Ann asked, clearly warming to her role as pretend heiress.

The Sikh man looked thoughtful. 'Let's see, there are a few Arab princes, a cluster of Japanese businessmen, and several members of an ultra-high-net-worth Malaysian family. Competition will be high. I should warn you that quite a few collectors from around the world have turned up today as well, though many of them are more interested in that set of diamonds over there.' He gestured to another cabinet, where five glistening jewels stood in velvet, cut into star shapes. 'They were all cut from the same rough stone, you see, a piece from a mine in Andhra Pradesh, not far from my home town.'

'Where's that?' Patti-Ann asked, frowning slightly.

'In the north of India,' the man said, bowing. 'The mine is on the bank of the river Krishna, very close to my family home.'

The man, Axel realised with a start, had clearly warmed to Patti-Ann.

'Cool!' said Patti-Ann. 'Are you going to bid on the diamonds?'

He burst out laughing. 'Oh no,' he said. 'I just work here.'

Patti-Ann laughed too, as if they'd shared a very funny joke. 'So you can give us insider info! What's the average price of one of these pieces?'

'Good question. I'd say most of the jewels here are between 50,000 and a million.'

'Dollars?' Axel managed to ask. They were the first words he'd spoken since they'd arrived.

The Sikh man and Patti-Ann both laughed. 'Of course,' the auctioneer replied. 'About a dozen of these pieces are worth more than two million, and the diamond set is worth seven million. Or at least, that's the reserve price: who knows how high it could soar once the bidding begins.' He glanced up towards the podium. 'Speaking of which, you two should take your seats. I think the auction is about to start.'

Axel wanted to slink to a corner in the back of the room, but Patti-Ann dragged him towards the front, and so they found themselves more or less in the middle, with an excellent view of the auctioneers at their table, their assistant standing in her slinky black dress, and the screen onto which gigantic photographs of the glittering pieces were being projected.

'Welcome, ladies and gentlemen,' the head auctioneer began. 'Our first piece today comes from the private collection of Luna della Zabello, an Italian countess from Sicily: it is a gold ring set with three Indian diamonds. Bidding will start at 30,000. Yes, the gentleman in the corner, 35,000. The gentleman in the front, forty.'

The first lot of jewels was followed by a diamond 'river' necklace that once belonged to a Hollywood movie star: 'The lady in the blue coat, 100,000.' Then came yellow diamonds, and pink diamonds, and necklaces encrusted with opals. After the first five or six, they all began to blur together in Axel's mind, but Patti-Ann's eyes were as bright as the jewels themselves. Suddenly, he heard her gasp, and throw her hand up in excitement. 'And now,' the auctioneer was saying, 'a truly exceptional *parure*, from the hands of a late twentieth-century Russian collector.' The jewellery, he had to admit, was spectacular: a silver necklace composed of five heart-shaped rubies, surrounded by tiny sparkling diamonds. But surely she hadn't meant to bid?

'The lady in the sequin shirt,' the auctioneer said, checked with his assistant, and nodded. 'Sold for 10,000 dollars.' He brought his hammer down.

Patti-Ann's jaw dropped open. 'I won?' she whispered.

'You meant to do that?' Axel whispered back, horrified. 'Do you even have 10,000 dollars?'

'I'll call my father!' she whispered back. 'I'll wear it for the wedding!'

It dawned on Axel that Patti-Ann was pleased with this turn of events. He felt his stomach twist. But there was no time to argue further, for a woman with a clipboard had arrived at their row of seats, and was motioning them over to ask for their information. They followed her to the back of the room, and Patti-Ann gave her address and phone number. In the background, the orange-sized rough sapphire appeared, and was sold for eight million. By the time Axel tuned back into the conversation Patti-Ann and the clerk with the clipboard were having, she was talking about a thirty per cent auctioneer commission plus VAT.

'That's just fine,' Patti-Ann was saying, having slipped apparently effortlessly into her role of pretend heiress.

Axel, losing patience with this charade, grabbed her by the arm. 'We're leaving,' he hissed. Patti-Ann shook him off with an aggrieved look.'I still need to pick up my necklace,' she hissed back at him, then turned back to the clerk, who smiled sympathetically. 'Unfortunately, madame, you won't be able to collect your purchase until the price is paid in full.'

Patti-Ann's face crumpled. 'But I live in America?' she pleaded.

'Oh, we ship internationally,' the clerk said kindly. 'Don't worry: your jewellery will arrive two to three weeks after we've received your payment.'

Patti-Ann smiled wanly. 'OK,' she said. 'Thank you!' This time, she let Axel drag her away from the auction. Behind them, the price of the five star-shaped diamonds had risen to twelve million.

* * * *

'That was so embarrassing!' Patti-Ann hissed as soon as they arrived back in the lobby, shaking off Axel's arm.

'What, your performance in there? I sure think so.' Axel was livid.

'Oh, because my fiancé dragging me around like a puppy, that's really grown-up and European.'

'We didn't belong in there!'

'I was doing just fine! I bid on a necklace, and I got it!'

'You didn't have to go through with it! You could have explained that you made a mistake!'

'A mistake?' Patti-Ann asked, sounding genuinely shocked.

'Did you even mean to bid?' Axel asked, confused.

'No! I just got overexcited.' She paused. 'But I'm real glad I did.'

'What are you going to tell your dad?'

Patti-Ann shrugged. 'I'll tell him what happened, that it was an accident. A happy accident. It's only 10,000.'

'Only 10,000? Sweetie, how much do you make in a year?'

Patti-Ann glared. 'Can we not have this conversation in the lobby of the Royal Palace Hotel, please?'

'Fine.' Axel began marching towards the elevator, not caring who overheard their fight. 'Let's go to our ridiculous 700-dollar suite, then. Because that suits us much more.'

Patti-Ann caught up with him at the elevator and stared at him, her mouth trembling slightly. 'You're not happy I came.'

Axel cursed himself inwardly. 'Of course I'm happy,' he said, but it was too late. Patti-Ann was crying, right there in the lobby, the tears splashing down on her ridiculous sequin top.

'I spent so much money on my flight, and this room; I tried to make everything perfect for you, and you just want to be back with your professor friends in his stupid house.'

'That's not true, honey,' he said, gently shepherding her into the golden mirrored elevator. 'You know I'm happy you came.'

A little sob escaped her. 'I had to get a passport made!'

'I know you did, sweetie. Please don't think I'm not happy you're here. I couldn't be happier. I was just upset about the auction. That's... a lot of money.'

Patti-Ann wiped her eyes as the elevator dinged their arrival on the fifth floor. 'What do you care?' she said. 'It's my Dad's money.'

'It's still money,' he tried to reason with her. 'Listen, I know it's very beautiful, but can't you just go down there and say you made a mistake? Surely they'll understand. They can't make you buy something if you can't afford it.'

'You want me to give my necklace back?' Patti-Ann sounded genuinely horrified, then she began to cry again. 'I just wanted something beautiful to wear for our wedding.' She pulled a tissue from her jeans pocket and blew her nose noisily. 'You weren't such a spoilsport when we were together at home,' she added bitterly, before dissolving into tears again.

They entered the hotel room, and Axel pulled her close. 'I'm so sorry, sweetie. I know you were excited about the auction, and the necklace. I didn't mean... I don't mean to do everything wrong.'

'I want to go home,' Patti-Ann murmured into his shoulder, sniffling. 'Let's just go home.'

Axel hesitated. Maybe she was right: they'd been happy together before. Why would this trip spoil everything? But Safiya and Schmidt Hennessey, they were waiting for him at the chalet... and his ticket back to Texas was for the following week. 'I promised the others I would work with them,' he said hesitantly, and felt Patti-Ann stiffen in his arms.

'Promised?' she asked, her voice trembling.

It wasn't worth it, he suddenly realised. If he left his fiancée now, and went to Safiya, the growing distance between them would turn into a rift. He needed to make things right. It was time to make a choice. 'But that doesn't matter,' he said at last. 'The others can talk to Bohmann without me.'

Patti-Ann flung her arms around him and held him tight. 'I'll call the travel agency,' she said, her voice still muffled by his shoulder.

'I just need…' Axel hesitated, then said: 'Just let me stop by the chalet to say goodbye.'

★ ★ ★ ★

With the taxi motor idling in the background, Axel found himself standing in the gravel driveway of Schmidt Hennessey's chalet less than an hour later, a light snowfall descending from the grey-blue sky. It seemed like a million years before that they had arrived there, he and Safiya. Since then, the euphoria of their trip together had faded away into nothing but a memory. He rang the doorbell.

Helmut Schmidt Hennessey opened the door, grinning. 'Axel! You should have called, I'd have come pick you up! Come in, come in, Safiya and I have so much to share with you.'

Axel hesitated. 'Actually, Professor, I'm afraid I have to go. I won't be able to work with you this afternoon.'

Schmidt Hennessey's eyes travelled to the taxi, and to the figure in the backseat, typing on her phone. 'Trouble in paradise?' he said, a little sadly.

Not trusting himself to speak, Axel simply nodded. Then, to his surprise, Schmidt Hennessey pulled him close into a bear hug. 'Well, I am very sad to see you go, but I can't tell you what a pleasure it's been having you here. Your research with Safiya, it is simply fascinating.'

'You two can Skype Bohmann together,' Axel said sadly, letting himself lean into the hug for a moment before pulling back.

'Of course.' Schmidt Hennessey nodded. 'And I can call you when you're back in Texas to fill you in on everything. I'll email you a summary of our discussions'

There was a silence. 'Is… Safiya there?' The rumbling taxi motor kept on spinning, like a ticking clock.

Something kind and sad travelled across Schmidt Hennessey's face. 'I'm sorry, Axel, but she's gone out for a walk. I'm sure she'll be back soon – why don't you and your girlfriend come inside for a coffee?'

But both men knew that wasn't possible. 'Tell her I said goodbye,' Axel said, not daring to meet Schmidt Hennessey's eyes. 'Tell her I'm sorry.' His heart was racing.

Schmidt Hennessey laid both his hands on Axel's shoulders, so that Axel had to look up into his fierce blue eyes. 'I will,' he said. 'I will.'

CHAPTER SEVENTEEN

Blazing sunlight was raining down on the day of Axel's birthday party, but there was a sinking feeling in his stomach as he stood at the back door of Patti-Ann's childhood home looking out at the preparations. Across the sprawling backyard lawn, his fiancée was bustling around joyfully, shepherding the last caterers and florists away. He felt a heavy hand fall on his shoulder. 'Excited?' a booming voice asked, and Axel turned reluctantly to face the crimson bulk of Rudy Boswell, Patti-Ann's father.

'Yes, sir,' he said stiffly.

Rudy laughed. 'This isn't an interrogation, son. Don't worry, I wouldn't be too excited 'bout one of these big fancy affairs myself. Who on this dang earth needs lace tablecloths for a birthday? But you've got to let the women have their fun, eh?' He gave an exaggerated wink, and Axel did his best to grin in response.

For a man of such intimidating stature, it was hard to take Rudy seriously: his cowboy swagger was too affected, his *nouveau-riche* trappings too tacky, his moustache too enormous, like a bristling animal that had accidentally landed on his face. Rudy was currently wearing a chequered yellow shirt and black jeans, a wide belt with a big silver buckle, and a black leather bolo tie decorated with a huge chunk of gold-flecked turquoise. He was also wearing gold rings, a gold star lapel pin, and a thick gold chain. Subtlety, Axel thought to himself, was not Rudy Boswell's forte.

'How are things out West?' he asked his future father-in-law politely.

Rudy made a hawking noise in the back of his throat, as if he wanted to spit, then seemingly remembered he was indoors. 'Business is incredible,' he said. 'I haven't had to work a day in months. Just sit at my desk counting the cash as it rolls in. Cattle are magic, you know: they just breed and breed and breed! I just tell my guys to put the best ones together and... boom!' The expression on his face was quite unpleasant.

'How much do the cattle sell for nowadays?' Axel asked, in a desperate bid to act interested.

'My heifers are about two grand, calves a little less,' Rudy said – his tone bombastic, although his eyes narrowed suspiciously. 'And they're worth every penny! When you factor in the cost of yardage, pasture and feeding the damn beasts, it's a fair price.' He paused. 'My boys, my team, they work really hard,' he added, a little defensively.

Axel nodded. It occurred to him that perhaps Rudy was just as ill at ease in his presence as he was in his future father-in-law's. 'I'm sure you all do,' he said as warmly as he could.

'I miss my girl, though,' Rudy said suddenly. 'It's always nice to be back here in Lake Salvation. Brings back a lotta memories.'

Axel nodded again, unsure what he could say. Rudy and Joycie-Lou Boswell had been divorced since Patti-Ann was a little girl. Her father was a nebulous presence, a generous absence, raining down gifts from his ranch complex in East Texas.

'Well, I guess you should go freshen up, huh?' Rudy said, his voice loud again, as if wanting to erase his confession.

'Yes, sir,' Axel said again, without meaning to, but Rudy only laughed.

'You try to enjoy your own birthday, son,' he added ruefully.

★ ★ ★ ★

The sun was even more violent outdoors. How bizarre it felt; thirty degrees in November. Had it really only taken him a few weeks to adjust to European temperatures? The idea was absurd – it was an uncharacteristically warm winter, even for Texas – and yet American weather felt like an assault on his body. Texas as a whole, in fact: the sunshine, the howdys and plastic smiles, the terrible diner food. Patti-Ann came sauntering across the grass towards Axel, interrupting his miserable train of thought. She was wearing a very short turquoise satin dress, and the necklace from Saint Moritz. The gaudiness of it took his breath away: it was beautiful, yes, glittering with silver and diamonds and rubies in an almost dangerous way.

'Are you sure you want to wear that today?' he couldn't help asking, regretting it at once as Patti-Ann's smile sunk away.

'Don't you like it?' she asked, crestfallen. 'I thought your birthday was a nice occasion.'

'Of course I like it,' he lied. 'It's just that I thought you were saving it for the wedding!'

'It's maybe a bit colourful for a wedding, don't you think?' she asked, cheering up a bit.

'You look beautiful, honey,' Axel added, then he leaned forward and kissed her cheek. Patti-Ann giggled, then reached up and pulled him in for a real kiss. The warmth of it felt suddenly suffocating; he pulled away.

'Shall we get some drinks?' he asked, taking her hand and pulling her towards the picnic tables before she could register the abrupt ending to their embrace.

'I made punch!' Patti-Ann said happily. 'See, my mom and I made one of those old-fashioned ice bowls?'

Axel did indeed see: she had purchased a carved-out block of ice and filled it with bright apricot-coloured drink and cut fruit. A silver ladle was sticking out of it, and there were little paper cups and umbrellas to serve it with.

The punch was sickly sweet, but the hit of alcohol helped soothe his nerves, and he gulped down half a glass. Patti-Ann beamed. 'It's really good, right?'

'It sure is, honey.' He finished the cup and set it down, a little unsteadily, on the side of the table. Something quite like panic was rising in his chest, and he wondered whether he was going to faint. 'I think I saw my mom's car,' he lied. 'Let me just go check.' He walked as calmly as he could to the path that cut between the neighbours' house and the Boswells', but instead of following it to the front of the house and the driveway, he took a smaller trail that doubled back to the little hill behind. Turning back, he saw that Patti-Ann hadn't noticed his defection, and he let out a sigh of relief. There, beneath the trees, he crouched in the greenery and tried to quiet his breathing, watching the stream of guests arrive from his vantage point.

His birthday, Axel observed from a distance, had begun in earnest: there were Wally and Bob, and Jim and Pete from the fraternity, and Patti-Ann's friends in a brightly-coloured mob, like parakeets: Nancy and Gloria and what was the redhead called, Julie? There was Joycie-Lou Boswell by the cake table, and Rudy lighting up the barbecue, strategically positioned at opposite ends of the lawn. There too, Axel saw with a sinking heart, was Pamela, linked arm-in-arm with a girl who looked like her pale shadow: younger, blonder, her face sprinkled with freckles, her eyes shyly to the ground. Her sister Carol, Axel worked out. The one who'd invited Patti-Ann to the Defenders of Grace meetings. From a distance, she certainly looked nice enough, though he wasn't quite sure why she was at his birthday. Then all thoughts of Carol vanished from his mind, for a group of three young men in smart shirts and ties had appeared: two of them he recognised from Bohmann's lecture, and from the TV news. Defenders of Grace. The third was Bohmann's son.

Jesus Christ, Axel thought. What on earth was Kyle Bohmann doing at his birthday party? He watched him sidle into the crowd, casting his gaze from side to side, then greet Patti-Ann with a hug. Axel's eyes nearly fell out of their sockets. Patti-Ann had some real explaining to do, he thought, a wave of fury rising in his chest. He prepared to march down there self-righteously… then something made him pause. Relations were already tense with his girlfriend – fiancée, he corrected himself automatically. If he started a fight in the middle of this party, the consequences would be incendiary. No: this was neither the time nor the place to confront Patti-Ann about her new friends. He was going to have to grit his teeth, eat his cake, and try to avoid anybody other than his college buddies.

With a sudden wave of relief, Axel saw his mother walking over and waving to Patti-Ann. He scrambled from his hiding spot, brushing the leaves from his clothes and walked quickly back to the party.

'What happened to you?' Patti-Ann asked, squinting a little. The ruby hearts on her necklace glittered.

'Had to pee,' Axel offered vaguely.

Felicia laughed, and he turned to his mother and clasped her in a tight hug. 'Try not to miss your party,' she said heartily. The scent of her perfume, the softness of her bosom, were so comforting that for a moment he thought he might cry.

'I won't.' He pulled away and did his best to smile warmly.

'Isn't your wife-to-be's necklace just out of this world? It's so sweet of you to have invited Patti-Ann along to Saint Moritz!'

'I just love that damn necklace so much,' Pamela gushed, appearing at Patti-Ann's side and saving him from an awkward response. 'It's so… European! So did you guys go skiing? Did you eat fondue?'

'We just visited,' Patti-Ann replied modestly.

'I actually had fondue in Geneva,' Axel added, unable to resist the urge to show off.

'Sweet!' said Pamela.

'Isn't fondue just melted cheese?' Felicia asked.

Biting his tongue, Axel nodded. 'Pretty much.' *With garlic and crémant*, he thought to himself, savouring the foreign word, as if this were a private secret.

'So where did y'all go?' asked a new, small voice. Axel saw Carol hovering shyly at her sister Pamela's elbow. 'I've always wanted to go to Europe,' she added, and when she smiled, he found himself sympathising with Patti-Ann. The young Defender of Grace seemed like a sweetheart.

'Well, I started off in London,' he replied, a little proudly. 'Then I flew over to Switzerland, and visited Geneva, Bern and Saint Moritz.' Packed into a single sentence, it sounded like a short trip: he had to focus hard to stop the flood of memories from overtaking him.

'And you travelled that whole way on your own?' Carol was looking up at him, glamour-stricken, her eyes wide as saucers.

'Well actually,' Axel found himself unable to withhold, 'I travelled some of the way with a professor I met on the road.' He was very conscious of Patti-Ann's eyes on him, and of Carol's. What would his new conservative Christian fan think if she knew how tempted he had been to stray from the path of commitment to his fiancée?

'She was a real interesting gal,' Patti-Ann added loyally, and Axel's heart went out to her. 'Very smart.'

'Well if you ever feel like travelling with another *smart* woman back to Saint Moritz,' Pamela said coarsely, 'you better take me!' She winked. 'Especially if you stop by those auctions again.'

Axel's stomach was churning, but he did his best to take the comment lightly. 'Not every woman is worthy of a piece of jewellery like this!' Then he felt awful: it sounded as if *he* had bought the necklace for Patti-Ann. But Patti-Ann was beaming, reaching up to the strands of diamonds to caress them lightly with her fingertips.

'It's just so beautiful,' said Carol reverently. 'Can I touch it?'

'Of course!' said Patti-Ann, unclasping the precious piece.

Carol giggled as the rubies and diamonds ran through her fingers. 'I know the Lord has stern views on vanity,' she said, 'but surely He can't have any trouble with something as perfectly beautiful as this?'

She and Patti-Ann laughed gently, conspiratorially, and although it was an innocent moment, something chilled Axel's blood. Or perhaps it was the fact that he glimpsed Kyle in the background, hovering by the cake. A protective instinct towards his whole birthday party set in.

'Sweetheart,' he said to Patti-Ann, 'do you think it might be time to cut the cake?'

She laughed, putting her necklace back on. 'You haven't even tried the barbecue! There's pulled chicken and Sloppy Joes as well.'

'Oh! Well I will now.' Taking his fiancée's hand, he marched confidently towards the picnic tables laden with food. He should have known Patti-Ann wouldn't just stick to cake: there were platters of grilled beef sausages and corn on the cob, piles of buns, bowls of several kinds of coleslaw, including Axel's favourite with pineapple. Sneaking a glance over towards the cake table, he saw that Kyle had vanished into the crowd. *Good*, he thought, scooping up a healthy spoonful of slaw.

'There you are!' boomed Rudy, appearing with a fresh trayful of grilled goods. He was now wearing a ten-gallon hat and an apron streaked with burnt grease. 'Enjoying yourself?'

'Yes, sir,' said Axel. 'These sausages are great.'

'Daddy!' Patti-Ann squealed, running into his arms, narrowly missing the tray he was setting down.

'Oof!' said Rudy, as his daughter collided with him. 'Whoa now,' he added, obviously pleased.

'I'm so glad you came,' she said, her face shining in an echo of her ruby necklace.

'Well of course I came! And I'm glad you're wearing them jewels,' he replied.

When they were both smiling like this, Axel observed, it was disconcerting how alike they looked. Rudy plopped down into a lawn chair, and Patti-Ann sat down on his lap. Axel was used to these odd displays of affection but wondered if everyone at the party felt the same – something about the divorce guilt had led Rudy to treat his daughter like a child well into her twenties, and Patti-Ann to relish the attention. Looking around, he saw that everyone was milling around in small groups, sipping from their cups and eating platefuls of barbecued food. Nobody seemed to be paying them – or him – any attention. He noticed a pang in his stomach, though he couldn't have said of what.

'Did you know I had to pay thirty percent fees to that auction place of yours??' Rudy was saying. He shook his head in mock disapproval. 'And VAT!'

'Fat? Chicken fat?' asked Patti-Ann, playing dumb.

Rudy laughed. '*Diamond* chicken fat for sure,' he said. 'The way they tax you over there in Europe, it may as well be blood.'

'And are you still driving that ridiculous car?' Patti-Ann asked affectionately.

Rudy owned an enormous red Cadillac with two horns attached to the front grille, a Fleetwood which he nicknamed 'The Bull.' It was a vehicle equally impressive and ridiculous.

'I sure am,' said Rudy. 'Thinking of getting a second car for the long-distance hauls, though. The Bull don't like the Midwest. Gets cold up there.'

'Business is booming, huh,' said Patti-Ann, sounding pleased.

'It sure is, darlin'.' Rudy planted a loud kiss on her cheek. 'We got these new Mexican labourers in, they work for peanuts. Gives me a much cheaper unit cost. Some people are selling their cows to Brazil now, to make leather. I guess I gotta think about that too. I mean, if you can't ride it, breed it, or eat it, I guess you wear it!' They laughed.

Patti-Ann reached up and stroked his moustache. 'I don't know how I'll ever thank you for the necklace, Daddy,' she said suddenly, and Rudy looked embarrassed.

'Anything for my honeypie,' he said. 'Anything at all. Ten thousand, who cares?' His voice had risen several notches in volume, and his eyes looked a little damp. 'So is it time for that birthday cake yet, or what?'

'You boys just can't wait, can you?' said Patti-Ann, but she sounded pleased. 'Come on, then!' She walked over to the cake table, then stood up on one of the lawn chairs and raised her voice. 'Everybody! It's time for the cake!'

Axel immediately regretted his keenness on this part of the birthday ceremony, for now the crowds were gathering and moving towards him. If any part of him had been feeling slightly peeved at not being the centre of attention, it was panicking at the prospect now. Luckily, Patti-Ann clearly intended to run the show.

'This is Axel's favourite kind of cake,' she announced: 'pineapple upside-down cake. It has three layers and a cream cheese frosting made with pineapple juice.' She bowed modestly as a scattering of applause greeted this announcement. The cake, Axel had to admit, was impressive: a towering, sculpted masterpiece, covered top to bottom in fluffy white icing and decorated with candied pecans. 'Those of you who know anything about my culinary achievements will know I didn't make this cake – I ordered it from the Bee Hummingbird Bakery in town. Thanks to the bakers over there, then, who made me look good for the first part of the party.' She grinned, and the crowd laughed with her. 'I want to thank my dad, too, for taking care of the barbecue.'

'If anybody knows about dead animals, it's me!' Rudy boomed.

Patti-Ann tittered. 'I'd like to thank my new friends in particular for making the effort to come celebrate my fiancé's birthday with me. It means a lot to me.' Axel stared. Was Patti-Ann really thanking the Defenders of Grace for crashing his birthday party? But of course they weren't crashing: she'd invited them. He swallowed the now-familiar wave of anger rising in his throat. 'Above all, though, I'd like to thank Axel Parker – my Axel, my sweetheart, and soon to be my husband – for letting me share his life all these years. I can't wait to share the rest of our lives too.' She met his eyes, and his anger melted away. 'To Axel Parker, the love of my life… and the birthday boy!'

'The birthday boy!' the crowd echoed, raising their glasses of punch and cheering. The sun blazed down, and Axel kissed Patti-Ann in front of all these people, then took a swig of his warm punch. Patti-Ann bustled away to cut the cake, and the crowd reorganised like a swarm of bees, with him no longer at the centre.

'So when are you going to make her an honest woman, huh?' Rudy asked, his hand crashing down on his shoulder. Axel opened his mouth to answer, hoping something cheery would come to him spontaneously, but his girlfriend's father was only joking. He pulled him into a smoky-smelling bear hug and pounded on his back. 'Now you're a man… and she's a woman. I remember when you were just a little kid,' he said, sounding emotional. 'When you were both just little kids, running around in our backyards. Back when everything was

easy. Back when times were good. Back when me and Joycie-Lou...'
Was he... drunk? As if on cue, Rudy pulled a half-empty glass bottle
of bourbon from the vast pocket of his barbecue apron. 'Want a swig?'

Axel hesitated. 'Sure,' he said, tipping the bottle up and filling his
mouth with sour, warm liquid. He did his best not to grimace, but
Rudy wasn't looking anyway. He was looking for lawn chairs, and
pulled two up. Axel sunk into the second one.

'She doesn't even call these days,' he was saying, gazing across
the lawn to where his ex-wife was talking with some of Patti-Ann's
friends. 'I don't even know if she's got somebody in her life. Does
she?' He looked up at Axel, his eyes watering, but didn't seem to
expect a reply. 'I know I wasn't always good to her. I know I liked my
bit on the side. Lot on the side.' He gave a sloppy grin. 'But I never
meant... Hell!' He took another swig from the bottle and wiped his
mouth on his sleeve. 'What you doing here, kid?' he snarled. Axel
looked up and, to his surprise, found Kyle hovering on the edge of
their little group.

'I thought I saw a bottle going round,' he said, squatting down in the
grass like an animal. His voice was surprisingly thin and reedy: Axel
realised he'd never heard it apart from that day in the town hall when
Bohmann had given his lecture. The memory sent a lightning stroke of
fury through him, but before he could give Kyle a piece of his mind,
Rudy had handed him the bottle. Axel was surprised to see Kyle grab
the bourbon bottle and take a long drink from the neck. He'd assumed
the boy had been coming over to lecture them about drinking.

'Thought you holy rollers couldn't take your liquor,' Rudy said,
sounding impressed.

'What,' Kyle drawled, 'you think a Christian kid can't sin? I'm off-
duty.' He gave an unpleasant laugh.

Axel clenched the lawn chair's armrests until he couldn't feel his
fingers. His fury had reached such a pitch that he could hear a whistling
sound in his ears. 'Off-duty?' he repeated in a low voice. 'Sure you're
off-duty. Off-duty caring for your dad. Off-duty studying, or doing

anything at all worthwhile with your life.' He was surprised at the viciousness of his tone. Axel Parker had never knowingly picked a fight with anyone in his life.

Kyle raised an eyebrow and leaned in, accepting the challenge. 'Oh, cause you know my dad so well,' he sneered. In this light, he looked far older than nineteen. 'You spend a few minutes every Sunday talking to him about his stupid, blasphemous book...'

'That "stupid book" is your father's life's work. A masterpiece.'

'A life's waste, yeah.'

'It's fascinating. Revelatory. It's the sort of work that wins Nobel prizes.' This was over-egging the pudding a little, Axel knew, but he was angry.

Kyle didn't let it slip, though. He stood up slowly, menacingly, resting his hands on his knees. 'Oh, this book you're helping him write is going to win a *Nobel prize*?' He imitated Axel's emphasis.

But Axel wasn't so easily cowed. 'Don't you dare talk that way about something you can't possibly understand. Do you always break the toys you can't play with? You're just a child.' He took a breath. 'Yeah, I know about the hacking. I know what you did, Kyle. Don't you know you damn near killed him?'

Kyle made a disbelieving noise in his throat. 'What, because he got fired? He had that coming for years. Everybody in town hates his guts.'

'He had a heart attack! Because you deleted his files! Don't you understand? Don't you have any sense of responsibility? You come in here all high and mighty, pretending to do the Lord's work...'

'Hey,' said Rudy, sensing this conversation spiralling out of control. 'Kids. This is a party. Your party.'

But Axel couldn't be stopped. All his frustration with what had happened that year, all his anger at the Defenders of Grace, at the close-minded town of Lake Salvation, at that stupid Chancellor Langdon, was bubbling out of him. 'All of you, you goddamn God-botherers, you fucking idiots, you think science is the enemy, you think you know better than every university professor, you think you can just shout over us on TV and delete our files…' His words were getting mixed up, what was he trying to say? Kyle just stared, at him calmly, blankly, until he ground to a halt. Then Bohmann's son delivered his final blow:

'My dad's the stupidest man I ever met.' His lip curled in a sneer, and his voice took on a truly teenage intonation: 'I wish he were dead.'

Axel's fist had hit Kyle Bohmann's mouth before he'd even realised it had left his pocket. The boy crumpled to the ground, then scrambled to a sitting position, his eyes burning. Rudy stood up unsteadily and grabbed Kyle by the shoulders, but the kid was stronger than him, and Rudy had been drinking. In a second, Kyle had knocked Axel over and had him in a chokehold, his knees pressing into his stomach. Axel's arms were flailing wildly, his heart racing, and even in his anger, even as Kyle's fingers tightened around his throat, he was hissing just four words: 'You – don't – deserve – him!'

Suddenly, Kyle's hold released, and Axel was looking up at the night sky. The stars were blurred and uneven. He felt like throwing up. 'Your dad loves you so much,' he whispered to no-one in particular.

In the distance, he could hear Patti-Ann squealing, or screaming, and for an irrational moment he thought *I hope she doesn't find me*. Then his mother's face was above him, whispering 'Oh sweetie, oh sweetie,' and her arms were gathering him up, and at last, at long last, his birthday party was over.

CHAPTER EIGHTEEN

'Some birthday, huh.'

Axel rolled over woozily, his head thumping, to find Patti-Ann staring down at him, her face brimming with love and concern. The first emotion to pass through him was disappointment, in a sharp wave – where was his mother? – and the second was even more painful for its unexpectedness: he missed Safiya. He missed her voice, her intelligence, the warmth of her smile and her dark eyes. He missed every single thing about being in her company, so suddenly and so desperately that it made him want to curl up in a ball and cry.

Axel did his best to smile at his fiancée. His heart hurt. His throat hurt. His ribcage hurt. A vision of Kyle's enraged face flashed into his mind, and he winced. Patti-Ann leaned in and kissed him softly on the lips, then drew his hands to her breasts. Axel pushed her away very, very gently.

'Do you… Do you think you could get me a glass of water, honey? I just woke up… and my head really hurts.'

This was not a lie. Patti-Ann smiled and climbed out of bed, beautiful in her nakedness. Axel closed his eyes, feeling the throbbing of his heartbeat through his various bruises. He heard the swish of material as she pulled on her dressing gown, and the creak of the door. Murmurs came from downstairs, the thud of footsteps – some of the guests had slept over, he realised. He listened to Patti-Ann and Joycie-Lou cheerfully bidding some of them goodbye, to the sound of the front door closing, then to her returning footsteps. He closed his eyes and pretended to have fallen back asleep.

Patti-Ann was giggling to herself. 'Honestly, some people. Your pal Wally slept in his car! I guess he got in there and worked out he was too drunk to drive home… And you'll never guess who Pamela left with.' She stopped, as if embarrassed. Axel opened an eye, unwillingly.

'Who?'

'Well it's still funny, even given the circumstances, I mean...' Patti-Ann looked genuinely embarrassed.

'Well, who was it?'

'Kyle,' she whispered.

Axel stared at her as if he'd never seen her in his life. 'Kyle,' he repeated slowly.

Patti-Ann couldn't help but dissolve into laughter again. 'I mean, after we carried you to bed, your mom and I, I guess somebody had to look after him. You beat him up pretty good, you know.' Did she sound proud? 'I mean, I don't approve of fighting, but that smug kid had it coming.' Yes, she was proud. Axel felt his stomach twist with conflicting emotions. A part of him felt proud, too, but mostly he felt sick.

'I thought the Defenders of Grace were your pals now,' he couldn't help saying.

Patti-Ann looked crestfallen. 'Hey, you picked a fight with him,' she pointed out. 'Or at least, that's how my dad told it.'

Axel had to admit that this was true. 'He had a hell of a lot of nerve, turning up at my birthday party. I can't believe you invited any of those awful people, Patti-Ann.'

'What, awful people like Carol? You seemed pretty charmed by her when she wanted to hear all about your glamorous trip to Europe, batting her eyelashes at you...'

Axel stared at his girlfriend incredulously. 'You're jealous of that little nutjob?' he asked. His anger from the previous night was still there, he realised, coalescing around Carol, and colouring Patti-Ann. 'Well, it's your own damn fault for inviting her.' He crossed his arms, feeling ridiculous as he did so.

'I organised the whole party, all the food, the drinks, everything!' Patti-Ann burst out. 'If I couldn't invite a few of my new friends... That's just ridiculous. You can sort out your own damn birthday party next year.'

'Good,' Axel shot back, no longer caring if he was hurting her feelings. 'I don't even *like* pineapple upside-down cake! It hasn't been my favourite for *fifteen years!*' With this parting shot, he sprang up out of bed, but his injuries cried out, and he had to sit back down again, which rather deflated the effect. With a groan, he sunk his aching head into his hand.

'You love pineapple upside-down cake,' Patti-Ann said mournfully, sitting down beside him.

Axel was silent. 'I really wish you hadn't invited those people, Patti-Ann. And I really need you to think hard about whether you want to be friends with them. I'm working with their sworn enemy. When the book comes out...'

'Axel, there were just three people who happen to go to that church. Three people, and Carol. OK, maybe I shouldn't have invited Kyle, but he just seems so lonely and miserable all the time! I won't invite him again, I promise.'

Axel let out a bitter laugh. 'I don't think he'd come.'

Patti-Ann leaned in sympathetically and traced the red marks on Axel's neck. 'Does it hurt very badly?' she murmured.

'It does.' Axel felt himself putting on a noble expression, as his anger drained away. 'It was quite a tussle.'

She kissed his neck very softly. 'Does that feel better?'

'Yes,' he said pathetically.

Patti-Ann stroked his arm, then gave his shoulder a wet kiss. 'How about that?'

'Yes,' he said more quietly, peeking inside her robe.

She laid a hand on his chest, and then lowered her head and kissed him there. 'And that?'

'Yes,' he said, pulling her down onto the bed.

★ ★ ★ ★

Even with his eyes closed, Axel couldn't keep Safiya from his mind. It was Patti-Ann's mouth kissing his mouth, Patti-Ann caressing his skin, Patti-Ann lying heavily on top of him, and yet... 'Ouch,' he said, breaking away. 'Sorry,' said Patti-Ann, rolling off him and looking disgruntled. 'Bruised,' he muttered, deciding that the best course of action would be to initiate again. *Focus.* He wrapped his hands around Patti-Ann's lower back and pulled her to him. She arced into him, smiling sweetly, drowsily. Lying on their sides, the atmosphere was a little less stifling, and still it was Safiya whose soft hands he imagined touching him, Safiya whose voice he wanted to cry out as he entered her. His eyes flew open, and he tried to focus on Patti-Ann: so pink, so soft, so familiar, her scent like peaches and cotton candy. Meanwhile, another part of his mind desperately tried to remember Safiya's musky sandalwood perfume, her freckled tan shoulders, her breasts in a silk blouse, but the effort distracted him. Patti-Ann looked over at him sadly as he slumped. 'Are you OK, honey?'

He rolled back onto his back and stared at the ceiling. 'I guess I had one too many bourbons with your dad,' he lied.

'Maybe I can help!' Patti-Ann said cheerfully, scooting down the bed on her knees.

Axel scrambled up into a sitting position. 'Thanks, honey,' he said hurriedly, 'but my head just hurts so much…' Safiya's image appeared for one perfect, burning second in his mind, and Axel couldn't stand this any longer. He flung himself out of bed, wincing as his feet hit the floor. 'I'm just gonna go for a walk, honey,' he babbled a little wildly, picking up his clothes from the floor. 'Get some fresh air.' Why was it so hard to get his legs into his trousers? Backwards, that was why.

He could feel Patti-Ann staring at him from the bed. 'Don't you at least want a clean shirt?' she said feebly.

'I'll be back soon,' he said, leaning in and giving her a peck on the cheek like a distant relative. Before her hurt expression could register he was already through the door, down the stairs, out into the backyard where Joycie-Lou was cleaning up paper cups… He waved and smiled apologetically, beelining for his car, and drove away from the Boswells' house before his thoughts could catch up with him.

* * * *

His favourite window booth at the Cherry Pie diner offered some respite, with its familiar oilcloth tablecloths and paper placemats. Sipping warm, weak coffee from a mug, he felt his heartbeat begin to slow. Was he losing his mind? No, he was tired, he was hungover, he was maybe a little jet-lagged... He was engaged. He was faithful. He was a good person. The waiter interrupted his attempt at comforting himself by setting down a big plate of waffles, a fat square pat of butter melting on top. 'Could you heat up my maple syrup, please?' he asked mournfully, and the waiter smiled. 'Of course. Would you like some more coffee?' Axel nodded. He stared in silence at his waffles for a while, watching the butter disintegrate and disappear. He was hopelessly in love with Safiya: there was no escaping it.

The waiter returned with a hot silver jug of syrup and a coffeepot, refilled Axel's mug and vanished. Axel pulled his phone out of his pocket, and opened the thread of messages with Safiya. *Dinner with us at the Royal Palace, 6.30?* his last message read; hers: *Of course*. The memory of that awful dinner made him shiver, and he slurped his $1.99 coffee for comfort. *Dear Safiya*, he typed, *I'm so sorry...* He deleted the text. What kind of a way was that to start? *Safiya*, he tried again, *I can't stop thinking about you*. But maybe that was too much: what if she didn't feel the same way? What if all she felt for him was an intellectual connection? Sadly, he cut himself a forkful of waffle. But it hadn't felt that way, not when their eyes met, not since the avalanche. Something had changed, he was sure of it. He cursed himself for being too stupid to see it before now, when it was too late. *I want you*, he typed experimentally, then let out a snort of laughter. He set the phone aside and tucked into his waffles. It was useless: he hadn't flirted with anyone since grade school. Patti-Ann had a Valentine's card from him pinned up on the board above her desk, all pink felt-tip pen and cut-out hearts. He didn't even remember what she'd looked like as a kid. For the first time, it occurred to him that Patti-Ann was still living with her parents because she was waiting to move in with him. And here he was, promising her the wedding of her dreams, pushing the date further and further away... Was he treating Patti-Ann unfairly? What was he going to do? Bohmann would know, he thought suddenly. He would go see Bohmann. He dialled Bohmann's number, dropped ten dollars by the side of his half-eaten plateful of waffles and left the diner decisively, phone pressed to his ear.

★ ★ ★ ★

Stepping out of the air conditioning into the bright sun of Lakeshore Drive was difficult, but Axel had to admit the lake looked gorgeous in this weather: a deep, clear blue with ripples sparkling on the surface. There were a few boats bobbing near the other shore, and a few people windsurfing. In the distance, he could see families spread out across the sand, reading books and picnicking. Bohmann had sounded good on the phone, not as frail as the last time he had spoken to him on Skype: Axel suddenly remembered that Patti-Ann had invited him to the birthday party, but that he'd said he was too unwell to attend. *Thank God*, he thought. What an unpleasant coincidence that would have been!

He rang the doorbell. After a moment, Bohmann opened the door in a silk kimono. 'Good morning, Axel!' he said, smiling.

Axel was suddenly embarrassed. 'I'm sorry,' he said. 'Am I too early?'

'Not at all, my boy! Come in, come in. I was thrilled to get a call from you. I figured I'd let you recover from your party before bothering you with work, but if you're feeling up to it…'

Axel followed him down the hall, wondering whether he should mention his run-in with Kyle. Arriving in the living room, he remembered the dusty photographs on the shelves and decided against it.

'Coffee?' Bohmann asked. 'I've just made a fresh pot.'

'Yes please,' said Axel, settling into an armchair.

He looked around the cozy space, feeling very at home amongst the bare wood, the dusty bookshelves, the reams of National Geographic magazines. A moment later, Bohmann returned with a tray.

'So how have you been, my boy?' he asked, pouring out two cups of coffee.

'You go first,' Axel smiled. 'How are you feeling?'

'Oh, I've been well,' Bohmann replied. 'Resting, reading, pottering around in the garden. I can walk a mile now, and do a few pushups if I really have to, and you must see the flowers!'

'And the Defenders, are they leaving you alone?'

'More or less,' Bohmann replied, frowning. 'Why do you ask?'

'I was just wondering...' Axel said, suddenly embarrassed, 'if you ever run into your son... into Kyle at social events?'

Bohmann looked sad, and Axel wished he hadn't asked. 'Very rarely,' he replied. 'We don't really run in the same circles, and those of our circles that do overlap, well, I tend to avoid.'

'He came to my birthday,' Axel burst out.

Bohmann looked surprised. 'Your birthday?' He blinked. 'You invited him?'

Now Axel really felt bad. 'Oh no, no,' he hastily assured the professor. 'Some crazy idea of Patti-Ann's. She's kind of fallen in with the Defenders of Grace crew, I guess... While I was away.'

'I see,' said Bohmann, quietly. 'Well, I have no right to judge. It seems like some of them are perfectly nice, respectable young Christians. But pack mentality is a dangerous thing...' He shook his head.

'I know. I'm worried about Patti-Ann. I think she sort of just drifted around when I was away.'

'Does she not have a job to do, something to fill her days?'

'She works in a clothing shop in town. I guess her main purpose is... me.' The words tasted bitter in Axel's mouth, and he gave a small, sad laugh.

Bohmann smiled sympathetically. 'And you're not sure how you feel about that.' It wasn't a question.

'I'm committed to Patti-Ann,' Axel said firmly, defensively. 'We're engaged. We're going to get married next year.'

'I thought you were waiting until the end of your PhD?'

'But I haven't even started! I can't keep pushing this away into some uncertain future, keeping her waiting for me...'

Bohmann raised a hand, and Axel fell silent. 'It was just a question,' he said gently.

There was an awkward silence. 'The truth is,' Axel confessed, 'I've been having doubts.'

Bohmann nodded. 'Is there someone else?' he asked.

Axel frowned. 'It's not that. I mean, Patti-Ann and I, we met when we were eight. We're like... one of those arranged marriages, where they check our constellations align when we're babies. Our families spent all this time together, and then of course we started dating, and then...'

'And now you're questioning this sequence of events,' Bohmann finished for him.

'Yes.'

The two men sipped their coffees.

'Surely it happens,' he burst out, 'that you might become infatuated with someone... That it might be only a passing thing, that it might go away?'

Bohmann laughed, a warm sound. 'Oh, Axel. Why don't you just tell me the whole story here?'

Axel looked at the floor. 'The truth of the matter is, Professor,' he said at last, 'I think I'm in love with Safiya.'

Bohmann smiled. 'Safiya! And you want that feeling to go away?'

'No!' Axel burst out. 'Yes. I mean yes. I'm engaged. I owe Patti-Ann... My whole life is here...' His thoughts were a tangle. He rubbed his eyes.

'I'm not asking you about your sense of duty, Axel. I'm asking what you feel in your heart.'

'My heart... My heart feels very stupid.' He lifted his eyes and met Bohmann's to find them brimming over with warmth. He laughed, at last. 'Oh God, Professor, what am I going to do?'

'And this Safiya, does she feel the same way?'

Axel was quiet for a moment. 'I don't know,' he said finally. 'I haven't told her. The last time... I didn't even say goodbye. I don't know if I'll ever see her again.'

Bohmann nodded slowly. 'It seems to me that you're missing quite a key variable here, my boy.'

Axel's face cracked into a grin. 'Always the scientist!' he said, Safiya's voice floating through his mind.

'Well, maybe science might be a helpful way to tackle this problem. I mean, have you tried that old chestnut, the list of pros and cons?'

Axel looked at the floor. 'I feel like it might be too heavily weighted.'

'What do you mean?'

'Cons of being with Safiya: break Patti-Ann's heart and ruin her life,' he said bitterly.

'Pros,' Bohmann shot back, 'true love. Maybe.'

Axel couldn't help smiling. 'True love, maybe. OK, I guess those are both strong.'

'Tell me some more pros and cons.'

'Well, Safiya can be kind of cold. Snobby, even. She's religious, a Sufi – I don't know if I'd ever be able to understand that.' He paused. 'She lives in Istanbul, I've only known her for a few weeks, and I don't know how she feels about me. Her culture, her family, her background and her religion are all totally unknown to me.' He was quiet for a moment. 'But when you hear her talk about the soul, it's like she's baring her heart to you. It's so beautiful. There were times when we were talking and we just fell into this sort of natural... harmony. I've never experienced anything like it. And she's beautiful, so beautiful, in this soft way; her voice, her eyes... Intelligent, too; fiercely so. I don't know what I could possibly do to deserve her.'

'Love has nothing to do with deserving,' Bohmann said sternly. 'Now tell me your arguments for – and against – Patti-Ann.'

Axel took a long drink from his coffee cup. 'Patti-Ann is a perfect girlfriend: devoted, loving, faithful. She'd do anything for me. I've known her since we were children: I know everything about her, and we've always planned to spend the rest of our lives together. I trust her completely.' He felt a pang in his chest. 'How could that not be enough? She's beautiful and sweet and kind; we share a common heritage and education. I'm the luckiest man in the world and I'd throw it all away? For what, for some... exotic creature I've barely spent any time with?'

'Don't be angry with yourself, Axel. Emotions are human. Why don't you tell me some of the cons on Patti-Ann's list?'

'She's boring.' The words were out of Axel's mouth before he could stop them, startling them both. 'So boring. We have nothing to talk about. She's horribly materialistic and concerned about appearances. She's not intellectual – almost anti-intellectual – and unambitious. Her father is this ridiculous redneck, her friends are a terrible influence – and that's before she started hanging out with the Defenders of Grace! Sometimes I feel like we're putting on a nice show but there's nothing real between us anymore. And she wants so much: so much love, so much affection, so much sex...' He blushed. 'She *thinks* I'm the only thing she wants in this life, but what if I'm just fooling her? What if I'm just stringing her along, all these years down the line?'

Bohmann didn't answer his question. 'If I've understood correctly, it's a choice between a person you know by heart and a person you barely know. The known and the unknown.' His eyes were twinkling. 'From what I know about you, Axel, I find it hard to imagine you really wanting to pick the known. The known bores you, as it should any bright and inquisitive mind.'

Axel laughed. 'I've certainly learned a lot about embracing the unknown from researching your book,' he had to admit.

'Tell me more!' Bohmann said excitedly, leaning forward. 'Why don't you give me a kind of report on your trip?'

Axel hesitated. 'Well, Professor Bohmann, I have to admit that I've been nervous about trying to sum up how I did on everything I was supposed to cover. I'm pretty sure I failed you on several accounts on this trip. If I really give you a report, I don't think it'll be worth more than a C minus.'

Bohmann laughed. 'Boy, nobody is grading you. Research is never, ever wasted – it just might take a little time for everything to fall into place! Why don't you tell me what you thought was most interesting?'

'Well, I really liked Helmut Schmidt Hennessey. A wonderful man.'

'Yes, so did I. He sent me a message – in fact, we had a conversation on Skype right after you'd left Saint Moritz. He seemed in excellent spirits. And CERN, that was a success also, right?'

Axel nodded. 'Yes, we met some really helpful folk, Straussfeld and de Grand-Maizelle in particular, and they gave me pretty much unfettered access to the labs. I'll have to come over with the materials some other time – I hadn't really planned this visit properly.'

'That's quite alright.'

'Fabien de Grand-Maizelle took us to see some private libraries in Geneva as well. There were all the ancient manuscripts, and original sketches by Galileo!'

'How wonderful!'

'So there were some points where... our theories were met with support, approval, even encouragement. But Bern was a complete disaster. This guy we were meant to be meeting... Well I guess I got confused about who we really should be talking to, and CERN put me in touch with this Althauser...'

Bohmann groaned. 'I should have been clearer,' he said. 'Althauser's a pill.'

Axel laughed, relieved. 'But the secretary there at the university put us in touch with Schmidt Hennessey. And you know the rest.'

'Well! Congratulations, boy. An A+ summary, if I may say so. Of course, we've barely scratched the surface of the actual work on the book, but hopefully that will happen easily when we look over the materials you brought over. I've read through all your emails, of course...'

'Actually, Professor,' Axel cut in, 'there's one more thing.'

'Go on...'

'When we were in Saint Moritz, Safiya and I witnessed an avalanche. It was... incredible. It kind of blew my mind. I've never seen anything so powerful, so beautiful in my life. This tsunami of snow hurtling down the mountain... and then it just stopped! All that energy, gone into nothing. It didn't make any sense; didn't seem to fit with the laws of physics as they are usually understood... I couldn't help but think of you. I wrote some notes – maybe I can show them to you sometime.' He stopped, embarrassed.

Bohmann leaned across and, unexpectedly, took his hand. His voice was emotional. 'I could feel a change in you, Axel, even across the ocean, even on the grainy Skype video. I knew I could trust you with this project. I knew you would come to see eye to eye with me, that you would see the Hand of God in action.'

'I still don't believe in God,' Axel said hastily, removing his hand in embarrassment, and Bohmann laughed.

'I wasn't expecting a conversion. After all, my book – my work – is not aimed solely at the religious. It's aimed at scientists and laymen, atheists and believers alike. But this avalanche of yours, perhaps we can integrate it into one of the chapters...'

'It's Schmidt Hennessey's idea, really,' Axel said quickly, his cheeks still pink.

'But I'd heard his energy theories before, and never thought how they might impact on my own work,' Bohmann said kindly. 'I will need to think more specifically about this "stop" of yours, Axel Parker. Not mine; not Schmidt Hennessey's.' He leaned back in his chair. 'I believe you've just earned yourself a co-authorship credit. Well done.'

Axel felt a slow grin spreading across his face. 'Thank you, Professor!' he said. 'I won't let you down.'

'We still have a lot of work to do,' Bohmann cautioned. 'It sounds like with the notes from CERN, and through your conversations with Schmidt Hennessey, we might be able to put together five or six of the chapters. My first chapter has always been called "The False Laws of Thermodynamics" – controversial, I know, but then things can hardly get any worse than they've been, can they? Besides, it's good to kick off an academic work with something a little fun. Then we'll slow things down a bit, pull back to the religious side: "The Hand of God and the Balance of the Universe," this one might be called.'

'At some point,' Axel chipped in, 'we'll have to discuss the limits of the current approaches to both science and religion.' A bubble of pride was rising in his chest: this was his project now, too. This was his work.

'Indeed!' replied Bohmann, whipping out a minuscule notebook from his shirt pocket and scribbling furiously in it with a tiny pen. 'That's a good point. How much guesswork is involved, how much trust.'

'We talked about all that at CERN: I'll show you my notes.'

Bohmann nodded enthusiastically, still scribbling. 'Which brings us to our next chapter, of course: "The Unseen and the Unknown," in which we'll discuss gravity, relativity, the Higgs Boson and various modern discoveries of energy studies.'

'And God.' Axel grinned.

Bohmann grinned back. 'And then we can work on this new chapter of yours – the stop.' He underlined something emphatically.

'"What is Lost,"' Axel blurted out, and Bohmann looked up in surprise.

'"What is Lost!"' he repeated, then went back to scribbling. 'I love it. We'll have to conclude with a chapter titled "What is Found," then.'

Axel grinned happily. 'I can't wait to find out what that one will be about.'

CHAPTER NINETEEN

Safiya, Safiya, Safiya – her name throbbed in his mind like a love song. Axel leaned his head on the warm aeroplane window, gazing down at the sea and the city below. There it was: Turkey! It seemed utterly crazy that he was here. *Maybe it is crazy that I'm here*, Axel reminded himself. But the memory of her smile, her eyes, her voice erased all of his doubts. Soon, he would be with her again, in her home: Istanbul.

What body of water was he looking at? The Black Sea? Or the Sea of... yes, Marmara, that was what it was called. He couldn't see the Bosphorus Strait, the thin ribbon of water he'd read separated the European side of the city from the Asian one. Now he could only see high-rises and houses, stained bright gold with the light of noon, and there was the cupola of a mosque, and there was a highway... and now, with a bump, the plane was touching down.

Safiya! he thought again, almost without meaning to. Axel couldn't stop marvelling in mingled joy and terror at the sequence of events. The last time he had seen her, her eyes had been filled with disappointment, disapproval, and a touch of something else – sadness. How his heart had ached when he had been unable to say goodbye! He had thought he would never see her again. Then she had written. A single email; no personal note or anything, just a forwarded flyer for a lecture Dr Midana would be giving at the Sultan Ahmed Mosque, or Blue Mosque, in Istanbul. *Death and the Soul*: the words had been printed in a simple, serious font, no images or accompaniment. But his mind had filled with the image of Safiya speaking in London, Safiya laughing and drinking wine, Safiya falling asleep on his shoulder on the train... Safiya wanted to see him again: she had invited him to her lecture. It had been impossible to resist. He'd booked a ticket two days before the talk.

It had been hard, lying to Patti-Ann and his mother, telling them Bohmann had some new research for him to do. It had been hard, taking a taxi to the airport alone, his heart pounding in his chest. And the hardest part was still to come, he thought to himself, rising from his seat.

It was cold, and the air smelled like the sea. He stepped out of the plane into the strange wind, the unknown mix of languages. Dazed, he collected his bag and made his way through security. A crowd of unknown faces seemed to surge in. 'Hotel?' they were saying. 'Taxi? Taxi?' Eventually, he let himself be guided to the front of the airport and into a cab. 'Sultan Ahmed Mosque,' he said politely, fiddling with the envelope of Turkish lira he had collected from his bank. It was a full hour and a half before Safiya's talk, but he didn't want to waste time stopping at his hotel. He just wanted to see her.

The driver either wasn't very chatty or didn't speak much English: either way, Axel was glad for the opportunity to sit a while longer with his thoughts. He watched the city stream by the window: first along a wide highway, curving along past fancy hotels, banks and apartment blocks, then into the smaller streets of the centre. It was a beautiful city, he thought to himself, right there by the sea, sparkling bright and blue, its light hypnotic. He was here, he truly realised at last. Here in Istanbul, with Safiya.

★ ★ ★ ★

'Hey. American. Hey.'

Axel opened his eyes with a start, to find his taxi driver's grinning face right in front of his.

'You asleep,' he explained. 'Welcome to the Blue Mosque!'

Guiltily, Axel scrambled out of his seat and groped through his banknotes, trying to wake up and calculate a tip at the same time.

'Thank you, thank you!' The driver's grin widened. Perhaps he had calculated a little generously. 'You like good coffee, sir?'

Axel laughed. 'I think I need some, yes.'

'There is very good place very close: the one with the green door.' Axel looked in the direction the driver was pointing, and saw a quiet café terrace in the shade of an old stone wall.

Gratefully, he wandered towards it, pulling his scarf tight, his case trundling along behind him. A scrawny cat emerged from the dappled shadows, then disappeared into a doorway.

An ancient man with a fuzz of white hair came to greet him. '*Kahve?*' he asked. 'Coffee?' Deep creases formed smiling parentheses around his mouth. He was obviously very pleased to have a tourist as a guest.

Axel nodded, and let himself be guided to a little table in the corner.

'*Az şekerli? Orta şekerli? Sekerli?*' the man asked, before frowning. 'Sweet?' he finally added, as if remembering the word. 'You like very sweet?'

'Yes, a little sweet,' Axel replied.

Seemingly pleased with this reply, the man vanished, leaving Axel surrounded by quiet old men with newspapers and cigarettes. After a moment, he reappeared with a tray and a steaming cup. Axel thanked him, and stared into the thick brew. It looked like a cup of coffee grounds. Did they not filter their coffee in Turkey? Hesitantly, he held the cup up to his nostrils and inhaled. The smell was incredible: rich, pungent and earthy, with a touch of spice. Realising the owner was still standing there, waiting for his reaction, he took a sip and smiled.

'This is really special coffee,' he told the man. 'Very good.' He added a thumbs up for good measure, which made his interlocutor roar with laughter.

'You need more sweet?' he asked, and Axel shook his head. 'You have sweet already!' Seeing Axel didn't understand his joke, he leaned in closer. 'You have a wife? Or some special lady, yes?'

Axel blushed, which earned him an approving slap on the back. 'A very special lady,' he said quietly.

Safiya, Safiya, Safiya, the song in his head began again, and this time he let his chest swell with hope.

★ ★ ★ ★

The cool late afternoon sun of Istanbul poured through the latticed windows, illuminating the speaker with a pattern of interlacing stars. Axel's heart was pounding. There she was, standing on the podium, dressed in a serious dove-grey suit. At last, Safiya: her voice, her eyes, her hands.

'Death is a difficult subject,' she was saying seriously, 'but this does not mean we should shy away from it, either in our studies or in our daily lives.' Above her, the smooth marble walls soared up, opening into the luminous cupola of the Blue Mosque. Arriving a full hour early for the talk, Axel had gazed up in wonder at the cream and blue tiles decorated with floral patterns, but now he could barely take his eyes off Safiya, almost too giddy to listen to her words.

Everything was unfamiliar here: the weather, the music, the taste of the coffee. But the face of the woman he loved, he knew by heart.

'How could it just all end, all of a sudden? How could life, in an instant, be over? It isn't, of course – we all know that instinctively. The key to understanding why lies in understanding the concept of the soul. The Arabic word for soul is "ruh". Etymologically and historically, as well as throughout the Quran, this word means "Holy Spirit," but is also used to mean the human soul. This linguistic overlap suggests a broader existential one: that our souls and the Holy Spirit are in fact one and the same; that the flame that gives us life and light is but a fragment of a greater, luminous and fluid whole.

'This fluidity and godliness are one: the soul has an existence which extends far beyond the boundaries of the body, a power which lies in Allah. God, in other words, is in all of us. In verses 76:1 and 2 of the Quran, we are told that God "created Man from a drop of mingled fluid." Personally, I like to interpret this verse as a metaphor for the soul: shortly afterwards, it is suggested that this drop of fluid "gave (Man) the gifts of hearing and sight."

'More explicitly, verse 32:9 states that "Allah fashioned Man in due proportion and breathed into him something of His spirit." Clearly, the human soul is a part of the eternal soul of God. When God brought the human race into life, he breathed into them some of his spirit – "ruh" – and that spirit has never left the earth. Each of us keeps the soul of God alive: each of us becomes an essential part of this whole. When we are born, we receive our chosen fragment of soul. When we die, we breathe it back into eternity. To put it simply, the soul never dies.'

Axel felt so moved, so uplifted by these comforting and poetic words. She had seen him; he was sure of it, though her face hadn't changed. Pushing away any thoughts that she might not be as thrilled to see him as he was to see her, he let himself be carried away in the flow of her words. Reality could wait.

'The Quran is very clear on this point,' Safiya continued: 'life does not end with death. Life does not end when our heartbeat stops, or even when our bodies grow cold. No, life does not come from nothing, nor does it vanish into nothing. The soul is the form in which life carries on outside our bodies, in heaven and on earth, in wind and sunlight and water.'

Axel caught himself grinning. Some of this sounded like the first lecture he had heard Dr Midana give in London, but some of it sounded like she was speaking just for him. Was this not an unusually science-inflected talk for her? Was she not offering a metaphysical take on their new and precious theory of the stop?

'One fascinating aspect of the Quranic conception of the soul is that it is not only shared by the men and women that walk this earth: this eternal, infinite soul also inhabits the animals and plants of this earth, the mountains and the oceans, – even the stars. In this way, every living thing worships God in its own way, bound together by their shared soul. Thus, the soul is infinite and omnipresent – it inhabits everything and everyone, always – but it is also inaccessible, unknown.'

"The Unknown and the Unseen," Axel thought to himself, thinking back to his meeting with Bohmann and smiling. He wasn't sure of the sequence of events: had their research together influenced Safiya, or had he just learned enough to understand what she had seen all along – that they were tackling the same questions in their work? Not that he understood all this talk of stars and mountains being infused with the spirit of God: but perhaps Safiya would be able to explain it to him.

'No matter how much we may study the subject, our human minds do not have the capacity to comprehend our human souls,' Safiya continued: 'such is the paradox of our existence. Trust, then, comes from faith: faith in the balance of the universe – whether through the will of God or the laws of physics, faith that every life is a part of a plan. Faith that we are where we should be, doing what we should be, living good lives, and that our death will come when it was supposed to. That is how we accept the immortality of our souls.'

Axel wondered if what he felt burning in his chest and stomach was comparable to faith. Love was an irresistible force, which seemed to operate entirely independently of his will. He could not control it, not even determine its intensity at any given moment. Perhaps faith could happen like that...

He suddenly became aware that polite clapping was happening all around him. Was it over already? Perhaps she would repeat some of it for him later. *Later*. The word sent a shock through him: it was time. He stood up slowly, and walked towards Safiya as if in a dream.

'Axel!' she exclaimed, turning pale, then blushing. She grabbed his hand, then turned it into a fierce handshake, obviously aware that people were watching. 'How did you... What are you...'

'I got your invitation,' he said lamely, feeling his own face turn red. 'I... wanted to hear your talk.'

Safiya gave an astonished version of her gentle birdlike laugh, and Axel felt his heart melting. At last, her eyes met his. They stood in silence for a moment, their hands still together. Axel felt the hopes and visions he had nurtured all throughout the flight breaking through his bloodstream like a wave.

'Well, what did you think?' she teased, finally letting go of his hand. 'Did you like the talk?'

'I thought it was wonderful,' he began, but Safiya had already turned away.

'Mother, Father, you must meet Axel Parker,' she was saying excitedly, and two inquisitive faces had turned his way. *Mother? Father?* Now he was shaking hands with them, as they nodded gravely.

'It's so very lovely to meet you,' Safiya's mother said in a lilting accent. 'I am Fariha Midana, and this is my husband Abdullah.'

Safiya's father grunted. Axel's heart was pounding.

'When did you arrive in Istanbul?' Fariha added.

Axel just stared at her for a moment. 'Er, two hours ago,' he said.

Safiya caught his eye quickly.

'I came straight here,' he added, unnecessarily.

'Well, why don't you come home and have tea with us?' Safiya asked him politely, and Axel felt a wave of something quite like terror go through him. This had not been the reunion he'd imagined.

He swallowed. 'Of course,' he replied. 'Thank you so much!'

What *had* he imagined, he wondered as they walked across the mosque courtyard, chiding himself: that he could turn up without warning and expect her to drop everything and… come back to his hotel? The fantasy seemed utterly ridiculous in retrospect. Of course she already had plans – for that afternoon, and maybe for the rest of her life.

What was he doing here?

CHAPTER TWENTY

Emerging from a jumble of alleyways, ducking under a final archway draped with vines, Axel found himself guided into a quiet courtyard. Against his will, he gasped: Safiya's house was breathtakingly beautiful. There were arches everywhere, dripping with beautiful white blossoms and vines, and every window seemed to have an ornate stone balcony. The very walls were built out of smooth black and white stone, and decorated with mosaics in cream and burgundy and gold. A monumental marble fountain was filling the courtyard with its quiet music. It felt very peaceful.

'This is our ancestral Ottoman family home,' Fariha said proudly, as Abdullah locked the front gate with a heavy key. She motioned Axel towards the door, and he followed, his suitcase trundling along behind him. 'Come in, come in!'

Inside the house, the atmosphere was dark and quiet. Fariha guided them down a long corridor, the walls of which seemed to be rippling: after a moment, Axel understood that they were covered with woven silk. After a moment, they emerged into a luminous room. The carpet was the first thing he noticed: an immense piece woven with Arabic characters, with a central medallion depicting a forest scene in green and gold. Noticing his gaze, Fariha smiled. 'This is a Hereke carpet,' she explained. 'Abdullah had it made for the family: see how the five names are the names of Safiya, her siblings, me and my husband?'

It occurred to Axel that he knew very little about Safiya's family. 'I have a brother and a sister,' Safiya said softly, as if reading his mind. 'Hamsa and Radiya.'

'The carpet is seven metres by four,' Abdullah barked suddenly. 'Made of silk, wool, cotton, and gold threads.'

Startled, Axel nodded. 'It is very beautiful,' he said.

Abdullah grunted. 'My name, the name of my wife, and the name of my three children,' he explained, pointing.

'Let me go make some tea,' Fariha said. 'Please, sit down!'

Axel settled onto one of the couches, arranging himself amongst the luxurious cushions. It had never occurred to him that Safiya might be rich.

'We call this room the *majlis*: it is the traditional salon,' Fariha added, smiling as she crossed the enormous family carpet on her way out of the room.

'How big is this house?' Axel couldn't help asking.

'Twelve bedrooms,' Safiya's father replied, a little bombastically, 'though we only use five.'

There was a silence. 'And what do you do, sir?' Axel asked politely.

'I own land,' he answered shortly.

'OK,' said Axel. 'Er, what kind of land?'

Safiya laughed softly. 'He leases the land to fruit growers,' she explained. 'It's quite a successful business. He works with the local banks, as well.'

'Fig, almond, pistachio,' Abdullah added. 'The peasants give me seventy percent of the produce, and then I sell. It is a successful life.'

'My husband is also on the municipal council of the city of Istanbul,' Fariha said proudly, reappearing with a tray. 'And what do you do, Mr Parker?'

'Please, call me Axel.' He paused. 'I'm… currently working on a book,' he finally said.

Was he imagining it, or did Safiya seem ill-at-ease? Perhaps it hadn't been so wise, coming back to her home like this… Axel felt his heart-rate accelerate.

'Lovely, lovely,' said Fariha, setting out the teacups. The scent of fresh mint rose from the silver pitcher as she poured, and she had brought a little plate of biscuits, too, decorated with almonds and rose petals.

'You have other job?' Abdullah asked gruffly. 'Good, American job?'

'I'm afraid I am still a student, Mr Midana,' Axel replied. 'I'm starting my PhD studies in the fall.' He accepted his cup of tea and breathed in the steam.

'A bookworm, just like our Safiya!' Fariha said warmly. 'My daughter takes after my mother, you see.' She handed her a cup of tea, then rested a hand briefly on her daughter's head.

Safiya sat very still, like a small child, then smiled up at her mother. Axel remembered her stories about her grandmother. How far away it seemed, their time in Schmidt Hennessey's chalet!

'What hotel are you staying?' Abdullah asked Axel.

'A small one near the Dolma... Dolmabahce Palace,' Axel replied.

'Small,' Abdullah repeated disapprovingly.

'Small?' Fariha asked, sounding sad.

'I'm sure it'll be very nice,' Axel said awkwardly. 'It was kind of a last-minute booking. Luma, I think it was called, the Hotel Luma.'

'Luma has cockroaches,' Abdullah commented. 'We send our bad international clients to Luma.'

Fariha murmured something in Turkish, then turned to him. 'Axel, you must stay with us. Look, you even have your suitcase with you! It is a sign.'

'Oh, I couldn't possibly!' Axel replied, his cheeks flushing. 'This is very kind, the tea; it's so lovely to meet you, but...'

'Yes, stay,' said Safiya, and Axel looked up from his flustered attempt at a reply.

Really? he asked her with his eyes, and the old familiar wave of hope came back, but she did not meet his gaze.

'We have twelve bedrooms!' Fariha added. 'It would be a pleasure. With us, no cockroaches.'

Abdullah growled something in Turkish, and Fariha said something sharply back. Safiya's father, it seemed, wasn't too keen on her American friend staying the night. For some reason, this made Axel's mind up.

'Thank you so much,' he said. 'I would love to. You have a beautiful home.'

'We have a beautiful library, too,' Fariha added. 'If you like, you can work there. You are here for research, yes?'

Axel did his best not to blush. 'Yes,' he said. He reached for another honey and almond biscuit. 'These are delicious,' he added, to change the subject.

At that moment, the sound of heavy footsteps came echoing down the hall towards them. Safiya looked up in trepidation, Axel noticed, whilst Abdullah's face spread into a slow smile.

'Fariha! Abdul!'

A young moustachioed man entered the room, his arms spread wide in greeting, his heavy boots clunking on the parquet. Safiya's brother? But Safiya was sitting very still, her face plastered with an unfamiliar smile. Safiya's... boyfriend?

Whoever he was, Abdullah stood up and embraced him, then he and Fariha traded a sort of bow. There was a rapid exchange in Turkish, which Axel suspected concerned his introduction. This gave him time to take in the new arrival's quite extraordinary appearance. The man was wearing a long royal blue shirt over bouffant royal blue trousers, topped with a red silk coat and red leather belt. There was a dagger shoved into his trousers at a nonchalant angle, and several medals glinting on his chest. His dark hair was slicked down in movie-star waves, and his moustache had been twisted into two fine points. He looked, to Axel, like a figure that had stepped straight out of a storybook.

The man's face suddenly split into a grin. 'My goodness gracious me!' he said, his Turkish accent coloured with an East Coast one. 'A fellow American!' He marched over to the couch and stuck out his hand for Axel to shake, which Axel did, slowly.

Axel was confused. 'You are... Where are you from?' he asked.

The man laughed brightly. 'I am a son of the Ottoman Empire,' he said proudly. 'But I spent two years in Boston. Horrible place, of course. Very cold.'

'Yusif has American degree,' Abdullah contributed.

Yusif, for this was his name, laughed politely, and the two men made several jokes in Turkish. Fariha made a tutting sound.

'He has a BA in international relations,' Safiya contributed, her voice neutral.

Yusif gave a high-pitched laugh. 'You know this does not matter in Turkey, my darling,' he said. Axel bristled at his patronising tone. 'Only the Americans we trade with care about this sort of thing. Here, it is only your roots, your heritage that truly matter.' Theatrically, he clapped his hand to his mouth. 'But I am forgetting myself, how rude! In front of your guest.'

Axel laughed politely, but was pleased to note out of the corner of his eye that Safiya remained stony-faced.

'I'm a PhD student,' he offered, slightly competitively.

'And I, Yusif al-Katib, am a descendant of Sultan Bayezid. My ancestor is Naili Abdullah Pasha, the chief scribe of the Ottoman court who became the Grand Vizier of Osman III. That is why my last name is al-Katib, it means "scribe". You see? Different things matter in different countries – with no offence to your P... h... D.' Yusif smiled widely, but his eyes were narrow.

Axel's blood was, ever so slowly, beginning to boil. 'So you're an old friend of the family's?'

Yusif looked offended. 'Dear boy, I *am* family!'

'He is family soon,' Abdullah offered, with something that quite resembled a wink.

'Yusif is the son of one of my husband's colleagues,' Fariha explained, her tone neutral.

'Tragically,' Yusif replied, smiling up at Fariha, 'we are divided, you see, by the ocean: I live on the European side of the city, my love lives on the Asian side.'

Axel bristled. Fariha giggled. Safiya remained quiet, as she had since Yusif had arrived. Axel had never seen her so subdued.

Yusif, who, it seemed, had quite a taste for the monologue, continued. To Axel's horror, he seemed to be using him as the springboard – as if he were confiding in a fellow man. It made Axel's skin crawl. 'I can travel here easily, in the most beautiful vehicles on this earth. I'm a very rich man, you know. My dad just got me the latest imported Mustang, a special edition: there were only fifty made in the whole world! 500 horsepower.' He beamed. 'But I don't ride it in this filthy city, oh no. Somebody might scratch it. When I own something, I just like to ride it and ride it around my property.' There was a nasty undertone in his voice that suggested he wasn't just talking about cars.

'So how did you get here, then?' Axel asked, not caring if he sounded rude. Safiya stifled a laugh.

Yusif blinked at him, unused to being interrupted. 'What?'

'Oh, I was just wondering! If you don't like to drive your cars outdoors, how did you come here today, across the Bosphorus?'

'Taxi,' Yusif replied, suspiciously.

'Yusif will make a good husband,' Abdullah said, rather unsubtly.

'More tea?' asked Fariha.

'Thank you, Fariha,' Axel said, carried on a wave of something unfamiliar – anger, love, confidence? – 'but I'm quite tired after my flight. Do you think I could perhaps take a rest in my room?'

Yusif made a strangled sound.

'Of course!' Safiya trilled, in a sweet, put-on voice he'd never heard before. Joyfully, Axel realised they really were on the same side. 'Let me show you to your quarters.'

Fariha, who had half risen from her seat, sat back down. Was she hiding a smile?

'Bye, Yusif!' Axel added with a wave. 'So nice to meet you.'

And without a glance back, ignoring the murmuring men's voices, Axel and Safiya swept out of the room.

★ ★ ★ ★

If Axel had been expecting them to burst into laughter as soon as they were out of earshot, he was once more disappointed. Safiya's shoulders slumped as soon as they left the living room, and he realised that this wasn't just a game for her.

'Safiya,' he asked hesitantly, 'are you… engaged to this guy?'

'Oh God, no,' she replied. 'Though my father certainly wishes I was.' There was a silence, as they descended a dark silken corridor. 'I've turned him down more times than I can count, and still he keeps coming back.'

'Why?' Axel asked.

'Because he's a stubborn ass, that's why.' A smile had appeared at the corner of Safiya's mouth.

'But your parents, they keep serving him tea and cookies?'

'My dad's terrified I'll end up a spinster. It's very unusual for a woman not to be married by thirty here in Turkey. Yusif is rich, as you may have worked out: that's all my father can see.'

'And your mother? She seemed a little less encouraging.'

Safiya smiled. 'Yes, she is. She… wants me to be happy,' she added softly, not looking at him.

They reached a huge oak door and she fiddled with the lock. They entered the bedroom, and Axel's breath caught in his throat. The bed was an immense four-poster made out of shining dark wood – walnut, Safiya would tell him later. It was swathed in delicate silk awnings, the most beautiful mosquito nets he had ever seen.

'Wow,' said Axel.

'My mother likes you,' Safiya added, a new twinkle in her eye. 'I think she's kind of relieved to have a nice guy in the house. So if you're planning on ravishing me, you'll probably have her support.'

It was a joke, Axel knew, but still his heart leapt into his throat. 'Your dad would kill me,' he said, keeping his tone light. 'Does he have a dagger like Yusif?'

'No,' Safiya said wickedly, 'but he does have a sword.'

Axel laughed.

'Let me show you the best thing about this particular room,' Safiya said, changing the subject. 'The balcony!'

She threw open the French windows, letting the sun pour into the bedroom, and stepped out. 'All the rooms in the house have balconies,' she said, 'but this one has the advantage of wrapping around. We're at the very top of the house, you see.'

Axel followed her in the glowing afternoon sun, following the wall to its angle.

'And here, you can get up to the roof.' Motioning for Axel to follow, she reached up to the gutter, placing her foot on a convenient stone, and pulled herself up to the crenellated rooftop.

'Is this safe?' Axel asked.

'Come on,' Safiya said. She pulled him up onto the flat bed of the black and ochre roof-tiles. 'You have to be careful for this part, but over here by the chimney, there's a place we can sit.'

Axel staggered after Safiya, then sat down carefully next to her. Taking in his surroundings, he was once more astounded by the beauty of the city stretching out around them.

'I used to come here a lot when I was a teenager.' Safiya sighed deeply, then pulled a packet of cigarettes from inside her jacket. 'What?' she asked, seeing Axel's face.

'I... didn't know you smoked.' He paused. 'Do your parents know you smoke?'

Safiya laughed. 'What do you think?' She lit a cigarette and took a deep drag. 'Do you want one?'

Axel shook his head. 'They're bad for you,' he said without thinking, and they both laughed.

He watched Safiya smoke for a moment, outlined against the slowly descending sun. 'Do you know, when I first met you, I thought you were so grown up and serious. Pious, even. Dr Midana, the Quranic scholar.'

Safiya laughed. 'And now you've seen me with my family...'

'Now I know you're a rebel!' he finished, smiling. 'A rebel with a PhD and a love of nicely tailored suits.'

'I was always the wild child,' she confirmed. 'Always running around the streets barefoot, stealing fruit from the little markets, reading books up here on the roof...'

'For some reason, it's easier to imagine you as a child than as a teenager.'

'I don't think I made life for my parents particularly easy. Even now, I hear them arguing...' She was quiet for a moment, smoking. Axel still couldn't get used to the sight. 'My older sister was married nine years ago – an arranged marriage, of course – and my older brother is a businessman working in Germany. Married too, four years ago.'

Axel shook his head in wonder. 'I know it's not the same, culturally speaking, in Texas,' he said, 'but I think Patti-Ann feels the same pressure. Like it'll be a terrible disaster if she's not married next year.'

Safiya was quiet for a long time. 'I really hate coming back here,' she finally said. 'It's like slipping back into my miserable, awkward childhood. My father treats me like I'm nine years old – my mother too, even though she means well. They think giving a talk at Sultan Ahmed Mosque is just some cute thing I do. Oh, let her have her little *bookworm* games!'

'Your talk was amazing.'

'I know.' Safiya laughed softly. 'It's just... Nobody knows who I am outside the university. It's like my achievements mean nothing here.'

She took another drag from her cigarette, and Axel took her other hand in his. 'Your achievements are your own,' he said. 'What does it matter if people on the street can't tell you're Dr Midana? Your colleagues, your professors, your students, they know. Isn't that what matters?'

'And that asshole Yusif!' she said with surprising viciousness. 'He pretends to be supportive of my studies, but I know, I just know if I gave in, he'd have me pregnant within a year, and then again, and again, until I was raising ten children. I'd never open another book in my life.'

'Don't marry that guy,' said Axel. 'Please.'

She made a choked noise, something like a sob. 'I hate him. I hate him! *Oh, I'm going skiing with my friends from San Francisco! Oh, I'm going diving with my friends in Izmir!* I mean, the man hates being outdoors. It's all for show. He may as well be burning the banknotes with a cigarette lighter. If he had his way, he would just lounge around all day on his silk cushions.'

'How did you meet this guy?' Axel asked, the horror in his voice barely disguised.

She breathed out smoke. 'His dad is basically a feudalist, like mine. He's never had to work a day in his life.'

'A dilettante.'

'Yeah. But you've never seen a dilettante like this. He just walks around the streets of Istanbul all day in his costumes, with his medals and his hats – they're all family heirlooms, you see. Then he goes home to his thirty-room villa overlooking the Bosphorus, and throws another disgusting party.'

'And drives his car around in the courtyard.'

Safiya stubbed out her cigarette on the roof tiles. 'Exactly.'

Axel paused. 'My mom would kill me if I brought home a smoker,' he joked.

Safiya's laugh trilled out. 'I'm not really a smoker,' she said. 'I only smoke when I'm stressed.' She paused, a mischievous light entering her eyes. 'What about a Muslim?' she asked casually.

Axel's heart was pounding. He didn't know what to say, waited too long, and the moment passed. Safiya looked away. 'My mom would love you,' he finally blurted out, and he was rewarded with a slow smile. She met his eyes, and he felt love spreading through him, as warm and golden as the sunset descending across the city.

Overwhelmed, Axel reached over and pulled Safiya close. 'Oh Safiya, I'm so sorry I showed up without warning. It was a stupid thing to do.'

Safiya's warm laugh was muffled by his shoulder. 'Yeah, it was,' she said. 'But I can't tell you how happy I am to see you.' She pulled back and met his eyes. 'Look, this can't have been what you were hoping to spend your time in Istanbul doing, hanging out with my family and my suitor.'

'I didn't exactly factor Yusif in, no.'

'Let's go somewhere tomorrow, just the two of us. Let me show you the city.'

'Show me your city,' he said, squeezing her shoulder, smelling the warm sandalwood perfume of her hair. 'Show me the university, and the libraries you like, and the cafés you go to with your rebellious professor friends.'

In his arms, she was very still, as if afraid to break the spell. 'I would like that very much,' she said.

Somewhere, the call to prayers rang out, mingling with the car horns and the sound of the pigeons.

CHAPTER TWENTY-ONE

It was pigeons again that woke Axel the next morning with the silken sound of their wings. Light drifted in from the street outside, through the curtains surrounding his bed. With a start, he remembered he was in Safiya's house; remembered the rooftop and the almond cakes and the Blue Mosque and the airplane journey. He stopped the retrospective there: right here, right now was a good place to be. He climbed out of bed and pulled on his jeans and a clean shirt, then walked down the carpeted hallway to the stairs.

'Good morning!' He heard the two women's voices before he saw them. The smell of freshly-baked bread greeted him as he entered the kitchen. Fariha and Safiya were sitting at the table – no Abdullah, he noted with pleasure. He smiled. 'My father likes to take his breakfast with his friends,' Safiya said, as if reading his mind.

'He likes very strong coffee,' Fariha added.

'I don't understand how anyone could turn down your coffee,' Safiya replied, taking her mother's hand. It was clear that she had almost physically relaxed since the previous day. 'It's so delicate! Axel, you must try it.'

'I'd love to,' he said, sitting down. His eyes widened as he took in the spread offering itself to him: next to the crown of fresh bread sprinkled with sesame seeds, there were platefuls of glistening olives, hardboiled eggs and creamy wedges of cheese. Fresh tomatoes and cucumbers had also been sliced up, bright and fresh, and sweet dates, dried figs and almonds filled a silver bowl.

'What's this?' he asked curiously, pointing at a platter of dried meat.

'Pastirma,' Safiya replied. 'Air-dried beef: a Turkish speciality. You must try some!'

Axel wasted no time in filling his plate with everything on offer.

Fariha laughed with pleasure, returning with his cup of coffee. 'I am glad you like Turkish breakfast,' she said. 'I thought maybe Americans only ate burgers.'

Axel shook his head vehemently, though it took him a moment to reply, his mouth being so full. 'They're missing out,' he finally said. He sipped his coffee and his eyes widened. 'It's spiced!' he said. 'Wow!'

'Cardamom,' Fariha explained, blushing. 'Another Turkish tradition.'

He sipped carefully, savouring.

'I see you've got the hang of Turkish coffee already,' said Safiya. 'Some people make the mistake of gulping their first cup down.'

'Well, this is my second cup, but one is enough to know to be careful.'

'So you are doing research together today?' Fariha asked warmly.

'Yes,' Axel replied, exactly at the same time as Safiya said 'No.' Their eyes met and they laughed.

'I'm taking Axel on a tour of the city today,' she explained to her mother. 'Work can wait.'

There was a twinkle in Fariha's eye as she nodded. 'You two young ones enjoy yourselves,' she said.

Axel blushed and busied himself with a fresh piece of bread.

★ ★ ★ ★

'So what kind of a tour would you like?' Safiya asked as they stepped out into the street. Axel pulled his coat tight around him: the wind had grown a little colder than the previous day. 'Intellectual, or touristic?'

'Personal,' Axel replied, remembering the previous evening's discussion on the rooftop. 'I want to see your Istanbul. Safiya Midana's Istanbul.'

Safiya beamed. 'I won't let you down,' she replied. She pulled her hair out of her scarf, letting it fall over her shoulders, and frowned thoughtfully. 'Well, you've already seen the Blue Mosque, so to balance things out, culturally speaking, I think you should see the Hagia Sofia: a Byzantine church. There are really beautiful mosaics there. And of course you must see the Grand Bazaar.'

'I'd like to see your university,' Axel contributed.

'Alright,' Safiya replied. 'Let the tour begin!' She made a grand gesture, as if the little street they found themselves in was a historical avenue, and for the soaring feeling in Axel's stomach, it might as well have been.

They walked down the crooked cobbles, past the walled enclosures surrounding the finer houses in the neighbourhood, past trailing jasmine vines and pigeons pecking at the dust. They walked past dilapidated storefronts, and gates chained shut, and past a series of cheap electronics shops. Finally, they emerged into the tree-lined avenue leading to the impressive facade of the Hagia Sofia. Rising between the palms and red maples and dark cedars, there it was: a cascade of pink brick and grey-white stone domes, ringed in by four blocky minarets.

'Like many Byzantine churches, it was converted into a mosque during the Ottoman Empire,' Safiya explained. 'Of course, it's a museum now.'

It was still early morning, and the queues were short: before long, the two visitors had crossed under an archway decorated with mosaic rosaces in white, crimson and gold, and entered the museum. They stood in awe as the golden light poured through the windows.

'It still feels like a sacred place,' Axel said softly.

Safiya nodded. 'I don't think a place of worship such as this could ever lose that spirit.'

'It's crazy,' Axel mused aloud, 'that a place could be converted. You'd think the fact that Christians and Muslims happily worshipped here, just in different eras, would be a good argument for different religions accepting each other...' He felt himself blushing, but Safiya put her hand on his shoulder and squeezed.

'Many pools, one moon,' she murmured, and he knew she was smiling.

The interior was breathtaking, painted ochre and gold, decorated with geometric designs and immense painted medallions of Arabic calligraphy.

'What do those say?' Axel asked, pointing upwards at the swirls of gold on black.

'Those represent the names of important figures in Muslim culture: Allah, the prophet Muhammad, peace be upon him, Islam's first four caliphs, and the two grandsons of Muhammad, peace be upon him.'

'They're very impressive.'

They wandered slowly around the museum, admiring the impressive architecture and gilded mosaics. One in particular caught their eye: a scene in which the Virgin was sitting on a throne, baby Christ in her lap, while two men offered her miniature models.

'Is that this church?' Axel asked, squinting at the scene.

'Yes! That's the emperor Justinian offering up the Hagia Sophia, and the emperor Constantine, offering up the whole city of Istanbul.'

'Extraordinary!' Axel exclaimed.

'It's a shame, really,' Safiya said. 'Many of the mosaics were covered or removed; some of them were sent to Venice and never recovered: some of them were destroyed in an earthquake. And some are still whitewashed over, for their protection.'

'How come?' Axel asked. 'Was it when the church became a mosque?'

'It wasn't, actually. Have you heard of iconoclasm?'

Axel shook his head, smiling. It was clear that Safiya couldn't wait to tell him all about it.

'Iconoclasm was a movement against religious images,' Safiya began.

'A Muslim movement?' Axel asked, remembering their London discussions about calligraphy.

'A Christian one,' Safiya corrected him. 'There's a different name for the Muslim proscription against the creation of images of living beings: aniconism. It means the same thing, of course: no icons! And Byzantine Christianity was actually highly influenced by Islam. In fact, the whole of Byzantine culture was a meeting between the East and West, with fertile cross-pollination in the arts, architecture... But I'm digressing.'

'No, keep going! This is really interesting. So this iconoclasm, isn't that what happened with Swiss Protestantism as well, destroying statues and all? I remember seeing traces of that in Geneva...'

'Exactly. The fear of idolatry has cropped up throughout Christian history: fear of worshipping "graven images," which was expressly forbidden in the Ten Commandments. The King James Bible explicitly says "Thou shalt not make unto thee any graven image, or any likeness of any thing that is in heaven above, or that is in the earth beneath, or that is in the water under the earth".'

'So wait, I'm confused. It's not just images of God or Jesus that are forbidden?'

'Everything on Earth is made by God, you see, and therefore sacred.'

'So we're not allowed… any representative art at all? That's crazy!'

Safiya laughed. 'Well, *we're* allowed anything we want,' she reminded him. 'We're not iconoclasts. And neither are most Christians; certainly not in this century.'

Axel was quiet for a while, processing. 'And the Muslim laws about religious art, do they say the same thing?'

'They don't, actually,' Safiya clarified, 'though the reasoning is the same – that we as mere mortals should not be allowed to create, as God creates. That should be His prerogative, and His prerogative only. But in Islamic tradition, it is the living, sentient form which is most explicitly prohibited from being represented: God above all, and then in descending order of graveness Muhammad, peace be upon him, the prophets, and any human being. So you'll rarely come across human or even animal figures in a place of worship.'

'Because you'd be at risk of trying to represent a part of God in the house of God,' Axel thought aloud.

'A part of God's soul,' Safiya agreed.

They were silent for a while, staring at the mosaic: the saints' placid faces, the hands raised in blessing, the crooked black letters, the halos of gold.

'It's an interesting idea, that all of Creation is sacred,' Axel finally said. 'I still don't really see why that means we can't create art celebrating it…'

'*We* again,' Safiya laughed. 'You really are becoming a religious man! On a more serious note, though, there have been a thousand sectarian conflicts arguing over the details of this: Orthodox versus Catholic church, Sunni versus Shi'ite... In the end, a lot of it is just religious leaders trying to claim they are better worshippers than their rivals.'

'Holier than thou!' Axel laughed.

'Just like your Defenders of Grace.'

Axel rolled his eyes. 'Just as destructive, certainly. Although I guess they just graffiti buildings, rather than actually destroy them.'

'Still. They're using an art-form as a weapon. It's worth thinking about.'

And they did, as they left the museum and walked back out into the cool winter sun.

★ ★ ★ ★

With every minute he spent in Safiya's company, Axel felt as if his mind were expanding. It was incredible, this intellectual companionship, he thought to himself as they walked down the busy streets. He felt blessed. Startled, he paused to turn the thought over in his mind. Blessed! Safiya's teasing words echoed through his mind. *You really are becoming a religious man!* Was he? He'd certainly not felt an ounce of cynicism the previous morning in the Blue Mosque, watching the wide eyes of the faithful as they drank up Safiya's words. He'd felt himself oddly moved by the imposing calligraphic medallions spelling out the name of God in the old converted church. He'd even felt his heart lift at the sound of the *muezzin* echoing out across the rooftops, calling the city to prayer. Was this all just love, love colouring the experience of Istanbul with unspeakable beauty, or was Safiya opening his mind up in other ways? But surely this was just religious tourism, a kind of cultural awe rather than any sort of awakening... He brushed the train of thought away, but a pleasant unease remained in his breast.

'Here we are!' Safiya exclaimed happily. 'The Grand Bazaar!'

'Will there be food in the Grand Bazaar?' Axel asked, gazing with her at the entryway. 'I'm starting to get a bit peckish...'

Safiya checked her watch. 'You're right, it's almost lunchtime. We stayed in the Hagia Sophia for hours!'

'I'm not sure if that makes you a terrible tour guide, or the best I've ever had.'

She beamed. 'The best, of course. And to answer your previous silly question, of course there is food in the Grand Bazaar. Don't you know what a bazaar is?'

'Not really,' Axel confessed. 'I guess I imagined a lot of guys selling rugs and shoes?'

Safiya giggled. 'You're not wrong! But they also sell pistachios, and honey, and hummus, and spiced sandwiches made with grilled aubergines...'

'Now I'm really hungry!'

Axel's self-proclaimed tour guide led him through the gate and into the bustle. The air smelled like leather, burning wood, and fresh coffee. There was a musty scent, too, like old stone. 'This must be a really old market, huh?'

'You could call it the oldest shopping mall in the world,' Safiya replied with a twinkle in her eye.

'How old? Come on, tour guide, I'm hungry for facts.'

'Five hundred years old,' she replied, 'or so. Though in its current incarnation, as a whole quarter, it's existed since the start of the seventeenth century. Before that, there were several buildings, and one of them was for slaves.'

'Whoa,' said Axel.

Safiya laughed. 'You're too easy a target, my little American.'

'So what else did they sell here, historically speaking?' he asked, looking around at the array of soft, billowing cloth.

'Well, we're currently standing in the centre of the silk trade, as you've probably guessed.'

'It's beautiful.' The silks on display were dyed every imaginable shade, from dusky gold to deep indigo blue.

'This is the part of the market that has always sold luxury goods: so we'll find plenty of jewellery and crystal here. In the old days, you'd have been able to buy armour here, too.'

'Armour!'

'Then there are the leatherworkers, the pottery and china stalls, and all the food merchants.' She waved a hand in the air. 'You'll get the picture soon enough.'

They walked past a shop selling only gold bangles: the collective shine was almost too much to look at. They passed shops selling ceramic beads, brightly-coloured shoes, and elaborately tooled leather bags. Walking down the little covered streets was like wandering through a labyrinth, discovering new delights around every corner. Here was a stall selling garlands of dried chilli peppers – black, red, yellow and purple, the smell intoxicating. Here were baskets and baskets of dried apricots and figs and bright red berries, piled high into pyramids. Here was a man selling tray after tray of Turkish delight, studded with pistachios and sprinkled with rose petals. By the time Axel and Safiya left this part of the market, they had accrued quite a collection of snacks, as well as two generous doner kebabs.

'I really feel like I should be trying something they don't have back home,' Axel argued as Safiya ordered the two sandwiches.

'Trust me, you don't have this back in Texas,' Safiya shot back.

They watched as the man sliced thin strips from the rotating cone of savoury lamb, then packed them into flatbreads with salad, a thick yogurt sauce and pickled beets. It was, Axel had to admit, a far sight from the greasy meat sandwiches he had occasionally acquired at the end of a night out with his Zeta Delta Pi brothers. He made a moaning sound as he bit in, then wiped his mouth on his sleeve. 'This is amazing!'

Safiya shook her head. 'You're getting it all over yourself.' Her tone was affectionate. 'Here, let me.' She pulled a tissue from her breast pocket and wiped the corner of his mouth. Their eyes met.

'I think I'm in love with this sandwich,' Axel declared, to break the silence, and they laughed and walked on.

★ ★ ★ ★

By the time the sandwiches were finished, the wrappers had been thrown away, and little sweet bites of lemon- and rose-flavoured Turkish delight had been consumed, they unexpectedly found themselves in a quiet street of the bazaar. The tourists had faded away, leaving only the two of them standing amongst the lamp shops. Axel found his breath taken away once more, just as it had been as he stood in the Hagia Sophia as the light streamed in; just as it had been when Safiya was speaking in the Blue Mosque, the pattern of the windows falling down on her in woven shadows. Stained glass and copper lamps were hung from every visible shopfront, cascading from the lintels and tangling from the ceilings. Fragments of soft light glinted in every direction, peacock green and gold and blood-red. Somehow, it was utterly silent.

'*Salah*,' Safiya breathed, as the sound of the call to prayers was heard ringing out.

Axel checked his watch: it was half past two, time for the afternoon prayers. Everyone had vanished.

'A lot of people go to the squares to pray,' Safiya whispered. 'Although I've seen men standing in rows on the narrower streets…'

They could hear a faint murmur, like many voices speaking together. A few voices were audible nearby, distinct from the mass chorus.

'I think there's a man praying in that shop,' Axel whispered back, having noticed a hunched figure in the back of one of the rooms.

They tiptoed down the narrow alley, then stopped and leaned against a wall, the light raining down all around them. Axel kept his eyes turned up to the hundreds and thousands of lightbulbs, each glowing steadily in their own shape and colour and intensity, all joining together to form one great, united light. He swallowed, feeling something coming together in his mind. Fragments of Safiya's talk at the Blue Mosque came back to him, jumbled and vague: *our souls and the Holy Spirit are in fact one and the same... the flame that gives us life and light is but a fragment of a greater, luminous and fluid whole.*

'Safiya,' he whispered, 'what do you really think the soul... is?'

She didn't laugh. They stood in silence, bathing in the great light made of tiny lights. 'I've studied the soul my whole life,' she finally said, 'and still I don't know. All I know is that I am a part of this world, a part of life on earth, and that my own humble soul belongs to a greater whole.'

'Like these lamps,' Axel breathed.

Understanding dawned on Safiya's face, and she slipped her hand into his. They turned to each other, the light from the lamps reflected as delicate pinpoints in their eyes. Then Axel's phone rang. Startled, he let go of Safiya's hand and pulled it from his pocket. Patti-Ann, his screen was flashing. After just a moment's hesitation, he rejected the call, switched his phone to silent, and smiled at Safiya. 'So, where to next?'

★ ★ ★ ★

The sea air whipped through their hair, cool and soft with salt. The sun glinted off the waves of the Bosphorus, like gold coins scattered across the blue waters.

'It's so beautiful,' Axel murmured, his hands wrapped around the boat's guardrail.

'I grew up on these waters,' said Safiya. 'It always fills my heart with joy, just being out here.'

'I just can't get over the fact that we're crossing between continents. Between the East and the West; Europe and Asia...'

The gleaming estuary of the Golden Horn was vanishing into the distance, leaving Axel's eyes free to roam from dome to minaret to gleaming high-rise.

'That's Dolmabahçe Palace, right there,' said Safiya, pointing. 'The one we just visited.'

The palace was beautiful from here, an orderly assemblage of columns, wings and porticoes, all made of white stone. They had roamed around the gardens for half an hour on the boat's first stop, soaking in the history and architecture, admiring the fountains and statues; yet it looked even more impressive from the water, like a great white bird unfolding its wings along the banks.

'Wow,' said Axel.

'Wow indeed,' Safiya echoed mockingly.

'Can you see my hotel?' Axel joked.

'Yeah, I think I can see some cockroaches...'

They giggled, as the boat sped by beaches and office towers, their chrome spears piercing the sky. He felt his phone vibrate in his pocket, but ignored it.

'Istanbul has seen so many changes,' Safiya murmured thoughtfully, almost nostalgically. 'So many names: Byzantium, then Constantinople, then Istanbul; so many cultures, Greek and then Roman, Ottoman and Turkish. So many conquerers.'

'You sound like you've lived through them all,' Axel said tenderly.

Safiya shrugged. 'I'm a scholar,' she said. 'Sometimes it feels as though I have, as if I've lived through these revolutions and renamings and religious transformations. So many dreams! Always dreaming of expansion, dreaming of empires, always wishing for more land... and then change comes all the same, over and over.'

'But you stay the same, just like your beloved Istanbul.'

Gazing at Safiya's profile, so noble, so soft against the backdrop of sea and the ancient city, Axel was quite overwhelmed by her beauty. Her dark hair had been tangled by the wind, adding a salty note to her sandalwood scent.

All you have to do is tell her.

The words tumbled into his head, quite unbidden.

'Safiya,' he murmured, as the boat moved slowly through the waves towards the shore, and she turned to him, a question in her eyes. He reached for her arms and took them in his. There was a bump as the boat docked, and startled, Axel almost lost his footing.

'Rumelihisarı,' a man announced over a loudspeaker. 'The Fortress of Europe! You have forty-five minutes to visit.'

Safiya was already walking towards the exit. Cursing himself, Axel followed. Every time he tried to touch the woman he now knew he loved, she seemed to be just out of reach.

★ ★ ★ ★

'And just over there is the Fatih bridge, the narrowest point of the Bosphorus.'

Safiya's voice had switched into its most neutral register, but still Axel clung to her every word. 'This is a slightly unusual place to stop,' she said. 'Our captain has made some interesting choices. Still, Rumelihisarı Castle, or Boğazkesen, as it's also known, is of profound historical interest.'

Axel looked up at the towering crenellated walls, so smooth and high. 'It's impressive,' he said. 'If this guy was my enemy, I wouldn't try to attack him.'

Safiya laughed. 'Well, "this guy" was more of an attacker. The fortress was built by Sultan Mehmed II, as he was preparing to conquer Constantinople. He wanted to stop aid coming in from the Black Sea once he began his attack. He won, of course, taking over from the Constantines.'

'That was the beginning of the Ottoman era then?' Axel was getting better at piecing the history together. He was learning so much, he realised with a swell of affection and pride.

'The Fall of Constantinople,' Safiya replied. 'The end of one era – the Roman – and the beginning of a new. A great victory for Islam, of course, insofar as Islam is seen as a conquering force rather than a private religion.'

There was a bitterness to her voice, and Axel was about to reply with some comforting words when he felt his phone ringing in his pocket again. A terrible surge of anger swelled in his breast. What was *wrong* with Patti-Ann? Couldn't she go a few hours without telling him all about her latest outfit? Guilt flooded through him. He kicked a stone.

'Careful,' said Safiya, 'that's medieval.'

Everything melted away as he laughed, and she smiled. When he was with her, Safiya was the centre of his universe. It was like a halo of golden light followed her everywhere, coloured everything she touched, like the rings of Saturn. Or gravity! And maybe he was her satellite. He blushed as these thoughts filled his mind. With Patti-Ann, he hadn't even liked writing 'I love you' on cards. Now, he felt like he could write whole books of poetry.

They walked on amongst the rough stone towers, Axel trying to keep his feelings in check. But they surged and ran through him, like a mountain stream bursting from the ground, and could not be stopped.

A bank of wild white roses was growing amongst the stones. 'How beautiful!' Axel exclaimed, bending down to pick one. A thorn pricked his skin, and he brought his finger to his mouth to suck the blood away, the rose held in his other hand.

Safiya appeared by his side and gently took the rose from him. Bending her head down towards the blossom, she breathed in and closed her eyes. 'I love roses,' she said, and in a rush of emotion, and partly to stop himself from blurting out *and I love you*, Axel tilted her chin towards him and, yes, without thinking, softly kissed her. Their first kiss smelled like roses and tasted faintly of blood. It lasted a long time. Axel's heart was pounding.

Then there was the sound of a bell clanging, and a man's voice shouting, 'three o'clock!'

'Goddamn this stupid boat,' Axel said out loud, giddy with joy, and he and Safiya laughed.

* * * *

Safiya, Safiya, Safiya. The song began again in his heart as they sat in happy silence, side by side, making their way slowly back down the blue channel of the Bosphorus. The buildings were the same – the high-rises, the minarets, the domes – but seemed infinitely more beautiful. The light had changed. Everything had changed.

He didn't dare reach for her hand. Did he? His heart was swimming in his chest.

His phone rang again, and his hand started guiltily back. Feeling quite ready to throw the stupid thing overboard, he pulled it out of his pocket. Seven missed calls, a host of text messages in his inbox, and Patti-Ann's name flashing on the screen. The laugh he'd been putting on to dismiss the gesture in front of Safiya died in his throat. This wasn't like his fiancée at all. Maybe something terrible *had* happened. He picked up.

'Where the hell have you been?' Patti-Ann was hysterical, on the edge of tears. 'Goddammit, Axel Parker. I've been calling and calling and you can't be bothered to pick up just for one single minute?'

'I'm sorry,' Axel said awkwardly, standing up and turning back to the guardrail. 'I didn't realise.'

'Didn't realise? Didn't realise?' Patti-Ann wasn't on the edge of tears, she was well over the edge. 'Where are you?' she sobbed. 'Who are you with? I thought you were working, but there's no way…'

'I've been in the library,' Axel lied, feeling very small. 'I had to keep my phone on silent.'

'Don't you lie to me, Axel Parker.' Patti-Ann's voice had taken on a warning edge, but it quickly broke into a new wave of tears. 'Oh God, Axel, we'll talk about this later, I mean, I'm still angry, but that's not the important part, oh God, Axel, your mother—' She took a ragged breath.

Axel's heart stopped in his chest. 'My mother? What's wrong? What happened?'

Patti-Ann made her voice calm. 'Your mother has been in a serious car accident, Axel. She's in the hospital. She's in a coma.' There was silence as all the colour seemed to drain from the waves surrounding the boat. 'The doctors are taking good care of her, but there's a real danger…' Patti-Ann stopped again, sniffling. 'We don't know if she's going to be alright,' she concluded instead. 'She needs you here, Axel. I need you. I really need you to come home.'

CHAPTER TWENTY-TWO

'Mom? Mom?' Axel came crashing through the door to the hospital room, then froze on the spot. His mother was motionless in the bed, her face drawn and bruised. A pale green sheet was pulled up to her neck. 'Oh Mommy,' he whimpered. 'Mom!'

'Shhh.' Startled, Axel now noticed, for the first time, a figure hunched in a chair in the corner: his aunt Charlene, Felicia's older sister.

'I'm sorry,' he whispered. 'I didn't... I mean, I came straight from the airport...'

Charlene just stared at him, as he slowly lowered his case to the ground. It occurred to him in a wave of confused anger that his voice wouldn't disturb his mother: nothing would disturb his mother. She was deep in a coma.

'How is she?' he asked, hesitantly.

'Same as when she came in,' Charlene replied sourly, adjusting her pantyhose at the knee. 'Less blood, of course.'

'Charlene!' Axel was appalled at her coarseness.

'What?' said Charlene. 'I'm just tellin' it like it is. Where you been anyway, young man? Where were you when it happened? That fiancée of yours has been here day in day out, but we've not seen hair nor hide of you!'

'It only happened yesterday,' Axel said defensively. What was it about Aunt Charlene that made him feel like a naughty child? Maybe it was her taste in clothes, he noted sourly. Today, she was wearing a light blue suit and a white blouse, black patent leather shoes with a one-inch heel and thick brown pantyhose covered in little snags, like flies.

'I was in Istanbul. For research,' he added, willing himself not to blush.

'Two days ago,' Charlene corrected him. Of course: his flight had been almost twelve hours, with the layover in Atlanta. 'But I guess you're here now, and that's the important thing.'

Their eyes met, and Charlene's expression softened as she saw Axel's face. 'Did you get some sleep, at least?' she asked, her voice still sharp though the tone had softened.

'Not really,' he replied. His thoughts had been chaos, he dimly recalled, jumping back and forth from idyllic visions of Safiya in gardens to terrifying ones of his mother in pain. Several times, he'd thought he felt his phone ringing in his pocket, even though he'd switched it off for the flight. He needed to send Patti-Ann a message, he knew, to let her know he was here – but he wasn't ready to see her. He wasn't ready for any of this. His mind was like a wild horse, no, a pack of wild horses, all running in different directions. He hadn't had time to think, to decide what he was going to do, though of course he knew what he had to do – his heart had chosen – but how could he even be thinking of such things now, with his mother in such grave danger? 'I tried to watch some movies on the plane,' he added, 'but I couldn't really focus.'

'Not many good movies nowadays anyway,' Charlene said tartly. 'It's why I never got one of them devil boxes in my home.'

Axel nodded vaguely, leaning back against the wall. He was so tired. He wondered distractedly if Charlene too had fallen in with the Defenders of Grace – but that was ridiculous, his aunt was from out of town and mostly kept to herself anyway.

There was a knock on the door. 'About time!' barked Charlene, adjusting her polyester blouse. Axel rubbed his eyes, sleepily, then stood up straight as two doctors entered the room in a gust of disinfected air.

'Charlene, hello,' the older doctor said smoothly. He was a tall man in his late fifties, his tight dark curls sprinkled with white. 'And you must be the son – Alex, was it? I'm glad you made it. My name is Leonard McThomas.'

'Axel,' he replied. 'Parker.'

'He's the brain surgeon,' Charlene commented. 'And a good one, too. Your mother's in good hands.' Was she blushing?

'Yes, so glad,' the younger doctor chipped in, practically bouncing up and down with – nerves? enthusiasm? He was a redhead, and looked like he was barely out of high school. 'So glad.'

Axel stared at them both. 'My mom,' he said at last, 'is she going to be OK?'

McThomas smiled sympathetically. 'We'll do everything we can for her,' he said, not answering the question.

'Yes, everything, everything we can,' his assistant repeated. His superior gave him a look, and he blushed.

'What... happened to her?' Axel asked McThomas, somewhat desperately.

The surgeon looked surprised.

'I just got here... I've been abroad,' he explained guiltily.

'And nobody...? Well.' McThomas removed his glasses and polished them on his sleeve, then put them back on. 'Your mother was in a serious car accident,' he began.

'She hit the windscreen,' Charlene contributed, 'went right through.' A look from McThomas silenced her.

'Her brain has suffered quite a serious haemorrhage,' the surgeon continued. 'She's in a deep coma.'

'A very deep coma,' his assistant echoed, like a shadow.

'Can she hear us?' Axel couldn't help asking. He looked over at his mother, at her sweet, pale face bloated beyond recognition, her lovely red hair in bedraggled strands across the pillow. 'Does she know I'm here?'

'I'm afraid not,' McThomas replied. 'In the first few weeks after a brain injury, bleeding or swelling can seriously affect the way your brain works. Most patients are entirely unconscious: they do not respond to visual or aural stimulation, and are unable to communicate or show emotional responses.'

'Of course,' the assistant added, 'comas are rarely permanent. Usually, patients end up in a vegetative state within three to four weeks.'

'Vegetative?' Axel repeated. That sounded bad.

'That's when they're able to respond to some stimuli,' McThomas explained, 'and start showing signs of falling back into a cycle of waking and sleeping. Right now, however, your mother is just sleeping.'

'And you can do something? Wake her up? Make her better?' Axel asked, trying to stop his voice from cracking.

McThomas nodded. 'There's an operation,' he said, spreading his big hands in the air. 'It's risky, of course – anything that requires cutting open a human skull is, as I'm sure you realise.'

'What are the chances of success?' Axel asked. This seemed to be what people asked in the movies.

McThomas was quiet for a moment. 'I don't like to deal in statistics,' he said hesitantly, and Axel felt his stomach drop.

'Is she going to die?' he asked, and this time his voice did break.

'There's a thirty per cent chance she'll recover completely,' McThomas said at last. 'We have many different kinds of therapy available nowadays...'

'Many kinds,' his assistant repeated, like a morbid parrot.

But Axel was already at the door, fleeing the room, crying his heart out.

★ ★ ★ ★

Charlene found him sitting by the vending machine, his head in his hands.

'Oh, Axel,' she said, sinking down into the plastic chair by his side. 'Why don't you go home and get some sleep?'

'Can't,' he moaned. 'Have to stay here with Mom.'

'You need to process,' his aunt said crisply. 'You need some peace and quiet.'

'There's no way I can sleep,' he murmured, hearing the whining tone in his voice and disliking it intensely. *I need to stay here in the hospital*, he thought. *I need to talk to my mom. I need to talk to Safiya – no, Patti-Ann. Oh God, I need to talk to Patti-Ann.*

'Why don't you come fishing with me?'

Axel looked up with a startled laugh, and met Charlene's unblinking stare. She was serious.

'Look, there's no point you sitting in there moping and weeping your eyes out. Your mother can't hear us anyway. You'll be spending plenty of time in that room over the coming weeks, son. Why don't you catch your breath first? And maybe a little catfish on the side.'

The more he considered it, the less extraordinary her suggestion seemed. 'Alright then,' Axel said, standing up slowly, 'let's go fishing.'

They walked down the hotel corridors in a gaze, past the dull framed photographs of flowers, until they emerged into the sun. Axel blinked, his brain frazzled with jetlag. 'What time is it?' he asked.

Charlene checked her watch. 'Just after three,' she said. 'Plenty of time to take a nice break before you head home for supper.'

Home. Patti-Ann would be expecting him back at hers, wouldn't she. He felt the weight of his phone in his pocket like an anvil, and ignored it. They reached Charlene's car, unlocked the doors and climbed in.

As they drove away from the hospital, soothed by the blast of the AC, Axel leaned back in his seat and watched the familiar roads stream by. Sheldon Road and Maple Leaf Avenue, the corner of Morgan and Birchwood, the library. The Lake Salvation Town Hall and the First Lake Salvation Church of Grace. He closed his eyes and rubbed them with his fists.

'Aunt Charlene, how did you find out what happened?' he asked. 'To Mom, I mean.'

'I called the police, of course,' she said tersely. 'Wouldn't hang up till somebody explained to me what the hell was going on. Of course, with your dad gone and all, there was nobody here for her, so I was next of kin.' Seeing Axel's face, she paused, then redirected the stream of her chatter. 'But we're all here now, of course. She's had plenty of friends stopping by, bringing flowers there's not a chance she'll see. Somebody even brought her cake! Can you imagine?' She shook her head.

'I bet that dwarf of an assistant ate it,' he replied bitterly.

Charlene laughed, a short bark. 'He thinks he's so smart, that one. Of course, you can understand how anybody could be awed by somebody like that McThomas.'

Axel was silent. Charlene, taking this as unspoken dissent, continued. 'Now I've met a lot of them charlatan doctors in my time,' she said, shaking her head. 'But Leonard has a reputation. I have not a single doubt he's going to save my little sister. It's a good thing we've got insurance!'

Axel looked over at her balefully.

'What?' Charlene was unfazed. 'Who knows what your family would be doing without it? This kind of operation can cost millions.'

Chastised, Axel nodded. 'You're right, it is good.'

'Good if it works, I guess,' Charlene concluded, with a truly phenomenal lack of a sense of timing.

He sat for a while in silence, thinking of his father. Matt Parker had died of cancer when Axel was just a boy: his last memories of him were vague visions of hospital gowns, flowers and antiseptics. Would it be the same if his mother...? He pushed the thought from his mind. He needed a change of pace, a change of scene.

The car slowed, and Axel focused on his surroundings as shadows striped the bright sunlight on the dashboard: they were in the woods on the northeast side of the lake, he realised, a place he hadn't come since he was a boy.

'Is this where you always fish?' he asked as Charlene threw off her suit jacket and assembled her equipment from the trunk, muttering methodically under her breath. He stepped out into the warm sun under the birch trees. The air smelled green and fresh.

'Rod, reel, tackle, net. Yes, it is. Well, it's one of my favourite spots,' she said, zipping up the bag and slinging it over her shoulder. 'I like the Tawnee River, too, a couple miles up Waco-wards.' She paused in front of the open trunk. 'Your Ma and I used to come here a lot when we were just little,' she added.

'Mom used to fish?' Axel asked, grinning against his will.

Charlene laughed, shaking her head. 'It's hard to imagine it nowadays, isn't it, with her nice dresses and house slippers...'

'Hey!' said Axel. 'She only wears those on the weekend.'

'You sure about that?' her sister teased. Charlene's clothes looked completely incongruous in this muddy setting: her cheap polyester suit, her white blouse and pantyhose. A moment later, she kicked off her heels, wriggled out of her skirt and climbed into a waist-high pair of rubber waders.

For a moment they walked cheerily in the sun, but by the time they reached the water's edge Axel's spirits had sunk again. He was so tired. He needed Patti-Ann, no, Safiya, no...

'Hey,' said Charlene, prodding his shoulder, 'no nodding off on the job. I need you here with me.'

Axel shook her hand off irritably. 'I don't need a babysitter,' he snapped. 'And it's not like catfish are hard to catch.'

His aunt gave a belly-laugh. 'You're sure right about that! But it's a lot of fun all the same.' She reached into her bag and pulled out an extendable pole. 'Here, hold this.' She kept rustling around, explaining as she went. 'Catfish are the easiest, you see, the most satisfying to catch. I take all the newbies catfish fishing, cause they're big, they bite hard, and they taste good.' She gave a predatory smile. You just need to find a nice, deep quiet spot – like right over here, this swimming hole. See how it's full of weeds? Catfish just love to hang around in there. But they can't resist my worms!' She held out a wriggling plastic box, and Axel wrinkled his nose like a kid. 'Come on now, make yourself useful!'

Axel poked the worm onto the hook with a grimace then handed the fishing pole to his aunt. 'You go first,' he said. 'I'll just watch.'

How old was Charlene? Axel found himself wondering. In her late fifties, no doubt, maybe even early sixties. She looked old, far older than her little sister: a thin, outdoorsy presence, skin wrinkled and browned by the sun. She waded a little ways into the muddy water, pulled the fishing pole back over her shoulder, then tossed the line out far. It hit the lake water with barely a tremor. 'Now we wait,' she said with a satisfied smile.

He leaned back against a birch tree trunk, feeling the tension in his shoulders release. 'How often do you go fishing, Aunt Charlene?'

'Oh, a couple times a week in season... I probably catch two or three catfish a week, depending on my luck. Just last week I ended up catching two cottonmouth snakes!'

Axel laughed. 'And you eat all the fish you catch?'

She shrugged, her eyes still on the lake. 'Sometimes I give it away to friends or neighbours. Once or twice I've gone to sell it at the farmer's market for a little extra cash. To tell you the truth, I'm not really in it for the eating part. I just like standing out here in nature, in the quiet.'

Axel was silent for a moment, letting the stillness wash over him. He could hear crickets chirping, and a few birds in the distance, and the sound of the waves lapping at the shore. He could see the appeal.

Then there was a sucking sound in the mud, as Charlene stepped back in excitement. 'They're biting already!' she said. 'You must be bringing me luck.'

Shaking his head, Axel watched as Charlene reeled in her line. He wasn't sure his aunt had brought *him* any luck, but he had to admit she'd brought him a little peace. It felt like his body clock had aligned with his watch, and like his feet had understood they were on Texan soil now. With a sigh, he pulled his phone from his pocket and began to text Patti-Ann, understanding now that he was home.

★ ★ ★ ★

Patti-Ann had wanted to meet back at the hospital, so Charlene had driven him back there – albeit unwillingly. 'You need to get yourself some sleep!' she muttered, her eyes on the road, but Axel was making his own decisions now, and setting his own schedule. Patti-Ann had been at the hospital every day, looking after his mother: now he needed to look after her in return. It was the responsible thing to do.

Entering the pale blue front lobby, with its antiseptic smell, Axel paused in the neon light. It was starting to get dark outside.

'Just call me if you need anything,' Charlene said one last time, and he nodded.

'Thanks, Aunt Charlene.'

As soon as he'd seen Patti-Ann, he would go home and get some rest.

His fiancée was sitting in the corner of the lobby waiting for him, her hands twisting in her lap. She leapt up when he came through the door, her eyes wide, her face drawn.

'Where you been?'

Axel pulled her into his arms, overcome with guilt. 'I…' *I went on a fishing trip. I needed some time to think. I came here as soon as I could.* 'I'm here now,' he finally said, and he felt Patti-Ann's arms tighten around him.

'I needed you here,' she said fiercely, pulling back to look him in the face, but her eyes were filled with tears.

'I know,' he said, overcome with gratitude for her presence, her love. Who was he to push this marvellous, caring woman away?

'The caterers need our final decisions for the menu, and the pearls for my wedding dress have arrived – you know, the ones my Dad had flown in from the Arabian Gulf – but the seamstress doesn't know what to do with them, do you know they don't have holes in them? And on top of that I've had to handle all this darn hospital paperwork, and—'

Walking with her as if in a trance, Axel felt a knot in his stomach tightening. He'd been mistaken. He didn't want to marry this woman.

'— they need your signature on a whole bunch of stuff, as next of kin, so I'm so glad you're here now, honey, so you can handle all this.' She slipped her hand into his and practically pulled him down the corridor towards his mother's room.

'Do we need to do the paperwork now?' he asked, hesitating. 'My brain's pretty fried.'

Patti-Ann turned towards him, and though her voice stayed sweet, there was a sharp glint in her eye. 'Your flight got in four hours ago,' she said. 'Where were you all that time?'

Axel sighed. 'I went fishing. Aunt Charlene... thought it'd be good for me to get out of the hospital for a while.'

Patti-Ann stared at him in disbelief. 'Get out of the hospital?' she repeated. 'I've been here for hours every day, trapped in that stinking little room! And you know I love your Mom, but it's really creepy, the way she's there and not there at the same time.'

'I know, honey,' he said, trying to placate her, squeezing her hand. 'I really appreciate everything you've done.'

She smiled a little, as if against her will. 'Well OK, then. But I really need you to sign a bunch of things.'

'OK,' he nodded. 'Let's go find the doctors.'

As he walked down the corridor, he felt as if he were shouldering a mantle of responsibility. This is my life, he told himself. This is where I belong.

CHAPTER TWENTY-THREE

A week after his return from Istanbul, Axel had lost any sense of pride or joy in being back home. As the sun crossed from one side of the hospital window to the other and then disappeared, days bled into each other. He stayed at his mother's bedside for the full length of visiting hours, spending whole hours just staring at her, willing her to wake up – partly out of a stinging sense of guilt, and partly to avoid Patti-Ann. It was growing increasingly difficult to hide his distaste for his fiancée: even now that he was sleeping back at his mother's house and spending most of the day at the hospital, somehow she always seemed to be around, asking about salmon rolls or profiteroles or lace tablecloths. The wedding had become her entire *raison d'être* – just as, it occurred to Axel, his mother's illness had become his. If his mother would just wake up, he kept telling himself, he would know the answer to his questions. He would tell her about Safiya, and she would know what was best for him. He would know what to do about Patti-Ann, and how to do it. Everything would become clear.

On the second day, he'd received a simple text message from Safiya – *are you all right?* – but hadn't replied. What could he say? After they'd kissed in Istanbul, for those few blessed moments in the wind and sun, speeding across the waves, it had felt as if a whole new life was opening up for him. Now that life was put on hold, or had perhaps been cancelled, he couldn't tell. He was needed here, that was all he knew. This was no time to indulge in a fairy tale, or to break what wasn't broken. And so he focused all of his energy on caring for his mother: or at least, he sat at her bedside, not even reading or listening to music.

This Sunday morning had started out just like the others: a quick cream cheese bagel and a coffee on the road, then settling into his chair for a long wait. He spent a lot of time watching the light settling on his mother's auburn hair – how had he never noticed the tiny silver streaks? The bruises were fading ever so slightly, and changing colour. He jumped, his contemplative reverie interrupted by a knock on the door and Patti-Ann's brusque arrival.

'I've brought breakfast!' she trilled, setting a grease-stained paper bag on the corner table, along with two coffees.

'I've already—' Axel began, before interrupting himself. What was the point? 'Thanks, sweetie,' he said, leaning over to take a sugar-glazed doughnut from the bag.

'I have an idea,' Patti-Ann said. Her eyes were shining. 'Why don't we go for a walk?'

Axel looked up wearily from the doughnut in his hand. 'A walk?' he said. 'Why?'

'You need some fresh air,' Patti-Ann said briskly. 'Now, I know I gave you trouble for turning up late to the hospital, but I didn't mean that you should spend your every waking hour here to make up for it. Your mother can't even tell you're here.'

Axel glared at her – he couldn't help it.

'What? It's true.'

He sighed. 'Where do you want to go?' he asked.

'How about Lovers' Lane?' she asked innocently.

'Lovers' Lane? There's a Lovers' Lane in Lake Salvation?'

'Yeah! Just the other side of Blackbird Alley.'

'Where's Blackbird Alley?'

'Just behind the forest. You know, the other side of the lake!'

'I have no idea what you're talking about,' Axel said blankly.

Patti-Ann shrugged. 'I used to go there all the time when I was a girl scout. Come on, it'll be nice!'

As he let himself be led out of the room, Axel's mind was spinning. Lovers' Lane? Did she want to make out with him in a car, like teenagers? They had a bed for that – although he'd been studiously avoiding that sort of scenario. Was Patti-Ann really so desperate for sex that she would lure him to the woods for it?

'Come on, silly,' she said, climbing into her car. 'I'll drive you back here afterwards.'

After what? Axel buckled his seatbelt with a sinking sensation in his stomach.

★ ★ ★ ★

Patti-Ann drove straight through the centre of town, and the knot in Axel's stomach began to relax as they neared the outskirts of town and the lake. So it hadn't been some kind of trick after all. He stared out the window, unseeing, until the car began to slow – then sat bolt upright. Surrounded by a low cloth fence, a huge white tent had been erected near the edge of the forest, not very far from where he'd been with Charlene a week previously. There were two men in suits guarding the entrance, and he could hear singing inside. Several neatly typed placards were resting against the walls, as if ready to be used in a demonstration: SAVE OUR CHURCH, one of them read. Others were printed: PRAISE GAZI THE MAGI! and LAKE SALVATION DEFENDERS OF GRACE.

'Patti-Ann!' He couldn't believe it. 'Why the… Why on earth have you brought me here?'

She smiled. 'Well, we're here now,' she said, not answering his question. Her confidence faltered as she saw his expression. 'Come on… Just for a bit!'

'No! No way. It's out of the question. I don't want to hear any of that hogwash.'

'How do you know it's hogwash if you've never been to one of the meetings? This is a really big deal. People come from out of state to see these!'

'I've watched the videos,' Axel said. 'It's a sect. Like the Ku Klux Klan.'

'It is not a sect!'

'Just… get me out of here.'

Patti-Ann swallowed. 'All right,' she said. 'Cards on the table. Just… please hear me out before you make your mind up. There's this healer—'

She held up her hand, stopping Axel from interrupting. 'This healer from the Holy Land. From Palestine, I guess, or Israel, I don't know. I know you don't believe in this sort of stuff, but I've been doing a lot of reading, there's so much evidence… A real miracle worker! And with your Mom being in the state she's in, well it can't do any harm, can it?'

Axel's glare softened as he understood Patti-Ann's reasoning. 'You want me to see this healer… to help Mom?'

She nodded earnestly. 'Look, I know you don't want to be here, it's why I said…' She faltered. 'Just come inside. Come see the guy. We can leave in… twenty minutes if you don't like it.'

'Fifteen.'

Patti-Ann switched off the ignition, unbuckled her seatbelt and stepped from the car. She walked briskly towards the entry to the tent, waving to the guards.

'Hi guys!' she said. 'I'm sorry we're so late!'

Trailing behind, Axel didn't hear the rest of what she said, only saw the two men glance up and nod. Then Patti-Ann turned, grinned, and beckoned him towards the tent. 'Welcome to the Tabernacle,' she whispered.

The inside of the tent was enormous: Axel felt dwarfed as he stepped inside, gazing up at the immense flat ceiling, stretched between long pillars of wood, and falling down either side towards the ground where it was pinned. It must have taken them weeks to build this, he thought, taking in the raised rostrum, the silk hangings in purple and gold. Another thought crossed his mind, making him giggle: he was far from the Protestant aesthetic here. Memories of his conversations with Safiya came flooding back to him so strongly he had to close his eyes for a moment. How he wished she could be here with him, witnessing this madness!

Patti-Ann grabbed his hand and pulled him in, wanting to move towards the middle of the tent, where a man was speaking, his voice echoing and crackling from loudspeakers in the corner. But Axel pulled back, towards a row of empty seats close to the door. Patti-Ann relented, and they snuck into place.

'Praise the Lord!' the crowd roared, so loud that Axel jumped.

Looking around the room, he was quite overwhelmed. There were two doors to the marquee, one on either side, and room to seat probably two hundred people. Vast banners hung down from the ceiling, embroidered with Gazi's name in enormous gold letters. There was a large table spread with books and brochures for sale, and several baskets for donations. It was crowded, too – Patti-Ann must have been telling the truth about people coming from far and wide: there was no way there were this many Defenders of Grace just in Lake Salvation. Unless, Axel reflected wryly, he'd missed some kind of apocalypse during his time in hospital.

Patti-Ann jabbed him in the ribs. 'Pay attention!' she hissed.

Axel focused his attention on the speaker, a short man in a white robe with a microphone wired to his head. He sighed. 'Who is this joker?'

'Don't you sigh!' Patti-Ann hissed, loud enough to attract a few head-turns from their neighbours.

'Sorry, sorry,' he murmured.

One of the head-turners, a man with a full head of white hair, didn't turn back, but instead kept on glaring, jabbing a finger at a flyer in his hand. Axel eventually understood that he was meant to take it, and did, nodding with an expression meant to convey gratitude.

GAZI THE MAGE! the brochure proclaimed in colourful text: *Worker of Miracles, come to the USA from the sacred deserts of the Levant! Descendant of the people of Nazareth!*

Great, thought Axel, Jesus's second cousin twice removed.

'Listen!' Patti-Ann whispered once more, and catching the despairing note in her voice, Axel relented.

'I have come to bring light to your life,' Gazi was saying, 'and to answer your questions. I have come to pull you out of the darkness of the misery of your lives, here in the beautiful state of Texas. I want everyone who leaves this tent to feel purified and new. I want everyone to feel like they deserve a miracle.' He gave a bow, as applause crossed the room in waves.

Axel had to admit that this sounded appealing, even to him.

'And I want to thank my dear friend Ichabod Potts,' Gazi added, 'thanks to whose generous sponsorship I have been able to come here, to Lake Salvation, today.'

Potts, who was standing to the side of the rostrum like a bodyguard, gave a gracious wave. His face looked even redder than usual. Any momentary forgiveness Axel might have been feeling towards the whole charade faded away into nothing.

'We all suffer the consequences of our sins daily,' Gazi continued. 'All the modern ailments: depression, ulcers, heart disease, cancers, all the way down to nut allergies... Do you ever wonder why nobody talks about them in the Middle Ages, or in pioneering days, and certainly not in the Bible? It's because we were healthier in the days of yore. Now we've all gone soft and sinful, our sin rotting us from the inside out like a disease. Our kidneys, our livers, our brains and hearts and lungs – I can help you heal them. All I ask in return is that when you leave the Tabernacle, you make a small contribution to Mr Potts's collection box, so that the First Lake Salvation Church of Grace can continue its good works.'

A smattering of applause filled the tent. Axel did not clap.

'But enough about me,' Gazi continued, standing in the centre of a tent dedicated to him, under banners emblazoned with his name. 'Now it's time for you to come to the forefront. To the front of the tent! Come now, step into the spotlight: it is time for you to be healed!' His voice took on a thunderous intonation. 'So do not fear, for I am with you; do not be dismayed, for I am your God. I will strengthen you and help you; I will uphold you with my righteous right hand. Isaiah 41:10, and today, Gazi,' — he checked his watch— 'at eleven thirty.'

Potts barked with laughter, and the room followed, nervously at first, then more genuinely. Gazi held up his hand and continued: 'My compatriot Jesus was well known for his healing powers. They have long run in our family. Generations of lepers and blind men have come to us, the epileptic and the paralysed. Today, you who come up to me, you will go down in history too.'

'Compatriot?' Axel couldn't stop himself from muttering. 'Where is this guy even from? Egypt? Iran?'

Patti-Ann swung towards him and crushed her finger into her lips. 'He's from the HOLY LAND,' she mouthed very slowly, before turning back towards Gazi, rapt.

'Now, can I have my first volunteer?'

Hands shot up all over the audience. Axel looked back down at his pamphlet, embarrassed for everyone present. *In many of the ancient languages of the Holy Land,* the text read, *Gazi means conquerer. Conquerer of sins! Let Gazi conquer all your sins, so that you can move forward, free from your mistakes, free from the weight of your past.*

'You there!' Startled, Axel looked up, but Gazi was pointing at a blonde woman a few rows in front of him. 'Yes you, in the blue sweater. Why don't you come on up here?'

'Oh sure,' Axel muttered, 'the prettiest girl in the whole audience.'

Patti-Ann didn't even look over at him.

Gazi motioned the girl up to the stage, and handed her a microphone. 'What's your name, lovely young creature?'

Axel's skin prickled.

The girl murmured something inaudible, and Gazi encouraged her to hold the microphone closer to her lips. 'Elizabeth,' she said at last.

'Elizabeth! Can we give Elizabeth a warm welcome?'

The crowd erupted in cheers and applause.

'All right, Elizabeth. So tell me, why did you raise your hand?'

'To confess my sins.'

Gazi threw his head back and laughed. 'I'm not a priest,' he said. Elizabeth turned bright red. 'I'm a miracle worker!' he corrected her. 'I'm here to conquer your sins, to make them go away.'

Elizabeth nodded earnestly.

'So go on,' Gazi said, lowering his voice conspiratorially. 'You're safe here: why don't you go on ahead and confess your sins?'

'Well,' Elizabeth began hesitantly, 'when I was six years old I stole scissors from my brother.'

Gazi nodded. 'That's nothing. What else?'

'When I was eleven,' she said, as if reciting memorised text, 'I had to kill a rabbit at summer camp.'

'Did you eat the rabbit?' asked Gazi.

'No,' said Elizabeth. 'We were just hunting. I still feel bad, though. I still think about—'

'Right,' said Gazi. 'Go on, then. Don't hold back. Tell us all your most serious sins.'

'When I was fourteen I lied to my mother.'

'Ooh,' said Gazi, and a few people laughed. Elizabeth looked mortified. 'What did you lie about?'

Elizabeth moved the microphone away from her mouth and said something to Gazi, but he shook his head. 'Yes, tell us!'

'I lied about a dream that I had,' she said.

'About what?' Gazi prompted.

'About a boy. A boy in my class.' Her face was crimson, and her hands were shaking.

'Good girl!' said Gazi, although he seemed disappointed. Were the sinners of Lake Salvation not sinful enough for his taste? Axel wondered in amusement. 'Unburden yourself to us! Every sin you confess here today is a sin that will no longer weigh on your conscience. You will be free! You will be healed!'

'Healed!' the crowd echoed.

Gazi perked up at the sound of the voices. 'What did you say?' he asked theatrically. 'What did you say Elizabeth was going to be?'

'HEALED!' the crowd cried out.

It was quite intimidating.

'Every one of us is a sinner,' Gazi began, giving up and turning away from Elizabeth, his eyes sweeping the crowd. 'Every one of us gives in to temptation from time to time. Every one of us is dirty, and every one of us is ashamed when we stray. If we are to be freed from a life of sin, we must confess, so that we can be healed and move on. This is the only way to progress from a life of sin into a clean and holy life. Only through confession and healing can we purified.'

Elizabeth was crying now.

'How old are you, child?' Gazi asked her very gently.

'Nineteen,' she sniffled.

'There is still plenty of time for you to return to the way of God,' he said. Pushing the wire of his microphone down from his mouth, he put his hands on the girl's shoulders and turned her towards him. He was murmuring to her now, as she looked up at him with wide eyes, her shoulders trembling. Then she began nodding, and her answers became audible: 'Yes, Gazi. Yes.'

Gazi pushed his microphone back up in front of his lips. 'Now Elizabeth, I want you to go home and think about what happened today. Tomorrow morning, I want you to take a hot bath, and a cold bath in the evening. After the cold bath, you'll pray and read thirty pages of the Bible. The next morning you'll take a hot bath and read another thirty pages. And so on and so forth, until you've finished the whole Bible. You'll feel so good. You'll feel so cleansed.' He paused, and raised his voice again. 'Daughter, your faith has healed you. Go in peace and be freed from your suffering.'

Axel was pretty sure this was something Jesus had said. He rolled his eyes.

'Any other sinners in the audience?' Gazi was saying, but Axel had already stood up and was walking towards the door.

★ ★ ★ ★

'Axel!'

Axel continued to walk, speeding up his pace. He didn't want to speak to Patti-Ann. He didn't want to see her face.

'Axel Bartholomew Parker!' Patti-Ann was yelling now, ignoring the men at the door of the tent making shushing noises. 'Don't you dare walk away from me!'

Reluctantly, Axel slowed and turned around. 'What?' he asked sharply. 'What do you want, *Patti-Ann Boswell*?'

Patti-Ann stopped in her tracks and stood panting for a moment, her bosom heaving, rage and disappointment chasing across her face.

'I said I'd come in for fifteen minutes,' Axel continued.

'You didn't even see anything!' Patti-Ann pleaded. 'That wasn't even a real miracle, that was just a warm-up, that girl didn't have any—'

'That poor girl,' said Axel, 'is wasting her time, and ours. That man, your Gazi, is a bone fide charlatan. Potts should be ashamed of himself, putting on a show like that, raking in the cash. It's sick.'

Patti-Ann's face was crimson. 'You're so cynical, you wouldn't know magic if it happened right in front of your face. Can't you just tell he's a holy man, the way he's dressed, the way he talks? I mean, didn't you see what just happened? That was a real, live miracle. He saved that girl. He could save your mother.'

Axel took a step towards his fiancée, his own anger rising to match hers. 'Don't you dare let that man anywhere near my mother. You don't have the right.'

'Why, you'd be so lucky... Even if I dragged Gazi to the hospital to see your mother, and he woke her up from her coma, and she was so happy, you'd pretend it had nothing to do with religion. You're just a sad, sad man, Axel.'

The pair were briefly interrupted by a group of men emerging from the tent for a smoke. 'This is just what America needs,' one of them was muttering gruffly to his neighbour. 'It's all going to the dogs, what with political correctness and all these Mexicans everywhere...'

'Not to mention the gays,' another chimed in.

'The South needs to band together,' his moustachioed friend agreed.

Axel shook his head and lowered his voice. 'Look at the kinds of people who come here,' he hissed at Patti-Ann.

'What, you think you're better than everybody all of a sudden, just cause you spend a couple days in Europe? That's Alan, from the garage!

You get your car fixed over there! And Luke, he volunteers weekends at the library. What's wrong with them "kinds" of people?'

'They're suckers. Every one of them. And it's not just their political views, it's the way Gazi's getting them all riled up. He's just putting on a show for money! It's like... a pantomime of religion! There's nothing real there at all. Everybody in there's just a bunch of fools. Even if they work at the library.'

Patti-Ann narrowed her eyes, and began using her fingers to mark sneer quotes in the air. 'Who's the one writing a book about the soul, huh? How come some people interested in religion are "scientists" or "philosophers," like your little Muslim friend over there, and some are fools, huh?'

She had a point. 'If by over there you mean Turkey, and if by interested in religion you mean a Quranic scholar...' Axel ran out of breath and energy at the same time. Also, he had no desire to talk about Safiya. Not here, not now, not with Patti-Ann this angry. But he couldn't calm down, even though he knew he should. 'OK, maybe you're right, Patti-Ann. Touché. Maybe it's not religion I have a problem with – maybe it's the Defenders of Grace. Maybe it's the embezzling of funds and lying to good, honest people. Maybe it's the computer hackings and the violent graffiti.'

Patti-Ann was staring at him. 'Are you saying you think the Defenders are worse than terrorists?'

'I don't want to have an argument about this,' Axel said firmly. 'And no, that's not what I'm saying.'

'Look, sweetie,' Patti-Ann said after a moment, clearly trying to deescalate the situation, 'I don't want to have an argument either. I'm sorry you hated it so much. But don't you see, Axel, even if it is just a show, he's giving these people hope?'

This was the final straw. 'You want to give me hope, Patti-Ann? Give me some space to breathe. Stop nagging me about the wedding all the livelong day. Stop trying to have sex with me every five minutes when I want to sleep. Don't trick me into going to some stupid show with some lie about Lovers' Lane.'

'I didn't…'

'Why don't you go back inside,' he interrupted, harshly, 'for another dose of hope? I can walk home from here.'

Patti-Ann physically shrank back from him. The three men were staring at them. Axel swallowed as he turned on his heel and began walking away from the Tabernacle. Had he gone too far? But it was too late: there was no going back. Better to leave things on this note and enjoy a few blessed days of his fiancée sulking. Maybe it would give him some time to think.

CHAPTER TWENTY-FOUR

Walking fiercely away from the Tabernacle and the confrontation with Patti-Ann, Axel found himself following the edge of the lake north instead of heading back into the centre of town. He needed to think. At first, he thought he might just walk back to the spot where he'd been fishing with Charlene, but that wasn't far enough. For a moment, the wild thought of wading right into the lake crossed his mind – a purification! – but he knew the waters were murky and warm. No, he needed another kind of absolution entirely, he realised, as his footsteps took him to the far end of Lakeshore Drive. He needed to talk to Professor Bohmann.

As he neared the front door, he slowed. Was this visit too impetuous? Should he have called first? The professor was still in recovery, after all. But before he could make up his mind either way, the door swung open.

'Well, the stars do align!' Bohmann was beaming. 'I was just talking about you!'

Relieved, Axel gave the professor a hug. 'Who with?' he asked curiously. 'It wasn't Patti-Ann, was it?'

Bohmann laughed. 'Oh no, fear not. I was just talking to Helmut on Skype – Professor Schmidt Hennessey, I mean.'

'Oh! That's great! Were you talking about the book?'

'Do bears poop in the woods?' Bohmann was clearly in a jovial mood. 'Yes, indeed. We were talking about "The Unseen and the Unknown" – that's the working title.'

'Chapter three,' Axel said happily.

Bohmann closed the door behind him, and the two retired to the study.

'Coffee?' the professor offered. 'Or maybe a spot of lunch?'

'I've had too much coffee already,' Axel replied, 'not to mention all the energy I seem to have generated out of sheer anger at the Defenders of Grace.'

'The Defenders?' Bohmann looked worried.

'Oh, not like that,' Axel hastened to reassure him. 'No, nothing personal. It's just... Well, Patti-Ann dragged me to one of their idiotic meetings.'

Bohmann wrinkled his nose. 'The Tabernacle?'

'Yeah. The Tabernacle. Have you been over there? They're putting on quite a show.'

'Is that where you came from?'

Axel nodded.

'On foot?'

Axel looked sheepish, but Bohmann only smiled. 'Ah, the energy of the young. Well, in that case, I'll definitely find us a bite to eat.'

He led the way towards the luminous kitchen. 'I read about it in the paper,' he added. 'The Tabernacle, I mean. Gabe the Mage or something ridiculous like that, is that right?'

Axel nodded. 'Gazi. He... It wasn't what I was expecting.'

'What were you expecting?' Bohmann opened his ancient fridge and began rummaging around inside like a rodent.

'I've watched some of the YouTube videos,' Axel explained, 'so I was prepared for that sort of thing: you know, a ridiculous performance, with some audience member faking a broken leg, the spotlight dancing everywhere...' He reached out to receive the food Bohmann was extracting from the shelves: a block of cheddar, Miracle Whip, a pack of sliced turkey breast, a half-eaten bag of grapes.

'Yes,' Bohmann said, nodding without turning around. 'The slapstick, the performance, the repetitive phraseology... It's fascinating, really.'

'Riling the crowd up into a frenzy... But this was somehow worse,' Axel continued. 'He called this poor young woman up on stage, and we all had to watch her desperately seeking some sins to confess that would be interesting enough for Gazi, the celebrity. It was like he was disappointed she wasn't sinful enough! He had to squeeze her like a lemon. Not very Jesus-like, if you ask me.' He set the food down on the formica kitchen table.

Bohmann laughed sadly, closing the fridge. 'A friend of mine went to one of those meetings, you know, for the... anthropological experience. I remember him telling a story once about Gazi having quite the opposite problem: some tattooed convict, I believe, coming up front and confessing all his crimes in gory detail... Pretty sure the Mage didn't have to squeeze that lemon very much; more like trying to contain him! He probably rushed right through it: OK, twenty hail Marys and off to bed!'

Axel laughed. 'I guess he's playing it safe now, then.'

Bohmann retrieved a loaf of sliced wholegrain bread and untwisted the bag, then set out two mismatched floral plates. They sat down at the table and began assembling sandwiches.

Axel couldn't set the subject aside. 'I mean, it's bad enough tricking people, preying on their religious sensibilities, but all of this for money? You should have seen the collection baskets, huge things everywhere!'

Bohmann shook his head. 'I've heard that in some places, they call out the amounts being donated over the loudspeakers, to shame people into giving more.'

'Unbelievable,' said Axel, angrily spreading Miracle Whip on a piece of bread.

'And Patti-Ann, what did she think of it all?' Bohmann's tone was neutral, but his words were further fuel to the fire of Axel's rage. 'Was she enraptured?'

'Yeah.' He mimicked his fiancée's voice, hating himself as he did so. '"Look at these modest faces, glowing with light! Why do we even need doctors or politicians or scientists or journalists? This is the truth, the only truth!"'

'You sound bitter,' Bohmann observed, unnecessarily. He paused, as if trying to find the most tactful way of putting his question. 'How are you two?' he asked at last.

'It's like she's gone off the deep end with all this God stuff. I mean, she's just trying to help – well, she frames it as trying to help my mom…' Axel shook his head, overcome with guilt. 'The worst part is, she's being lovely, keeping me company at the hospital, making me meals… OK, the meals are awful, and I'd frankly rather be alone with my mother, and she keeps talking about the most ridiculous details of our damn wedding…'

Bohmann's lips twisted into a thoughtful expression, but he said nothing.

'I mean, is this how it's going to be now, the two of us, in our lives, in our marriage? At loggerheads, arguing all the time, driving each other crazy?'

'I have this strange image of you two as parakeets,' Bohmann replied. 'The most beautiful birds, a perfect match in pictures, but always knocking their pretty green heads together.'

Axel laughed, an unpleasant sound. 'It just feels like I'm the one ruining things.'

'I highly doubt that to be the case. When there are troubles in a couple, they are very rarely just one party's fault.'

Axel let out a long sigh, staring down at his sandwich. 'I mean, I can see why she's drawn to this Gazi the Mage nonsense. I wish there was a magical way to wake my mom up too, you know? Some nights when I stay late at the hospital, I find myself… almost praying. Well, to her, not to some God, but just thinking over and over *please wake up, please wake up,* like a spell.'

Seeing Axel's eyes were filled with tears, Bohmann reached across and squeezed his hand. 'It's the hardest thing in the world, seeing our loved ones ill or in pain.'

'I guess what I'm saying is that I understand why people turn to religion in these sorts of circumstances. I just… It seems to offer so much comfort! And Patti-Ann, I know this sense of community really appeals to her too – I had to tell her not to let them bring over casseroles.' He laughed. 'I mean, casseroles, to someone who might not wake up or ever eat again!'

'People want to help,' Bohmann said evenly.

Axel nodded, trying to keep the tears back. He picked up his sandwich and bit in, and chewed for a while in silence. 'Professor Bohmann,' he said at last, 'I hope this isn't an insulting question, but don't you ever wonder if religion just seems too good to be true? Like it answers all our most profound fears, the deepest unknowns of the human condition: why are we alive here on earth, where do we go when we die, are we alone, do we have a purpose...'

'I hope working on my book has prompted this examination, rather than just your mother's illness!' Bohmann teased very gently, and Axel smiled. 'Speaking seriously, however, the question of the function of religion in our daily lives is one every believer must wrestle with. Personally, I don't find these questions invalidate any of what religion has to offer me: I think questioning should lie at the very heart of any belief. Blind, unquestioning belief leads you to end up dumping all your life savings into Ichabod Potts's collection basket, or drinking the Kool Aid.'

Axel frowned. 'Kool Aid?'

'My, my,' said Bohmann. 'Is that before your time? Jonestown?' He shook his head. 'It's a figure of speech,' he explained, 'relating back to a very horrible thing that happened to a cult in the late seventies – the Peoples Temple, I believe they were called. There were hundreds and hundreds of people, all following this crazy leader. One day, he asked all of them to kill themselves by drinking cyanide mixed in with Kool Aid.'

'And they did it?' Axel was horrified.

'They did. But be careful, my boy, before you go leaping to any conclusions: there is an immense difference between a religion and a cult.'

'Of course.' Axel stared at his half-eaten sandwich. 'Well, I sure hope the Defenders of Grace don't get up to anything like that.'

It was Bohmann's turn to laugh awkwardly. They finished their sandwiches in silence.

'I suppose,' Axel said, wiping his mouth, 'it's important to wonder what draws people to any of this. It's almost like it's a human instinct, to want to believe, to want to belong. I mean, maybe the professors who disagree with you, the hardcore scientists, maybe they're just part of a cult too. It's just a more socially acceptable one.'

'Not in Lake Salvation!' Bohmann shook his head. 'There's some truth in what you're saying, Axel. Especially the complicated dynamic between the two facets of belief – the personal and the social. Even the political.'

'It's like everybody has something missing,' Axel murmured, almost to himself.

'And what, my boy,' Bohmann asked very gently, 'do you think you are missing?'

'I don't know,' Axel replied honestly. 'It's just, for the first time, I think I understand why people go looking for it.'

Bohmann pushed his chair back from the table, stood up and picked up their plates. 'This sounds like a discussion for the study, to me. Why don't I make us some coffee?'

* * * *

It was nice to be back in Professor Bohmann's library, Axel reflected, leaning back in the comfortable armchair. It was a quiet, reflective space – a very different kind of quiet to the chill of his mother's hospital room. This room felt warm and welcoming.

He let his eyes roam over the bookshelves, feeling a familiar pang at the sight of the childhood photograph of Kyle. But this time, past the National Geographics, he noticed a new section: *Modern Studies: Ideas of the Soul. The Book of the Soul: Rational Spirituality for the Twenty-first Century. Spirit, Soul, and Flesh,* by E.D. Burton.

Entering the room with a tray of coffee mugs, Bohmann followed his gaze.

'Oh, a separate line of enquiry,' he said, setting down the tray on the table. 'Something I spent a lot of time thinking about, years ago. Before I began working on this book.'

'But you were planning on going to Safiya... Dr Midana's talk?'

'I was planning on attending the conference,' Bohmann corrected him, a twinkle in his eye. 'Yes, I suppose I still like to keep an eye on modern scholarship concerning the soul. But I've recently focused most of my energy on the Hand of God.'

'The soul, though,' Axel said, almost interrupting. Mentioning Safiya had made him light-headed: he didn't want to change the topic.

Bohmann smiled. 'Do you really want me to drone on about this?'

'I do,' said Axel, honestly.

'My, you are in an introspective mood! Well, I suppose it all ties in to our earlier conversation – what people think their inner life is composed of, or is missing, and the ways in which they conceive of the form it might take... The Hebrew and Greek words for the soul carry the same meaning: "nepesh" and "psyche" both mean 'breath.' Of course, much in the same way the word is used today, those terms were used to mean the inner nature of man: his personality, even his personhood. His essence.'

'But separate from the body.' There was something immensely comforting about listening to Bohmann switch into lecturing mode: Axel didn't want it to end.

'Or inseparable from the body, depending on your religious views. But certainly... intertwined with the body, yes. The term psyche in particular could be taken to simply mean life, in which case the soul could not be said to exist after a person's death. But in most historical and modern conceptions, the soul is imagined to extend beyond the body. Beyond life.'

Axel nodded enthusiastically. 'In Muslim culture as well, if I've understood Safiya's talks correctly.'

Bohmann nodded. 'An important element of the definition of the soul in both the Biblical and the Quranic sense is that this spirit is often seen as belonging to God, proceeding from God, pertaining to God. God is the one who... bestows a soul upon a body. I believe the Arabic word for soul or spirit is "ruh".'

Closing his eyes, Axel could only vaguely remember Safiya's talk at the Blue Mosque: the light filtering down, and the sound of pigeons; something about flames and fluidity... 'Safiya explained it so well, this idea that the human soul and the Holy Spirit were in fact one and the same. I just can't quite recall the wording.'

'Well, it's a good thing the two of you are working together, then!'

Axel swallowed, and didn't dare to look up, but he could feel the professor's expectant – even hopeful – gaze.

'Professor,' he said at last, 'there's something I'm not telling you, about the situation with Patti-Ann.'

Bohmann beamed. 'Go on, then.'

'It's... Safiya.'

The professor's smile grew even warmer. 'I really don't want to spoil this moment by saying "I knew it," but... I knew it!'

Axel smiled against his will. 'Something happened between us in Istanbul.' Was he blushing? 'We kissed.'

'Did you tell her you love her?' Bohmann was leaning forward in his seat like an anxious child.

'I didn't have time. We'd just kissed in the garden, then we got back on the boat – we hadn't even spoken! And I picked up the phone and there was Patti-Ann, telling me my mother had had a terrible accident.'

'You had quite a day,' Bohmann remarked.

'Yeah.'

'I take it you've not spoken to Patti-Ann about any of this?'

'I've not spoken to anyone about it. Except you, right now.' In despair, he picked up the mug of hot coffee and drained it. 'I feel like I'm trapped. Like I'm shuttling back and forth between this innocent, intellectual Eastern love and this vapid Western... hick love. Diner love. Church love.'

'So you're sick of Texas, or just sick of Patti-Ann?'

'I don't know. It's like they're all mixed up together. And maybe this is a terrible thing to say, of course I hope she'll recover, but if my mother didn't make it... I wonder what would be keeping me here.'

Bohmann nodded slowly. 'Well, you're the right age to spread your wings, cast off your shackles, all that.' There was a thoughtful silence. 'And Safiya, you have news from her? Does she know... How does she...'

'I've not dealt with any of it,' Axel said unhappily. 'I just don't know what to do. What am I supposed to do, jilt my fiancée when my mother's in a coma?'

'Don't be petulant,' Bohmann rebuked him. 'You're talking about other people's feelings, other people's whole lives. You're so worried about upsetting Patti-Ann; how do you think Safiya feels, with you vanishing without a word?'

Axel stared at the floor. 'I miss her,' he mumbled.

'Listen, Axel, you can't just keep people in limbo because you're too cowardly to do the right thing!' Bohmann's tone softened as he saw Axel's face crumple. 'I'm not yelling at you. Well, maybe I am. It's just too hard to watch a young man like you wasting his life because he's afraid to act.' He reached across the coffee table and gave his protégé's arm a squeeze. 'I just want you to realise that the situation's not an impossible one to resolve. Don't stay frozen by your inability to decide while time goes ticking by. I mean, haven't you made your choice already?'

Slowly, Axel nodded. 'I have. I know I love Safiya. I know what I have to do. I just don't know how to do it. Every time I see Patti-Ann she's making me a casserole or looking after my mom or worse, talking about our wedding.'

'Well why don't you start with Safiya, then? I can understand that the timing is a little difficult where Patti-Ann is concerned, but not Safiya. Why are you causing her pain?'

Axel blinked rapidly, waves of new guilt rushing over him. 'I don't... I didn't think...'

'I can see that, my boy.' Bohmann gave an avuncular laugh. 'Let me tell you about another interesting paradox concerning the soul: depending on which idea you follow, the soul is regarded either as a moral force or as the seat of the feelings, desires, affections and aversions of a human life – much like the heart is in popular culture nowadays.' He paused and took a dainty sip of coffee. 'It seems to me, Axel, that Safiya has taken over your soul.'

'She has,' he murmured, his heart aching. 'She has.'

'Well what are you waiting for, then? Call her!'

'Just like that?'

'Well don't you want to?'

'Yes! I just… But…'

'No more buts.' Bohmann sat back in his chair, satisfied, and picked up his cup of coffee. 'Besides, I'd really like to meet her.'

CHAPTER TWENTY-FIVE

Axel was pacing back and forth beneath the neon lights of Dallas Fort Worth Airport. Outside, the sky was orange and blue from the setting sun, and every plane that dipped out of it with a roar and a flash of lights made his heart jump. Was it her? Was she here? Maybe she'd missed her plane, stayed in Istanbul, stayed in New York. Maybe she'd changed her mind. He drank deeply from his iced chai latte, grimacing at the sweetness. His pale reflection in the window, flickering with clinical yellow-green light, reminded him uncomfortably of his mother's. At last, at last, the right sequence of letters and numbers crackled from the loudspeakers, and Axel rushed to the arrivals gate.

A long stream of strangers emerged first, but Axel barely noticed them, so focused was he on finding her. *Safiya, Safiya, Safiya.* There she was: her face drawn, her jacket wrinkled, her lips curved into a wide smile. More beautiful than anyone he'd ever seen. Axel ran towards her and clasped her in his arms. 'I can't believe you came,' he murmured into her neck.

Safiya pulled back. There was a stiffness to her. 'I can't believe how long it took you to call me.'

Axel gave a low groan of self-reproach as he pulled her back to him, her warmth, her sandalwood scent mingled with the bitter ones of aeroplane travel. Remembering himself, he finally let go. 'Would you like anything? A coffee? A doughnut?'

'A shower,' Safiya said decisively.

Axel nodded. He reached for her bag, but she adjusted the strap across her shoulder and led the way out of the airport. Trailing after her a little sadly, out into the darkening parking lot, Axel wondered for the hundredth time if he'd made a mistake. Was she regretting her decision? Had she just come to see him for some closure, to clear things up? But as he caught up with her and guided her towards his car, he saw the warmth in her eyes. She was here, here in Texas, by his side: that was all that mattered.

They sat in silence in the car for a long time, listening to the purr of the motor, watching the last rays of sunlight fade to blue.

'How is everything in Istanbul?' Axel finally asked, awkwardly, his eyes on the road.

Safiya gave a quiet laugh. The lights were switching on by the side of the highway, sending shadows flickering across her face as they drove. 'Good,' she said, and didn't volunteer any more information.

What felt like a very long time passed.

'I wanted to call,' Axel blurted out. 'I... It's just, with my mother in hospital, and everything, I just didn't know...'

'You could have answered my text message,' Safiya said crisply. 'I wasn't trying to get in your way.'

Axel was appalled. 'No, no, of course not!'

There was a softening to Safiya's silence. 'So you don't regret what happened? In the garden?'

Axel took his eyes from the empty highway and met hers with as much intensity as he could muster. 'I don't regret anything,' he said.

The atmosphere in the car was so transformed that he had to switch the radio on to break the tension. They drove on to the faint strains of old jazz tunes, as the sky turned dark around them, smiling.

★ ★ ★ ★

It was infinitely strange, seeing Safiya sitting at his mother's dining room table, in his childhood home. She'd showered and changed, and was towelling her hair dry. The intimacy of the moment made his throat catch.

'Tea? Coffee? Something to eat?' he offered, knowing even as he did that there was nothing in that fridge, just an old tub of butter and some crab-sticks.

'I don't know,' she answered. 'I have no idea what time it is. I feel really awake. Could we go walk around town? I haven't been to the US in years, I've forgotten everything.'

Axel could have laughed from sheer joy. 'I'd love that,' he said. 'And then if you're hungry we can pick something up.'

Safiya smiled knowingly. 'Nothing in the fridge?'

He shook his head. 'It's about seven p.m., by the way.'

'I'm not really hungry yet, but maybe I will be.' She pulled her hair back with her fingers and braided it quickly, then pulled on a cardigan. 'Let's explore your hometown, then.'

As Axel locked the door behind them, a strange thought crept into his mind. What if people saw them? What if one of Patti-Ann's friends – God forbid, Pamela – walked past them on the street and reported back to his fiancée? He shook his head. He was being ridiculous. His research partner was visiting from Istanbul: everybody knew he'd been working there. He wasn't doing anything wrong.

They stepped out into the twilit street. It was still warm. Safiya touched his arm, hesitantly, then linked hers through it. In the rush of feeling, something else occurred to him: everybody was going to know, at some point. Safiya was going to be his girlfriend. Wasn't she? As his heart-rate accelerated, something quite like terror went over him in a wave. What was he doing? Was he ready for this? What if he ran into Patti-Ann's mother?

'Are you OK?' Safiya asked, removing her arm from his. Something in her face suggested that his thoughts had been visible across his.

'I'm OK,' he replied, decisively taking her hand in his. Let them see us, he thought. The streetlights were flickering on around them, and the first crickets beginning to call out.

They walked down past the maple trees, and the catalpa, and the birches; past the library, past the Bells' house with the swing on the front porch, past the parking lot where he used to play baseball as a kid.

'So you've lived here your whole life,' Safiya said, gazing around at the perfectly trimmed front lawns, the sprinklers scattering droplets in the darkness.

'It's pretty suburban, I know.'

'It's lovely. Quiet, though. Are there even any bars?'

Axel grinned. 'There weren't when I was a teenager. Anyway, you know how it is in the States – twenty-one.'

'Of course,' said Safiya, 'I forgot.'

'Which doesn't mean I didn't sneak my share of beers with my fraternity pals. But bars, restaurants, that sort of thing; when I was a kid, there was just the one diner, the Cherry Pie. It's still my favourite place in town, I'll have to take you.' He hesitated, pushed the image of Patti-Ann from his mind. 'Now, there's a few new places that have opened up, trying to make Lake Salvation into some kind of city – a Mexican grill, even an Irish pub... But they're not doing too well.'

'It's a conservative place.' It wasn't a question.

'Yeah. And it's got worse since the Defenders have kind of taken over. I mean, when I was a kid, people were split fairly evenly between the three churches in town – the Episcopal, the Presbyterian, and the Church of Grace. But nowadays almost everybody follows the Defenders, whether or not they're members.'

They found themselves passing the red brick façade of the hospital, the familiar glow of the lobby. Axel paused.

'Is this where your mother is?' Safiya asked softly.

'Yeah.'

'Do you want to go see her?'

Axel nodded mutely. 'I'm sorry,' he said, 'it's just... I've spent so much time there lately, it feels weird to just walk by.'

'I don't mind at all,' said Safiya. 'As long as you don't think it's too soon to be meeting your mother...'

Axel smiled sadly and squeezed her hand, then let go as they pushed through the hospital doors.

There was nobody at the front desk, which was just as well: visiting hours finished at six, and though the friendly staff usually let family members stay as late as they wanted, he wasn't sure they'd have allowed Safiya in. What if she'd had to sign a book, and somebody had seen?

I have to stop being such a coward, Axel told himself firmly, taking her hand once more. The memory of his last conversation with Professor Bohmann spurred him on, giving him courage.

The floor squeaked under his shoes just as it always did, and the elevator hesitated after he punched in the floor number, as usual, but it still felt different from his other visits. Pushing away the thought that someone else might be in the room, he knocked softly on the door and entered.

Apart from the small bedside lamp, which had been left on, the room was in darkness. Axel always liked the nighttime visits best: a time when Felicia looked as if she could have been sleeping peacefully.

'She's beautiful, your mother,' Safiya said softly, as if echoing his thoughts.

Axel nodded, not trusting his voice. He leaned in and pushed a loose strand of hair back from her forehead.

'How long has she been like this?'

'Two weeks or so.'

'Of course,' she replied. 'Since you left Istanbul.'

'Safiya—' Axel began, but she held up a hand, a ghost of a smile on her face.

'Don't,' she said. She sat down in one of the chairs by the side of the bed, and looked down at Felicia benevolently.

I love having you here. The thought sprang into Axel's mind, unbidden, though he didn't dare utter the words. Still, it was wonderful, Safiya's silhouette outlined against the blue window, her dark eyes glowing in the lamplight.

'Do you mind if I pray?' she asked.

Startled, Axel shook his head. Why not? he thought.

'Out loud,' she added.

'Out loud?' he asked, before he could stop himself.

'It's a Sufi tradition,' she explained, almost bashfully. 'I don't know if I even believe, but… My uncle, in Turkey, had terrible lung cancer. They told him he had two weeks to live. We stayed by his bedside, staying with him praying for weeks... He lived another twelve years.' She looked at the ground, blushing. 'Look, I'm not asking you to believe, but it's meant to be more powerful if several people join together, share their energy.'

'OK.' Axel was smiling. 'I'll follow you.' In the light of her grateful glance, he added, 'it can't do any harm, can it?' He took a chair and sat down next to her. 'So how does it work?'

'You repeat the verses,' she said. 'It doesn't matter if it's the Bible, the Quran... I remember the monks in Nepal did the same thing, with Buddhist mantras. I think it's universal, the power found in repeating words.'

'What was the place called again, the lake you went?' Axel asked, chatter a nervous reflex.

She smiled, as if sensing his discomfort. 'Phoksundo,' she said. 'And we don't have to pray now, if you're not sure. It was just an idea.'

'No, I think I'd like to. It's just... It's been a long time since I've prayed.'

Safiya reached across and took his hand gently. 'I'd like to show you the temple,' she said softly, 'in Nepal. I think you would understand more easily there, the power of prayer.'

Axel's heart leapt in his chest. Nepal! With Safiya! 'I'd love that.'

She blushed and squeezed his hand. 'Your mother is a believer?' she asked.

He nodded.

'Then I think it will do her good to know you're praying for her. Even if it's been a long time. Even if you're not sure you mean it.'

Still stalling, Axel began again, hesitantly: 'I bet lots of non-religious people pray in hospital rooms, or when family members are ill.'

Safiya laughed softly. 'Yes, I suspect they do. What's that saying, no atheists in foxholes? The human mind really has an enormous capacity for dealing with illness, disasters, death, for accepting the terrifying reality of living in this world—'

'—but it's a lot easier if we believe we're not doing it alone,' Axel finished for her.

She nodded. 'Sufism chooses a middle way: to trust in the self, and in the superpower's guidance, without believing that some external force is going to take care of everything without us lifting a pinky.'

'Or if we just toss some coins into a collection basket.'

'Everybody wants a miracle,' she added sadly, not looking up at him.

'But there's no such thing.' For some reason, this exchange had comforted Axel. He wasn't trying some magical ritual: he was just being there for his mother.

'Do you know that the word Islam means acceptance?' Safiya said softly. 'Our entire lives are like the blink of an eye to God above.'

'More quantum physics!' Axel joked, and Safiya cracked a smile.

'Now, do you feel ready to begin?'

He nodded.

She sat forward, pushed up the sleeves of her cardigan, and smoothed down the stray hairs that had escaped from her damp plait. 'Now. Let's start with something simple: the verse from the Quran known as *al-Fatiha*, the Opening: "In the Name of Allah, the Merciful, the Compassionate. Praise be to Allah, the Lord of the worlds, the Merciful, the Compassionate, the ruler of the Day of Judgment. You we worship and You we ask for help from. Guide us to the right path."' Looking back up at Axel, she smiled. 'Of course, you do not know these verses by heart. Perhaps we can repeat simply the last section: "Guide us to the right path." Now repeat with me, seven times.'

'Guide us to the right path,' Axel murmured, a little embarrassed. 'Guide us to the right path.'

'Good!' said Safiya, when they had finished the first cycle. 'Wonderful. Now let us try another healing verse. She paused, as something occurred to her. 'Are there any prayers that you know by heart?'

'The Lord's Prayer,' Axel answered, almost embarrassed.

'I know that one,' Safiya smiled. 'Perhaps we'll be able to get into more of a rhythm if the prayer is familiar to you. Remember, what we are doing is channeling our energy towards your mother, filling her with our love.'

Axel looked at his mother's face, and his heart swelled.

'*Our father in heaven,*' he began, '*hallowed be your name.*'

He had to admit, there was something comforting to the rhythm of the words.

Your kingdom come, your will be done, on earth as in heaven.

Safiya's voice joined his, so that they formed a small chorus: both their voices soft and low, both their faces turned towards Felicia on the bed.

Give us today our daily bread. Forgive us our sins as we forgive those who sin against us. Save us from the time of trial, and deliver us from evil.

The experience was a profoundly strange one. Axel hadn't prayed since childhood; not since his confirmation. Even then, kneeling by his bed or closing his eyes on a church pew, it had been more of a reflex than a ritual. He'd barely listened to the words, mouthing them without feeling, and by the time he left for university, he'd given up on prayer entirely. But this was different.

For the kingdom, the power, and the glory are yours, now and forever. Our father in heaven...

Axel slipped into a more comfortable rhythm, and felt his soul joining his voice in honest, heartfelt prayer.

Your will be done. Forgive us. Deliver us.

Please save my mother.

Words. What a well of comfort they were! Millenia of love and grief, solitude and celebration, birth and loss, poured into them by souls all over the world. Axel found himself remembering something Bohmann had said to him a while back: that the root of the word religion was the Latin verb *religare*, to connect, to bind. His thoughts drifted back to hymns sung at church weddings, and prayers echoed by a hundred voices in Sunday services, even his murmured evening childhood confessions. What if they had meant something, all those words, even if they'd been mechanical? Axel felt a tide of something deep rising in him.

Please wake up.

I love you.

He was not alone.

As their hands clasped, the old familiar doubt came back to him – was this love or belief? Was this falling in love or a religious conversion, or were they in fact one and the same?

Your will be done.

Looking back and forth from Safiya's face to Felicia's, from his mother's back to his lover's, he was quite overcome. There was something in the room, in the sound of their voices mingling. It was powerful. It was as if it was bringing colour back to Felicia's cheeks, bringing breath back into—

'Axel?'

Felicia opened her eyes. Axel made a strange sound and scrambled to his feet, knocking his chair over.

'Mom?' he said. 'Mom?' He grabbed her hand, felt that it was warm.

'It's a miracle!' Safiya's voice was joyful, and close to tears, too. 'She heard us!'

Axel felt his eyes filling with tears. Did she? Had they really woken her? Had it worked? It was unbelievable, amazing, the doctors hadn't thought there was a chance she could wake up…

Felicia had said something, or rather, issued a series of incomprehensible sounds, smiling. 'Ol-in-va-in-leck-i-vet-pi-hal-la,' perhaps? Axel had no idea. 'Ha-lu-an- men-ne-jel-leen.'

He stared. His mother's eyes were wide open, a little glassy, as if she wasn't quite here. What was she saying? 'Why is she talking like that?' he asked.

'I don't know. Maybe it's the shock of waking up?' Safiya's eyes were wide. 'It's not a language I know,' she said.

'What do we do?' Axel was panicking.

'We'll call the doctor,' Safiya said decisively, reaching to the side of the bed and pushing the button.

'Se-oli-nin-kau-nis,' said Felicia, or something like it. 'On-se-ai-ka-lou-nas?'

The doctor. 'Yes, yes, good,' Axel said distractedly. Had they really woken her up? Was she going to be OK? Her eyes didn't quite seem to be focusing on them.

Safiya reached across and took Felicia's hand in hers. 'Felicia?' she said gently.

His mother was looking at her, but her eyes didn't seem to focus. 'Sisko?' she asked.

Safiya blushed, then laughed awkwardly. 'That sounded an awful lot like she was calling me fat in Turkish.'

'Sisko? Charlene?' Felicia asked again, and they both stared at her.

Axel laughed too, then, at the madness of the situation, then another rush of panic hit. He needed to tell Charlene, of course. He needed to tell Patti-Ann. Not feeling up to the phone call, he typed up a quick text message – *my mother is awake!* – and hit send.

'Where are the doctors?' he asked, his heart racing.

'It's late,' Safiya reminded him. 'They'll be coming soon.'

He checked the clock: it was almost ten. They'd been praying for hours. 'We didn't even have supper!' he remembered.

Safiya laughed, though there was a trembling edge to the sound.

Felicia let loose another stream of syllables, and Axel shook his head. 'Olin,' she seemed to be saying a lot. What did any of it mean?

Safiya leaned across and touched his shoulder. 'Don't worry,' she said. 'The important thing is that your mother is awake. She's going to get better. We're here with her.' Warmth swelled up in his heart, replaced by another wave of panic: why on earth had he texted Patti-Ann? *Oh God, are they going to be here together?* He couldn't leave, of course not, but what could he do? He would be trapped with his two women.

'I'll call Bohmann.' Axel's heart was racing. His first thought had been to call his father; perhaps Bohmann felt like the closest substitute. Surely he'd be able to explain.

His mother raised a hand – she was able to move! – and began speaking again. This time the words came in waves, the rhythm totally unfamiliar to him. 'Oli-me-pe-la-etti.' Eighty? 'Se-ei-ol-lut-mi-nun-vika!' As they stared at her, they heard the door open. The young doctor appeared.

'Doctor McThomas will be right along,' he said shyly, before stopping in his tracks.

'Oh, thank God!' Axel exclaimed. 'My mother's awake, you see, from her coma!'

'Se-ei-ol-lut-mi-nun-vika!' Felicia said again. The young man stared, his eyes popping out of his skull. Following his gaze, Axel understood his shock. 'Sis-ko-ni-ja-mi-nah-lay-ki-vat-pi-hal-la. Se-oli-nin-kau-nis!' His mother was babbling quite animately now, making similar sounds to before, both her hands waving in the air.

'Oh God!' said the doctor's assistant, all colour draining from his face.

'I know,' Axel said happily, 'it's unbelievable. It's a miracle!'

The doctor raised a shaking hand, until he was pointing at Felicia in her bed. 'It's the devil's work! The devil's tongue!' He dropped his folder on the ground, turned around and fled the room.

Axel blinked, then looked to Safiya for reassurance. 'What on earth was that about?'

Safiya looked rather shaken. 'Does he think she's speaking in tongues?' she suggested.

'What?' said Axel. 'Is that what she's doing?'

'Speaking in tongues is a miracle,' Safiya replied, 'according to the New Testament. You know those paintings where the apostles are standing around with flames spouting out of their heads?'

'Pentecost?' He distantly remembered the story from Sunday school.

She nodded. 'They were inspired – speaking in tongues. It was the first instance, in the Bible, of direct personal contact with God by believers. The fire, it's a symbol of the Holy Spirit filling them.'

'Filling them with what? What is she saying?' Axel, he had to admit, was kind of freaked out. He stared at his mother, as she continued to emit a string of mysterious syllables.

'Well, in the Pentecostal story, the Apostles were understood by everyone around them, as if they were suddenly speaking in the many languages of the people. But many people believe that speaking in tongues is actually a way of channelling a new, divine language.' She paused, as if embarrassed. 'Which would explain why some parts of what she's saying sound so similar to Old Arabic, or even Aramaic, or Turkish.'

'The ancient Biblical languages?' Axel's eyes were wide. 'So why was that guy panicking? Shouldn't he be saying hallelujah, trying to get my mother canonised?'

Safiya swallowed. 'Some people believe it's a curse rather than a blessing,' she said. 'I mean, from the outside, it can look rather like demonic possession. Not, of course, that there's any chance of that here. Even in the Bible story, some of the onlookers made fun of the Apostles, accused them of being drunk and unruly. It's not something many people are comfortable with, listening to holy words coming directly from God.'

Axel was quiet for a moment. 'I sure hope that idiot went to get McThomas.'

Safiya reached over and pressed the button again. 'Just in case,' she said.

They stood for a moment just staring at his mother. Her cheeks were pink: she looked healthy. Or was she filled with the Holy Spirit? Was that just her own soul shining out, Axel wondered, or something external – something come from God? And wasn't that the same thing, according to all of Safiya's studies?

'Do you really think she's communicating with God?' he asked, feeling a mix of emotions – excitement, embarrassment, confusion.

'I don't know,' Safiya replied. She met his gaze sympathetically. 'She's certainly communicating, I just don't know what... or to whom.'

The young doctor's voice crept into his mind, unwelcome: *The devil's work!* Surely not, that was just superstition. This was the twenty-first century. Axel didn't believe in any of this. Did he? And yet his mother was awake. Something had brought her back to life.

'Is that my mother's voice?' he asked, his voice cracking slightly. *It's not a demon or anything, right?* 'It sure sounds like my mother's voice.'

Safiya nodded uncertainly. 'She's awake. That's the important thing.'

His heart pounding, Axel reached across and took both of Safiya's hands gently in his. 'Yes,' he said. 'It is.'

CHAPTER TWENTY-SIX

'I'm freaking out,' said Axel, pacing up and down. 'Where is the damn doctor?'

Felicia had fallen silent, and did not react when they said her name or tried to speak to her. She was staring out the window, smiling, into the darkness of the night. From time to time, her hands rose to her face and touched her cheeks.

Axel's phone buzzed in his pocket, and he pulled it out.

Praise the Lord! I'm coming, sweetie. Hang in there. Patti-Ann. His stomach lurched.

'Do you want to call Bohmann?' Safiya asked softly. 'You wanted to earlier.'

Axel looked at her gratefully. 'Yes!' he said. Bohmann would know what was going on. Bohmann would know what to do.

He picked up on the second ring. 'Professor?'

'Well hello, Axel! I was wondering when I'd have news from you. So, did you call your lady friend, your Dr Midana? How are—'

'Professor,' Axel interrupted, his face flushing, 'this is important. Safiya is here with me now in the hospital – my mother has woken up. We were praying together, repeating prayers, I don't know, it's a Sufi thing, and now she's woken up and she's babbling in a language we don't understand.'

'Woken up?' Bohmann repeated. 'From her coma? How marvellous! There has been some truly fascinating research into the idea of healing through the repetition of spiritual texts. A certain Dr. Abdul Hai Al-Dabbadh, I believe, perhaps Safiya has heard of him. If I recall correctly, the idea is that the sick body has fallen out of balance, genetically speaking. Oh, a Professor Malintoch in Pennsylvania did some mathematical calculations on this subject, as well. In short, it's a question of energy – that the repetition of certain texts generates a sort of… energy, that shocks everything in the brain back into place. It's similar to acupuncture, or massage, really, only it's done entirely through the voice. It's fascinating, fascinating!'

'So it's not God,' Axel said slowly, in mixed relief and disappointment, 'it's energy.'

Professor Bohmann made a dismissive sound. 'Six of one, half dozen of the other,' he said. 'Some scientists measure this in ohms, some people talk about gravitational waves, and then there's all the people whose plants grow faster when they talk to them, or play opera on the radio. It's all the same idea. I mean, what's the first thing they do when you have trouble with your heart? Strap pads to your chest and give you an electric shock. Puts everything right back where it should be, like restarting a computer.'

'Professor,' Axel pleaded, then stopped, unsure what it was he was pleading for.

But the professor understood at once. 'I'll be right over, my boy,' he said. 'Just hang tight.'

When he hung up, he realised that the professor hadn't even mentioned the speaking in tongues part. Maybe he hadn't heard.

Speaking in tongues, Axel typed into Google. 'Glossalalia' – a Wikipedia article appeared:

Glossolalia or speaking in tongues, according to linguists, is the fluid vocalising of speech-like syllables that lack any readily comprehended meaning…

His heart-rate accelerated. That certainly seemed to be what was happening to his mother!

…in some cases as part of religious practice in which it is believed to be a divine language unknown to the speaker.

So was it was true? Was Safiya was right? Was it a miracle, a miracle, was his mother full of the Holy Spirit?

But this line of questioning was swiftly interrupted as, at last, the door flew open and Dr McThomas came in.

'Axel! I'm so sorry I'm late, I was in surgery…' He stopped and stared at Felicia, who was smiling peacefully.

'Ol-in-va-in-leck-i-vet-pi-hal-la,' she said.

'So it's true,' he said in wonder, taking off his spectacles. 'My assistant was pretty spooked. It's very unusual, someone waking up from a coma like this. Let alone two weeks after such a serious accident.' He put his glasses back on. 'Tell me, what language is she speaking?'

Safiya and Axel exchanged glances. 'I don't know, sir,' said Axel. He hesitated. 'My friend thinks she is speaking in tongues.'

McThomas sighed. 'Ah, so that's what Richie was yelling about. This superstitious old town...'

Axel suddenly, and acutely, felt foolish. He put his phone to sleep and slipped it into his pocket. 'What's wrong with her, then?'

'Traumatic brain injuries,' McThomas began, 'are a very particular type of injury. When you jostle your brain, well, it's a very delicate organ. In your mother's case, the temporal lobes – the hippocampus and amygdala – have been severely affected.' He paused, delicately, before continuing. 'A healthy person's brain is very, very carefully organised. When you slam that delicate thing into the front of a car – if you'll excuse the image – then the damage can cause some... misfirings, particularly where memory is concerned.'

'What does that mean?' Axel said, his frustration growing.

'It means that these sorts of injuries can change a patient's relationship to the temporal narrative of their memories. In other words, I suspect your mother is speaking a language she learned at another time in her life.'

'But that's impossible,' said Axel. 'Safiya said she was speaking something that resembled old Arabic, Aramaic or Turkish. My mother's never been to the Middle East!' *She's speaking in tongues*, he stopped himself from saying. *It's a miracle!*

The doctor was quiet for a moment. 'Well, there are cases – very rare cases – of patients waking up speaking an entirely new language. There hasn't been much evidence, the studies are inconclusive...' Axel could almost see the gears whirring in his head: visions of a prestigious case, a miraculous recovery, his name in the papers... It made him angry. He and Safiya had saved his mother, not McThomas. Prayer had saved her, not brain surgery. Hadn't it?

'You're the specialist,' he said. 'How can you not know what's going on?'

But before the doctor could respond, the door had opened, and Charlene appeared. 'What on earth is wrong with you, boy?' she said angrily, before stopping in her tracks. 'Jesus, Mary and Joseph,' she said. 'It's true.'

'I'm sorry, Aunt Charlene,' Axel said, abashed. 'I should have called. It all just happened so fast.'

Charlene was at the bedside in a few long steps.

'Charlene!' Felicia said happily. 'Sisko! Ha-lu-at-ko-le-kie-pu-tar-has-sa?'

Charlene went pale. She reached down and took Felicia's hand in hers. '*Sisko*,' she said. '*Hei*.'

Axel blinked rapidly, trying to process. Was Charlene speaking in tongues too, now? His aunt turned back slowly from the bed. 'Why is my sister speaking Finnish?' she asked McThomas, her tone accusatory.

'I might ask you the same question,' McThomas said mildly. 'Do you have any knowledge of your sister learning the language? A semester abroad, perhaps, or an old boyfriend?'

Charlene shook her head slowly. 'No, no,' she said. 'You don't understand. We lived in Finland for two years. When we were kids – little kids – our father worked in an office in Helsinki for a short time. But I don't speak a word of it now; I had no idea Felicia remembered it.' She sank into one of the chairs. 'It's a really long time ago.'

'*Charlene, tule leikkiä puutarhassa kanssani!*' said Felicia.

'Do you know what she's saying?' Axel asked, in wonder.

Charlene shook her head. 'We were just kids,' she said. 'I don't remember a word. Something about a garden, maybe? I mean, I was seven or so, but she was only three or four years old! There's no way she could remember.'

'Yes there is,' said McThomas, softly. 'As I was saying before you came in, Ms Parker, head injuries can have all sorts of odd effects on people's memories. Many people are unable to form new long-term memories; others forget whole decades of their lives. There are many documented cases of patients reverting to behaviour pertaining to other life stages, particularly childhood.' He leaned on the last two words, as if underlining them.

Axel's mind was racing. He darted an accusatory glance at Safiya, who was looking at the floor. 'So it's not...' He stopped. It's not a miracle. It's not a demon. It's not the Holy Spirit. It's not God. It's just medical science. He met her eyes, and she quavered.

'Axel,' she said, 'our prayers – we woke her.'

He swallowed, trying hard not to be angry with her for letting him believe.

'Yes, it's still quite exceptional,' the doctor said amiably. 'Though I'm not personally comfortable with using the word miracle.'

Now McThomas thought Axel was the crazy religious one! The realisation made his cheeks burn.

'Axel...' Safiya said again, softly.

'Excuse me?' Bohmann's voice was hesitant; Axel hadn't even heard the door open. 'Is... everything all right in here?'

'Professor!' Axel exclaimed in relief.

'I'm sorry, who is this?' McThomas asked.

'Professor Melvin Bohmann,' he said, holding out his hand for the doctor to shake. 'So is it true? Glossalalia?' He was asking McThomas, and the doctor hesitated.

But before either of them could speak, there came a strange sound from the hospital corridor. It was the sound of many voices singing.

A hymn, Axel realised, and then: 'Oh God,' he said. 'Patti-Ann.'

'What on earth?' McThomas began, but he got no further, for the hospital door was flung open, and Patti-Ann appeared, followed by a dozen members of the Defenders of Grace. Their voices mingled, loud and confused:

'Burn her!'

'Praise the Lord!'

'Corianthians, 14:2: "For anyone who speaks in a tongue does not speak to men but to God. Indeed, no one understands him; he utters mysteries with his spirit".'

'Exorcism! Save her soul from the Devil!'

'A miracle! A miracle!'

Axel's mouth went dry.

CHAPTER TWENTY-SEVEN

Chaos. A few of the women were singing as they marched into the hospital room, their faces angelic: Carol, and two of her friends, no doubt. Ichabod Potts, his toupée slightly askew, was reading aloud from a worn Bible in a stentorian tone: '*And these signs will accompany those who believe: In my name they will drive out demons; they will speak in new tongues.*' Patti-Ann, who had entered first, spear-heading the procession, was standing at the back of the room, by the wide window, her face shining. It was clear that she was of the camp that believed Felicia's healing was a miracle. The other camp contained Kyle Bohmann and the young doctor Richie, Axel saw with dismay, as well as Gazi the Mage. They crowded around the end of the bed, like wolves circling a lamb. A few older couples he vaguely recognised from the Tabernacle were cowering behind them against the wall, to the right of the door and perpendicular to the window – as far from Felicia's bed as they could get in such a small space. Patti-Ann moved forward, to behind Axel's shoulder, while Professor Bohmann and Doctor McThomas were on the other side of the bed, closest to the door. Both looked quite stunned.

McThomas cleared his throat. 'You can't all be in here,' he said. 'It isn't allowed.'

'But sir,' said Patti-Ann, 'it's a miracle!'

'*Siskoni ja minä leikkivät pihalla,*' said Felicia.

'We do not know what we ought to pray for,' Potts bellowed, 'but the Spirit himself intercedes for us with groans that words cannot express.'

'We must conduct an exorcism,' said Gazi the Mage, gravely. 'It is the only way to liberate the spirit of Felicia Parker from the demon that has taken hold of her.'

'It's not a demon!' Patti-Ann argued, her voice shrill. 'She's healed! She has returned to us, speaking in the voice of the Lord!'

'*The Holy Spirit fell on all who heard the word!*' said Potts, flipping through the pages rather desperately. '*And the believers from among the circumcised who had come with Peter were amazed, because the gift of the Holy Spirit was poured out even on the Gentiles. For they were hearing them speaking in tongues and extolling God!*'

'*Se oli niin kaunis,*' said Felicia.

'I'm going to get security,' said Charlene, leaving.

'Kyle,' said Bohmann, 'what in God's name are you doing here?'

'I'm here to help with the exorcism,' he replied snidely. 'What are you doing to help the afflicted Parker family, reading them bits from your science book?'

'Hey,' said Axel, 'we're not afflicted.'

'First we must ascertain if it is God or the Devil who is speaking through his mouthpiece, Felicia Parker!' Ichabod Potts was struggling to be heard over the din of voices.

'Wait a minute,' said Patti-Ann. 'What the hell is *she* doing here?'

The girls, confused, stopped singing. Safiya, who had been sitting very quietly in the chair next to Axel's, looked up shakily. 'Hello, Patti-Ann,' she said.

'*Sisko?*' said Felicia.

'AXEL BARTHOLOMEW PARKER!' Patti-Ann yelled at the top of her lungs. 'Get out of this hospital room right now and explain yourself!'

Axel stood up. 'She's *my* mother,' he said, 'and I'd like you and all your friends to leave. Please,' he added.

Fury was burning in his fiancée's eyes. 'I see it now! It's her, it's her! Your mother – is possessed by the devil,' she cried out.

'Oh, so all of a sudden you're in Gazi and Kyle's camp?' In his rage, Axel did his best to meet Patti-Ann's gaze, but the force of it was incandescent.

'And it's all because of that whore of Babylon!' she shrieked, suddenly lunging towards Safiya – Axel had to physically restrain her. 'That witch from the East, that terrorist, she's come over here to steal my boyfriend! And kill his mother!'

'Visiting hours end at 5.30 pm,' McThomas said weakly, backing towards the door.

'Or perhaps the Holy Sprit has descended upon her,' Ichabod Potts cried out, standing on his tiptoes, 'and we, the inhabitants of Lake Salvation, will all be saved!'

'*She's* the reason my mother is awake!' Axel shouted, pushing Patti-Ann back as carefully as he could, but finding his movements limited by the group clustered behind her. 'We prayed together all night!'

Safiya, next to him, was edging her chair towards the wall behind the bed, though there was no escape in any direction.

'Praise the Lord!' said one of the girls, timidly.

'You *prayed*?' Patti-Ann's voice could have shattered glass. 'What did you pray to, Allah? *Science*? Or did you pretend to believe in God, you lying, swindling, son of a…'

'Patti-Ann,' Bohmann said gently, trying to move through the crowd to her side of the room, 'why don't we go outside, just for a minute? Do you think you could talk these people…'

'The exorcism of Felicia Parker cannot wait another moment,' said Gazi, striding towards the bed. 'I have seen this many times in the Holy Land: soon, the demon will begin speaking to us all, convincing us to do terrible things. You see, already Beelzebub has convinced this man to be unfaithful to his future bride.'

'*Tuletko pelata kanssani?*' asked Felicia.

'I am not his future bride!' Patti-Ann yelled, suddenly swivelling so her fury was directed at Gazi, on the other side of the bed. 'If he thinks we're getting married after THIS' – she wildly swung her arms around to indicate the room – 'he's got another think coming.'

'Will somebody just exorcise the damn woman!' This was Kyle's contribution, Axel knew without looking.

Potts was still reading, raising his voice. '*Because the Spirit intercedes for the saints in accordance with God's will!*'

There was some muttering amongst the Defenders.

Ignoring Patti-Ann, Gazi lunged for Felicia and grabbed her by the shoulders. Before Axel had time to react, he had pulled her out of the bed and thrown her over his left shoulder.

'Mom!' Axel cried out.

'*Sisko*?' said Felicia.

Gazi began crying out in an unknown language – some form of Arabic, no doubt.

'Put my mother down!' Axel struggled to get around the bed, but Patti-Ann and the rest of the Defenders were in his way. Pushing his way up against the window, he began attempting to edge around the crowd.

'Oh my God,' said Patti-Ann. 'Is Gazi OK? Is he speaking in tongues too? Has the Devil got to him?'

'Heal! Heal!' the girls began shouting, and Kyle and Richie and the older couples joined in for good measure.

'That's not how an exorcism works!' Ichabod Potts, it seemed, was not enjoying having the spotlight stolen from his impromptu sermon.

'It is how it is done in the Holy Land!' Gazi explained, gasping for breath under the weight of Felicia's body. He was bouncing her now, like a baby who has finished a bottle of milk. It was a very strange sight.

'Mom!'

'Heal!' cried one of the Defenders.

'They're both Devils from the East!' shrieked Patti-Ann. 'That awful Sophie person, the Turkish one, she's infected everybody, she's ruined everything!'

'Get away from my mother! Help!' cried out Axel, having trouble pushing through the older couples, who stood like stone statues in his way, mesmerised by Gazi's performance.

'Is he hurting her?' one of the girls piped up from the window.

'HEAL!' cried Kyle and Richie.

'I've bought three kilos of pearls to sew on my wedding dress! We've picked the tablecloths! We have a cake tasting next Sunday!' Patti-Ann was getting increasingly hysterical.

'SECURITY!' This was a new voice, as two guards burst in through the door, almost running into Gazi. One of them tried to grab Felicia, but Gazi moved towards the crowd for protection, who seemed unsure how to proceed. The girls screamed.

'He's the Devil!' Ichabod Potts howled, switching camps. 'He has been possessed by the spirit of Felicia Parker! Get him out!'

'Devils!' squealed Patti-Ann.

'Devils from the East!' one of the older women bellowed, unexpectedly.

Kyle leapt forward as if to fight the guards off, but the older Defenders parted to let the guards through, so that he was trapped. Out of the corner of his eye, Axel saw Bohmann ushering Safiya discreetly out the door, his arm around her shoulder. *Thank God*, he thought, before turning back to the struggle at hand.

'Everybody! Please stay calm!' the first guard, a tall man with a beard, was yelling. 'Sir, please put the patient down. Sir!'

Gazi gave a howl, though Axel couldn't see what had happened – did hospital guards have tasers? In any case, the second guard had succeeded in wrestling Felicia away from him and was carrying her, pietà-style, towards the bed.

'Everybody out!' the first guard yelled, pushing through to the back window and herding everybody towards the door.

'No, please,' Axel gasped, pressed along with the movement of the crowd. 'She's my mother.'

The guard helped him break out of the crowd. 'This one can stay,' he instructed his partner. 'Everybody else: out.'

Putting his fists on his hips, he spread his legs, forming a muscular wall between the Parkers and the Defenders of Grace beyond.

'I'm his fiancée!' Patti-Ann screamed, pounding her fists on the guard's chest. 'I have to stay!'

The guard hesitated; looked back over his shoulder at Axel. Axel slowly shook his head, backing away. 'No,' he said, and he turned away from them all to where the second guard was carefully tucking Felicia back into her bed.

'You're all right, ma'am,' he was murmuring. 'No harm done.'

'Move along, move along,' said the first guard.

'Praise the Lord,' someone said weakly.

Axel clasped his mother's hands. 'Mom, are you OK?

'*Se on niin kaunis,*' said Felicia, smiling.

The sudden silence was eerie. There was the faint sound of shouting in the corridors, then singing, then silence. Axel's phone began buzzing in his pocket. He reached in and, without looking, switched it to silent mode.

'Are you OK, sir?' the first guard asked Axel. 'Do you need us to stay here?'

'Thank you,' said Axel. 'I think we'll be all right now.'

As a siren went whining past outside, something occurred to him. Safiya. Where had she gone? He whipped out his phone, but the three missed calls were from Patti-Ann. His heart dropped into his stomach as he realised that the mob might have followed his lover and Bohmann out of the hospital. They already hated the Professor: who knew what they might do to them both, worked up into a fury as they were?

'Actually, sir, do you think you can stay here with my mother for a while; just to make sure nobody comes back?'

The bearded guard nodded respectfully. 'Of course,' he said.

'I need to make sure someone is OK.'

CHAPTER TWENTY-EIGHT

'Safiya!' There was no-one left outside the hospital, and Axel shivered in the contrast between the warm neon-lit interior and the cool night air. 'Safiya!' he called out again.

He pulled his phone from his pocket and called her. Her name blinked in big white letters. No reply.

He tried Bohmann. No reply. Wind was starting to blow, whistling through the leaves of the trees above him – a strangely disembodied sound.

Where would she have gone? He began walking back the way they had come hours before, towards his house. Maybe she would have retraced her steps. Then again, why? Axel's mind began spiralling. Maybe she'd flagged down a taxi, headed straight back to the airport. Maybe the Defenders had caught up with her, and had taken her to the Tabernacle, tied her to a chair...

In the shadows ahead, he saw someone walking with shoulders down.

'Safiya!' he cried once more, and the figure slowed. 'I'm so glad you're—' He ran to her, but when she turned, he took a step back. 'Are you OK?' he asked.

Her face was pale. She'd been crying. 'What do you think?' she said.

'I'm sorry,' said Axel. 'I'm sorry I didn't... I had to stay with my mother.' He paused. 'Where's Professor Bohmann?'

'I let him go home. He offered to drive me somewhere, but I didn't know where to ask him to go.' She sniffled, and he saw that she was exhausted.

'And the Defenders?'

Safiya shrugged. 'They didn't even see us. They all went off in a pack together, singing their songs.'

'Did you...' Axel stopped, and decided to change the subject. 'Hey, do you want to get some food?'

She hesitated.

'I know you're angry and upset, and you've every right to be, but can we just go sit somewhere and calm down?'

'Calm down?' Not, Axel realised too late, the right words to use. 'Calm down, after what happened in there?'

Hesitantly, he reached for her shoulder. 'I've never seen them like that. It was pretty terrifying, huh?'

She glared at him and shook his hand off. 'The really terrifying thing was your *fiancée* calling me a whore in front of all those people, and you not stepping in to defend me.'

'I—'

'Didn't you notice Bohmann trying to help me? Did it even cross your mind that that situation might be genuinely dangerous for me?'

'That guy was throwing my mother around like a rag doll! I had to stay there and look after her!'

'I know! I know!' Safiya shouted, sounding close to tears again. 'I just can't believe you brought me to that hospital. Had you even told *anybody* that I was coming?'

Axel slowly began to understand her anger. 'I hadn't,' he confessed.

'You just thought you'd invite me to fly over all the way from Istanbul, to... hang out? To keep you company while you took your sweet time working out whether you still wanted to marry your girlfriend?'

Axel swallowed. 'It's not like that,' he said.

'Oh? So what is it like?'

'I mean, those guys are crazy!' Axel said, uncomfortable with the direction this conversation was taking. 'You know that. Surely you're not trying to blame me for that?'

She stared at him, her eyes wide and red. 'Oh, poor you. Poor little Axel. You don't want me to blame you? You just want to move through life hurting people, messing people around, and you want to be thanked for your cowardice?'

'What about the elephant in the room?' Axel cried out, desperately. 'Or rather, the team of elephants! I wasn't the bad guy in there! Even

Patti-Ann, I know she was horrible, and I'm sorry about that, but she was just riled up by those crazy holy rollers!'

'Hell hath no fury,' Safiya said, scathingly.

Now Axel was getting angry. 'And what about you, you're supposed to get off scot- free? I'm just as brainwashed as Patti-Ann! You used my distress over my mother to try to make me believe we'd witnessed a miracle! You let me believe in your stupid Sufi prayers, I let myself go along with it just because I'm so in love with you—'

His breath caught in his throat, and for a moment everything stilled. What felt like an eternity passed.

'In love with me?' Safiya asked, very softly.

'Well, yes,' said Axel, all his emotions rushing out of him like water. 'I am.'

The wind began to blow again, and the leaves rustled above them. Somewhere, a bird called out.

'I love you too,' said Safiya, 'but I'm angry.'

Axel laughed. 'Listen, Safiya, we're both really tired... Can we maybe just set this aside and get some dinner?'

'OK,' she said, a ghost of a smile appearing on her pale face. 'I guess that'd be nice. As long as we don't run into anybody.'

Axel gave a ragged laugh. Now he was the one who felt like crying, out of pure emotional exhaustion. He took her hand, and began walking.

'We could go get hamburgers,' he offered, 'from this stand by the library. Or maybe just milkshakes and fries? I don't know how hungry you are.' He took a breath. 'Or if you want to sit down, there's this nice diner, the Cherry Pie. They have great meatloaf, and their pies are out of this world. I could really use some sugar right now...' It was a peace offering, a babbled one, though she couldn't know the significance of it.

'Sure,' said Safiya. 'Let's go to the diner.'

'I mean, there are things for us to talk about, of course,' he said hesitantly. 'I have some serious explaining to do, and I owe you – well, several major apologies.'

Safiya laughed and tightened her grip on his hand. 'Explaining would be a good start.'

They walked for a time in silence.

Now something like euphoria was rising in his chest. Maybe they were going to be all right. Maybe Safiya would stay here with him, or maybe they could go somewhere, just the two of them... 'My Mom's OK!' he said, the realisation coming back to him out of the fog of his confusion.

Safiya smiled. 'Thanks to us,' she said. 'Thanks to you.'

Axel sighed.

'Look, I don't want to start arguing again,' she said, her tone placating, 'but I need you to know that I truly, in my heart of hearts, believe that we woke her. We did it together, through the strength of our prayers. I understand that you disagree with me, but did any of the doctors explain why she woke up?'

'No!' Axel paused. 'I didn't ask.' But it was hard to stop there. 'I mean, medically speaking, it's impossible.'

Safiya looked over at him and raised her eyebrows. 'When did you become so close-minded? Aren't you Bohmann's protégé?'

Perhaps she had intended it as a gentle tease, but the words stung. 'I'm not close-minded,' Axel shot back. 'I'm just a realist. Yeah, I do believe in science. I just don't understand how you can keep defending – how you think religion can be a good or useful part of what happened in that hospital room. I mean, you were there! You saw what it was like in there. Religion makes people crazy. All the singing and the screaming and the exorcising... It's insanity. I don't want to be a part of any of it.'

He hadn't meant to say so much. Sneaking a glance over at Safiya, he saw that she looked deeply hurt.

'I didn't...' He tried to backtrack.

She let go of his hand. 'If that's how you feel...'

'No, listen!' he stopped walking and grabbed both of her hands back. 'Surely we can agree on some— I mean, you saw how they all turned on Gazi the Mage. Like wolves attacking their alpha. Wasn't that horrible?'

'Do you really think I'm *defending* those racist maniacs?'

'No,' Axel relented, 'but I need you to understand how all this makes me feel about religion.'

'But that's just the thing, Axel.' Now it was Safiya's turn, he saw, to be unable to stop herself. 'You don't know a thing about religion. If you think those violent loons have anything religious about them, you're completely deluded. Let me tell you, I've seen things – censure, violence, rape, even a crucifixion in a desert village once – religion being used in terrible ways you can't even imagine. But the way bad people *use* religion is just one slender, meaningless aspect of what religion represents. And it has nothing to do with what religion truly *means*.' She managed to pause, and took a breath before continuing more slowly. 'I know you know better than that. I've spent time with you. I know your soul. Religion is a source of peace and comfort and acceptance. Religion can be life-changingly wonderful. You know that. You saw that in the room – I was there. I saw it in your eyes.'

'If you know me so well, why can't you just accept that I'm an atheist?' It was not a word he'd ever used before: it felt odd in his mouth.

Safiya shrank back, and something about this bothered him. Now that he'd upped the ante, he wanted to keep on going. Stick to his guns, even if he wasn't sure of what he was defending.

'Come on, are you so shocked?' he challenged her. 'Do you not want to be with me if I don't *believe*, like you?'

'I don't care what views you hold privately. I do care, however, about being able to talk openly with you – about our agreements and disagreements. About our beliefs, yes.' She hesitated. 'If we love each other, none of this should matter. We've always debated, that's our dynamic! That intellectual fire is a big part of this connection between us. Our work together...'

'When have you ever really cared about my perspective? Every time, you act like I'm some stupid child. Well I'm not.'

'I wouldn't treat you like a stupid child if you didn't act like one! Do you really think you're the one making this a reasonable conversation?'

Stung, Axel shouted back: 'You always make me feel like I'm your student! Or some kind of project. I mean, what do you want me to be, a convert?'

Safiya stared at him, and Axel had the distinct impression that he'd crossed a line. 'A convert?' she repeated, disbelievingly. 'You think that's what this is about? You think I flew halfway across the world to convert you?'

'Well, why *did* you come? You want me to jilt my fiancée after just one kiss, without us having even talked about it? Just so you feel more comfortable being here with me?'

'Holy mother of God. I've heard enough of this.' Safiya spun around on her heel.

Axel grabbed her arm. 'Wait, Safiya, I'm sorry. I didn't mean that.'

She flung his arm off her. 'Don't you dare,' she said. 'I clearly made a mistake coming here. About you. About us.'

'No, no,' he begged, 'I didn't mean that.'

'I do,' she said very quietly, and she turned and began walking back towards town.

'Safiya,' he pleaded, but she didn't turn around. 'Safiya!'

Axel stood and watched her go, until she had vanished into the darkness.

CHAPTER TWENTY-NINE

The mountains stretched off in all directions, the green valleys swooping up into the clean rock, the soft snow, the sharp peaks. Even with his eyes closed, Axel could feel them surrounding him. A bell rang, with a hollow golden sound that seemed to spread like ripples across a pond, and he opened his eyes. Wooden floors, plain stone walls, mantras circling the room in simple white paint. The small golden statue of the Buddha in its carved niche.

His knees were beginning to ache from his position, but he'd become a little more flexible over a week of early-morning meditation. Or was it ten days now?

'Good,' said Zhu Yong, returning the bell to its ledge and squatting down by his side. 'Now that your mind is completely clear, you are ready to let your thoughts return.'

Reluctantly, Axel unfocused from his meditative state, letting his thoughts come back to him in a tumultuous swirl: his aching feet in hiking boots, the first view of the mountains, the tiny Nepalese airport, his mother hugging him goodbye, the scent of peanut butter cookies, the Defenders in the hospital, Patti-Ann yelling…

He blinked, frowned a little. 'Slowly, slowly,' said Zhu Yong, smoothing his saffron orange robes over his knees as he sat down. 'Not all at once. You are the cowherd: do not let your yaks stampede down the mountain. Perhaps let one or two important thoughts come back at first.'

My mom is OK were the first words that came into his head, once the imagined yaks had disappeared. Then, involuntarily, *Safiya*. He tried to focus on the first thought, to fill his mind with visions of his mother's miraculous recovery: driving her home from the hospital with the radio blaring; checking her bedroom a few days later and finding her out in the garden, weeding; back in her beloved kitchen, baking peanut butter cookies. The sound of happy chatter that had filled the house the first time she had her old friends over for coffee. The kindness and enthusiasm with which she'd encouraged him to take some time away from everything.

'Good, good, I can see you relaxing. Stay with these happy thoughts.'

Safiya appeared once more: in the Turkish rose garden, with the sea breeze blowing in her hair. In his car with the streetlights streaming in, in the hospital room, pale and unhappy; disappearing into the Texan night, leaving him forever.

His eyes flew open.

'What did I say – happy thoughts!' the monk said reproachfully, and Axel laughed softly, rubbing his eyes.

'I'm sorry,' he said. 'It's much harder to focus when I am allowed to think again. When my mind is empty, I think I understand meditation, but when I let the thoughts back in… It's frustrating.'

'Don't worry,' Zhu Yong said kindly, 'I know you are very new.' He moved over so that he was facing Axel, not sitting next to him. Their eyes met, and Axel tried not to flinch at their piercing blue. The monk's tone was serious now: 'I need you to work on a more *mindful* form of meditation. You cannot simply push away the thoughts that are troubling you. You have to let them come to you, wash over you like waves, but not take over. You are still in control. Do you understand?'

'Yes,' said Axel, 'but it's not easy.'

'No,' said Zhu Yong, settling back into his yoga pose. 'It is not. Now, go back to the thoughts that were troubling you – the ones you are unable to push away.' His smile crinkled the corners of his eyes. 'Do not fear your own mind: it is yours to control.'

But Axel couldn't bear to think about Safiya any longer, so he forced his thoughts to turn back to Patti-Ann. He winced as the memories came back to him: his birthday party, her screaming in his mother's hospital room, her stony silences and desperate seductions since. Was he really a coward? Had he just run away from his problems again, instead of facing them? But Safiya was gone, gone back to Turkey, not answering his messages or emails or picking up her phone. And Patti-Ann was there every day, full of anger and love and hope. It was impossible to turn her away. After everything they'd shared together...

'Focus on the way things are,' the monk continued in his calm voice, 'not on the way you wish them to be. Only in truly understanding a situation can one hope to change it.'

Of course, he knew what he had to do. But he didn't have the courage. *I'm just a coward, a lonely coward.*

As tears began to leak from his closed eyes, his heard Zhu Yong sigh. 'That's enough for today, my young novice. No point in crying any more.'

Reluctantly, Axel opened his eyes. 'I'm sorry,' he said. 'I was doing better yesterday.'

'Meditation is not baseball,' the monk chided him gently. 'It is not about performance. It is about learning slowly and instinctively, not pretending you understand. These things cannot be rushed. Have you ever heard of a two-day meditation retreat? No, you have not. There is a good reason for this.'

Axel smiled and shook his head, then uncrossed his legs and slowly stood up. He stretched.

'There should be some new arrivals joining you for breakfast,' Zhu Yong explained as they walked towards the door of the ancient stone temple, his shaved head gleaming in the cool sun. 'Americans like you, I believe. They have just finished their trek.'

Axel smiled, trying to hide his disappointment. He had been the only foreign visitor in the small Buddhist monastery up in the hills above Phoksundo Lake since his arrival: as Zhu Yong had explained, he'd come at the end of what was usually the monsoon season, which most tourists did their best to avoid because of the heavy rains – and the leeches they encouraged. But with climate change, and a bit of luck, he'd had gorgeous weather, cool and dry, and the whole monastery to himself.

'You must learn to embrace change,' Zhu Yong said mysteriously, bowing slightly before he turned and walked away. From time to time, Axel couldn't help wondering if the monk could read his thoughts.

He walked slowly out to the ridge of the mountain that overlooked the valley. To his right, up on the second hilltop, the cluster of buildings where the monks had their simple lodgings, and where a simple meal of rice and lentils would shortly be served. Behind him, the main temple, its whitewashed walls shining. In front of him, the seemingly infinite expanse of the Himalayan foothills, with the sprawling turquoise waters of the lake nestled into a hollow below. Perhaps he would walk down to the waters again after lunch.

He'd been walking every day since he'd arrived in Nepal, soaking in the countryside, his eyes raised up to the peaks and the sky. It was the only time his thoughts seemed to leave him alone, his mind taken over entirely by the beauty of the mountains. When he was walking, he felt strong and sure. When he was sitting alone indoors, or trying to sleep, thoughts of Safiya and Patti-Ann so quickly rushed in to overwhelm his mind...

It didn't help that Safiya had walked these same paths, gazed up at these same peaks, more than ten years ago. He wanted so terribly to ask Zhu Yong if he remembered a young Turkish Sufi student. He wanted so desperately to tell Safiya he was here, that he'd gone on a kind of pilgrimage to seek the same enlightenment she had sought in her youth. He wanted nothing more than to be back with her, holding her in his arms. But he couldn't.

Yes, he would walk down to the lake again later. But now, he was hungry. He followed the path down the eastern hill, then climbed back up the western one, towards the main cluster of buildings. The prayer flags were fluttering in the wind with a sound like birds flying.

Entering the darkened room where the monks took their meals, he breathed in the familiar scent of spices, the clean smell of rice. He bowed at the two monks already eating, scooping up the green lentils and rice in their right hands. 'Namaste, Jhampa,' he said. 'Namaste, Choden.' They nodded in acknowledgement, two figures in identical shades of orange. There were two dozen monks currently living at the monastery, and Axel knew most of them by sight by now, if not by name. Some of them ignored him, going about their business with focused devotion; others asked him for chewing gum or ball-tip pens. And some, like Jhampa and Choden, simply acknowledged him as one of their own, seeking enlightenment in his own way, albeit with a few more tears. Laughing at his internal self-deprecation, he sat down and waited for his own metal dish. He listened to the rhythmic speech of the two monks, the murmured Tibetan words. They seemed quite animated: Jhampa kept holding out his hands and making them vibrate; a curious gesture, like jazz hands. It made him smile.

When the food arrived, he snapped a photograph of his dal bhat on his phone – not very Buddhist, he thought every time, but his mother would want to see as many photographs as she could when he got home. He smiled to himself, thinking of all the questions she would ask. Of course, up here there was no phone reception, and only a small data key in the library for emergencies. Early on, after Axel had broken down weeping for the first time, Zhu Yong had told him he was welcome to use it 'to ease the heartache of distance,' if he needed. He'd been grateful, but declined: what use was the internet if Safiya wasn't on the other end, answering his messages? His mother knew he'd safely landed and set out on the trek up to the monastery in good weather: she wasn't someone to be unnecessarily concerned for his safety, although he knew she'd be checking the news diligently and putting on a show of worry for all her friends.

He heard footsteps and looked up. 'Good news,' said Zhu Yong, sitting down slowly next to Axel. 'No guests yet: I heard from the boy delivering our new rugs that they are still at Chhepka.' He laughed. 'Maybe leeches make them walk slow.'

Axel smiled, pleased. He would have at least one more day's peace, then.

'You must learn to be more welcoming, my young apprentice!' Zhu Yong shook his head, but he was smiling. 'You know, this is a sacred place for many people. Almost all people who come here, over many years. This is a place of many religions: the ancient Bon religion, the Buddhism of the Tibetans like me, and all the Christians and Muslims and Jews who come travelling here nowadays to learn about meditation and appreciate the landscape.'

Many pools, one moon. Safiya's voice came floating back to Axel. 'I don't mean to be selfish,' he said. 'I just like the quiet.'

'Oh, monastery is always quiet. Otherwise, we make them walk back down.'

Axel laughed, then scooped up some of his rice with his fingers.

'You are getting better at eating,' Zhu Yong commented, as his own plate arrived in front of him. 'First day was like watching baby rat. Very sad baby rat.'

Giggling again, Axel dropped a bunch of rice back onto his plate.

'Then again, maybe I am wrong.' Zhu Yong gracefully composed a small bite of rice and lentils, and ate it tidily.

'You don't even have to lick your fingers!' Axel said in wonder, not for the first time.

'For this, we have napkin,' Zhu Yong reminded him. 'And what will you do this afternoon? The weather is very nice.'

'Yes,' said Axel, 'I was thinking I would walk down to the lake.'

Zhu Yong nodded. 'Good, good,' he said. 'I think you will learn more about meditation this way than in our lessons in the temple.'

Having finished his dal bhat, Axel bid the monks good day and headed out into the bright, clear sunshine. Stopping by the dormitories, he shouldered his pack, checked his water bottle, and set out. The path was an easy one to follow, a track worn smooth by the passing feet of monks, shepherds, trekking guides, and men and women carrying everything from fresh vegetables to modems, bags of snacks and footballs. On the way up, Axel had seen a woman carrying a whole fridge on her back, supporting its weight by a single strap looped around her forehead. She had been wearing flip-flops as well, which he'd stared at in disbelief, his own feet aching in his hiking boots. His feet no longer ached, after ten days of walking the mountain trails that surrounded the monastery, and travelling up and down to the lake. For a moment, he wondered if there were fish in the waters, and thought of Charlene, but he pushed the thought away. All he wanted was to be alone. All he wanted was to clear his mind.

He walked past a whitewashed stone stupa, or shrine, prayer flags fluttering in the wind. It made his breath catch in his throat, walking through these sacred places, as if the prayers of all those who had come before him still floated in the air… He shook his head, smiling wryly. If only Safiya could hear him now! Her absence haunted this place as surely as another woman's presence might have. What a fool he'd been to come to this place she'd visited – a heartbroken lover's choice. Of course he would sense her everywhere, wonder if she'd walked this trail, if she still knew the Buddhist mantras, if she remembered how to eat dal bhat… He missed her terribly. Sometimes he wondered if it would have been easier to get over her in Texas; other times he knew it would have made no difference.

His heart ached as he crossed a rickety wood and metal bridge across a small stream, then followed the track as it wound down among the rough rock, the scrub and pine trees. Once, a small animal skittered out of sight – some kind of weasel or squirrel, perhaps – and he could hear unknown birds calling out overhead. Otherwise, he was alone. Looking up to the mountain ridge in the distance, the high Himalayas, he smiled sadly. Some of the bare stone hills near the monastery had a sprinkling of snow, but the high peaks were capped with a permanent blanket of what looked like soft, pure snowfall. They were truly beautiful. 'Maybe you will see a snow leopard,' Zhu Yong had said once, and Axel hadn't been sure if he was joking. How he would have loved to travel up into those high peaks! Maybe the monks could find him a guide…

★ ★ ★ ★

The lake's vast expanse looked perfectly flat in the cool afternoon air, its turquoise so intense it seemed to glow. Axel sighed, took off his backpack and sat down on a flat slab of rock. The wind played in the pines above him, a whistling sound that reminded him vaguely of Texas. He took a swig of water, which tasted faintly of iodine from the purification tablets he had to dissolve in it every night. He wondered if the monks drank the water of the lake, but reasoned the water they collected in plastic tanks must come from a mountain stream higher up in the valley. Even through the medicinal flavour, it was fresh and cool.

The morning's failed meditation was still bothering him. These women, couldn't they leave him alone? Even when he was thousands and thousands of miles away from them, with no means of communication, they were haunting him. He sighed. Zhu Yong was right: he needed to learn to control his mind. It wasn't Patti-Ann or Safiya's fault that they were so present in him. It was his own fault for leaving the situation unresolved for so long. Galvanised into action by the sheer beauty of the blue lake, he pulled his pack onto his knees and rustled around inside for a pad of paper and a pen. Then he paused. It was Safiya he most desperately wanted to write to – to apologise, to plead with her to come back, to tell her how much he loved her. But before he would allow himself the torturous pleasure of this hope, he needed to stop being a coward. It was time to make the decision he'd been putting off for months, even if it meant losing both women.

The pen trembled slightly in his hand as he set the nib to the lined paper.

Dear Patti-Ann, he wrote, *this is a difficult letter to write, but as time passes, it's becoming more and more difficult not to write it.*

He closed his eyes, struggling. How could he do this to her? Focus, he murmured to himself, trying to channel Zhu Yong's meditative calm and determination. He thought back over the weeks since the incident in the hospital, to all the screaming fights with Patti-Ann and the miserable make-up lovemaking afterwards. On Monday she'd want him to buy her expensive jewellery to win her back; on Tuesday she'd be raging about calling off the wedding. One morning, he'd woken up to find her staring at him blankly, the pillow soaked with tears.

When he'd opened his eyes, she'd only smiled, and the desperation of it broke his heart. Worse, she had organised so many awkward diner suppers and parties with her friends – a flurry of activity to make things feel normal between them, he guessed. For him, it had been torture. Every time, he'd spent the whole time burning up with guilt, with the recurring feeling that everyone he talked to knew the real truth: that he wasn't in love with her anymore, but was too scared to leave.

I don't want to be ruled by fear, Patti-Ann, he wrote, *and you don't want to spend the rest of your life with someone who wants to leave but is too afraid to. I know we've been happy: blissfully so, at times. But we were just children when we made this commitment to each other. It seemed so natural, instinctive, the progression from being childhood buddies to being a couple. I had so little understanding of what any of it meant: love, companionship, trust, the rest of our lives… I don't want to say I was foolish, or that I regret it; only that I understand a little better now how serious it is, this business of love. I don't think it should be undertaken lightly. And I think I'm at risk of walking into marriage for the wrong reasons.*

A tear slipped down his cheek. His heart was pounding.

I have loved you, Patti-Ann, you know that. But that love has changed over the years into something weaker than it should be, something like a habit. I think love should be a choice, one you make together every day.

He swallowed. This was the hard part. A vision of his fiancée screaming in the hospital room – *that whore of Babylon!* – flashed into his mind.

Of course you'll wonder if this has anything to do with Safiya. It's important to me that you understand that I'm not leaving you for another woman. Yes, my time with Safiya has been very meaningful to me; maybe it's even been a catalyst to this decision.

He stopped. Patti-Ann wouldn't really want to read about his revelations or his new love. It would just send her into another of her flaming furies. After all, it was none of her business what happened or didn't between him and Safiya. He crossed out the last section.

This decision is about just two people: you and me. It's about the difference between thirteen-year-old you and me, and you and me now, in our twenties.

It's about the difference between true love and commitment. And it's about not getting married out of fear of letting go.

Patti-Ann, I want you to be happy, and I don't think I can make you happy. Go out and find somebody who will love you the way you deserve to be loved. Go out and meet someone who shares the same dreams, the same vision of the future. I wish I could be that man for you, but it's becoming clear that I can't. I hope you understand – I wish you all the best in the world.

Your friend,

Axel.

He stood staring at the paper for a while, then slipped the pad of paper back into his backpack. His chest felt light, as if a great weight had been lifted. He felt like he could walk to the top of the Himalayas right now. For a long time, he sat motionless on his rock, letting his thoughts wash over him like the calm waters of the lake. Then he stood up, shouldered his pack, and set off back up to the monastery.

* * * *

There was a box in the library where the monks and students could leave letters; to be collected and carried down into the valley every week or so. Axel had discovered this over the course of his evenings spent here, after dinner, working his way through the battered nineteenth-century novels and travel guides that various visitors had left behind.

'You're in luck!' a novice told him with a lopsided grin – Axel remembered his name was Hikmat. 'I'm leaving in ten minutes. Special delivery.'

'Maybe my luck is changing,' Axel replied, smiling.

'Yes, yes, very changing,' said Hikmat. 'You see the stars shake this night? Everything moving.'

Axel frowned, confused. The boy shrugged. 'Change is good,' he said, which Axel could only agree with.

He paid the boy generously for the task of finding him a stamp and envelope, then headed back down the hill, and up towards the temple.

He found Zhu Yong in his usual spot, sitting on the floor with his eyes closed, legs crossed. The sharp, warm smell of the yak butter lamps filled the place, and the light was different in the afternoon.

'Yes, Axel?' Zhu Yong inquired, without opening his eyes. 'What is it?'

Axel laughed. 'Hello, Zhu Yong,' he said. 'I'm sorry to interrupt your meditation.'

'It's OK,' he said, slowly uncrossing his legs and standing up without his hands touching the ground. He brushed some invisible dust from his robe. 'So, you have had a revelation? Achieved nirvana?' he asked, raising one bushy eyebrow.

Axel felt colour creeping into his cheeks. 'Something like that,' he said. Suddenly, his visit didn't seem so urgent.

Zhu Yong laughed. 'Don't look like that,' he said. 'I only sat down ten minutes ago. You have not kept me from enlightenment, or anything like that. Now, tell me what you want to know.'

Do you remember Safiya? I'm leaving Patti-Ann. I've made my choice. I've written her a letter. Everything's going to be OK. 'I was wondering if it was possible to find a guide into the higher mountains,' he said instead.

Zhu Yong's eyebrows crawled even further up his smooth forehead. 'This is what makes you so happy? Hiking?' He shook his head. 'Americans.'

'Yes,' said Axel, stubbornly. 'I was thinking by the lake.'

'Ah,' said Zhu Yong, more gently. 'And you thought you could think better up there, closer to the sky. Yes, I understand.'

Axel nodded. The monk wasn't entirely wrong. 'Well, a guide will be arriving soon, with the new Americans. But you know, there is a very easy trail leaving from behind the monastery. Well, easy for us, at least. Have you already walked up behind the eastern hill?'

He shook his head. 'No, I didn't know. I always go around the western one, down towards the valleys and the lake. The way I came up with my guide.'

'Ah, well that is a good place to start. It goes around the hill just behind this one, you see, so for a start you'll have a different view. New mountains to contemplate. Revelations,' he said lightly. 'The trail is quite a popular one during high season, October and November, so it's quite easy to follow. I doubt you'll encounter anyone there this time of year, though.' Zhu Yong paused. 'How are you with heights?'

'I don't have vertigo,' said Axel, 'though I'm not too fond of some of those mountain bridges.'

'There is only one bridge,' Zhu Yong said thoughtfully, 'but many of the paths have... views. Views down as well as views up.'

'Ah,' said Axel. 'OK. I'll be careful.'

Zhu Yong walked to the entrance of the temple, squinting up into the sun. 'No clouds,' he said. 'No crows, either.' He shook his head. 'Well, don't be gone too long. There is change in the air.'

'Rain?' Axel asked, wondering whether to take his heavier coat.

'No, not rain,' said Zhu Yong, still craning his neck up towards the sky.

There was a silence. 'Well, thanks,' Axel said at last, awkwardly.

Zhu Yong seemed to remember his presence. 'Take the left track behind the hill, not the right. Follow the cluster of pines. After that, there is only one path. And Axel—' He laid an avuncular hand on the boy's shoulder. 'Don't go too far. This is just exploring. We'll get you a guide for the real trek.'

Axel nodded. 'Don't worry,' he said. 'I'll be back in a couple of hours.'

CHAPTER THIRTY

The air was calm and still, the sky still a brilliant shade of blue. To Axel, it felt as if the world was in sync with his heart: quiet, at peace. He set one foot in front of the other, enjoying the springy feel of the grass and soil beneath his feet. Buddhism, he was coming to understand, had a great deal more to do with acceptance than with transformation. Whenever he tried to meditate seriously, he always felt like he was fighting his mind into some approximation of a peaceful state, but maybe he was doing it wrong: maybe it was alright to let his difficult, painful thoughts come flooding in. Only then would he truly understand himself. Only then would he be able to make the decisions that would free him from the troubling elements of his life. Only through acceptance, he realised with a wry smile, could he change.

The zigzagging track descending the back of the eastern hill came to an end at the foot of a set of rough-hewn rock steps, a few pine trees scattered around. This was the second hill, then, the one the trail wound around. He clambered up the rock staircase, glad he was wearing his hiking boots, and began walking into the small forest. The air smelled clean, like dry leaves. It was a comfortingly simple act, walking uphill: tiring for the lungs, purifying for the bloodstream. His thoughts always seemed to fall into something like order when he was walking. Again, he smiled at the realisation that this was far closer to successful meditation than his pained sessions with Zhu Yong. Sitting in the temple, in the glow of the yak butter lamps, he'd believed he was supposed to be purifying himself, straining towards a peaceful nirvana outside himself. How much more difficult and painful the truth was – how much more beautiful!

Axel stopped when the trees began to thin, wiping sweat from his forehead. He pulled out his water bottle and drank deeply, then clambered up a nearby rock for a better view. There it was, the monastery: the whitewashed stone buildings looked like toys from this distance, like building blocks tidily arranged across the two hilltops. It was a comforting sight. Axel smiled. Solitude, too, had been a blissful discovery here in the monastery. The monks seemed so happy just going around on their own, praying and eating together twice a day but otherwise alone. When was the last time he had been truly alone for more than a day? Arriving in London, maybe. Sure, he'd had moments on his own in hotel rooms, in transit, even walking or driving in Lake Salvation, but this was different. Here, he slept alone and woke alone, meditated in the temple, walked down by the lake, then spent a few hours reading in the library. It was a simple, solitary rhythm, and it felt quite blissful. He breathed in deep, climbed down from the rock and walked on.

Not that he didn't miss Safiya, and his mother, even Professor Bohmann. He wasn't planning on staying out here forever, after all. But there was something to be said for some distance from all of that; from all of his life, in fact. Suddenly, rounding a corner, he couldn't help but gasp as the towering white peaks came into view. He hadn't realised they were so close: it was all a matter of perspective. *More Buddhist wisdom!* he joked to himself, speeding up his pace, wanting to come closer to the high mountains. The next turn in the path brought him to a ledge overlooking the valley: he clambered up, hoping to look down over the monastery and the lake, but realised he was turned around. Instead, sprawling valleys of brown rock and soft green forest spread out in all directions, wild and craggy. A pale jade stream wound between them, with several tiny bridges slung across it. 'Wow,' he whispered.

Views, he remembered Zhu Yong saying. Beyond the green and bare rock, he could see the crests of so many nameless peaks, so white and wild: two twinned summits spelling out an M in the distance, a series of ridges like sharp teeth, one low-slung ridge like a salmon's tail. White clouds clung to their tips, dissolving into the air like a thin flag. There were two choices, at this point: follow a descending trail that plunged down towards the valley, towards the mountains, or follow the curve of the hillside around, completing a circular hike back towards the eastern hill of the monastery. At this point, he worked out from the geography, he must be halfway around the second hill. He shook his head and pulled his phone from his pocket. The white peaks trembled on the screen, reduced to a postcard. At times like these, he wished he was more of an artist, but a quick snapshot would have to do. Pocketing his phone, he knew he had to get closer. It was irresistible. He looked up at the sky, a sudden memory of his stormy Saint Moritz walk with Safiya troubling him, but there wasn't a cloud in sight. Shining blue as far as the eye could see. A line of buzzards appeared, squawking, their ragged line passing so fast overhead he could hear their feathers moving in the wind. He shuddered. Zhu Yong had been right: he hadn't seen a single crow, not even a little songthrush. The buzzards were the first birds he'd seen that day.

He began his descent. There was a different quality to the air in the valley, he noticed, even half a mile in: as if the air was stiller, more contained. An echoing silence. The rock rose up either side of him, higher and higher, until it felt as if he were entering a long tunnel. How far was he from the jade blue stream? He had no idea. The further down he went, the less perspective he had on his surroundings. The white mountains began to vanish, too, as he descended. Still, he was drawing closer to them, he knew. Even if the high stone was making him feel a little claustrophobic. Perhaps if he could just make it to the end of the long valley, he was thinking, he would see them again – when a sudden sound made him stop. A crack, and a tumble.

Avalanche! he thought, panicking, but no: it was a rockslide, far down in the distant end of the valley. He watched wide-eyed as the boulders tumbled down into the valley, innumerable stones of all sizes following them like a swarm of bees. *Thank God there's no-one down there*, he thought, before realising he had no idea if that was true. It was too early in the season for hikers, Zhu Yong had said, but what about the people who lived in these valleys? Maybe there were villages down there, ones he couldn't see from his vantage point. He swallowed. He needed to get back to the monastery. He'd walked too far already.

Axel turned and began walking quickly back up the valley, towards the crossroads he'd left not too long before. What was that noise? It sounded like some kind of motor. His t-shirt was clammy with sweat, and his breath was short. *Altitude*, he tried to reassure himself, but he knew he was frightened. What was he thinking, coming all the way out here without a guide?

The rumble sounded at first like a low-flying aeroplane – *it's crashing!* Axel thought wildly – then became a white wall of noise. Then he felt the earth begin to shake beneath him. He turned back towards the valley and could barely process what he was seeing: rocks falling everywhere, snapping trees. More surreally, the ice peaks were disintegrating from the distant mountains, slipping down into the chaos and darkness beneath. Frozen, he saw a boulder the size of a car come flying down towards him, then crash into the rockface on the other side of the valley, smashing into smithereens. Coming to his senses, he turned back to the path and began to run out of the valley, towards the hill.

The earth was buckling around him, moving, and still the sound was all around him. *Like jumping on a water bed*, he thought, the image coming to him murkily. A rift had opened up to one side, as if the earth was opening to swallow him up, but Axel just ran straight on, as fast as he could, back towards the hill. Time compressed strangely. By the fact that he was struggling to breathe, he knew he was going uphill, and understood that was a good thing. Then a great wave of something hit him, and all he could do was fling his arms around a pine tree. *I'm going to be buried alive*, he thought, not knowing if what was pummelling into his back was ice or dirt or snow. *This is it.* He had no idea how long it lasted, but when he opened his eyes, the ground was black and muddy. Dirt, he understood. His face stung, and something warm was running down his cheek. It was utterly silent.

Not even brushing off his clothes, he started running again. He had to get as far from this valley as he could. He had to get back to the monastery. The ground had stopped moving, and his ears were buzzing; a dull, hollow sound. He focused on the sight of his feet pounding the ground: first rock, then torn earth, then springy green grass. At last, he stopped, his hands pressed to his thighs, his breathing rough and painful. When he turned, he could no longer see the valley, only the peaks in the distance. It stunned him, how still and stable they seemed. Walking more slowly now, he began circumnavigating the hill. He was sure it was shorter that way, even if retracing his steps would have felt more comfortable. But the path was neatly traced, and there were almost no signs here of the shattering earthquake, only a fallen tree or two, and a large patch of bare earth where a rock must have once lain. It was comforting and uncanny in equal measure. As the buzzing in his ears gave way, he began to really notice the silence, too. As the path wound slowly towards the southern side of the hill, Axel found himself slowing down. Something was holding him back, although he didn't understand what: wouldn't he feel a wave of relief at finally seeing the walls of the monastery?

When he reached a lookout point, he finally understood what he'd known in his heart since the earthquake had begun. The monastery had been destroyed. The whitewashed buildings had been crushed, as surely as if a giant child had flicked them with his finger. Wooden beams stuck out like matchsticks from the piles of bricks, and a fragment of orange cloth was fluttering in the wind. Axel's breath caught in his throat, and he began to run down the hill.

★ ★ ★ ★

Somewhere nearby, a donkey was braying – a raw, dreadful sound. Axel slowed, a sense of foreboding in his stomach. From this point halfway down the hill, he could see a small hamlet, or what was left of it: a cluster of homes. Following the donkey's voice, he made his way painstakingly down the southwestern flank of the hill, following the track as it dipped down. He could no longer see the houses. How had he not explored more before today? he found himself thinking. How did he not know the valley better after all these weeks; the people that lived there, the villages? The cries were closer, now, and all at once he emerged from a small woods into the clearing. Half the houses had been smashed, he saw at once, and several more might have been swallowed by the ravine that had opened up, right in the grass. One side of the rift had risen up above the other, roots dangling from the ripped earth. It was eerily silent. He tiptoed past the two remaining shacks, one of which had lost its corrugated tin roof. There was no-one here. Not a soul. Then he saw the donkey: lying on its side, its eyes rolling white in terror. As he moved closer, slowly so as not to frighten the beast, he saw that it was strapped into an elaborate harness, which seemed to disappear down the ravine. Then he understood: there wasn't just one donkey. There had been two. This one, the living one, was tied to one that had fallen into the earth. Swallowing, Axel looked around him. There was no way he had the strength to pull a full-grown donkey up out of the rift, let alone a dead one. He knelt down very gently by the donkey that lay on its side. Very carefully, he laid a hand on its forehead. The donkey's eyes rolled, and it tossed its head weakly, braying, then submitted to his stroking.

Axel stood back up. There was only one solution: he had to cut the harness. He made his way over to the broken houses, not daring to enter the empty ones. He retched when he saw the blood, and pulled away. Suddenly remembering the monastery, he realised he had to act fast. He wouldn't be the only survivor in the valley: people needed help. Spying a fragment of twisted brown metal poking out from the corner of one of the houses, he pulled it up, not looking too closely. It was some kind of farm implement, broken into pieces when the house had collapsed. By the ravine, the donkey was still bawling. It made his heart ache. Their owner must have been preparing to travel down into the valley when the earthquake hit, for food or supplies. The donkey saw the sharp object in his hand, and brayed louder, but didn't have the strength to move. One of his hind legs kicked weakly. Axel knelt down by his side and began sawing at the harness. The leather was pulled tight by the weight beneath, and frayed in places from the accident: still, it startled Axel when it gave way. The donkey leapt to its feet, unsteady as a newborn colt, and Axel fell onto the ground. Braying, it ran off down towards the lake. Axel stood up slowly, brushing dirt from his legs. 'You could at least say thank you,' he yelled after the donkey, but his voice sounded strange in the deathly hush of the village, and after that he spoke no more.

He turned back towards the main track, focused on getting back to the monastery now. The sky was still a brilliant shade of blue, as if unaware of what had happened to the earth below. It was unnerving, somehow, that the sun should not be affected by what he had witnessed – the valley collapsing as if a nuclear bomb had detonated beneath it. What an enormous amount of energy! Enough to power all of Europe and America combined, he thought, dazedly. Hundreds, thousands times more than what he had witnessed with Safiya in Saint Moritz. And no doubt there had been dozens of avalanches around the valleys, snow lifting from the mountainside into a chaos of white, devouring everything. All of a sudden he felt sick to his stomach.

★ ★ ★ ★

The monastery was eerily silent. Could he even call it a monastery, now that most of the buildings were rubble? Two monks were walking slowly, one's arm draped around the other's shoulders. Their faces looked empty and blank. He didn't recognise them. Everywhere, the grass was matted with dirt and red dust. As he climbed back towards the eastern hill, he saw with a thrill of relief that the temple was still partially standing: one of its walls and the roof folded over like cardboard, but the structure still recognisable. 'Oh God.' The words escaped from him before he'd had time to clasp his hand over his mouth, and the standing monks looked up from their task wearily. The bodies were lined up on the side of the hill, wrapped in silk sheets. 'Choden,' Axel said softly, recognising one of the workers, his eyes welling with tears. 'Are you OK?' Choden looked at him blankly for a moment, then nodded, turned and walked away. Axel counted seven bodies. Almost half the permanent residents. Choden and the two strangers were still alive, but who else? Axel blanched and began running towards the temple, praying blindly and instinctively. *Please don't let him be dead. Please let him be OK.*

Zhu Yong smiled weakly when Axel burst through the doorframe. 'You need to wash your face,' he murmured, his voice rough. 'Very brown, not like American.'

Crying softly, Axel fell to his knees by his side. One of the wooden beams that once held up the ceiling lay over Zhu Yong's stomach, and his legs disappeared into a heap of broken bricks. There was blood on the corner of his mouth. The air smelled like dirt and rancid butter.

'Do you have... water?' he asked, and Axel scrambled to pull his water bottle from his pack.

Zhu Yong gulped thirstly as Axel poured the water carefully into his mouth, then coughed and winced. 'I told you change was coming,' he said.

Axel made a sound like a laugh, then wiped his eyes. 'I've never been in an earthquake,' he said.

'I'm so happy you are alive,' said Zhu Yong. 'I could not live with the guilt if I had let you go into that valley... You didn't, did you? You turned back, like you said?'

Axel hesitated. 'I went around the eastern hill,' he lied. 'Like you said.'

Zhu Yong nodded, relieved. 'I have experienced many quakes in my life,' he said, 'but none like this. I believe it marks a turning point for me.' He reached a shaking hand up and wiped a tear from Axel's face. 'Don't cry,' he said. 'This is only one life. In my next life I will be very handsome. Have many beautiful wives.'

Axel began laughing and crying again.

'I will watch over you. Don't worry. My soul will stay here, close to my body, during four days. I will make sure those idiots out there do a good job cleaning up. You make sure they read prayers over me, yes? It is the Tibetan way.' He sighed. 'I have heard, you know, that after this I may see a brilliant light. A clear light. It will be frightening. But if I can embrace it, welcome it, then I need not be reborn.' He shrugged, wincing again at the pain.

'Do you want to be reborn?' Axel asked quietly.

Zhu Yong smiled, showing his yellowing teeth. 'I am not finished here on this earth. No, I do not think I will embrace the clear light this time. But when the quake began, I saw something strange – saw the snow falling from the high mountains, and the sun seemed to fall down too, so bright. I wonder if it is like that, when it comes.'

They were silent for a moment. 'If I do not accept the light,' Zhu Yong finally said, 'then I will begin seeking another birth.'

'So you can choose your reincarnation?' Axel asked.

'I will be limited by my thoughts and actions in this life.' Zhu Yong grimaced. 'I have not been perfect.'

'You've been a monk all your life!' said Axel. 'Isn't that good enough?'

Zhu Yong made a strange sound, which Axel recognised as a laugh. A little blood seeped from the corner of his mouth, and he leaned down and wiped it from the monk's face with his sleeve.

'Our single lives are nothing in the face of the universe, my child,' Zhu Yong finally said, his eyes staring at the ceiling, or into some unknown beyond and above. 'Good or bad. I wish you could see, like me, how hopeful a message that truly is. Our insignificance is what makes our lives so beautiful. You must learn to appreciate the unknown.'

Axel slipped his hand into his and squeezed, trying hard not to cry. 'So the souls of all those who have died here today, they will stay here for four days?' he asked. Right then, it didn't feel like a strange thing to imagine. How could these people leave their temples, their families, their lives behind just because an earthquake had killed them?

Zhu Yong nodded. 'Each of them insignificant, each of them irreplaceable. Such is human life.'

When Zhu Yong closed his eyes, Axel sat for a long time, still holding his cool hand, trying to understand that his soul had left his body, and would not return.

CHAPTER THIRTY-ONE

Axel startled awake from a nightmare full of black dirt, his shirt stuck to his back. It was dark, and the air was dry, but he was warm – of course, he was on an aeroplane back to Texas, flying back home. He took a long ragged breath in and pressed the button to call the air hostess. The light blinked on over his head, glowing softly.

In his dream, he'd been back in the valley, running as fast as he could, except that his feet had been sinking into the earth as it wobbled beneath him, until the earth was around his waist like sinking sand. Then – and this part had really happened – he had turned around, and looked down the tunnel of the still, dark valley. The ice or dirt or snow had stopped coming in a wave, and the boulders had stopped crashing down. An eerie silence filled the valley. The terrifying energy had just… dissipated. Vanished into the air. Or changed, the scientist in him argued. Yes, everything he had ever learned about energy told him it had transformed. But into what?

Into death, he thought moodily, unable to stop thoughts of the dead creeping into his mind. Bohmann's Hand of God certainly hadn't intervened to save those poor villagers, their livestock, or the monks in the monastery. Then he chastised himself for the cynical thought, remembering Zhu Yong. The monk had accepted the end of his life – or of this particular life – peacefully. Where Axel had seen an ending, he had seen a time of change. He had been willing and ready to give himself up to the cycles of the universe: life and death, birth and rebirth. If Axel wanted to honour his memory, he would need to do the same.

The air hostess appeared in the soft green glow. 'Yes, sir?'

'Could I get a glass of water?' Axel croaked. 'With ice, please?'

'Are you alright, sir?' she asked, frowning in concern.

He nodded, clearing his throat discreetly. 'I'll be fine.'

Cleanup at the monastery had been slow. He had helped move beams, roll stones, gather the bricks into piles, ready for reconstruction. He'd helped dig graves. On the third day after the earthquake, some of the monks had decided that they were done with waiting: somebody needed to trek down into the valley for medical supplies, and to get help. Axel had stayed with the weak and the wounded, cooking dal bhat and trying to keep morale up. He'd helped pick up all the books that once formed the library, saving as many as he could. He'd walked down by the lake, staring blankly at the bright blue waters, missing his mother and Safiya. He'd waited with the others in the canteen, or pacing out under the dawn sky, scanning the sky for a helicopter. At last, one had come, whirring like a metal vulture, descending. Once the wounded had been carried up into the body of the beast, Axel had hesitated, the wind from the whipping blades in his hair, the noise of the motor deafening. Wasn't he needed here? Could he really turn his back on all this, never to return? Wouldn't it be betraying Zhu Yong to leave the monastery? It was Choden who had talked sense into him. 'Your family will be worried,' he had said, his face close to his ear, his strong hands squeezing his shoulders. 'They need you. Go home to them.' Axel had clasped him in a tight hug, a sob in his chest, then climbed into the helicopter. For a long time, his face crushed to the grimy windows, he'd watched the peaks fade into the distance.

Axel wiped his eyes and stared for a long time at the animated map in front of him, showing the plane's speed (900 km/h) and the outside temperature (minus sixty degrees Fahrenheit) – unfathomable figures. A long golden line showing the flight's trajectory appeared first, showing the aeroplane's progression out of Kathmandu, out across northern India and Pakistan, arcing down towards the Persian Gulf. This too seemed unreal, with the names of deserts printed out in several languages. The immensity of the Himalayan range reduced to a painted line of brown! Finally, a map of current weather systems appeared, blue waves and white trails of clouds swirling across the face of the world.

Axel wondered idly if hurricanes appeared on maps like these, then why earthquakes didn't. How strange it had felt that the earthquake hadn't affected the weather, so that the sun kept shining on even as everything below it was destroyed! There had been almost no warning signs – the birds, the rockslide, the rumbling noise like an aeroplane… With a twist in his stomach, Axel remembered both Zhu Yong and Hikmat mentioning change in the air. The novice had mentioned the stars shaking: perhaps Axel had slept right through the preliminary signs the previous night. He wondered what had happened to Hikmat. The earthquake had struck all across the country, following a vast faultline. It was impossible to know if the road back down the mountain had kept him safe. Axel hated the selfish thought even as it coalesced in his head, but he couldn't help wondering if his letter had made it out of the country, or if Patti-Ann was still in the dark as to his intentions. He supposed he would find out soon enough.

He shook his head, as if trying to dispel the gloom that hung around him. Most of the people on the plane with him had been in the earthquake, or were coming home because of it. The tiny airport at Kathmandu had been a scene of chaos, every one of the tourists thinking they were the ones who deserved to get home the fastest. How different their reasoning had been to the monks' in the monastery, who had accepted their tragic fate peacefully! Axel wasn't usually one to romanticise other cultures, but in this particular case he couldn't help but feel that the American and European tourists could have stood to learn something from Tibetan Buddhism.

The air hostess returned with a large cup of water and ice, which she handed to him with a smile. 'If you need anything else,' she said, 'just call me.'

Axel smiled gratefully and drank his cold water down. Ice water! There were, after all, some advantages to Western life. He wondered if Zhu Yong had ever had ice water, or Coca Cola. Maybe in his next life, Axel thought wryly. He found himself wondering, not for the first time, about the idea of reincarnation. Zhu Yong was the first person he'd ever seen die, and it had been shocking, how clear it was when his spirit had left his body. He'd been sitting with his friend Zhu Yong, and then sitting with an empty vessel. It was like the silence suddenly filling the valley. If life, if his soul left his body, why shouldn't one imagine that it could return to another body, another birth? Extreme as the idea was, its roots seemed quite logical. Couldn't some truth be lurking there, a kernel of something worth exploring? After all, as the laws of physics state, energy is not created or destroyed. Energy is simply transformed. If one believed in the transmigration of souls, then, the idea would be that a soul continued to exist after it left the body. The only flaw with this theory was the unlikely idea that a soul continued to exist after death in the same form as in a living body, rather than being absorbed into something greater – a higher, or wider, power. Wasn't the alternative exactly what Safiya talked about? Souls returning to God, continuing to live after death as part of a great mass of souls, then returning to earth in a different form? A circle or cycle of life. Axel sat up straight, a peculiar tingling in his chest. In a way, it was just like Zhu Yong: what appeared to be an ending was simply a time for transformation. Could it be that the principles of energy transformation applied to life itself? Could it be that the life forces they were studying – he, Bohmann, Schmidt Hennessey, Safiya – were in fact all one and the same? Could chemical, mechanical, solar energy, the energy of earthquakes and wind turbines and steam engines, be related to – or seen as – a kind of life force? A... soul? A force that powered the Big Bang and set the stars spinning across the universe. A force that crashed down mountains in a cloud of snow, or moved the very tectonic plates of this earth, or shone down in the form of sunlight, making crops grow. A force that filled men and women as they prayed, or walked by a clear lake, or fell in love. A force that gave life, that connected everyone on earth, that left bodies only to be reabsorbed into another kind of power. A transformative, living soul. He realised he had crushed his plastic water cup in his excitement, but he couldn't help it. Life itself! The gears of his brain were whirring. Bohmann, even Schmidt Hennessey, had spent so much of their careers trying to prove that the laws of physics were limited or wrong. He too had been deeply drawn to the idea of a 'stop,' or some idea of an uncharted and inexplicable loss of energy. But what if the key to understanding life wasn't some Hand of God, or some mysterious stop? What if everything was more connected and more coherent than he had previously imagined?

He punched the button and set the little light above his head glowing again, then rummaged for the pad of paper and pen in his backpack. The air hostess appeared almost immediately, still smiling.

'Could I have a coffee, please?' Axel didn't even look up from the notes he was already scribbling as fast as he could.

'Had your eureka moment, then?' she teased him, but he only smiled and kept writing.

CHAPTER THIRTY-TWO

Upon arriving in Texas twenty hours later, wired from five or six cups of aeroplane coffee and a chocolate muffin, Axel took a taxi straight to Bohmann's house. The morning sun was bright and strange, and his mind was in a state of tense calm. He no longer cared whether Patti-Ann knew he was leaving her, and his mother could wait for her hug and her little gifts. A pang of guilt went through him at this thought – Felicia had been so worried when they'd spoken on the phone from Kathmandu. She'd had to wait five days after the news of the earthquake to hear from him: there had been no means of communicating with the outside world left in the devastated monastery, so he had been unable to call her until the helicopter had carried him all the way back down the mountain. Then he'd taken a cross-country bus back to the capital, where the airport was, and in the ensuing chaos of crowds, he'd lost another two days. All in all, his mother had had to wait a week without knowing if he would be able to leave Nepal safely. It wouldn't be fair to let her worry any more. He relented and pulled his phone out of his pocket. *Hi Mom! Plane delayed*, he typed, feeling guilty. *I'll be home in a few hours! Love you.*

Then he set all other thoughts aside. He pulled his suitcase from the trunk of the taxi, paid the driver, and marched up to Bohmann's front door. Gosh, it was hot in Texas.

'Axel, my boy!' Bohmann exclaimed, opening the door sleepily, taking in the suitcase. 'Running away from home?'

Axel laughed, suddenly embarrassed, realising how rumpled his travel clothes were, and how tired he must look. 'I came straight from the airport,' he said. 'I have to talk to you about something. I've made a discovery.'

'Come in, come in.' Bohmann closed the door behind them, shaking his head affectionately. 'How was Nepal? Your mother called me to tell me you were all right, you know. She's such a sweetheart. Knew I'd be worried sick, watching the news.'

Without meaning to, Axel wondered if Safiya had felt the same. Then he remembered that she hadn't known he had been going to Nepal. She wouldn't know the monastery had been destroyed either. The thought made him feel almost infinitely sad.

'Coffee? Water? Advil?' Bohmann peered more closely at him. 'Shower? Nap?'

'A shower might be nice,' Axel admitted. 'And I could do with brushing my teeth.'

'My, you are a strange one. I can't wait to hear whatever you came all the way out here to tell me!'

'And I can't wait to tell you. Once I smell a little less gross.'

Laughing, Bohmann escorted him upstairs, found him a clean towel and a spare toothbrush, then padded back down the stairs. Axel could hear the coffee-maker bubbling as he stripped out of his sweaty travel clothes and climbed into the shower.

As the hot water cleared his head, he felt his thoughts settling into order. He wasn't crazy, coming here, and his theory came from more than grief and exhaustion. He could feel this life force moving through him: in the heat that warmed the water, in the motion of the water pressure, in the beating of his caffeinated heart. This was important – Bohmann would understand. Confidence washed over him in waves, soothing his rattled mind, and by the time he stepped out of the shower, he knew how he would start.

Bohmann handed him a tall glass of ice water when he arrived in the study, wearing his last clean clothes. 'Thanks, Professor,' he said, sinking into one of the leather armchairs. 'I'm sorry for turning up here like this without warning…'

'I'm used to it,' Bohmann smiled. 'Don't waste your breath apologising: tell me about your theory!'

Axel took a long drink from the glass of water, then set it down on a low table. 'Do you know that feeling,' he said, 'when you stare at a problem or a question for the longest time, and suddenly it clarifies? Like those magic eye puzzles, where you can suddenly see in three dimensions, and what you thought was a shapeless blue mass is actually full of 3D fish, or palm trees?'

Bohmann smiled. 'I remember those, yes,' he said. 'I used to do them with my son.'

Axel nodded. 'So, all the work we've done together has been on energy, more or less.'

'My whole career, more or less.'

'And even though we all agree that the world we live in is made of energy, we've kept up bumping up against these insufficiencies and frustrations, these parts of the mechanics or logic of that which we couldn't quite understand. Philosophers and scientists alike have wrestled with the question of the origin of the universe – after all, nobody knows *why* there is life on earth, and only barely *how*. Meanwhile, we think about energy – how it works, its cycles, its transformations, but we don't really study energy itself. What it is, why it exists, how it's here on earth. And where or how it might exist beyond our ability to perceive it.' He took a deep breath. 'Your frustration with the notion of the loss of energy during its transformations led you to come up with the idea of the Hand of God. It led me to contemplate the idea of... some kind of stop. Schmidt Hennessey, too, mostly works on these elements of the unseen and the unknown – what is difficult for us to understand.'

'Yes, yes!' said Bohmann.

'Like every scientist before us, we're trying to impose some kind of order on the universe, desperately trying to understand every minute working of its systems. But I'm beginning to think that this fight of ours is the wrong way to proceed. It's like we can't see the wood for the trees! We're analysing how the bark grows, how the roots collect nutrients, and somehow we've missed the fact that seen all together, from a distance, these trees are a forest. I'm talking about the universe, the cosmos, life on earth and in every single living organism! They're connected. What I'm saying is that I think the key to studying energy in a much more ambitious sense than anything we've undertaken so far may lie in something much closer to acceptance of the patterns of the universe as a whole. We need a new perspective: a different method of analysis or understanding, if you will.'

Bohmann frowned. 'Go on.'

Axel hesitated, gathering his thoughts. 'When I heard Safiya speaking in Istanbul, I remember thinking that she had begun to integrate some of our thinking, our scientific research, into the way she was thinking about the soul. I remember her saying that life does not come from nothing, nor does it vanish into nothing. Life carries on outside our bodies, in heaven and on earth, in wind and sunlight and water.' A vision of the light streaming in through the windows of the Blue Mosque came to him, but he pushed it away. 'I was thinking about this again in Nepal. The earthquake was tremendously powerful – there was this energy in the air. It was the same in Saint Moritz, when I saw the avalanche. Volcanoes, hurricanes, landslides, wildfires, all these natural catastrophes, well, they're so impressive because of this *power*. This life! It's like seeing – truly seeing – the universe in action for the first time. It's like being given a glimpse of the true and awesome power that lies all around us. Seeing the forest *and* the trees. It's... intoxicating.'

Like falling in love. The thought drifted into his mind, but again, he ignored it.

'That kind of energy, it's transformative, but it's also destructive. I saw a lot of people die in the earthquake, Professor Bohmann. The news says that tens of thousands of people died that day, and in the aftershocks that followed. More importantly for me, though, I saw someone I cared about, my mentor Zhu Yong, die. And he simply accepted his fate, his life lost to the devastating power of the earthquake, because he knew it was not the end. He knew the... energy of his life would not be lost. It would be transformed into new life. He died with a smile on his face.'

Bohmann was leaning forward, on the very edge of his seat, his coffee steaming, forgotten, on the side table next to him.

'And that was when I saw it. I began thinking about how everything on this earth is connected, but how little time we spend really acknowledging or appreciating those connections. I started thinking about energy. I saw that the energy of the earthquake was the same energy that kept Zhu Yong alive, and then left him. I heard, or felt, such destruction in the air, and I thought about how what caused the earthquake in Nepal was the energy, the heat at the earth's core. I thought about your sunlight, too, Professor. I thought about cycles, and connections. I thought about how the gravitational collapse of hydrogen clouds is what forms a star, gives birth to a sun. Then the energy from that nuclear fusion becomes sunlight. On earth, sunlight keeps operating as living, breathing energy, being stored and then set free: for instance, evaporating water to higher ground, from which it can become a stream, which can make plants grow, or tall trees that then burn down in a forest fire, generating heat and light. All of that energy is slowly recycled and released, right from the moment the hydrogen cloud collapsed. It's all connected, right?'

Bohmann nodded slowly, trying to follow. Axel wasn't ready to stop. He felt himself being carried away by the flow of his thoughts, which seemed to stream straight from his heart, bypassing his jetlagged head, like a river rushing down a mountain.

'And the human cycles we create, harnessing and transforming that energy, they're just our imitations and extensions of the larger cycles at work. For instance, Professor, that hydroelectric dam converts gravitational potential energy – water falling downhill – into electricity. That electricity can be converted by a motor, for instance, into mechanical energy, or into heat for a radiator, or light for a lightbulb. All from that same water, all from that same starlight, all from that same hydrogen cloud, that first big bang! Do you see where I'm going with this?'

'Yes,' said Bohmann, hesitantly. 'I think so.'

'Of course, the original energy is water, in this case, and before that, sunlight, but it transforms into heat and movement and light and sound. But there's yet another level of energy cycles going on in this living world, one we don't tend to think of as connected to those greater ones, although it mirrors them perfectly. And at this level, it's easier to pinpoint what I really want to hone in on and study. So, say that sunlight makes a sugar beet grow, which we then consume in the form of a doughnut, or stirred into coffee. That sugar goes into our stomachs, our bloodstreams, our hearts and brains, all moving in a million permutations of activity. So many little systems operating side by side that we can't even keep track of them! All of them powered by that sugar, grown by that sunlight, from that first big bang hydrogen burst. And still we've only covered the visible, physical part of what keeps us alive. I mean, why are we alive? Why can I move this finger, and why won't I be able to when I die? It's all about energy.' He stopped for breath, as the conclusion began to build in his chest. 'I mean... isn't it incredible, how this energy is everywhere, connecting everything?' Axel burst out. 'Chemical energy, thermal energy, mechanical energy, kinetic energy – it's all connected, it's all the same! Life! It's all connected, all never-ending, all utterly beautiful.'

'Can you explain what you mean by life in this context?' the professor asked, sounding a little overwhelmed.

'I'm talking about... a kind of life force. Not in a science fiction sense, but in a philosophical one. I mean, if we just look at human life, it's not really just eating sugar that makes me a living, functioning human being, is it? I am not alive simply because I have absorbed the energy from that big bang that created the sunlight that made the sugar beet grow. Eating some sugar can make me wiggle my fingers, or run a race, but it's not what makes me fall in love, or solve a math problem, or write a novel. That... life energy is something more. And it's not just a feature of the human cycles, it's a fundamental part of all of them. The cycles of the cosmos. The cycle of life and death. The cycle of the human soul. You and I and Schmidt Hennessey, we were all focusing on the right moment, but we were looking at it from the wrong direction. When an earthquake tears the earth apart, destroying thousands of lives, where does that energy go? When sunlight streams down on earth but doesn't burn those people, where does it go? It is simply transformed, concentrated into a kind of power outside the reach of modern science? And as we all know, just because you can't measure it doesn't mean it's not real.' Axel felt his eyes filling with tears. 'People think they understand energy because they can explain the science of what they perceive,' he said, 'or because they can give these different incarnations different names. But they don't understand. They don't see – really see – the energy of this world. They don't understand where it comes from, how it's all connected, and all meaningful. They don't see that that means that we're all a part of this energy, that we were all created together. That all life is interconnected. That all life is the same.'

He took a deep breath, and looked up at Bohmann, in whose eyes a light was dawning.

'Professor Bohmann, all of that energy, in space, in the stars, in sunlight, on earth, in all of us – it *is* the soul. It's all of our souls – this energy is life itself. That's the on switch, the origin, the connecting force. It's why we believe in heaven, that it all comes from heaven. From that first big bang hydrogen cloud collapse. It does! It's true! But our planet is a part of the heavens, just as Galileo suggested – a heavenly body, even with all its imperfections. Our little blue earth belongs to the eternal rhythms of the cosmos, and each of our lives belongs to those patterns, too.' A tear slipped down Axel's cheek.

Moved, Bohmann reached across and put a hand on Axel's shoulder. 'My dear boy,' he said, 'that's quite something.'

Axel slumped in his chair and wiped his eyes. 'May I have some coffee?' he asked.

Bohmann laughed, an emotional sound, and poured him a large mug, and sloshed in cream and sugar. 'The convert needs his energy,' he joked gently.

'I don't know if this is religious, Professor,' Axel said hesitantly, accepting the cup of coffee. He felt quite shaken by everything he'd just said, which went far beyond what he had scribbled in his notebook on the plane. In fact, he'd have been incapable of summing it up before.

'I don't know if religious is quite the right word,' Bohmann admitted. 'I mean, is Safiya's research religious? Is Schmidt Hennessey's research religious? No, although they revolve around concepts which most have considered religious – the soul, for instance – and admit their deep roots in religion. So does my research, although perhaps more explicitly, given that I use the idea of God to unify it. Of course, I've always explained that this is more of a metaphor for a higher power than anything – but we're not talking about my research. Your ideas about acceptance, about order in the universe; about coherence and connection, about the soul… Some will likely call them religious. You, however, are free to make your own mind up about that.'

Axel nodded and took a large gulp of his warm coffee.

'But there's another side to what you're saying, isn't there. Maybe that's what made you rush over to my house. You're saying, more or less, that mine and Schmidt Hennessey's controversial theories are, well, wrong. You're maybe saying that all of science is wrong!'

Axel snorted with laughter, spilling his coffee on his lap. 'I don't know if that's what I'm saying,' he confessed, accepting a paper napkin from Bohmann. 'I think I'm just questioning our instinct, as scientists, to get so wrapped up in our single theories, rather than aiming for a more general, all-encompassing understanding. Aiming to dissect and pin down this universe rather than just… live in it.'

'Holistic,' Bohmann commented. 'Perhaps you're right.'

'Or maybe I'm just proposing another crazy, single-minded theory of my own,' he shrugged. 'A holistic view of energy.'

'Well, you wouldn't be the first to suggest a major perspective shift is exactly what modern energy science needs.'

'But maybe you're right, Professor, that I am challenging your theory. I think you're on the right track, but you've not completed the equation. More generally, I think there's a common flaw to all of the theories we've been working on together so far – this attraction to the mysterious. We all want so badly to integrate something unseen and unknown into our theories, that none of us are taking the time to work on what it might be. And I believe this unseen thing can be known: the soul.' He smiled, getting excited. 'There's no Hand of God, Professor. There's no magical stop. There's only another kind of transformation, a new kind of energy conversion. And the key lies in what we've been trying to do all along: break down the separation between the work being done in the scientific and religious and humanities communities.' He rand a hand through his hair. 'I just find it hard to believe that nobody's studied the connection between all these energy cycles and human life or the soul before. It just feels so... obvious to me!'

'I'm sure it has been thought about a great deal. The connections and parallels between micro- and macrocosms of the living world certainly have. However, questions regarding the soul or the afterlife have always been sensitive ones. We're lacking in, how shall I put this, communication with the subjects. There's no proof.'

'Doubting Thomases!' Axel said suddenly, then began laughing. How desperately he wished Safiya was here.

Bohmann smiled, puzzled.

'OK, so I feel like it's important to clarify at this point that I'm not talking about the soul as a sort of ghost,' Axel said hastily. 'This isn't about reincarnation, or an afterlife where the dead are all floating around. Much as you use the notion of God as a kind of metaphor, I'm going to be using the notion of "the soul" as a way of thinking about these interconnected energy systems.'

Bohmann nodded. 'So what happens to a human soul when we die, then? According to this theory of yours. You say it's not a specific A to Z model of a human being that will simply change forms – as certain sects believe: all right. What is it, then?'

'It's transformed,' Axel answered, without having to think about it. 'It becomes a part of the universe, or God, or the cosmos, or however you want to frame it. A kind of eternal soul. Then, within that greater system, it's reintegrated into life on earth.'

'Recycled!' Bohmann grinned.

'The Defenders are really going to come after me, aren't they!' Axel added wryly.

Bohmann cocked his head to one side. 'I wouldn't be so sure about that,' he said. 'I haven't heard a peep out of them since we ran into them at the hospital. It seems to me they've realised they've been crossing lines. Or maybe they just ran out of funding, I don't know.'

'Well, that's a spark of good news.'

They sipped their coffees for a while in silence, each lost in their own thoughts.

'Are you hungry?' Bohmann suddenly asked. 'I'm hungry.'

Axel grinned. 'I have no idea,' he said. 'I've been travelling for so long, I don't even know what time it is.'

'It's pretty much lunchtime,' said the professor. 'Do you want to help me cook something?'

'The only thing I can cook is dal bhat,' Axel joked.

Bohmann's eyes lit up. 'Oh, would you cook me some? I haven't been cooked for in… well, years!'

'Of course I will,' said Axel, standing up. 'It's the least I can do after rocking up here all wild-eyed and jet-lagged.'

'Bright-eyed and bushytailed, as the saying goes. Well, I do like to see my young students fired up. Reminds me of my more ambitious days.' Bohmann hauled himself slowly out of his chair, and they walked to the kitchen.

'So, what do you need? Shall I run to the supermarket?'

'Well, mostly rice and lentils, let me think, an onion, some spices…'

Bohmann pulled open a drawer, and a musty, peppery smell billowed out. 'I used to have quite a good collection of spices,' he said, 'though not all of them are at their freshest.'

Axel began pawing through, looking for coriander, cumin, turmeric. 'Do you have any fresh ginger?' he asked, holding up a pale yellow bottle.

'I'm afraid not, my boy,' said Bohmann. 'But look at this! Red lentils! God knows how many years these have been up here…'

Axel accepted the heavy bag of lentils, hefting it in his hand. 'These'll be great,' he said, 'and dried ginger will be fine. Do you think you could find me an onion, and maybe some garlic? And a pan, a big pan.'

Bohmann mock-saluted and began scrambling around the kitchen. Axel lit the gas flame and began pouring little bits of spices into the pan.

'No oil?' the professor asked in surprise.

'Not yet,' said Axel. 'I'm toasting the spices.'

A rich, warm smell began to rise from the pan, soon mingling with the sharp scent of the onion Bohmann was chopping.

'We ate this twice every day,' Axel reminisced, 'and it was always delicious. It keeps you going all day, even when you're hiking for hours! Of course, some days I could have killed for a Mars bar…'

Bohmann laughed, carrying the onion and garlic over on the chopping board. 'What should I do now?'

Axel stirred the spices so that their aroma filled the kitchen, then he poured a little oil into the pan. 'I'm not sure this is the 100 per cent traditional method,' he confessed, 'but I did watch the monks in the kitchen a few times.'

'Better than buttered toast,' Bohmann commented, tipping the chopped vegetables in.

The sweet scent of onion and garlic mingled with the spices, and both men inhaled happily.

'I'm starving,' Axel suddenly realised.

'I've heard achieving nirvana has that effect.'

Axel shook his head and rolled his eyes. 'It's not like that,' he said. 'It's just a working theory.'

'I know, my boy, I know.' Bohmann's eyes were shining. 'But it does my heart good to see you like this. I can't help but be excited for you.'

'OK, now we can add the lentils.'

'Oh, I bet you're supposed to rinse these!' Bohmann rushed over to the sink, tipped the red lentils into a sieve and ran them under the tap. 'There you go,' he said, returning with the dripping sieve and adding its contents to the saucepan with a sizzle.

Axel stirred everything together. 'Now we wait,' he said.

'That's entropy for you,' Bohmann said, staring into the pan of lentils. 'Once you mix everything together, it can never be unmixed. Such is the balance of the universe.' Axel gave a startled laugh. 'What?' said the professor. 'It's true. If you mix cream into coffee, the cream will not stay in a tidy fern leaf or galaxy-shaped spiral. It will mix in until both are inseparable, and you cannot unmix it. That's called topological mixing.' He pulled out a chair at the kitchen table, and sat down heavily. 'I'm guess what I'm really thinking about is chaos theory, which was only acknowledged in the second half of the twentieth century. Chaos theory, you know, the butterfly effect.'

Sitting down across from him, Axel nodded. 'I know the basics,' he said.

'Shows that no matter how well we know a system, it cannot be predicted. Just look at our weathermen! The other day the weather app on my phone showed a black cloud raining, while I was outside by the lake without a jacket.' Bohmann made a harrumphing sound. 'We scientists are terribly resistant to what feels like it cannot be explained or controlled. In the case of chaos theory, this coffee-cream thing was just palmed off on imprecise measures, dismissed as incidental noise. It took a hundred years for scientists to acknowledge topological mixing as a full and valid part of the systems they were studying.'

'I think my jetlag is really setting in,' said Axel. 'Why are you telling me this?'

Bohmann laughed. 'There are two reasons chaos theory is on my mind right now. One: perspective is everything, and acknowledging our limits is an immense part of the work we do. Just look at scientists like Mandelbrot, and any study of patterns in data. And that was the 1960s! Recent stuff!'

'What was Mandelbrot studying?' asked Axel, struggling to keep up.

'Mandelbrot's argument was about perspective, broadly speaking. He noted that a ball of twine looks totally different depending on your own position: like a single point when viewed from far away (that's zero-dimensional), like a ball when viewed from up close (that's three-dimensional) or, from up really close, like a long curved strand, wound around, which would be one-dimensional. Order and chaos! Of course, the chaotic is different from the random. And therein lies the whole secret of the universe.'

Axel rubbed his eyes. 'I feel like what you're saying is very interesting, but I'm very tired and hungry.' He laughed, stood up and went to stir his lentils.

'I know, I know, my boy. We'll have all the time in the world to talk about all this. But I want you to understand that what you're undertaking is part of a longstanding and very honourable scientific tradition – lest you think your holistic theory is overthrowing all of science. Your theory *is* science. The separation between science and religion is an artificial one. That's important for you to remember. Or if you want to disagree with me, you'll have to work on a coherent argument.' He paused, his eyes twinkling. 'But maybe not today.'

Bohmann stood up, walked up towards the stove, and peered into the pan. 'How are we doing over here?'

'I think it's time to cook up some rice,' said Axel.

'I guess they don't have microwavable rice in Nepal, huh?' said Bohmann, retrieving an orange sachet from the cupboard.

Axel wrinkled his nose. 'That's not very traditional. But it is quicker than going to the store,' he added, relenting.

'Good,' said Bohmann. 'Then we can set the table.'

After popping the sachet in the microwave, the professor began pulling down plates from the shelves. Axel found the cutlery in a drawer.

'Really, if we were doing this in style,' he said, 'I'd make some kind of *achar*, or spicy tomato pickle, and serve some extra vegetables on the side, but today we'll live like paupers or monks—'

'Which is appropriate, given that we have gathered here today for a deeply intellectual discussion…'

The two men laughed. Bohmann retrieved the cooked rice from the microwave and spooned it into two plates, and Axel ladled some of his dal over the top.

'Now, for a truly traditional experience, we cut the power and eat with our fingers, OK?'

The doorbell rang, and both of them looked up in astonishment.

Bohmann blinked. 'Nobody ever comes over here this time of day. Must be Jehovah's Witnesses or something.'

'Don't worry, the dal bhat is pretty hot. I'll wait.'

Axel fished out his phone as Bohmann left the kitchen. *Stopped to see Bohmann for lunch — I'll be home soon*, he texted his mother, despite knowing how much she would yell at him for not coming straight home. *Love you!*

He could hear voices at the front door, but couldn't make out the words. Whoever it was was speaking quite softly.

Axel sighed, snapped a picture of his meal and sent it to his mother. *Guess my stomach is still in Nepal*, he captioned it.

After a moment's hesitation, the professor still not having returned from the front door, he texted Patti-Ann. *Did you get my letter?*

'Axel?' Bohmann's voice was hesitant. When Axel looked up, his jaw dropped.

'Hi Axel,' Kyle said sheepishly. 'Wow, that sure smells great.'

'It's all right,' said Bohmann softly, seeing Axel's hands clench around his chair's armrests. 'My son... comes in peace, I guess.'

There was an awkward silence. 'Listen, Dad, I didn't mean to interrupt. I can come back some other time.'

'No, no! Please, join us!'

Noticing the pleading note in Bohmann's voice, Axel stood up. 'Sure,' he said. 'There's plenty of food.' He pulled down a plate from the cupboard and spooned dal bhat onto it. 'I need to be heading home soon anyway.'

CHAPTER THIRTY-THREE

The three men ate in silence for a time, each unsure how to begin a conversation.

'So, I guess you guys are wondering why I'm here, huh,' Kyle eventually said, his eyes firmly on his *dal bhat*. His plate was almost empty, Axel noticed: the twenty-year-old was eating like he hadn't seen a homecooked meal for some time. Surprisingly, it brought a wave of something like pity rising up in Axel's chest.

'Well, it has been six or seven years,' Bohmann replied. He was keeping his tone light, but Axel could see the emotion brimming in his eyes. His hands were shaking as he brought bites of lentils up to his mouth.

Kyle bit his lip, his shoulders hunched forward. 'I don't really know where to start,' he said. 'Maybe I shouldn't have come.' He still acted like a wayward teen, Axel thought in dismay, wondering how old he really was. Twenty-two? Twenty-four? It was hard to tell under that thicket of dark hair, with that snarl of his lip.

'Why don't you start with what's going on with the Defenders? Have they ditched you?'

'Axel!' Bohmann said reproachfully.

Axel hadn't meant to make a dig, but he couldn't help it. The kid had destroyed his own father's research, been a part of a hate campaign that got him fired from the university, and generally gone around wreaking havoc every time Axel had crossed his path: at his birthday party, at the Tabernacle, at the hospital. Why did he have to turn up now? It was hard not to feel protective towards Bohmann, who was still visibly shaking.

'Sorry,' he muttered.

Kyle looked pained. 'Well, if you really want to know, they've disbanded, I guess,' he said defensively.

Axel raised his eyebrows, feeling bad about his question. 'Disbanded?' he repeated.

Kyle nodded. 'Yeah, Ichabod Potts has left the country,' he said sadly, the posturing draining out of him with each word. 'He's... fleeing from the law. There have been these charges, embezzlement, fraud, I don't know. I came downstairs this morning and he'd just gone, with all his things. The lights were on. He didn't even leave a note.'

Now that his face had unwrinkled out of its teenage sneer, Axel noticed how tired and pale he looked. 'Oh, Kyle! That son of a...'

'I shouldn't have been surprised,' he muttered, 'but I was. He was a nasty old fucker, but he really looked after me, you know, after...'

'After Mom died,' Bohmann finished gently. 'I know, son.'

Kyle's eyes were red, and the words began to flow as if they'd been pent up inside him for years. 'I didn't mean for anything to happen the way it did, Dad. I just missed Mom so much, and it felt like you didn't care that she was gone.' Axel flinched at the level of anger that was tangible in Kyle's words. These were old grievances, ones that had been fermenting inside him, driving the pitch and volume of his voice up as he continued. 'You just kept on with life. And I never felt like I was the son you needed or wanted – not smart enough, not interested in science. I felt like I was a constant disappointment to you. So when Potts took the time to ask me how I was coping, to talk to me about grief... he made me feel like I had a choice to do something big with my life, something new.'

Bohmann nodded, staying miraculously calm in the face of this outburst. 'A fresh start. I can understand that.' There was a silence. 'Even if it broke my heart,' he finally added.

Axel was frozen to his chair, unable to tear his eyes from the scene. It crossed his mind that he should get up and discreetly leave the room, but he didn't want to interrupt. Besides, he really wanted to see what happened.

Kyle seemed unable to look up from his plate and meet his father's eyes. His voice had dropped to a low murmur again. 'He made me feel like I was powerful, important, you know? He made me feel like I was flawless in God's eyes, like I would always be protected. Like I'd always belong. We made a lot of money, he always gave me a fair commission on my collection plate. It took me a couple years to figure out everything he was doing with that money wasn't above board, but by that time he was my family. The Defenders were, I mean. They were everything to me.' Now Kyle was crying in earnest, raw, guttural sobs escaping in between the words of his confession.

'Even when I saw what a scam it all was, even when I understood that this had nothing to do with Christianity in any good or moral sense, I was in too deep. Sometimes I'd be watching Potts humiliate some poor out-of-town guy up in front of a TV audience for money, and I'd feel sick with shame. But he was still my... well, he'd become a father to me.' He leaned on the word defensively, as if provoking Bohmann, but the professor didn't react. 'I didn't know how to leave; I didn't want to leave. I didn't want to be on my own. I'd already messed up one family, I couldn't risk another. I didn't think I had a choice anymore, after I burned all my bridges...'

'You could have come to me,' Bohmann said, reaching across the table and clasping his son's hand. 'You could have told me you were hurting. I didn't know you felt that way. I thought you needed me to be strong, to keep our house going like nothing had happened, like Mary wasn't gone. Of course I was hurting. My whole life fell apart that year. I lost my wife and my son.'

'I just miss her so much,' Kyle said, wiping his nose on his sleeve.

Bohmann stood up, walked over and wrapped his son in his arms. 'I miss her too,' he murmured. 'Every single day.'

As quietly as he could, Axel slid his chair back, attempting to tiptoe from the room.

Kyle laughed, the sound muffled by his father's shoulder. 'Dad, your guest is trying to sneak out. I think we've embarrassed him.'

Bohmann pulled back from the hug, his eyes red. 'You don't have to go,' he said.

'At least finish your food,' Kyle added, pulling a tissue from his pocket and blowing his nose. 'Or I will.'

'OK,' said Axel, sinking back down into his chair, embarrassed. 'But then I really need to get home to my mom.' He smiled at Kyle, a peace offering, and the youth smiled back.

'Seriously, can I have some more lentils?' Bohmann's son asked, and his father leapt up to fill his plate.

'There's cheese, too, if you want, and some olives.'

Kyle nodded gratefully. 'Thanks, Dad. I haven't really... I don't really have any money.'

'Don't you worry about that, son. You can stay here as long as you want,' Bohmann said at once, setting down more food from the fridge.

Kyle cut himself a huge wedge of cheese, then used it to spoon *dal bhat* into his mouth. 'So what were you guys talking about before I showed up?' he asked once he'd finished his bite. His voice was still shaky, but there was a softness to his expression that Axel had never seen before. He looked a lot younger.

'Axel was telling me about his idea for a new book,' Bohmann said with a smile. Relaxing for the first time since his son had turned up, he ate a spoonful of lentils.

'A book?' Axel looked up in surprise. 'I don't know about that. It's just a theory.'

'It should definitely be a book.'

'Well, I sort of thought it was going to be a chapter in your book. You know, the book we're working on together, aren't we?'

Bohmann laughed, startling everyone. 'My boy, your theory will take far more than a chapter to spell out. No, no, the tables have turned: you shouldn't be my assistant any more. Heck, I should be your assistant!'

'But what about your book?' Axel was still confused.

Bohmann waved a hand in the air dismissively. 'My book isn't going anywhere, it can wait. This, what you're talking about, this is what I want to focus my energies on. When you get to be my age, you learn to prioritise. No, no, no objections. You just make sure to send me your chapter drafts so I can look through them. I'd be thrilled to be your editor.'

'But—' said Axel.

'I'm so sorry about your research, Dad,' Kyle blurted out. 'Is that why you're not writing your book anymore?' He looked genuinely upset.

Bohmann shook his head gently. 'Who said anything about me not writing my book? No, I'm just firing Axel from the task.'

'We only… I was only supposed to give you a scare, let you know that the Defenders had their eye on you. It was my fault – I was the one who got carried away and wiped the whole disc.'

Axel saw that Kyle had tears in his eyes again. How fragile he seemed today, for someone who spent all his time playing tough! It was genuinely moving, seeing this new side to him.

'Of all the things you should be apologising for…' Bohmann grinned, hesitated, then reached over and laid a hand lightly on Kyle's shoulder. 'Son, you destroying that research was the best thing that could have happened to modern science. It made me work harder than I've done in thirty years, it put me back in touch with old friends all over the world, and it set Axel here on a path of discovery the likes of which I could never even have imagined. Now, I'm not saying you should go around bugging everybody's hard drives, but in this case, you did me a favour.'

Kyle looked like Christmas had come early. 'You really mean that?' Bohmann nodded.

'It's true,' said Axel. 'It all worked out just fine.'

Kyle smiled gratefully at him. 'Two books, huh. That's really something.'

'About what you said earlier, Kyle,' Bohmann said suddenly, 'I never meant to make you feel like you had to be… like me. I'd happily have supported you in any sort of career you wanted. And I plan to, from this day onwards. Go on, tell me, what are your plans?'

'I don't know,' Kyle mumbled, and for a moment a flicker of his grumpy teenage self appeared. 'It's not like I have a lot of options.'

'Well, if you need a job, I'm sure I can hook you up with something,' said Bohmann. 'But you don't need to worry about that straight away. Kyle, son, you've just broken away from a cult. You're allowed a little time to figure things out. Get back on your feet.'

The relief on Kyle's face was palpable. 'I don't really deserve...' he muttered, his voice trailing off into nothing, his eyes like those of a beaten puppy.

'Don't be ridiculous,' Bohmann said in his warmest, most professorial voice. 'Nothing you say today will be held against you, OK? I'm asking as your dad, who wants to know what you've been up to, not to force you into anything. If you tell me you're really into plumbing, I won't make you become a plumber. So tell me what you care about, what you're into. Tell me what's important to you!'

Axel couldn't help but smile, happiness welling up in his stomach. For some reason, he felt like a part of this little family, sitting at the table – *as if Kyle were my stepbrother, or something.* It occurred to him, not for the first time, that Bohmann had really been a father to him throughout his studies. Now that he was standing on his own two feet, perhaps the professor's energies could be directed back where they were always meant to go: into caring for his own son.

'Well, actually, I've been making a lot of music,' Kyle said very shyly. 'I... kind of sing, and I play the guitar.'

'The guitar?' Bohmann's eyes were shining. 'Just like your mother?'

Kyle nodded. 'I mean, it's nothing, really. I started out just doing hymns with the Defenders for the Sunday services, and then some friends brought me along to an open mic night over at the Trout Fisher Bar... Now I'm going to try out for a regular slot over at the Cherry Pie Diner on Fridays nights.' He was blushing. 'My first one is next week. Maybe you guys could come.'

'I'll be there,' his father said happily. 'I'll embarrass you just like a real dad.'

Kyle cut himself another wedge of cheese. There was another silence, as everyone finished their plates. 'She's really pretty, your girlfriend, I mean the new one,' he suddenly said shyly, looking over at Axel.

Instinctively, Axel flinched, but seeing the blush spreading across Kyle's cheeks, he backed down. 'Yeah,' he said, 'Safiya's a really wonderful woman. I think I lost her that night, though.'

Kyle's eyes went wide. 'Because of what happened at the hospital?'

Axel nodded mutely. 'I don't just mean you guys. I mean, what you – what the Defenders did was horrible, turning up in a sick old woman's hospital bedroom... But Safiya, I failed her too. I didn't defend her. I should have been there for her, and I didn't rise to it.'

'But you two, you had a connection! Even I could see it. Have you tried calling her?'

Axel couldn't help but smile at the young man's enthusiasm. 'I've tried,' he said, 'but she won't pick up.'

Kyle's face fell. 'Oh,' he said. 'That sucks.'

Something occurred to Axel. 'How's Patti-Ann been?' he asked.

Kyle looked surprised. 'You've not been in touch with her?'

Axel grimaced and shook his head. 'I had some things to work out first,' he said.

'Well, she comes to meetings a couple times a week now. She kind of replaced me as Potts's project, to be honest.' Kyle shrugged, but his voice was bitter. 'I guess she was a pretty new face, useful for the campaign. He wanted her to go on TV with him. Although who knows what'll happen now that he's run away.'

'Wow,' said Axel. 'I guess a lot of things changed while I was away, huh.'

'Wait, you were away?' asked Kyle.

'He was in Nepal!' Bohmann said, rather grandly. 'Finding illumination.'

'Taking some time out,' Axel corrected him, smiling.

'That's pretty cool,' said Kyle. 'So did you find what you were looking for?'

'I think so,' said Axel. 'Or I hope I did.'

★ ★ ★ ★

That night, Axel lay in bed, eyes closed, imagining stars floating through space, swirling like weather systems on an aeroplane map, the Milky Way like cream mixing into coffee. He imagined the Himalayas surging up out of the oceans as two tectonic plates were pushed together. He thought about how equivalently complex systems were operating inside every living thing, in plant cells and human chromosomes, all alive, all linked, all infinitely beautiful. He fell asleep with a smile on his face.

CHAPTER THIRTY-FOUR

An ordered universe: energy and the soul. The human macrocosm: an interdisciplinary study of the soul. Or did he mean a human microcosmos?

Looking up from his notebook, Axel drank deeply from his mug of coffee and shook his head. No-one could say he had chosen an easy topic to work on. He crumpled up the top sheet of paper and tossed it into the wastepaper basket. Preparing an introductory speech to give at Princeton was harder than anything else he'd done, academically speaking. He'd never written anything like it. He didn't even have a PhD! It was OK, he told himself, trying to channel his mother and Bohmann's encouraging, reassuring words of support. He was on the right track: he knew what he was talking about, and he felt passionately about the subject. Besides, he still had the rest of the day to work on his talk, as his flight out of Dallas wasn't until that evening. Axel leaned back from his desk and stretched. From his bedroom window, he could see his mother on her hands and knees in the garden, pulling up weeds and singing along to pop songs on her portable radio. It gladdened his heart.

He turned back to his notes. Princeton! Of course he was nervous. Who wouldn't be? The last three weeks had been a blur. Bohmann had encouraged him to begin drafting the book as soon as possible, to lay out his ideas, even messily, while they were still fresh in his mind. So he holed himself up in his childhood bedroom and wrote. And wrote and wrote and wrote. Bohmann had been more than helpful, sending back chapters printed out and covered with scribbled notes and highlighter. They'd spent whole afternoons sitting at his kitchen table or his study, working through difficult theoretical points while Kyle quietly practised the guitar in his bedroom. Axel couldn't believe how involved the professor had been – he felt guilty and grateful in equal measure. It had been Bohmann, in fact, who'd sent the first draft of the first chapter to *Scientific American*. Astoundingly, the magazine had accepted to publish the final version, giving him three months to polish it up. Axel hadn't been able to believe his luck. It was unheard of, a publication of this calibre accepting a first draft of a chapter – of an unwritten book, no less, from some Texan unknown! And yet the academic community had begun buzzing – both the scientific community, especially after the *Scientific American* news, and the more spiritually- or philosophically-minded departments. Once more, Bohmann had played a large part, Axel had to admit, emailing colleagues across his generous and eccentric network spread all over the country. This technique had borne its first serious fruits, career-wise, in the form of an invitation to give the introductory speech for an interdisciplinary conference on science and religion. And as of the previous weekend, an agent had been in touch to discuss optioning the rights to his book. It felt more and more like Axel was riding a wave of something exciting sweeping the country, an opening of minds, a cross-pollination across subjects and departments. Or perhaps it had already been happening for years, outside Texas at least, and now he got to be a part of it.

Not for the first time that morning, he thought wistfully of Safiya. So much of this was the fruit of their work together. How he wished he could tell her all about it! Long before him, she'd seen the potential that it had taken him months to uncover, the crossover between her work on the soul and his work on energy. Even Nepal, the trip that had changed everything and led to his first sparks of a revelation, had been inspired by her. He'd stopped sending her messages, embarrassed by the wall of silence with which she replied. If she wanted to forget what had happened between them, who was he to force her to remember? And so he sat alone with his melancholy – and his as yet unfinished speech – he suddenly remembered.

Axel sighed and swigged the last, cool dregs of his cup of coffee. His book was still a vague, unformed object, and trying to condense its argument into a short talk was no mean feat. Perhaps if he worked some more on the conclusion, the order of the rest of the talk would naturally fall into place... The cosmos, that was the key to it all. Macrocosms and microcosms, all mirroring each other, all connected. He just needed a good, clear metaphor. Yes, that was it!

Axel was right in the middle of jotting down a crucial point when he heard the doorbell. He thought nothing of it, concentrating on his work, until a hesitant knock came on the door.

'Axel, sweetie?' It was his mother.

'Yeah?' Axel kept scribbling, intent on not losing his train of thought.

'I know you don't like to be disturbed when you're working, but... it's Patti-Ann.'

'What about her?' Axel mumbled, his mind still on his speech.

'She's in the living room.'

Axel stopped writing. He hadn't seen his ex-fiancée in weeks. Since she'd texted him back *What letter?* he'd more or less blanked her, refusing her calls, letting her know by email that he was extremely busy with a new book project. He told himself he wasn't just being cowardly, that everything was spelled out in the letter, that he just needed to wait for it to be delivered. But in truth, it was entirely possible – likely, even – that the letter had been lost in the aftermath of the earthquake, and if not, then he couldn't imagine that the Nepalese postal service was renowned for its speediness. If Patti-Ann knew nothing of his confession; thought he just needed some space... The thought made his stomach sink.

His mother came into the room. 'Come on, Axel, you've not spoken to her since you came back from Nepal. That's no way to treat your fiancée. Or is she your ex-fiancée now? Does she even know?'

Axel glared at her, and she held up her hands. 'All right, all right, you young people do things however you think is right. Just... come downstairs and have a darn cup of coffee with her, will you? I've made cookies with macadamia nuts. Your favourite.'

Axel relented. 'OK,' he said. 'I'll come talk to her. You'd better not be lying about those cookies.'

He stretched and slowly, unwillingly, left his desk and his piles of notes, closed the door and headed down the stairs.

Patti-Ann was sitting on the couch, her back ramrod straight, her eyes bright as a deer in the headlights. Her face was glittering with makeup, and her hair had been carefully curled: she'd obviously spent hours getting ready to see him. The sight made his heart melt.

'Patti-Ann!' he said, his voice coming out as something of a squeak.

She stood up quickly. 'Axel! Your hair, it's so long! And your beard!'

Axel brought a hand up to his face self-consciously. 'Yeah, I guess I kind of kept it that way when I got back from Nepal.'

'No, I like it!' said Patti-Ann, a little too enthusiastically.

They stood facing each other, unsure what to do. After a moment, Axel went in for a brusque hug, then sat down in a chair across from the couch. Patti-Ann stood for a moment, as if stunned, then sat down slowly.

Felicia coughed quietly from the doorway, then bustled in with a tray of steaming coffee and cookies. 'Just let me know if you need anything,' she said cheerily, looking at Patti-Ann.

'Sure, Mrs Parker,' she replied, nodding mechanically.

There was a long, heavy silence after Felicia left the room. 'Your mother's doing really well,' Patti-Ann eventually said, before blushing, as if realising any mention of her recovery would be inextricably tied to the complicated events at the hospital.

'She really is,' Axel said, forcing himself to smile. 'It's just amazing. She's out in the garden every day, cleaning, cooking... I've tried to tell her to sit still but she won't listen.'

'You're darn tootin'!' Felicia hollered back from the kitchen. 'I'm not gonna waste my miraculous recovery!'

Patti-Ann and Axel laughed, and something in the air softened.

'So you're still here,' she finally said. 'I wondered if maybe you'd left town.' She managed something like a weak smile.

'No, still here,' Axel said. 'For now. I'm not really sure what's going to happen next. Things have really been happening fast with this book of mine.'

'So you said,' said Patti-Ann hollowly. 'In your email.'

Axel winced internally. 'It's nice to be back home,' he babbled, to fill the silence, 'as long as this transitional phase lasts. It's likely I'll be looking for teaching positions come this fall, but for now I'm focusing on my book.'

'So you gave up on the PhD?'

'Well, on the Lake Salvation one, at least. I think I've drained that place of everything it had to offer.'

'I see.'

There was a long, long silence.

'You haven't called,' she said, finally. Her tone was not so much accusatory as a statement of fact.

Axel hesitated. 'I've been really busy with my book,' he finally lied, hating himself for it. To his horror, he saw Patti-Ann's eyes fill with tears.

'Don't you lie to me, Axel Parker. I got your letter. You coward!'

Axel swallowed.

'If you want to dump your girlfriend – no, your fiancée! – by letter, you could at least mail it from someplace with a reliable postal system.' This was obviously a line she had prepared. It made Axel feel terrible.

'I know,' he said. 'It's just… I felt like I'd said everything so neatly in writing, I thought I would spoil it by coming to talk to you. And yeah, spelled out like that, it does sound pretty lame,' he admitted.

'Not as lame as your darn letter,' she spat, pulling a battered envelope out of her bag and unfolding its contents. 'I mean, what is this crap? *Our love has changed over the years into something weaker than it should be, something like a habit.* What a horrible thing to say!'

'I'm sorry,' Axel said weakly.

'*I can't be the man for you! I can't do this!* I can't, I can't! You sound like such a coward. I mean, are you afraid of me or something? All you talk about in this letter is fear. Fear of commitment, fear of letting go, fear of being a decent human being! I mean, what do you think is going to happen when you come out and say it? Go on, say it.

Say it to my face.' Patti-Ann was leaning so far forward, her hands gripping the edge of the couch, that he was worried she would fall off, or begin to levitate from the sheer force of her emotions. When Axel didn't reply, she continued: 'See, I think you don't want to have this conversation because you don't really want things to be over. You want to keep me waiting, in limbo, on the back burner, until you figure out if things are going to work out with that little bitch over there in Iraq or wherever.'

Axel began to protest, but Patti-Ann kept talking over him. Her tone softened, gained a new pleading note. 'The thing is, it's not really about her, is it. You're getting cold feet about marriage. That's why your whole letter is about fear. You're frightened of moving forward. You could have just told me! Axel, these are the kinds of things that people in relationships talk about together. They don't go behind each other's backs, or run away to Tibet, or write a goddamn letter!'

'Nepal,' Axel corrected her without thinking.

'What?' said Patti-Ann, thrown.

'I was in Nepal.'

Patti-Ann stared at him, as if he was someone she didn't recognise. Axel realised it was time to step up.

'Patti-Ann,' he began, 'you're right. I should have come to see you, to tell you in person instead of writing a letter. It's just that it took me a long time to come to this decision. I've really thought hard about it. This isn't about Safiya, or about you joining the Defenders, or even about anything that's happened between us recently. This is much bigger than anything like that.'

'Is it about the wedding?' Patti-Ann's eyes had filled with tears again.

'It's not,' he said. 'Or maybe partly. Maybe you're right that fear is a big part of what I'm talking about, or feeling. But it's not fear of change. It's a fear of things continuing as they've been going now. Listen, Patti-Ann, do you remember what it was like when we were kids? Do you remember how... easy everything was between the two of us? It just doesn't feel like that for me anymore. It's a lot of work.'

'Well of course it's work! Love isn't just a pair of slippers, or a chocolate cake. Love isn't meant to be easy every day.'

'You're right, of course. But, Patti-Ann, I'm not... happy anymore. I'm not excited about moving into the future anymore. I'm not...' He swallowed, the movement hurting his throat. 'I'm not in love with you anymore.'

'You don't mean that,' Patti-Ann cried out. 'That's impossible. After everything we've been through together!'

'That's just the thing, though. We've grown apart. Our plans, our desires, they're not the same.'

Patti-Ann wiped her cheeks with a kleenex, then gave a wobbly version of a coy smile. 'A lot of our desires are the same,' she said.

Axel sighed, exasperated against his will. 'Patti-Ann, you can't build a life, a successful marriage, around sex.'

'Well, it's an important part of it!' That sultry pout! How many times he'd seen it, been charmed by it. Now it just annoyed him.

'Look,' he tried to explain, taking another tack, 'it's more than that. This evening, I'm flying to Princeton to give a talk. Can you even understand what that means to me?'

Patti-Ann's eyes went wide again, that deer in the headlights look of hers. 'Princeton? You're moving to Princeton?' She paused. 'Where even is that?'

'It's in New Jersey,' Axel explained as patiently as he could. 'It's an Ivy League school. It's a really big deal for my research.'

'What the hell are you going to do on the East Coast? Is that Sophie girl going to be there too?'

'No,' Axel said, a little more loudly than he'd meant. 'This has nothing to do with women, any women. It's about my work, my career. This book is everything to me.'

'So I've been replaced by some damn book?'

'I'm focusing on my work,' he said, not answering the question. 'This is my first major speech. This is my future.'

'You're obsessed with your work.'

'Maybe I am. Maybe I'm in love with this book now.'

'Are you going to make love to your book now too?' Patti-Ann taunted, the tears finally brimming over and slipping down her cheeks.

'Yeah,' said Axel, an inexplicable wave of anger going over him. 'I'm really into paper and ink now. It's my new thing.'

'That's a weird thing to say,' said Patti-Ann, shrinking back into the couch, still crying.

Axel took a deep breath and ran a hand through his hair. 'Patti-Ann, I'm sorry, I don't want us to fight. I'm just trying to show you... to say that we don't understand each other any more.'

'But I do understand you,' she sobbed. 'That's why I'm here. Don't you remember all the good times we've had? At the diner, or that time we drove to Austin, or when we made love behind that old oak tree?'

'Of course I remember,' Axel said as softly as he could, 'but that's the past, not the future. We need to think about the future. And I don't see my future here in Texas.'

'But you're Texan born and bred!'

'I know. But I've grown away from it all.'

'OK,' Patti-Ann said desperately, 'then we'll go somewhere together! Somewhere far, like... Houston!'

Axel groaned.

'Or Princeton! I could do the East Coast, I could learn. Is it really cold out there?'

'Patti-Ann, it's not like that. It's more than that. The future isn't just tomorrow, or next week. The future is the rest of our lives.'

'And that doesn't make you excited anymore?' For the first time, Patti-Ann sounded like she was hesitating.

Axel plunged into the breach. 'It doesn't,' he said honestly. 'Look, everything we've shared, all of our past together, I'll treasure forever. But we have to think about the future. I... have a responsibility to be honest with you, especially because of everything we've shared. I don't want to be responsible for ruining your future. I don't want to follow you blindly into a bad marriage, just because it feels like the right thing to do.'

Patti-Ann began to sob again, a heartbreaking sound.

Axel kept going, willing his resolve not to falter. 'You deserve so much happiness, Patti-Ann. You deserve everything you've ever dreamed of, a family, babies, barbecues on the patio, going to church on Sunday. If we get married, I'll spoil all those things for you, because I won't be happy. Look,' he said desperately, 'isn't it better that we figure this out now, before we get married and have kids?'

'But it's all I've ever wanted,' Patti-Ann moaned through her tears.

'And you can still have it! Just not with me. You deserve so much more than me!'

Patti-Ann suddenly curled over on her side on the couch. She looked like a miserable baby animal.

'Oh, sweetie, you mustn't take it like this!' Axel knew all he had to do was sit down next to her on the couch and everything would be all right. But for how long? He had to be strong. A strange bit of inspiration came to him. '*When I was a child*,' he said gently, '*I spoke as a child, I understood as a child, I thought as a child; but when I became a man, I put away childish things.*'

Patti-Ann reared her head up, an expression of pure rage crossing her face. 'How dare you use those sacred words to hurt me! You unbelievable, selfish...' The anger crumpled into sorrow. 'This just isn't like you at all. This intellectual thing, this Princeton nonsense, it's all just some thing you're trying on. Like you're trying to pretend to be a grown-up, or something. Think of all the fun we've had together! Things were simpler when you were just enjoying being alive.'

'Maybe things were simpler, Patti-Ann, but they're different now.'

'Why do they have to be different?' she began, then something occurred to her. 'Wait,' she said, a manic light coming into her eyes, 'I get it. You're just messing with me. It's a trick! All of this, it's just so we can get back together and have really hot make-up sex. Right? Right?'

The desperation in her eyes exhausted Axel. All he wanted was to be back upstairs in the quiet of his room, writing his speech.

'It's not a trick,' he said.

'I don't believe you,' Patti-Ann sobbed, her makeup melting all over her lovely pink cheeks. She put her face in her hands.

'Patti-Ann, I think you should go home,' Axel said softly, finally standing and laying a hand on her shoulder.

His ex-fiancée's shoulders shook as she cried and cried. After what felt like an eternity, she stood up shakily and looked him right in the eyes. 'You think real hard about what you're doing, Axel Parker,' she said, her breaths short, her eyes red from crying. 'There's no coming back from this. So I'm gonna go home and pretend none of this happened, OK?' She straightened her shoulders.

'Don't do that,' Axel pleaded, feeling desperate, but Patti-Ann ignored him.

'Goodbye, Mrs Parker!' she shouted up the stairs, then turned and went out the front door.

'Wait!' said Axel, but it was too late. 'Jesus Christ,' he muttered under his breath.

'Are you two OK?' his mother called down from upstairs.

'No we're goddamn not!' Axel shouted, so loudly he startled himself.

Felicia slowly came down the stairs. 'I will not have you swearing at your mother,' she began sternly, but her expression softened as she saw his face. 'Oh honey,' she said, pulling him close to her breast. 'Well, look on the bright side: I guess you don't need to share those cookies now.'

★ ★ ★ ★

Axel sat at his desk, trying to focus on his work. The unexpected conversation with Patti-Ann had left him shaken, particularly her parting words. What a stubborn girl she was, to continue not to see what was happening! It exhausted him, having to tell her again and again that it was over. And yet it was his fault, leaving it this long, not coming to see her immediately upon returning from Nepal. How could he be angry at her for being hopeful? He stared at his notes. *An ordered universe.* It certainly didn't feel very ordered right now! Inside, it felt downright chaotic. He sighed and ate another macadamia nut cookie, then pushed his chair back from his desk. He might as well finish packing first, then have another go at the speech. He was too distracted to do good work on it now.

The rest of the afternoon passed faster than he'd expected, a flurry of ironing shirts and finding books, and before he'd realised it, it was time to climb into his mother's car with his weekend bag, a tupperware full of cookies and a satchel full of notes. 'You sure you have everything you need?' his mother asked for the twentieth time. 'Axel, sweetie, you know it's cold over there on the East Coast. Shouldn't you be bringing another sweater?' He smiled against his will. 'I already have two, and I'm only going for a week,' he said. 'Besides, I'll mostly be indoors, at the conference. I think it's pretty unlikely I'll get pneumonia in the hotel lobby.'

His mother laughed, and they drove north, the warm evening light diminishing to a soft blue around them. At the airport, his mother hugged him tightly. 'I know you'll be great,' she said. 'My smart boy, all grown up and going to Princeton!' Axel buried his face in her shoulder. He didn't feel very grown-up right then. His mother pulled back from the hug and looked him in the eyes. 'You make sure you send me a message when you get there, OK? Now hurry up, or you'll be late!' Shaking his head – his flight wasn't for another hour – Axel walked into the neon glow of the airport. There were so many memories here, all overlapping in his mind: picking up Safiya, his heart pounding with excitement; leaving for Nepal, his mind in miserable chaos; returning after the earthquake, on fire with his new theory. Once more, his nerves were jangling. Too much coffee, perhaps. He walked towards a kiosk, wondering wryly if many people were entirely calm in airports. Maybe a bottle of water would maybe help him relax.

'Axel?'

Confused by the soft feminine voice, Axel turned around, and felt his heart drop into his stomach. Patti-Ann had taken off her makeup, and was wearing a simple cotton dress. Her eyes were shining with tears, and she looked beautiful: like the sweet young girl he'd fallen in love with all those years ago.

'Don't say anything yet,' she said gently. 'I couldn't just let you go like that. Axel, I just had to tell you that I love you with all my heart. I've never wanted anyone else, and I never will. I can't be happy without you. I can't live without you. I'll love you till the day I die. And I just thought you should know that.'

She stopped, looking at him expectantly. There was a silence. 'Well, aren't you going to kiss me?' she finally asked.

'No,' Axel said simply. 'I can't.'

Patti-Ann reached for his hands and took them in hers. 'Can't we just go home?' she pleaded. 'Forget Princeton. Let's start over. Let's go ride down the highway, east to Tyler, west to Waco, wouldn't you like that? It'll be just like the old days. We'll make love three times a day, if you like, and stay up all night talking.' She squeezed his hands tighter. 'We'll love each other, and we'll get married – whenever you're ready, sweetie, and then we'll have babies. We'll grow old together, just like we always planned. Because we're family.' She stopped, hesitating, tears springing to her eyes.

'That's not what I want anymore,' he said. It was hard to say, so hard, and yet he knew he had to. 'You don't understand me, Patti-Ann.'

'Oh honey, but I do. That's why I'm here!'

'It's time to let go,' he said, gently releasing her hands. 'It's time to leave our past behind us.'

'This isn't about the past,' she argued. 'It's about the future!'

'Yes, it is, you're right. It's about our futures, our separate futures. We're not getting married, Patti-Ann. We're not driving to Waco, or Tyler. We're not having babies, ever. And we're not growing old together. Today is the start of the rest of our lives apart. And I really need you to understand that.'

Patti-Ann physically shrank back from him. 'This doesn't sound like you. This isn't the Axel I know.'

'Maybe I'm not the Axel you knew anymore.'

'What happened to us?' The words were so simple, so heartfelt, that it was all Axel could do not to start crying too.

'Time passed,' he finally said. 'We changed.' After a long silence, he added: 'My plane is leaving in twenty minutes.'

'So go, then,' Patti-Ann said calmly. 'Cool down. Go to the East Coast or wherever. Take your time out, and then come back to me. I'll give you all the time you need.' Suddenly, and without warning, she flung herself into his arms. 'It could be good again,' she murmured against his ear. 'We could be close again, if only we just took the time. We could get to know each other again. Just give me a chance!' Before Axel could react, she'd begun kissing his neck softly, then his ear. He felt her teeth on his ear, and squirmed out of her grasp.

'No,' he said, as firmly as he could. 'This is no time out. I don't need any more time to think. This is really it, Patti-Ann. It's over between us.'

'I came all the way out here for this? Didn't you hear all the things I said?' There was a note of desperation to her voice.

'I have to go,' he said again, adjusting the strap of his bag over his shoulder.

'Don't leave me!' she pleaded, pulling it down to the ground. There was something so childish in the gesture that his heart hardened, for the last time.

He picked up the bag and took a step back from her, willing himself to stay calm. 'Goodbye, Patti-Ann,' he said, and he turned and walked to the gate without looking back.

CHAPTER THIRTY-FIVE

Axel's mother had been right: it was chilly in October on the East Coast. He was grateful for the warmth and golden light inside the café he'd found, and for the rich coffee and almond croissant that were helping him wake up on this grey morning. He checked his watch: only nine hours to go till his talk. He frowned at his notes, and sighed aloud. Almond croissants always made him think of Safiya, and Geneva; another autumn that felt like a hundred years ago. How he wished… but there was no point in wishing, he told himself sternly. That was all in the past.

He pulled a flyer advertising the conference from his notebook. SCIENCE VS. RELIGION, the text proclaimed, slightly tongue in cheek. He had to hand it to them: Princeton wasn't afraid of playing with controversy. Still, he hoped it was stirring up academic interest, rather than baiting any opponents. He still had uncomfortable memories of the graffitied front of Lake Salvation University after Professor Bohmann's talk. The subtitle, *a friendly interdisciplinary conference*, went some ways towards putting his doubts to rest.

'Oh my gosh, is that him?' The two young students at the table next to his were suddenly staring at him, wide-eyed. 'He's so young!'

Seeing he'd noticed them, the undergraduates blushed and giggled. The older of the two bit her lip, then leaned across. 'Excuse me, but are you Dr Parker, from Texas?'

'I'm no doctor yet,' he said, 'but I am from Texas, and yeah, I'm Axel Parker.' He couldn't help but grin.

'Everybody's talking about the conference, and how you're giving the opening talk,' the student said gravely.

'It's basically insane,' her friend piped up, pulling idly on a silk scarf. 'Last year they had Richard Dawkins!'

The older student rolled her eyes. 'You mean Stephen Hawking,' she hissed. 'Don't you pay attention?'

'She's a theologian,' the second student added, ignoring her friend and batting her eyelashes, 'and I'm a biochemist.'

'Well that's amazing!' Axel exclaimed. 'And you're both coming to the talk?'

The girls stared at him. 'Oh no,' the older one said, blushing now. 'The opening speech is only for special guests and heads of departments.'

'Oh!' said Axel. Then, remembering he was a serious academic now, he made his expression stern. 'I'll look forward to seeing you at other events during the conference, then.'

Turning back to his notes, he was ashamed to realise he was blushing. He hoped the girls hadn't thought he was flirting with them. The attention was something of a novelty. He drained his coffee, packed away his notes and marched purposefully towards the door.

Stepping out of the café, he began walking in the direction of the central quad. The buildings looked almost medieval, with their old stone shining in the morning sun. Orange and crimson leaves lined the ground, crunching under his footsteps. His breath formed a little white cloud in front of him. It was turning into a lovely morning, and he decided to head to the library. He walked past the crenellated walls draped in dark green ivy, light glinting off the windowpanes, under stone arches and gigantic oak trees. It was like wandering through a fairy-tale vision of an Ivy League school, he thought to himself, a little starstruck. A gaggle of passing students, their laughter hanging in the air like steam, startled him from his reverie.

The reading room in the Firestone Library was a luminous space in between buildings, light flooding down through the angled skylights. It was beautiful, and quiet this early in the day. The polished oak tables seemed to float under the glass arches, like boats on a canal. Axel sat down at the table and pulled out his notes once more. He still wasn't quite satisfied with the conclusion. Perhaps somewhere amongst the leather-bound volumes, he would find some inspiration. Some ancient book on cosmology, perhaps?

'Axel Parker?' A deep voice interrupted his thoughts, and he turned around to find a tall, handsome man in a red cardigan smiling down at him. He had thick, dark stubble, and thick rimmed spectacles. 'This is just tremendously exciting!' the man continued. 'I'm David Mossaz, a philosophy professor here. My graduate students and I have been working all week on preparing questions for the Q&A!'

Axel went pale. 'Q&A?' he repeated.

The man blinked at him. 'Well yes, after your speech,' he said. 'You don't know about it? For God's sake, my colleagues are so terribly disorganised. Come, come, we must discuss this.' Seeing Axel was hesitating, looking wistfully at his notes, he added: 'There's good coffee where we're headed.'

They crossed the library, and headed back across the quad to one of the older buildings Axel had noticed before. Mossaz pulled open a heavy wooden door, and they walked up a flight of worn-down stone stairs, before arriving in a bustling common room. 'Everyone, I'd like you to meet Axel Parker,' Mossaz announced.

Every professor in the room swivelled to look at Axel, making him blush bright red. It was warm in the room, which was lined with bookshelves and tall oil paintings, no doubt of former professors or deans of the school. Five beat-up leather armchairs stood in a circle in the centre of the room, around a table covered with magazines and sheets of paper. There was a huge fire roaring in a carved stone fireplace, and the air smelled like fresh coffee.

An old man in a tweed jacket slowly walked over, his eyes magnified by his thick opal-rimmed spectacles. 'Steady on,' he said. 'You'll scare the poor boy!' He held out an unsteady hand, which Axel shook gratefully. 'I'm Professor Nightingale. Astronomy.'

'And I'm Professor Vernet,' a young lady with long dark hair added in a lilting French accent, holding out a slender hand. 'I teach chemistry, mostly.'

'Maurade, physics,' a plump woman with a pompadour of white hair said, adding: 'Head of department.'

'Axel!' The voice was familiar, as was the smiling face, but Axel couldn't quite place the man in his blazer, chinos and white sneakers... 'Chester Mackenzie, remember? We met in London!'

'Professor Bohmann's friend! Of course!'

'I've heard so much about your talk, I just can't believe it. You were just a kid when I last saw you, an engineering student! And now you have this beard, and you're writing a book...' He shook his head. 'How long has it been, a year?'

'About that,' Axel admitted.

'Now, now, don't look embarrassed,' Mackenzie smiled. 'I'm tremendously impressed! You've come a long way... And Melvin, he's not with you?'

Axel shook his head. 'He used his health as his excuse, but really I suspect he wanted me to stand on my own two feet.'

Chester Mackenzie laughed, a friendly sound. 'Looks like you're doing just fine to me!'

'That's because I haven't given my talk yet...'

'Won't you give the poor boy some coffee?' Mossaz interrupted. 'Turns out nobody told him about the Q&A,' he explained to Mackenzie.

'I should have checked with my secretary,' Nightingale said regretfully. 'It's quite possible I may have forgotten.'

Vernet laughed, laying her manicured fingernails lightly on his sleeve. 'You, forget? Impossible,' she said.

Flustered, Nightingale muttered something Axel didn't catch, as Professor Maurade had returned with two cups of coffee, a silver pitcher and a silver dish of sugar cubes on a tray. 'Milk? Sugar?' she asked. He nodded, then accepted the cup.

'Where is Philip?' Vernet asked. She pronounced it *Philippe*.

'Nederhauser's bound to be busy on a day like this,' said Maurade.

'Nederhauser's bound to need good, strong coffee on a day like this,' Mossaz corrected her. 'I mean, the good news about a Q&A session is that it more or less carries its own weight. All we need is a few words to kick it off, and it should be under control. Mr Parker's introductory speech should serve just that purpose.'

'Besides, I think they're serving wine afterwards,' Vernet commented. 'That should help keep it short.'

The men laughed, while Maurade frowned. 'Are we really serving wine at the end of a twenty-minute event?' she asked disapprovingly. 'My, this conference really is turning into a rock festival.'

'Oh cheer up, Maurade,' Professor Nightingale said affectionately. 'It'll help everybody get into the spirit of things.'

'So, who's going to be at my talk?' Axel asked.

The professors looked at each other, considering.

'Well, we are,' Mossaz finally said. 'All the heads of departments, and probably one or two professors from each school. Then you add in the four or five visiting professors, one from Harvard, one all the way from Oxford, a graduate student or two… You've probably got yourself twenty-five people altogether. A small, specialist crowd, really.'

Axel nodded. Twenty-five people didn't sound so bad. Even if they were all leaders in their fields, and many of them had tenure, or had published books he hadn't read. For all he knew, he thought nervously, one of them had probably been nominated for a Nobel Prize. He took a swig of coffee. 'And is there anything I should know about giving a speech at Princeton? The Q&A session, particularly – are there any sorts of… rules I should follow?'

Maurade smiled approvingly. 'Well, we usually try to make sure that no one person hogs the floor. And of course if you can discourage the discussion from veering into an outright fight, that would be ideal.'

'Our dear Professor Maurade here is a little uncomfortable with the whole subject of this conference,' Mossaz commented.

'Nothing of the sort!' she retorted. 'I love a good intellectual debate. I just don't wish to encourage… shouting. You never know who's going to turn up to these things.'

'With all due respect, Professor,' Mossaz said, 'it'll mostly be faculty. The spirit will be more reminiscent of a round table, or a seminar, than a public talk. And I don't think either the philosophers or the astronomers have too much of a reputation for brawling.'

Axel coughed. 'I'll do my best to discourage anything like that, ma'am,' he said, and everyone laughed and smiled.

'Well there you go,' Vernet said with a charming giggle.

'And there he is!' Mossaz exclaimed, as the door opened to reveal a tall, stopped figure with cherry-red cheeks.

Philip Nederhauser entered, rubbing his hands together for warmth. 'Ah, Axel!' he said warmly. 'So nice to meet you at last!'

It had been Professor Nederhauser who had invited Axel to Princeton: the two had exchanged a series of emails over the last few weeks, setting out the topic and specifics of Axel's introductory speech.

'You too, Professor,' Axel said, shaking his hand enthusiastically.

'Well, I for one am glad you found your way up here. It'll no doubt make this evening much less intimidating.' He smiled. 'I've also prepared several nice and neutral leading questions, in case the Q&A session dries up.'

'Or gets out of hand,' Maurade commented.

'Oh, good,' said Axel, relieved. 'I was wondering about that.'

Nederhauser laid a hand on Axel's shoulder. 'Don't you worry, Axel,' he said. 'Everything's going to go just fine. And don't feel you have to hang around all day with us old farts, either,' he added with a smile. 'Though of course you're welcome here.'

'Thank you, sir,' Axel said gratefully. 'I was actually thinking of heading back to my hotel for a little nap before the talk.'

'That sounds like a grand idea. And if you're stuck for a place for lunch, I can highly recommend the Rib-Eye Grill, on the other side of the river. They have the most fabulous roast potatoes...'

'Philip, he's from Texas!' Chester Mackenzie intervened. 'That's like offering an Eskimo snow!'

'Well he'll appreciate it, then.'

After exchanging a few more jokes with the professors and finishing his cup of coffee, Axel decided it probably would do him good to take a walk and clear his head. Bidding everyone good day, he left the common room to a chorus of 'see you tonight!' Outside, though the sun was nearing its apex, the biting cold surprised him, and he pulled his sweater close. He left campus, heading towards the river, its waters a shining grey-green, rippling in the autumn wind.

There was no peace like the kind he felt walking by the side of a body of water. It made him think of Phoksundo Lake, and the lake in Saint Moritz, even the roiling waters of the Thames in the rain in London. It made him think of fishing with his Aunt Charlene. Most of all, it made him think of Safiya. He remembered standing with her on the bridge in Geneva, looking down at the rush of the Rhône, thinking about transformation. That was where she'd first told him of her love for the mountains; a love that would lead them to Schmidt Hennessey's chalet, and that would bring him to Nepal. No matter how he looked at it, he owed everything to Safiya. She was the love that had carried him to his philosophical revelation: there was no way around it. He would be grateful to her forever.

Axel stared mournfully into the waters, watching the fallen autumn leaves swirl in the current. He felt homesick, though for where he wasn't sure. Slowly, he turned and walked back to his hotel.

★ ★ ★ ★

The hotel where Axel was staying was a well-known villa from the 1700s, which had been restored in its historic glory, all crumbling red brick and beams, with crocheted lace curtains in the windows. From his bedroom, he could see the silver river snaking by, and the tops of the stone turrets of the university. The rooms were small, the atmosphere was cosy, and in his bed, wrapped in starched cotton sheets and a handmade knitted blanket, he quickly fell into a deep sleep.

Birdsong startled him awake from a dream in which his mother was helping him escape from the earthquake. Sweating, he sat bold upright and checked his watch, then took a deep breath. He still had plenty of time before his talk: time to grab a bite to eat, revise his notes, and walk back along the river to the campus. Maybe he could Skype Professor Bohmann briefly, though, just to set his mind at ease. He set up his laptop on the narrow antique desk, and breathed a sigh of relief as the professor's grainy photo appeared with a green tick next to it. He pressed the button, and the call sound rang out.

'Axel, my boy!' What a strange thing long-distance communication was; that the professor's familiar voice should sound as faint and digital from the East Coast as it did from Europe. Another stab of homesickness went through him, an almost pleasant sort of pain.

'Hi, Professor,' Axel said, smiling.

'Nerves already?' Bohmann checked his watch. 'I guess it's coming closer.'

Axel nodded. 'Turns out I have to lead a Q&A session as well as give a speech,' he said.

Bohmann's eyes went wide. 'What a tremendous honour!'

'Everybody here is, like, the head of their department!' Axel blurted out. 'And I'm not even a doctor yet!'

'Well, my boy, if everything goes well, it seems likely you'll get an invitation to study there. Just be yourself, and if you can talk about your subject with even the tiniest bit of the passion you showed me when you came back from Nepal, you'll blow them all away.' He shook his head and smiled. 'It's always a mystery to me, why bright young minds like yourself are intimidated by old farts like me. You're the future! Our job is just to stand around and shepherd people like you to glory, Axel. I mean, have you met any of the Princeton lot?' Axel nodded. 'And were they friendly to you?' Axel nodded again. 'Well then! What are you worrying about? Any one of that team, they'll have your back if anything goes wrong. And nothing,' he continued quickly, before Axel could think too hard about that, 'is going to go wrong. You just have to believe in yourself, Axel.'

'It's just... It feels like I shouldn't be out there alone, presenting all this like it's my idea. It's yours, Professor Bohmann, and it's Schmidt Hennessey's, and it's Safiya's.'

'And have any of those people shown any sign of wishing they were in your place?'

'Well, no. I guess not.'

'And wouldn't all of those people be absolutely thrilled to hear how things were going?'

'I guess they would.'

'Indeed, I can vouch for two of them personally myself! And I'm quite sure your lovely Safiya would feel the same.' Bohmann's expression softened. 'Go easy on yourself, my boy. Just go up there, and share your ideas. If anyone challenges you, that means people are interested in your ideas. Any question is something you can answer in your subsequent work.'

'You're right,' Axel said, more confidently than he felt.

'Besides, there's usually wine afterwards,' Bohmann added, 'in case you need to loosen up.'

Axel laughed. 'One of the professors said this conference was beginning to feel like a rock festival,' he said.

'That's what old farts like me say when things get too exciting. It's a good sign for your field, my boy. A very good sign.'

They exchanged a few more pleasantries, then Axel sighed and checked his watch again. 'Well, I guess I should read through these notes one more time, or ten.'

'You'd do just fine without 'em,' Bohmann said affectionately, 'but do whatever you need to do. I'll be thinking of you.'

'Thank you, Professor. I'll tell you all about it when it's over.'

★ ★ ★ ★

The next few hours speeded by in a blur, and before he knew it, there he was, standing up on the podium in front of a sea of smiling faces. He'd never stood this side of an auditorium before, looking out over the semicircle of audience members, and it was actually less intimidating than he'd feared. There couldn't be more than thirty people in the room: the size of a Lake Salvation University seminar, or a primary school classroom. The thought made him smile.

Nederhauser was speaking, introducing him, but Axel was having trouble concentrating on anything but the lights on the ceiling, shining down so bright and hot. 'Marvellous interdisciplinary work... Revolution... Earthquake in Nepal...' The words came to him in fragments rather than strung together in a speech. 'And Axel, if you're ever interested in undertaking a PhD at Princeton, you just let me know.' He tuned in just in time to catch these words, and nodded mutely, his cheeks turning pink. So Professor Bohmann had been right! These people really felt like he belonged among them, no matter how far along in their careers they were. The thought buoyed him to no end. 'Now I believe it is time for me to withdraw, and leave the stage to our young star guest. Ladies and gentlemen, please welcome Axel Parker!'

Small as the audience was, the sound of the applause took Axel's breath away, and as he stepped up to the microphone, for a moment, his mind went entirely blank. Images started flashing through his mind, and he wondered if he was about to pass out: mountain goats running into snow, rifts opening up in the quaking ground, the rippling surface of a lake. A voice in the audience gave an encouraging whoop, and a few people laughed – a friendly sound. 'Thank you, everyone,' he began, his voice sounding less shaky than he felt. 'It's a tremendous honour to be speaking here at Princeton. I'm particularly moved by the presence of so many heads of departments: astronomy, philosophy, theology, mathematics, chemistry, physics... It's quite overwhelming, being surrounded by so much knowledge in so many domains. I'm very much looking forward to seeing how everyone's research – everyone's energies, if I may – intersects throughout this conference.'

'In fact, much of the subject of the book I'm working on, whose central thesis I gather you are all aware of thanks to Professors Bohmann and Nederhauser's enthusiasm for my work, has to do with opening up questions across different subjects, crossing borders so that science and literature, science and economics, or science and religion can communicate more honestly.' He took a deep breath. 'It is my sincere belief that some of the more esoteric approaches or visualisations favoured by the writer and the believer might actually be tremendously useful to the scientific community. I'm not saying that one model is better than the other, but simply that all the systems on this earth should be able to speak to each other – and that we're lacking translators. To many hardcore scientists, the language of religion is incomprehensible; to many devout believers, science seems to make no sense. I want to show that this lack of discussion comes down to the framework rather than to the content of the theories on both sides, from the most ancient and traditional values to the most cutting-edge.'

'Thus, in my own work, for a long time I was confronted with various paradoxes having to do with the very nature of energy. As an engineering student, if you'd said the word "soul" to try to explain any of this to me then, I'd have laughed in your face. But I'm ashamed of that attitude now. So many of us have so much to learn from each other. I could not have accomplished any of this work without the help of my friends.' His voice caught in his throat, and he moved away from this tack. 'The conclusions I've come to are ones I would have been unable to imagine within the limiting framework of my engineering degree. In particular, it was in working with a theologian, a dear friend from the University of Istanbul, that I began to consider this idea of the soul. Now, every one of us is aware that we are alive, and that there is life all around us on the planet, but few of us spend much time thinking about the interconnectedness of that life. Those of you who study the cosmos in an astronomical context will know what I'm talking about when I say that the world around us is simply brimming with life, all of it connected and ordered.'

Axel was beginning to relax into his subject, seeing all the faces in the room turned to him, many of them smiling. 'Now, given the length of this talk, I may not be able to venture into as many specific examples as I'd like concerning the possible applications of my theory. This introduction may remain a little abstract, just long enough not to annoy my detractors too much and, hopefully, short enough to make the rest of you want to read my book!' There was a scattering of laughter around the room. 'The good news is, though, that there will be a Q&A session when I finish, in which I hope that we'll be able to explore some of these possibilities together.'

'But before we move on in this way, I want to talk a little bit more about this notion of order – or coherence, as I prefer to think of it. It is here, I believe, that religion has been most useful and simultaneously most problematic to scientific advances in the study of the cosmos. When we think about energy, the bursts of energy that punctuate all life across the universe – be they shooting stars or the millions of stars absorbed by black holes, tsunamis or earthquakes – we have spent most of our life on this little blue planet classifying these disasters as inexplicable, or only explicable by the intervention of some external superpower. This is what makes the workings of the world we live in seem frightening, even supernatural. For instance, my own dear friend and mentor Professor Bohmann, also of Lake Salvation University, has studied the application of the laws of thermodynamics to sunlight at great length, considering the loss of energy between the time when rays of sun leave the burning star and when they hit the surface of the planet without burning us all to a crisp. This is not my theory, so I won't expound on it any further, even though this theory has puzzled me since freshman year, although I will suggest that anyone who enjoys my work will enjoy his as well: it is where my roots and my inspiration lie, and I owe a great deal to him.'

A burst of applause across the room startled and pleased him; he held up a hand for silence. 'That said, there is something about Professor Bohmann's theory with which I disagree, and that is calling in the idea of an external superpower or Hand of God as the explanation for this phenomenon. Of course, no one disputes the laws of thermodynamics – energy emitted must equal energy absorbed. The larger point I would like to make in this instance, however, has to do with how we consider these forces at work, seeing them as dangerous and destructive, when really there is always hope in transformation, and always consistency in change.' Axel paused, gathering his thoughts. 'As the laws of physics teach us, nothing is ever truly lost or created, and everything is always in a state of transformation. This is another way of looking at coherence and acceptance in a more religious sense: that every part of life belongs to life, from the beam of sunlight to the treefrog, from the crashing waterfall to the sleeping baby. When we eat something sugary, when we meditate, when we die, we are manifesting the power of the eternal just as surely as an earthquake, or tectonic plates shifting to create new mountains. Think of sunlight, and lamplight, and the love that swells our own beating hearts. Where does the light come from? Where does the light go? Every manifestation of energy, from the innocuous to the apparently destructive, is a part of this cycle: and this is why it's important to recalibrate our way of thinking about so-called natural disasters, to stop seeing them as inexplicable, and to see them instead as belonging to the natural order of the world – to the soul, if I may. Life doesn't come from nothing, nor does it vanish into nothing. Every death, every great burst of energy, every catastrophe, is part of the same energy cycle as every birth, every quiet moment, every natural disaster slowing or coming to an end so that life may begin anew. All of these are part of the same cycle of the soul, the same coherent order of life in the universe. In so many ways, the most essential philosophical question governing human life is "why are we here on this earth?" Considering energy through this new angle goes a long way towards answering this question.'

He paused, and listened to the thoughtful silence of the auditorium. You could have heard a pencil drop to the floor. He smiled. 'And now I believe it's time for me to move away from philosophical and religious abstractions, and to bring you all back to a more concrete visualisation. If you're willing, I'd like to try a little exercise: I'd like you all to close your eyes and imagine the Milky Way, that perfect swirl of stars, billions of lightyears away. Think about the fragile balance that maintains these macrocosms. Think about the energy of the entire universe, in scientific or religious terms, whatever you're comfortable with! Then zoom in, and place yourself at the heart of this galaxy. Just like Google Maps! Zoom in until you're at the centre of the solar system, then zoom in on that little blue planet we call home, and on the landmass we're standing on right now, and zoom right in to Princeton, and this university, and this very room, and the chair you're sitting in. Now, with your eyes still closed, try to keep the energy of the universe present with you. Imagine that you're still at the very heart of that Milky Way. Imagine that beautiful energy, that perfect balance, still poised and moving all around you. Now I'd like you to zoom in again, into the centre of your head, or into the beating heart in your chest, whichever you find easiest to visualise. Think about the energy that moves within you, beating in the cycle of your bloodstream, flickering in your synapses. Inside each of our cells, there is a microcosm just as complex and beautiful as the Milky Way we were imagining at the start. That's where the light comes from, and where the light goes. Now, if you can strain your mind back to the bigger picture, and reach back out, and pull the strands of that beautiful macrocosmic balance in, then you might start to understand what I mean by coherence. And yes, I'm sorry, this is a bit like meditation.' Again, people giggled, but he noticed that almost everyone kept their eyes closed. 'What I want you to think about is the reciprocity of this balance, this energy. While each of us lives in space, it is important to realise that space also lives in us. The soul is the key to this idea of integration. Every burst of energy, whether in the nebulas, the galaxies, or right here on earth, comes to a sudden stop, and then goes into storage; the great "potential energy" of the cosmos, to be converted as needed into the soul. The difference between my theory and all other theories is the "missing link", which is the storage and subsequent conversion of energy. The soul itself contains this energy, without contravening the second law of thermodynamics, of energy in equals energy out. Through this lens, the soul is a way of visualising our human energy as part of the energy of the whole universe. A way of understanding life in terms of cycles of energy, from birth to death and back again. A way of understanding both human death and natural catastrophes in terms of natural energy release, and seeing these imbalances as way of restoring a coherent balance in the universe. But that's a bit much to cover in an introductory talk, and so I believe it is time for me to open to floor to your questions.' He paused, unsure what to say next, and finally added: 'Thank you for listening.'

The room erupted into applause, and hands began flying up all around the auditorium. Axel felt himself grinning. Everything had gone well!

'Yes, Professor Mossaz?' He decided to start with the friendly philosopher.

'I'd love to hear more,' Mossaz began, 'about how you came up with this theory. Is it true that the catalyst for your work was the earthquake in Nepal?'

Axel nodded, relieved. An easy, personal question. 'Yes, it's true,' he said. 'It was the first time I truly understood the bursts of energy that are released across this earth in various forms, or saw the interaction between the loss of life and the possibility of transformation. It was a difficult time, and my heart still grieves for the people of Nepal, but I will never forget what I learned on the banks of Lake Phoksundo, in the company of the Buddhist monks who are rebuilding their monastery there even as we speak.'

'Thank you very much,' said Mossaz, giving a sort of bow.

Time for the next question. 'Yes, Professor Vernet?'

'I would be very interested to hear how you think your theory applies to the field of chemistry. Are you currently studying its applications?'

Axel froze. He knew nothing about chemistry. His heart began to pound. Then, remembering what Bohmann had said to him on Skype – every question he couldn't answer had the potential to feed into future research – he decided to be honest. 'I'm afraid chemistry is not my field,' he said, 'but I would love to discuss this further!'

Professor Vernet raised an eyebrow flirtatiously, and he blushed.

Professor Nightingale spoke next. 'I think perhaps an email list might be an excellent way to explore some of the more complicated questions raised this evening, across all of our fields. After all, it will be much easier to bore Mr Parker with specifics this way!'

'Well, I think we should organise a regular round table on the subject,' Vernet piped up next. 'Assuming Axel accepts Philip's offer of a scholarship and joins us next year.'

Nederhauser nodded in an avuncular fashion. 'Yes, I think this is an excellent idea. In fact, I've been thinking of launching a weekly round table during the spring semester, with different guests every week. This is a fast-moving field, and I want Princeton to stay at the very cutting edge of the research that's being produced by the country's brightest minds.'

A scattering of applause went around the room. A weekly round table? A scholarship? Axel's mind was reeling. He hadn't realised he was being offered a scholarship. Did that mean they would fund his PhD? Would he be teaching as well? But this wasn't the time to think about this: he decided to take on one of the questions from the younger graduates in the front row.

'This may be kind of an abstract question,' the young man said, 'but I was wondering how you, personally, visualise the soul?'

Axel smiled, pleased by the question. 'This is actually something I think about a lot,' he said thoughtfully. 'After all, even once we've admitted that the soul is a useful framework, that doesn't answer the question of what it actually might be: is it chemical, biological, or more abstract than that? Is it some kind of steam, like many religions have said? I suppose my own vision runs along the lines of what I was trying to get everyone to visualise: a kind of energy or glow, perhaps. What about you?'

The student looked startled and pleased to have the question come back to him. His cheeks pink, he thought for a moment, then said: 'I guess I think of it kind of like a cloud, maybe. I don't know.'

Another man's tweed-clad arm shot up – one of the visiting professors, no doubt – and Axel nodded. 'Wouldn't different people's souls look different, though? Aren't all human beings individual?' The man's voice was deep and reedy, the voice of someone you might enjoy listening to on the radio.

Axel laughed lightly. 'That's a more abstract question than I'll be able to answer very well – maybe someone in the philosophy department might be able to help you out a little better!'

There was laughter in the back of the room. 'Dr Alexander is actually a professor of philosophy at Harvard,' Mossaz called out, and Axel grinned.

'Oh! Well in that case, I'll simply say this: no matter how one might imagine or perceive the individual soul, in terms of my work, its most essential quality lies not in separateness, but in connection; not in individuality, but in its belonging to a greater whole – the great and eternal energy of this earth.'

Dr Alexander nodded, as if satisfied, and sat back, scribbling on a pad of paper.

The questions went on for well over an hour, though to Axel it seemed to pass in the blink of an eye. Eventually he noticed that Professor Nederhauser had stood up from his chair on the side of the stage, and gathered that his time must be up. 'One last question, then,' he said, 'and I'd be happy to continue the discussion with you all over the coming days in the seminar and study groups we are planning.'

He scanned the room. One hand in particular, towards the back of the room, had been raised since the start of his talk. He couldn't see the person very well, but pointed in their direction. 'You, yes you, in the back.' He smiled, in case they were nervous.

'Mr Parker,' a soft voice began, and his heart leapt in his chest. 'I was wondering how you felt about the more explicitly religious conceptions of the soul. Is there room for them in your research, or are you still a scientist at heart?'

It was everything Axel could do not to rush across the room then and there, to see her face. Could it really be...? It was impossible. *Safiya Safiya Safiya*. He didn't dare say her name, in case he was wrong, but in his heart he knew. 'I believe,' he began, then had to stop and clear his throat. 'I believe that the religious notion of the soul was absolutely crucial to the genesis of this theory. And I believe that it is the interaction, the... synergy of a scientific approach and a religious vision, that lies at the heart of what I'd like my work to achieve.'

'So perhaps you would be open to discussing this further with, say, a Quranic scholar?' Safiya had leaned forward into the light, and he could see she was wearing a white silk scarf and her favourite dove grey suit. She was so close, and he wanted to be closer to her soft voice, her dark eyes, her scent of sandalwood and musk.

Axel's heart was melting in his chest. 'Yes, I would, Doctor Midana,' he said. 'Yes, I would.'

CHAPTER THIRTY-SIX

Dazed, Axel couldn't keep his eyes off Safiya. Around him, the quiet bustle of the drinks reception was in full swing, with voices murmuring and glasses clinking and the occasional burst of laughter. It was hard to believe any of this was real: that he was still at Princeton, in this room with its golden pine panelling; that his talk had gone so well, that Safiya was here, amongst the professors, like a ghost from another world. Yet it was true: there she was, in her soft dove grey suit, getting them drinks at the drinks table. It was miraculous and mundane in equal measure. He didn't want to waste a moment more away from her, and yet a part of him wanted this limbo to last forever. Right now, everything was still unknown, still possible...

A hand clapped down on his back, interrupting his wistful train of thought. 'Fantastic speech!' It was Chester Mackenzie. 'It was just like watching Melvin speak back in the old days. That fire, that passion! Really great stuff.'

Professor Mossaz had appeared by Mackenzie's shoulder. 'Yes, really wonderful. This intersection of scientific and religious thinking, it's really a rich area, ripe for exploration... We've been held back by cultural taboos for far too long. I look forward to learning much more about the soul in the coming years!'

'Yes, and in person, too, right?' Mackenzie nudged him. 'Surely you'll be accepting that scholarship?'

But Safiya had reappeared, and Axel's mind had gone blank. It was difficult to see more than five minutes into the future.

'Give the poor boy a break,' Mossaz intervened, sensing his discomfort. 'Let him rest on his laurels for twenty minutes, won't you?'

'Of course! Of course! Why don't you get yourself some wine, dear boy?'

'I will.' Axel smiled gratefully as Mossaz took Mackenzie by the elbow and manoeuvred him over towards a table of hors-d'oeuvres.

Safiya handed him a glass of sparkling water. 'I thought you might like this more than any of that cheap, warm wine...'

'Thank you,' Axel said, or tried to say – the words sort of stuck in his throat and came out sounding foreign. He blushed, swallowed, tried again. 'You're here.'

Safiya nodded, seemingly unperturbed by his awkwardness.

'How?' he blurted out.

She laughed, and the familiarity and strangeness of that sweet, birdlike sound made Axel's heart lurch in his chest. 'Well, I owed you an unexpected visit, didn't I? Ever since you turned up to the Blue Mosque...' Seeing Axel's wide eyes, she hesitated, her expression growing serious, then seemed to relent. 'Our department receives invitations to this conference every year. "Science and Religion" – of course I'm on that mailing list! And they made quite a big deal out of this exciting young professor giving the keynote speech...'

'I'm not a professor,' Axel said, reflexively.

'But you're going to be!' Safiya corrected him, then, seeing his hesitation, peered at him more closely. 'Aren't you? Surely you're not considering turning down a fully-funded scholarship?'

'No, no!' Axel said hastily, then, 'I don't know.'

There was a silence. 'Oh,' said Safiya, looking down at her water glass. 'I see. Are you... Is there something holding you back in Texas, then?'

'No!' Axel said, so fast and so loud that several people around them turned around. 'No, it's not that,' he added, more softly, seeing a gleam of something warm in Safiya's downturned eyes.

'So you and Patti-Ann...?' she asked, her voice trailing off, as if she didn't dare ask the question.

'It's over,' he said firmly, then nodded for a while, unsure what to say. 'We talked,' he finally added.

'Axel!' a feminine voice trilled, startling him. He felt a slender hand on his waist, and turned to find Professor Vernet smiling at him. She smelled like cigarette smoke and perfume. 'Congratulations! You handled everything so smoothly.' There was a silence, in which Axel couldn't think of anything to say except 'Thank you.' His thoughts were a million miles away.

'So can we expect you to be joining us in a few months' time?'

'I'm considering my options,' he said flatly, then turned back to Safiya.

After a moment, with a flutter of her hands and a disappointed little moue, Vernet left. Axel sighed in relief. 'Can we get out of here?' he asked Safiya. 'Please? I can't think straight with all these people around, and sooner or later someone is going to get offended.'

To his relief, she nodded. 'We have a lot to catch up on,' she said, turning towards the door with a smile. Still unable to believe any of this was really happening, Axel followed Safiya out into the world.

★ ★ ★ ★

The cool night air felt wonderful: it had been boiling at the reception, Axel suddenly realised, and full of people he wasn't ready to talk to. There was only one person in the world he wanted to be with right now, and here she was walking by his side, the sound of her heels echoing on the pavement. He pulled his coat around his neck and shivered happily. Glancing over at Safiya, he found her eyes were straight ahead, dark and beautiful as ever, her hair loose over her shoulders. How he still loved her! A stab of fear went through him, almost simultaneously – he couldn't stand to lose her again. What if she'd only come out of a spirit of academic support, or to encourage him in his career?

'You look like you've seen a ghost,' she commented, her arm softly threading itself through his. 'Are you OK?'

Axel nodded mutely, too overwhelmed to reply. 'It's... Seeing you again...' He shook his head, trying to clear his thoughts. 'It's very emotional,' he finally said.

It was Safiya's turn to blush. 'Yes,' she said, without hesitating. 'I'm sorry,' she added after a silence. 'Maybe I should have given you some notice.'

'Yes, instead of giving me a heart attack...' But he was smiling. 'At least you kept your questions till the end. I don't know if I'd have been able to finish my speech if I'd seen you earlier.'

Safiya squeezed his arm, and they walked on, a thousand unsaid thoughts and feelings tangible in the air around them.

Axel let out a long, slow sigh, his breath crystallising in the air. 'So why didn't you answer any of my messages?' he asked. 'I know that's a big question,' he added.

'I suppose you have a right to know,' she said. They had reached the side of the river, and either side of them the walkway stretched off into the distance, lamps winking either side like a ribbon of lights.

'Let's sit for a minute,' Axel suggested, and they made their way to a bench.

'I don't really know how to explain,' Safiya finally began. 'I know that the fact that I turned up today without warning isn't going to fit very well with what I'm about to say... But I hope you can try to understand.'

'You were angry,' Axel prompted her.

'Yes, very angry. Disappointed. Hurt. And I also felt very, very foolish. How could I have thought that you would give up your beautiful little blonde fiancée for me?' Axel opened his mouth to speak, but Safiya didn't let him interrupt. 'I felt tricked, betrayed, by the fact that you didn't tell me you were still with her. You really should have told me,' she added, turning towards him. But the spark in her eyes was a gentle one.

'I know,' Axel replied. 'I was such a coward. I was... terrified. Of losing you, and yes, of losing Patti-Ann, of making a choice and changing my whole life. But I made such an awful mistake, Safiya, I see that now.'

Safiya held up a hand. 'It's my turn,' she said calmly. 'Then you can apologise. As much as you like.'

They laughed, and something in the air loosened between them.

'OK,' said Axel. 'I won't say another word.'

'As the days went by, after I came back home, the more I started feeling like the whole thing had been a pipe dream, something dreamed up by two fools. We'd never talked about it, what could really happen – there was just one kiss...' Unbidden, the memory of the Turkish rose garden fell into Axel's mind: that beautiful day he'd tried so hard to forget. 'Everything before then had been this intellectual connection, this sweet friendship... I thought maybe I'd made a mistake, thinking it could be anything more. After all, we come from such different worlds. And you were engaged.'

Safiya paused, looking out over the lights reflected in the river. 'My mother knew something was wrong. Even after you left Istanbul I think she suspected there was something between us. She kept making these speeches about choosing a partner who really understands you, about family and tradition, telling me I should be really sure...' Safiya sighed. 'And I couldn't help but listen, even if it made me angry, or scared. I mean, you and I are so deeply different; the worlds we come from, how we were raised... Then my father started inviting Yusif around every single weekend. I started to think maybe it wouldn't be such a bad life, making my family happy, giving them grandchildren...'

Axel nodded, biting his tongue. There was so much he wanted to say, but first he needed to listen.

'But I couldn't stop dreaming about you. I dreamed about the avalanche, and about our late nights working together, and do you want to know something funny? Once or twice I dreamed that we had gone to Nepal together, to Phoksundo Lake...'

'That's crazy!' Axel burst out. 'I was there! I went there.'

Safiya smiled, as the understanding dawned, then blanched. 'But the earthquake!' she said.

He nodded slowly, unwilling to change the conversation's track. 'I was there,' he said. 'I'll tell you all about it. But first you need to tell me you told that Yusif to go fly a kite.'

Safiya laughed. 'I did. I don't know what happened. It was an afternoon like all the others; I was working on preparing a talk for the next week, quite a difficult topic about mythical dichotomies in religious poetry, I really would have liked to stay in my room working, but of course my father wouldn't accept that. So I was sitting there, half listening to Yusif drone on about his new cars, half working on the conclusion for my paper, and all at once it occurred to me that I was free to choose my work. Why was I sitting here, when I wanted to be anywhere else? I was a grown woman, a professor, not a child! So I stood up – right in the middle of a sentence of his – shook his hand, bid him good day, and told him I was not interested in seeing him anymore.'

Axel laughed out loud in joyful surprise.

'My father still isn't speaking to me,' Safiya added, ruefully, 'so my mother has to pretend to be angry with me too. But I saw her face when I left the room. She was trying not to smile.'

'Surely they should know you've always been a rebel,' Axel said affectionately.

Safiya shook her head. 'Tradition has a stronger hold on all of us than we're ever willing to admit.'

Axel nodded, sobered. 'Yes, that's true.' They stared out at the water in silence for a while. 'I wonder,' he said at last, 'how many people get married just because they know it'll make their parents happy.'

'There was a boy I knew at university,' Safiya said after a while, 'Naz. A smart kid, always very popular. He met an exchange student from Germany when we were both at the University of Istanbul. Fell in love, over the moon, couldn't wait to introduce her to his parents. It didn't go well. Our parents were friends, you see, so I had the news secondhand from both sides: Naz devastated, and his parents horrified, confiding in mine.' She shook her head sadly. 'These East-West alliances, they aren't easy. There's a tremendous amount of cultural baggage – history – against us. And that's without bringing the religious element into it. The German girl converted to Islam, and still that wasn't enough. Eventually they moved to Europe together, and I lost touch with Naz, but I know it broke his heart, disappointing his family like that. It's a heavy weight to carry into a relationship.'

Axel took a deep breath and a leap of faith. 'If you're trying to talk me out of being with you, you'll need more than that,' he said. Safiya looked up at him, her eyes warm and sad, but he couldn't stop. 'I've thought about you every day since you left. I've never met anyone who made me feel so… full of life. I feel more like myself in your presence, and I feel incomplete when you're gone. And my work, everything I've accomplished, I could never have done any of it without you. Sometimes I felt like you knew all along, you know, like you were just waiting for me to see the light?'

Safiya shook her head. 'I knew there was more to our work together than met the eye,' she said, 'but I didn't know what form it would take. And I thought I would be the one to come out of this with a prize-winning theory.'

Axel laughed, surprised. 'Maybe you still will!' he said.

'I'm joking,' she said. 'This theory of the soul, it's all yours.'

'No, it's not,' Axel said fiercely. 'It's Bohmann's, and it's Schmidt Hennessey's, and it's yours. Nothing, none of this would have seen the light of day if Bohmann hadn't asked for my help; if we hadn't met at that conference in London; if you hadn't decided to come with me to Switzerland. Everything that happened was part of some greater pattern, some plan – I know, I know what that sounds like. But I believe it. And I'm not just talking about my work. I'm talking about meeting you, and being with you at every one of those crucial moments: London, Geneva, Bern, the avalanche… Even in Nepal, you were so present in my mind it was as if you were by my side every day, every time I looked out at that beautiful lake. You're the one I have to thank for this whole theory, my career, Princeton, the book, everything. But I don't need any of that if I can just have you.' He stopped, breathless.

Safiya raised an eyebrow. 'Are you kidding?' she said. 'Don't you dare give up Princeton for me!'

Axel laughed, but the silence that followed made his heart ache so badly he could barely stand it. Then Safiya took his hand. 'I'm yours,' she said simply. 'I don't know how we can make this work – if I should move to Princeton, or if we should try some kind of long-distance thing for a while…'

'No,' said Axel, surprising himself with the strength of his response. 'I need you here with me. I mean, of course, you can go home and set things in order. But as soon as… I mean, if you were willing… If you want…'

Safiya's eyes, Axel realised with wonder, were brimming with tears. 'Yes, I want that very much,' she said, her voice trembling. 'I want to be with you.'

'I can't promise you any easy solutions to this, but I can promise you that I'll do everything in my power for us to be together,' Axel said in a single breath. 'You are my first priority.'

They sat side by side, breathing shakily, staring into each other's eyes as if stunned by everything they had just managed to say. 'I love you,' Axel finally said. Then, very gently, he leaned in and kissed his beloved Safiya.

'I love you too,' she replied quietly. 'But you'll have to lose the beard.'

He laughed. 'OK,' he said. 'I only kept it because it reminds me of Nepal, which reminds me of you…'

'Oh, I want to hear all about Nepal!' Safiya said, leaning towards him.

'Would you like to go out for dinner?' Axel asked.

Safiya laughed. 'You sound like you're asking me out on our first date.'

'Well maybe I am,' said Axel. 'Maybe we're starting over.'

Safiya's expression softened, and for a moment the sparkling lights on the river were reflected in her eyes, like the spiral of a galaxy, like the energy of human atoms, all in movement, all connected. 'You're right,' she said. 'We are.'

EPILOGUE

Axel stood at the window, looking out over the city of Geneva below. There were the two rivers, snaking across the landscape – one drawing a curved line across the French countryside, the other twining down from the lake. There was the diamond of Plainpalais, and the spire of the cathedral rising above the old town, and beyond, the long flat blue expanse of the lake. He sighed deeply, and raised his cup of coffee to his lips, then turned back towards the bed.

Safiya was still sleeping, her face turned towards the window and lit by the gentle glow of the rising sun. The sight of his wife still made his heart leap in his chest, even five years on. Resisting the urge to climb back into bed with her on this sunny Saturday morning, Axel yawned, stretched, and went to sit down at his desk, setting his cup of coffee down. The deadline for the collaborative paper he was currently working on was looming, and he needed to finish his section before his next meeting with his partners at CERN. Then there was the talk he was giving at the University of Lausanne, where he had tenure, and next month he would be giving a speech about his third book at Princeton… Axel shook his head, looking through his diary. I'm a very lucky man, he thought to himself, and a very busy one. He glanced up at his wife once more, as if to give himself courage, then checked the clock on his laptop. He still had two hours free to work, before he had to drive to the airport to pick up his mother. Axel took another sip of his coffee and began work.

★ ★ ★ ★

Later that same day, Axel, Safiya and Felicia were sitting on the terrace outside their chalet, sharing a pot of melissa tea and a plate of almond cookies.

'I just can't believe how beautiful it is!' Felicia was saying, gazing up at the slope of the hillside behind them, around at the scattered pine forest, then down across the valley. 'I mean, your place in Princeton was really nice, with that patio and everything, but this is just something else. Even if it takes me a lot longer to get here.'

Axel smiled happily. 'I just love living in Geneva,' he said. 'I can't imagine moving anywhere else. The air is so pure, the atmosphere is so peaceful... and in the summer, we can swim in the lake.'

'And from up here on the Salève,' Safiya chimed in, 'I feel like we're on top of the world.'

'You two always did love your mountains,' Felicia said affectionately. 'Do you have any big hikes planned this summer?'

Safiya and Axel exchanged a shy glance. 'Well, we'll be doing our usual weekend trips,' Safiya finally said, 'but I probably shouldn't be exerting myself too much.'

Felicia frowned for a moment, not understanding, then her eyes widened as Safiya's hand descended protectively to her belly.

'Oh my goodness!' she exclaimed. 'Oh my gosh!' Before Axel understood the movement, the couple found themselves clasped to his mother's bosom, which was heaving with happy sobs. 'I'm just so happy for you both!'

Safiya extricated herself gingerly, smiling, a tear slipping down her cheek. 'Me too,' she said.

Axel wrapped an arm around his wife's shoulders, pulling her close. The familiar sandalwood scent of her still made his heart squeeze in his chest.

Felicia had gathered herself together. 'So that's why you invited me to come stay! I was wondering about that. You're going to have the baby here?' she asked.

Axel and Safiya nodded in unison.

'So you're really settling here for real,' Felicia mused aloud. 'Wow. And now you're a consulting professor here and at Princeton?'

'It's actually in Lausanne, not Geneva,' he explained. 'They have one of the best technical universities in the world. But yes, I really like the teaching work,' he added.

'And you work with CERN on various scientific papers,' Safiya added.

Axel smiled gratefully. 'I do. I guess they decided they could use a bit more of a philosophical perspective in some of their work.'

'And you've also been doing voluntary work for a green energy foundation,' said Safiya, grinning now.

Axel blushed. 'They're doing very interesting work,' he said. 'I'm just giving them a hand.'

Felicia reached across and mussed his hair, like she used to do when he was a child. 'Your wife's right. You don't have to be so humble,' she said. 'With everything you've accomplished, you can be damn proud. I certainly am!'

Axel looked back and forth between the two women smiling back at him, and a wave of happiness swelled up in his chest. This was his family – and soon there would be one more!

'And what about your old colleagues?' Felicia asked. 'Are you still in touch with that professor over there in the Alps?'

'Schmidt Hennessey came to visit us this winter,' Axel replied. 'We went on a long snowshoe hike, it was great.'

'I'm so glad,' said his mother. 'You know Melvin asks about you all the time.'

'All the time? So you're seeing a lot of each other?' Axel asked, a twinkle in his eye.

Felicia blushed furiously. 'It's not like that!' she said. 'But his son, that Kyle, has turned out to be such a sweetie, so I go to all his concerts. He's got a real following in Lake Salvation – I've even heard him on the county radio! And Melvin and I have dinner every… every once in a while.'

Axel hesitated. 'And Patti-Ann?' he asked. 'Do you ever hear from her?'

Felicia shrugged. 'I see her on the TV,' she says. 'You know she has her own show now?'

Axel nodded. 'I watched it once, just to see. You could barely recognise her with all that makeup! But I guess the show's pretty successful.'

'She's not as bad as that awful Potts man, that's for sure,' Felicia said philosophically. 'Anyway, who are we to judge, as long as she's happy?'

'Yeah,' said Axel, 'you're right.' He paused, dipping a cookie into his cup of tea. 'It's strange,' he said finally, 'how far away it all seems. I mean, I spent a huge chunk of my life in Lake Salvation, and it all seems like a dream! Even Princeton, and we've only been gone three years! All these people, everything I had over there, it seems like it belongs to a parallel universe.'

'Don't you start using your science words on your mother,' Felicia chided him affectionately. 'But it sure feels to me like you're a million miles away.'

'I understand,' said Safiya, softly.

There was a contemplative silence.

'It's hard to feel sad about the past,' Axel finally said, 'when I'm so excited about building a future here, with my family.'

'So you're not planning on moving back to the US anytime soon?' Felicia asked, a note of sorrow in her voice.

He reached across the table and squeezed her hand. 'We'll make sure your granddaughter gets to visit you every year,' he said.

Safiya raised an eyebrow. 'Granddaughter?' she asked, amused. 'What makes you think it's a girl?'

'Oh yeah, you're right.' Axel laughed, giddy. 'I don't know, I just have this feeling about it.'

'Well as long as it's a good feeling,' Safiya said warmly.

'It is,' said Axel. 'It definitely is.'

VINCENT GARNER

Vincent Garner is a scholar from Ireland, specializing in areas of physics and chemistry. His research is of interest to many eminent universities and institutions in the United States and Europe. He now lives with his family in the Lake Geneva region of Switzerland. This is his first novel.